I0817858

ÎNVIEREA

by Bruce T. Jones

ISBN 978-1-63393-349-1

Published by

The Twisted Pen

310 30th Street

Virginia Beach, VA 23451

TwistedPenPub@gmail.com

In association with

köehlerstudios™

This book is dedicated to my family and friends.
If you have ever shared a laugh or a smile, tears or anger,
or even a hangover, you have influenced me
more than you know.

To my publisher John and editor Joe, thank you for
your patience, wisdom and faith.

The roads we travel and tales we shared, all go into the creative
process that unwinds in the pages that follow, and will follow
for years to come.

I am grateful for the time spent and The Lord for bringing each
one of you in my life

For the memories and those yet to be,
Thank you.

ÎNVIEREA

The Legend of New Orleans Continues

Bruce T. Jones

Journal of the Ursuline Guardians
27 August 2010
Final entry

Învierea, in native Romanian tongue, is *The Resurrection*. It is the raising of Lazarus, Jesus Christ, the Son of Man, and at the Final Judgment, the multitude of our beloved dead. But it can pertain to an unholy curse, an enslaving misery that can only beget darkness ... or does it? I have lived a lifetime, serving the affirmations of my ancestors, bearing true witness to the miracles of Învierea, both the good and the evil. It is from this duty, I take my leave, the obligations of my ancestors now fulfilled.

Daniel Constantine
Order of the Dragon
The Old Ursuline Convent
New Orleans, Louisiana

CHAPTER ONE

CAST INTO THE bowels of Hell—Dante's words so understated my torment. For three days I willed myself to die, but God would not answer, nor did Satan. With each hour I grew weaker, decimated by a lack of the forbidden nutrition my body yearned. Curled up in darkness on the bathroom floor of this vacant room, I was consumed with rage, self-pity, and thoughts of self-destruction. All of my grand plans for a life renewed with Samantha would never come to pass. My fate was sealed.

There had been many opportunities for the Reaper to claim me. Cheating death, this retribution was cruel beyond compare. I deserved this fate, but Samantha did not. Why must she suffer love's callous heartbreak again? Not knowing what evil I was capable of, I could not trust my ability to control this growing, unrelenting appetite. For her safety, I could never see her again.

Renaldo had given me the key to this room two days ago. In the process of being refurbished, the workers were not scheduled to return for another week. Laying in the dust and scraps of construction debris, feebly, I battled to repulse blood lust. Into the darkness of night I would venture for quarry, but first I needed to seek out Daniel. After nearly fifty years of attending to the vampires of the convent, surely he could help supply the sustenance I required.

Secondly, I would track down those responsible for my hideous transformation and finish my work. Then, when all was done, I would decide how to end my own miserable existence.

My senses of smell, hearing, and vision were intoxicatingly keen. I pushed my key card into the lock of my original room, returning to the scene of now bitter memories.

Before the door opened, I sensed I was not alone.

"Good evening, Mitch."

"How'd you know I was here?" Lacking the stealth he desired, his voice was tempered with disappointment. "Renaldo tip you off?"

I should have been happier to see Mitch. After all, it's rare having a seasoned cop on your side while committing murder. True, arresting me at the Chamber proved to be a rocky start, but once convinced of the lethal blood-sucking tendencies of our adversaries, his assistance with the NOPD and Sam proved invaluable. "I have not seen Renaldo in two days," I replied wearily.

"Where in the hell did you disappear to? We've seen no signs of the others. Did you kill them without me?"

"No, I have not seen them, and I have been just down the hall the entire time. The million dollar question you're about to ask is *why*." I walked to the dresser and tossed the contents of my pockets on it. "How long have you been waiting?"

"About six hours. I was determined to find you. Your boy in the lobby, I don't think I could have beat the information out of him," Mitch smiled. "Fortunately, I know a certain lady that was more than eager to assist in locating you."

"Please don't tell me she is back in New Orleans."

"No, she's still safe in New York. What the hell's wrong? You look like shit."

I pushed past Mitch and stared through the window. I knew I had to return to the world outside. "Something has gone wrong, Mitch. Horribly wrong." I glanced to him, as he searched my expression for a clue. "I do not know how … but I am one of them now. I am a vampire." The words rolled off my lips all too easily, lacking any apparent anguish.

"You're kidding … right?" Mitch nervously smiled.

"Look at me. Does this look like I am kidding?" I pointed to my face, directing him to study the image surely altered by the newborn evil within.

Mitch studied my appearance, then tensed as he saw …

something. "How? *When*?"

"I blacked out after I killed Monique. It must have happened then. But as far as I can tell, she never drank my blood, and I do not recall drinking hers. I don't know how I became ..." The repeated confession proved to be too painful to vocalize.

"Are you sure?"

I walked back to the dresser. "Come here." I waved him towards me.

Mitch looked uneasy. Having seen the viciousness *we* were capable of, I did not blame him.

"It's okay, Mitch, if I wanted to kill you, you would already be dead." As we gazed into the mirror I held onto a fading hope; two familiar faces would be looking back.

"Holy shit," Mitch exclaimed as he waved his hand in front, and then behind me, observing the anomaly with fascination. He turned and poked me in the arm, while watching in the mirror. "Damn Brian, what in the hell are we supposed to do now?"

"I need to ... feed ... then I need answers, then retribution. Then you will have to finish me."

"Finish you?"

"Yes, you know what I am saying. I cannot be left like this." I knew Mitch was going to have a problem with the concept, but at this point, he was the first person I thought capable of actually completing the task.

"You'll forgive me if I seem less than enthusiastic, at the moment. You don't seem so evil to me, yet."

"Yes, I know. But keep the *yet* in mind."

"I'll think about it, if you promise to do me a huge favor," Mitch said as he stepped back and studied my familiar attributes. "Let me know if you start feeling hungry," he smiled uneasily.

"Mitch, I am incredibly hungry."

"What can I get you?"

"How about some O negative?" I joked, trying to lighten the mood.

"Forgive me if I refuse to acknowledge that request, in fact, I'm going to pretend like I never heard it," Mitch said, shaking his head.

"You do that Mitch." I stepped away from the mirror scoffing, "I can only assume I need to clean up a little. Mirrors are pretty damn useless now."

"You have looked better, my friend, or should that be 'my fiend'?"

I hissed at Mitch, revealing my canines. "You are killing me, Mitch." I opened the drawer and pulled out some jeans. "Oh never mind, I forgot. I am already dead."

We both grinned and tensions eased. "Seeing as how you are refusing to pick me up some dinner, I could use your help with something else."

"Name it."

"Find Isabelle. Have her bring what I need to their secret playhouse. Make sure she understands it is not an option. Maybe she can shed some knowledge as to how this happened to me as well."

"I don't think she will voluntarily acknowledge the existence of said nutrition or the location of their secret crib. We've raided the Chamber over the years, and have never found one single drop. Doing so would confirm our suspicions, and she knows that would eventually lead us to close down their clubhouse."

"Try your best, Mitch, but don't tell her what it's all about. With or without the blood, I need her there." I picked up my cell phone and scrolled through the missed calls.

"You might want to call that pretty lady and those friends of yours. They're really worried." Mitch had his hand on the doorknob to leave. "Brian, get yourself cleaned up, you look, and worse yet, smell like one of the homeless right now. And that pains me more than knowing what happened to you."

I flashed a crooked smile. "Hey Mitch, if the dispatcher calls about a Red Cross break-in, how about taking care of it buddy. I'm ready to bite the first ..."

"Don't even think about it. We'll hook up after I have corralled Isabelle. I'll get you what you need. Last thing I need is you committing any more crimes. That will only make more work for me."

Leaving the door slightly ajar, Mitch left me in a somewhat better mindset than I had arrived in.

I gazed at my phone. Samantha, Phillip, and Jimmy had all called, multiple times. Jimmy would be first, as he and Chuck would be instrumental in completing clean-up duty. As for Samantha and Phillip, I was ill prepared to speak with either, if I chose to speak with them at all. What could I possibly say but goodbye?

CHAPTER TWO

I CALLED JIMMY while en route to the Old Ursuline Convent to find Daniel.

The call could have gone better. He and Chuck were pissed off over my disappearance. Jimmy sounded relieved, but he was not about to concede it. I did not elaborate, other than I would meet them at Crawdads at twenty-three hundred.

Having discovered it painful to tread before the sacred symbols of the Ursuline Convent, I was forced to leave a phone message for Daniel. Would he receive it, or respond to my request? I didn't know. But I knew I would have to adapt to my newfound limitations, and I needed help.

Passing through the French Quarter, scents I once found appealing no longer aroused my desires. The variety of rhythms, which previously blended, were now isolated, down to a single stroke of a guitar string. I could pinpoint the origins of conversations deep inside crowded bars. The night had a new brilliance, the darkness exploding in hues previously undetectable. These phenomena occurred in microseconds, previously impossible to fathom, much less comprehend.

As I traversed Bourbon Street, one element was painfully absent; the presence of another of my kind. They were gone. Quite possibly, Chuck and Jimmy had completed our mission. A more somber thought: The remaining vampires had fled from New Orleans. Either way, I could send Chuck and Jimmy packing. With Samantha safely in New York, there was nothing more to lose. Gone was my anxiety; no loved ones or innocents to suffer my foolishness and fate. Approaching the safe house, I spotted Daniel standing a block away. Once he recognized me, he approached.

"Daniel, I am glad to see you got the message. It is good to see you again."

"Likewise," he said, as he extended his hand. "I have missed you over the past few days."

Extending mine out to greet him, he withdrew his hand and stepped back. "Apparently all is not well with you." His hand retreated into his trademark Armani sport coat.

"Please don't. I mean you no harm." Obviously he could sense the curse and was preparing to defend himself. "All is not well, and for that, I am prepared to die. But first, I need answers."

"Then you are as I suspect, one of the undead?"

"Yes."

"How did this happen?"

"I don't know. Three nights ago, before I killed Monique, she drugged me with something. It burned inside with excruciating pain. I was so disoriented, but never passed out. She never drank my blood—unless she drank it through some kind of telepathic osmosis. I have no bite marks, anywhere. Believe me, I checked."

"How did you kill her?" Daniel stepped cautiously forward.

"She took me to an abandoned house. We had sex," I explained, images flashing like a broken movie reel.

Daniel cut his eyes in a glare of disapproval.

"I was drugged. I would never have done it otherwise. I was completely under her powers. But somehow, when she tried to bite me, I overpowered her and killed her with my bare hands and maybe, my teeth ... I think."

"Did you drink her blood?"

"Drink no, swallow ... maybe. When I defended myself, I think I may have bitten her neck, attempting to sever an artery." Justifying my actions, I foolishly hoped he would tell me it was okay, just a temporary thing. Something a transfusion would fix.

"Vampires use their own blood for two purposes. The first is mind control. She must have had you ingest her blood at some point. When did you first begin to feel ill?"

"In the bar, I let her have some of my drink. She must have spiked it then, shortly after the burning set in."

"I am unaware of any painful effects. Usually, the victim becomes acutely susceptible to the vampire's will for several days. In larger doses, the effects can last for weeks or months and sometimes, bring on complete madness." Daniel paused, allowing me to absorb his wisdom. "The other purpose is to turn its victim into the undead. But to succeed in the process, the victim's blood must be drained to the point of death. I am thinking you probably would have remembered such an event. Unlike simple ingestion, as I told you before, this process is most painful."

"Is that it?" My disappointment was obvious.

"It is all I know," Daniel said "But a book exists, *The Journal of the Ursuline Guardians.* It's locked away in the Convent. It contains much history surrounding the ten women. We have no need for it anymore. The book is yours; there you may find the answers within its pages."

I turned my head away, distraught with my predicament.

"Do not be downcast. All is as it was meant to be. Remain true to your purpose."

My expression did not convince Daniel I was onboard with his optimism. "Have you located the remaining four?"

"No, I was hoping you would tell me they were dead," he replied. Daniel added more rain on my parade. "If they are, I am unaware of it."

"Great! They are gone, and I am ... I am a fucking vampire. And you want me to believe this was God's grand design for my life."

"You walked the steps that led you down this path. At any time, if this was not your destiny, God would have intervened. The fact we are here is all part of a scheme too divine for either of us to comprehend. Monique's death could not have been accomplished by just any ordinary man. You must look past your own perception of circumstances, and forge ahead with the task that is of your own making. In that journey you will answer the call of your purpose, my friend."

"Play the hand you are dealt. Always comes down to that, doesn't it?"

Daniel nodded, confident I would follow through with my mission.

"You will bring the book to me?"

"I will leave it with Renaldo, at the front desk," he said.

"Is there anyone in this town you do not know?"

"I do not know Samantha, yet," he confessed. Daniel turned to leave.

"Daniel?"

"Yes," he replied, turning back.

"I don't suppose you might know where an average guy with a drinking problem might find a little type A?"

"As a matter of fact, I had not thought about disposing of the Convent's supply, just yet. Do you know of someone that might be in need?"

"Possibly." I pulled the office key out of my pocket. "There is a fridge inside." Daniel snared the key with cobra-like reflexes. "Just leave the key inside, I have a spare."

Daniel hesitated as he began to leave. "Brian, I know God's purpose, although shrouded in mystery, will ultimately reveal goodness in the end, when all has come to pass."

With his parting words of wisdom, Daniel turned and walked silently away. Dumbfounded, I stood and watched his departure. I just could not wrap my arms around this whole *destiny* concept. Certainly Samantha did nothing to deserve any part of this. Why did my dark and twisted fate have to be so tangled with her seemingly innocent life?

I remained in the street, aimlessly staring into distant shadows when my cell phone rang.

"What's up, Mitch?"

"We're at the house," he said.

"Send her inside. Wait for me outside. I'll be there in ten minutes."

"We'll be here," Mitch assured.

I made it across the Quarter faster than expected, surprisingly not even breaking a sweat in the stagnant heat. O'Reilly was waiting outside the house, motionlessly leaning on his car, watching my rapid approach.

"Hey Brian. You sure got here quick."

Mitch was doing his best to make small talk with a vampire.

"I've got a little something for you," Mitch teased. He reached inside and pulled the trunk release. Inside the cluttered trunk lay a white and red Igloo Cooler.

I pulled the bag of blood from the trunk as Mitch produced a knife and straw from his pocket. "Thought you might need this," he said, offering the utensils. "Brian, I gotta know you won't harm her. I can't let you go in there if you plan on killing her."

I poked a hole in the bag and stuck the straw in. "Let's just say I am not in a huge hurry to give you any excuse to stake me, just yet. Cheers." I raised the bag and turned away. I was not particularly ready for this whole blood consumption thing, much less in front of Mitch. As I headed to the opened front door, I pulled the straw to my lips, struggling with the thought of what I had to do. Inevitably, to remain strong enough to defeat the remaining vampires, I would have to drink in the evil I once deplored.

With a deep breath, I drew the cool crimson fluid into my mouth. The sweet nectar quenched the unfamiliar newborn desires. I accelerated my consumption as I entered the house. Now drinking frantically, the blood filled voids beyond a physical hunger. The strength and confidence that shrouded me could only be described as supernatural.

I did not have to look; Isabelle's presence in the upstairs bedroom was revealed in acute sensory perceptions. I glided up the rickety stairs, silently, almost floating until I gazed upon the backside of her silhouette.

"I knew you would return to me," Isabelle announced in a sultry voice.

She turned; her eyes filled with all the desire a man could ever crave to command. Fantasizing the softness of her neck, the rapture of puncturing her flesh, savoring the first drop of her blood, these involuntary thoughts raged like a wildfire. "Are you alright?"

She saw it, the wild gleam, the insatiable hunger. For the first time I saw a fear inside her. How could I concentrate on my purpose? I summoned every ounce of strength. "Isabelle, how can a person become a vampire if they are not bitten?"

She tipped her head to the side, and stepped toward me. "Why do you ask, Brian?"

"Monique, the woman I warned you about, she was truly vampire. I do not know how, but ... she ... changed me."

"Monique? She and I are one in the same."

"No, Isabelle, you are not. You are nothing like Monique."

"I am," she protested.

"No Isabelle." Angered by her fantasy-world beliefs, my voice bellowed. "Do you have these?" I flashed my newly altered glistening canines. Grabbing her jaw and forcing her mouth open, I sought my validation. "Can you do this?" Without thought, I raised my hand in the air and without laying a hand on her, Isabelle's airway constricted. I forced her backward by sheer will. Terror welled in her eyes, attacked by a force she had never experienced. My actions were channeled by some inner force, one that suddenly overpowered my conscious thoughts.

"I see what you are, Isabelle. And you are not like Monique, or me." I reached out, tenderly clutching her jaw, and turned her face to the mirror. I placed my face beside hers. "Tell me, Isabelle, what do you see?"

Speechless, she stared in the mirror. Witnessing the evaporation of her fairytale existence, her mouth agape, she stared at her solitary reflection. Perhaps, for the first time in her life, the truth of what she was, or was not, was an inescapable reality.

With her satin-like flesh against mine, the scent of her body aroused my appetite once more. I allowed my face to caress hers.

She melted into the sensation as a tear trickled down her cheek.

"Tell me ... why I have been married twice and the men I love grow old and die. Tell me why everyone I know grows old and dies. *Everyone except me.* I have seen sailing ships and horse-drawn carriages. I have seen the light bulb invented and a man walk on the moon. I have lived through plagues and famines."

Her tears grew in intensity. She turned to my face, her lips quivered. "Tell me why I thirst for blood." Isabelle's lips met mine. "Make me like you," she pleaded softly as she brought her hands to my face.

"I cannot," I insisted.

"Then end my life. I do not want to live this way anymore."

"Isabelle, I cannot end your life, and I will not make you like me."

My connection to Isabelle intensified. Its origins held some invisible clue. She honestly believed she was over a hundred years old.

I was, in fact, over sixty. Yet we both appeared no more than thirty-five. Was there some piece of a puzzle I had overlooked, something unknown buried deep in my past, and hers?

Her lips pressed against mine again. "Isabelle, I cannot do this," I pleaded.

"Please," she whispered, turning her neck to my mouth. Her veins bulged in anticipation of my weakness.

I pushed her away. "Isabelle, I won't deny I have an incredible desire to consume you, a vexing need to be with you. But I cannot do this. For me to take you, I would lose control of myself. I would lose everything."

"I understand. I feel it too. But I do not wish to contain my desire. I want to explore it to the end of time, to be yours forever," she pledged.

"What we feel, and what we allow to happen are two entirely different issues. Our fates *are* intertwined. I think I have known it all along." I explained, searching for any shred of reason to fight off the overwhelming desire that burned inside of me.

My love for Samantha was forced to end. But that love was entirely different from this blood-lust rage. This was primitive and instinctive, more akin to my desire for Monique. I desperately needed a distraction. Memories of my first night in this room flashed back. "The first night I met you, you drugged me, you brought me here. What was that all about?"

"Initially, that was Cindy's mischief. She decided to drug you. She wanted you for herself. As I danced with you, I began to realize that you were different. There was something about you that I could not grasp. It was while we were dancing I decided to take you for myself."

"Okay. But what the hell were you trying to accomplish by biting my leg?"

"I told you already. I do not know why, but periodically I crave for blood, especially the blood of a lover. You aroused my desire."

"Why not just cut my arm? Why the puncture wounds, down there?" I asked uncomfortably pointing to my crotch.

"The fang, as we call it, is mainly a symbolic device for those of us born without."

"And down there?" I prompted for further explanation. It

occurred to me, this was the only occasion that I received a bite wound.

"That was all of my doing. I knew you would not remember any of the night. I wanted to ensure you knew where I had been," she said with a lustful gleam.

Ready to walk with me, or die by my hand, her truthfulness was now apparent.

"Isabelle, I do not know what my life holds beyond the next hour, but I will make you this promise: if I survive, I will not leave you to a life of isolation and despair."

"If you will not take me now, then stay. Be my lover, just for tonight."

"Isabelle, I love another. I cannot be with you."

"Is she like you?"

I did not dare divulge the honest answer. I knew the danger it would bring Samantha.

"She is very much like me."

"Then she is the luckiest woman I know."

If only that were true.

"I have to go; Mitch will take you back to the Chamber." With Monique dead, there was no reason for her not to return to the only place she belonged.

Isabelle drew near and hugged me securely. The fragrance of her skin intoxicating, the warmth of her body exhilarating. Placing my hand behind her head, I pulled her close. Holding her tightly, a soulful connection ignited. I pushed back enough to look into her eyes.

"I will come back for you, I promise." I kissed her forehead softly, left the house and passed out to the street.

Mitch was still standing vigil by the car. "Tell me you didn't kill her?" he asked sarcastically.

"Not yet," I joked, as I looked back to see her staring out the transom window.

"Keep an eye on her for me, Mitch."

"As best as I can," he replied. "What's next for you?"

"I think the others left the night after I killed Monique. First thing I would do, contact all of the casket shops and have them check their inventory. If they have any missing, I would check traffic or surveillance cameras near the shops. I would be looking for a rental truck or anything big enough to transport them."

"Sounds like a good place to start. I'll put a few guys on it tonight. We should be able to know something by tomorrow."

"Thanks," I said, as I checked my watch.

"You want me to see if I can get you a good deal on one while I'm at it?"

"No thanks, Mitch. For now I will settle for the bathtub and a blanket. I am not quite ready for casket life, just yet."

"Just let me know," he offered with a smile.

"Call me if you get any more bodies, or missing blood supplies. I honestly think they are gone, but if anything suspicious should turn up, I need to respond quickly."

Mitch nodded.

"If you don't mind, Mitch, I think I might grab a pint to go."

"Help yourself, I'm trying to cut back." Smiling broadly, he popped the trunk.

Grabbing a pint and a fresh straw, I turned my back and quickly drained the bag. With every swallow, my strength magnified.

I dropped the empty bag in his trunk and closed the lid. "I appreciate it."

"Call me if you need a delivery. I'd rather be the delivery boy than fill out morgue reports all night," Mitch winked. The feisty detective was not about to quit busting my chops.

"Will do," I said, as I turned my attention in the direction of Crawdad's.

CHAPTER THREE

THE BLACK ESCALADE pulled up to the Maison Dupuy; Samantha, her sister Dee, and Phillip were ushered into the balmy evening by the sharply dressed driver. The sleepless nights and stress were beginning to show on Samantha; gone was the glow of happiness.

Taking leave from his publishing empire, Phillip had reluctantly agreed to return to New Orleans to find me and help clean up what remained of his ill conceived blockbuster story.

Entering the lobby, dazed and exhausted, Samantha spotted Renaldo behind the front desk and headed in his direction. Phillip and Dee lagged behind, affording her a private conversation with the tight-lipped employee.

"Mrs. Denman, it is good to see you again." Alarmed by her distressed expression, he tempered his customary enthusiasm. "Is everything okay?"

"Renaldo, have you seen Mr. Denman?"

"Not for three days, ma'am. I thought he might be with you."

A tear of desperation rolled down Samantha's face. "Renaldo, I left him here with you three days ago. When was the last time you saw him? Who was he with? Please tell me."

Renaldo knew he had promised to keep my business private.

But he had not planned on facing Samantha's desperate plea. Aware of Phillip and Dee's attention, he walked around the counter, took Samantha by the elbow and led her to a secluded corner.

"I'm not sure what happened, but I did not see him until tonight. He left here alone, about an hour and a half ago. And if you'll forgive me for saying, Mrs. Denman, but Mr. Denman and you both look as if you could use some rest."

Samantha nodded. Renaldo was right.

"Yes, I could use some sleep. But I have been very worried about Mr. Denman."

"Might I suggest you wait in your room for him. I am not positive, but I think he will be back later tonight. Meantime, you could get a little rest before he returns."

Silently, Samantha considered her options.

"Let's go to the bar. I'll buy you a glass of wine. It will help you rest."

"Thanks, Renaldo. Let me tell my sister I'm staying here."

Phillip and Dee were immersed in conversation as she returned. "I'm going to stay here, and wait for Brian."

"Do you want to go to your place?" Phillip asked Dee.

"Not a chance. We'll get a room here," Dee insisted, her hands resting on her hips, announcing her mind was set.

"You don't need to do that," Samantha objected.

"With everything we know, there is no way I am leaving you here, alone," Dee countered.

"I will be okay. I am just going to wait for Brian in his room. I'll be fine."

"Tell you what," Phillip interrupted, "You can both stay here. I will go down to Bourbon Street and see if I can find him."

"No," Samantha objected. "Dee can go with you. I'm going up to the room to try and get some sleep."

"Alright," Dee reluctantly agreed. "Just promise me you'll stay in the hotel. I do not want you out there by yourself."

"I promise. Renaldo and I are going to the bar for a glass of wine, then I'll go straight to my room … Mother," Samantha pledged, forcing a halfhearted smile.

"See that you do, or you'll be grounded for a week, young lady," Dee joked, trying to lift her sister's spirits.

Once outside, Phillip placed his arm around Dee as they walked down the rugged, sun-baked street.

"Dee, I was wondering," Phillip began, but paused to consider his words.

"Yes?"

The words he was contemplating would not come easily, but for once Phillip decided to abandon reason. "Dee, when this mess is over, I was wondering if you would consider coming back to New York with me."

"What, for another week?"

"No, more like an indefinite stay." Phillip's voice was seriously lacking its self-assured swagger.

"Why, Mr. Wilder, are you propositioning me?"

"No, no, no," he rattled off unconvincingly. After a brief pause of uncomfortable silence and a bewildered look from Dee, Phillip continued. "Well maybe. It depends on your definition of proposition."

"That would depend on the offer. What are we talking about here, Phillip?"

"Exclusivity, just you and me."

"And all this time I was hoping this was nothing more than unadulterated lust," Dee said with a coy smile.

"Ouch, that hurts," Phillip responded, rejection sweeping across his face. "I was actually hoping we were becoming something more."

Dee mulled Phillip's words. "Have you ever said that to anyone else?"

"Never," Phillip replied quickly and confidently.

"Have you ever felt this way before?"

"Absolutely never, and I'm not planning on leaving New Orleans without you."

Grabbing him by the shirt, Dee kissed Phillip madly. Gasping for breath, she pushed back and whispered, "You won't have to."

Phillip smiled broadly. "Come on. Let's go find Brian so we can get the hell out of this town."

Taking to the dark and quiet streets, my newfound love of the night blossomed; a place where prying eyes held no concern, a place where in the quiet I found peace. Eventually winding my way to Crawdad's, I stood outside and stared at Jimmy and Chuck throwing back a couple of cold ones.

Laughter from inside sparked memories of happier times. Just days earlier we were planning the mission like it was just another day in the jungles of Colombia, killing the bad guys and plundering their spoils. How it had changed so drastically. Jimmy and Chuck were out of sorts, worn thin by the stressful days of the hunt. Hoping they had had some success but dreading the conversation to follow, I walked with trepidation.

"Well look what the hell the cat dragged in," Chuck started when I arrived. "I hope you and the little Missy have been having a good time while Jimmy and I have been doing your dirty work."

Without reply, I remained somber. I could not look directly at either, as crucifixes dangled from their necks.

Jimmy cut his eyes, meticulously studying every detail of my face.

"I must say you look well rested," Chuck added.

"Guys, I am sorry," I began to explain.

"You're damn right you're sorry," Chuck jumped back in. "I'll have you know, while you've been ..."

"Shut up, Chuck," Jimmy interrupted. "Brian's got something he wants to say."

I pulled out the chair, away from the table. "Guys, I'll explain in a second, but first I need you to do me favor. Lose the crosses."

Exchanging puzzled expressions, they turned back to me.

"Just do it, please," I insisted.

They looked puzzled but tucked them under their shirts. I bowed my head in shame, ill prepared to look either in the eye.

"Guys, I don't know how, but I am one of them. I ... I am a vampire."

Staring in disbelief, Chuck picked up his beer and chugged the remainder. Jimmy continued reading my expressions.

"Shit," Chuck objected, "there ain't no way you're a fucking vampire, Brian. I mean, look at you. You don't look anything like one of them."

I glanced at Jimmy before turning away.

"What happened?" Chuck calmly asked.

"I don't know. Nobody knows. It happened the night you were locked down in the church. The night I killed Monique. She did it. I just don't know how."

"Well, fuck it all. I guess I've got to stake you now," Chuck beamed.

You just might get your chance, I thought. *But not yet.*

"Chuck, shut the hell up," Jimmy implored.

Chuck crossed his eyes at Jimmy and looked back at me. "I just don't want him sucking my blood if he needs a quick snack. Okay? You know how fast those bitches were."

"So what's the deal, Brian?" Jimmy asked. "Are there any others left?"

"Six are dead, and not coming back. Angelique, Celine, and Gabrielle are all in the wind. And then there's the issue of the tenth. We don't know a damn thing about her."

Jimmy slid a tepid beer in my direction. "It *was* cold."

"Here's what I think. I believe the bitches have flown the coop. I am going to track them down and finish what I started. You guys can stay and help me or you can get your ass out of Dodge. If you stay, there's a local cop who will help with whatever we need."

"A cop?" Chuck's shocked expression relayed his disbelief.

"Yeah, I know. But he has already helped eliminate two of them and he knows about the rest. He will provide intel and manpower if needed."

"That's it?" Chuck asked.

"Not quite." At this junction, the boys had well exceeded the initial payment for services rendered. With my days numbered, if Phillip would not cover the increase, I would. "If you stay, your cut goes up to five hundred K. But I need a couple of promises from you."

"Like?" Chuck inquired.

"After you are sure all of the vampires are gone, I need you to go to LA and wrap up Rob's affairs. I was going to, but things just did not turn out like I planned."

"Rob's affairs," Chuck grimaced. "You know, after all the years of bullshit we survived, if you had told me he was gonna check-out at the hands of a bunch of blood-sucking skinny bitches, I'd have laughed you right off the planet." Chuck drained his beer. "God damned vampires, go figure."

"Anything else?" Jimmy chimed in.

Lost in a moment of self-pity I hesitated. "Yes, one other thing. Once I am satisfied our job is done, I will call for you. I need to know you will make sure *all* of the of the vampires are dead."

Staring in silence, their expressions said enough.

"Guys?"

Still nothing was said. Chuck's mouth dropped open as implication of my request, no longer a joke, hit home. Jimmy groped for his beer, not taking his eyes off of me.

"I need to know I can count on you to do the right thing, like I did with Rob."

"Reality check," Chuck began, "Rob was already dead."

"And so am I."

"Whoa there cowboy, you look a lot healthier than Rob did," Chuck argued.

"Brian, let's just say for the sake of discussion, we can find a way to reverse the damage. Or perhaps you can find a way to control your urges, much like you are doing now. I think it would be prudent to take a wait and see approach," Jimmy suggested.

"I don't think there is a cure, and I can't conceal *this* forever. I have been the hunter all of my life. I do not want to spend the rest of my days in solitude, on the run, always looking over my shoulder."

"What about what's her name?" Chuck inquired.

"Her name is Samantha, Chuck." I cast an evil glare at Chuck for his continued ribbing. "I love her in ways I can't even begin to articulate, but there is no place in my life for her now. I will not live eternally consumed by regret."

"Why don't you just ..."

"No Chuck, I will not share this curse with her, or anyone."

"Not even me? I think I could really dig this vampire culture thing." A sly grin of twisted sincerity crossed Chuck's face.

"Forget it. That will definitely not happen, ever."

"Killjoy," Chuck pouted.

Jimmy nudged a beer closer. "I know it's not what you're craving, but it would make me feel better just to see you faking it."

I could not help but smile. "So what's the verdict, guys? You in or out?"

"Let's just say we're staying to take care of business. The other thing, we'll take a rain check," Jimmy offered.

"I suppose that will have to be good enough for now."

"So you gonna have that beer and seal the deal?" Chuck asked.

"Buy me a pint of O negative, and I'm in," I said with a half-hearted smile as I picked up the sweat-laden bottle and studied it.

"Damn," Jimmy sighed, "So this is it. The end of the road."

"Yeah." Exasperated, I returned a prolonged sigh. "I guess it is." I swallowed the beer, which lacked the taste or satisfaction I desperately craved. "When my time comes, I'll make sure you know where to find me. I would prefer not seeing you ... when it happens."

"Shit, Brian," Jimmy began to say, "I don't ..."

"Save it, Jimmy. Whatever it is will only lead to regrets. I don't want to go out that way." Rising to leave, Chuck and Jimmy followed my cue. "You guys have always been there for me. That's why I love you like brothers."

I walked out of Crawdad's not looking back. Buck, the owner, with his soiled white T-shirt and greasy apron stood on the sidewalk smoking a Camel. The memories of this place, our time together, and Buck's simplistic wisdom would replay in my mind for the remainder of my days. In a fitting gesture of admiration only Buck would understand, I muttered, "Up yours, Buck," as I walked away into the musty night.

CHAPTER FOUR

I WALKED THE darkened streets aimlessly, wondering what in the hell to do with Isabelle. Snap her neck tonight and end her delusional misery? But within her delusions, she possessed a sense of understanding the villain I had become. How long could I cage the desire to do the evil now festering within?

Circling the outskirts of the Quarter, attempting to remain far from the crowds, I suddenly perceived a familiar scent. Then it vanished. In the midst of dealing with vampires, I had developed the uncanny ability to detect their presence. Suddenly, the scent intensified. I turned off Decatur Street, in the direction of its origin. Quickening the pace, instincts steered my course.

The scent was familiar, but altogether different than the malodorous stench of the undead. Instantly, reality hit. Phillip had returned to New Orleans, and he was not alone. Inhaling the air, I searched for clues of Samantha's presence. Closing the distance between, I arrived on Bourbon Street and turned left, hard on the trail. Samantha was near!

The rush of raw emotions brought me to the brink of collapse. The faint pulse of love, clinging to a now bitter memory, versus rage, hate, and worse yet, the untamed desire to feed. Could I stand in her presence and do no harm? I yearned to hold and kiss her, to lie beside and feel the warmth of her body next to mine. To witness the glow of her skin as the sun reflected in the morning light. This was never to be, ever again.

But what of this hunger? Passing dozens of hapless people in the street without this sudden yearning, it was clear. It was for Samantha, and her alone. I continued down Bourbon in the direction of the Maison Dupuy, instincts foretelling of Samantha's presence. Less than a block from Toulouse, I spotted Phillip and Dee. I had no time or purpose for them, only for Samantha. Without thought or effort, the pace of Bourbon Street grinded to the speed of a slow-motion video as I became one with a mysterious breeze that swept me down the street. In a blur of holographic light, I passed directly between Phillip and Dee as they looked at each other. Within an instant, I gazed back over my shoulder at my oblivious friends.

"Did you see that?" Phillip asked, bewildered by the sensation.

"I thought I saw something, but I'm not sure what it was." Dee shivered, chilled by the passing of my presence.

A frown crossed my face and my spirit sunk. I knew that chill. Angelique ... Monique—the frigid presence of our kind.

"Are you okay?" Noticing Dee's sudden change in demeanor, Phillip put an arm around her.

Dee nuzzled in. "Yes. I just caught a chill."

"I felt it too. You want to call it quits for the night?"

Dee looked at her watch. "Not yet. For better or worse, I need to find something out for my sister." Dee's determination echoed down the street. "Hey, I just had an idea. I don't know why I didn't think of it sooner. That bar where we first met, Brian was friendly with the bouncer. Let's go see if he knows anything."

Just out of their sight, I watched as they turned and then passed. I wanted to call out, but what could I say?

Standing in the hall, staring at the door, the last barrier of protection, I knew Samantha waited on the other side. My hand quivered, the last sign of resistance, as I extended it toward the lock. Losing the futile battle, I slid the key into the lock. Twisting the handle and slowly opening the door, I wished by some small miracle the light on the lock had remained red. Moving like some freakish stealthy demon, I glided to the bedside. Samantha's body was aglow in the moonlight.

The vision was like a downpour of holy water, suppressing my thirst for her blood. Evident, even in her sleep, the apparent distress I created, delivered an onslaught of guilt and pity. I stood over her body and tears rolled down my face. My only love, my greatest failure, how I silently prayed for some kind of miracle. How desperately I yearned to hold her.

Samantha had fallen asleep fully dressed on top of the sheets. Folding the comforter in half on top of her, I carefully slid onto the feathery mattress. Sitting with my back against the headboard, I wrapped my arm around her shoulder and ever so gently pulled her close.

At that moment, it became apparent for the first time in my life, the true power of love. Though the deepest imaginable misery consumed me, all thoughts of harming Samantha vanished. I could somehow become her guardian, using my supernatural abilities to protect her for the rest of her days.

"Mmm," she mumbled as she barely stirred. "I thought you were dead." Softly spoken, amidst the sea of Ambien unconsciousness, she nuzzled into my chest.

"I was," I whispered, "but you saved me."

Sam settled in tighter. I would hold her until sunrise, and die in her arms if not for the gruesome ending she would have to witness.

"Mmm," she purred again, "you're cold."

"Sleep now. *Odihneste te acum suflete oboist.*"

"Somebody help me!" a distressed voice cried out faintly, stirring me from my sleep. Having slept only briefly, I carefully slid to the side of the bed, not wanting to disturb Samantha, who was sleeping peacefully. "No!" the voice cried again. Instantly, I recognized the distant cry for help. Dee was in danger. Instincts driving me, I blazed in the direction of The Chamber, at a speed so incredible, I scarcely perceived the journey. I had achieved the same supernatural speed of my adversarial vampires, without any conscious effort.

The Chamber; after being drugged and abused by Isabelle upon my first visit to this wretched house of debauchery, I should have torched it to the ground. But I ignored my instincts, even after witnessing Monique's resurrection, her blood-spattered skull withstanding my Beretta's best. And now, the charm of strike three. This haven for vampire wannabes had ignited a wrath within unlike never before.

Slowing my pace, I stormed through the narrow door and charged up the alley. Kirk the bouncer rose to challenge my trespass. I spoke not a word, but thrust my hand in the direction of his chest. Without laying a hand on him, a burst of energy hurled him ten feet backward into the far end of the bar.

Kirk's collision alerted everyone surrounding the bar to my presence. With the rage a wild animal in my eyes, I turned my attention to any who dared stand in my way. Horror stricken, the bar flies parted like the Red Sea.

Behind the bar, the words *Dracul has risen* were scribbled in large, looming, blood-dripped letters. Indeed, he had! I unleashed another explosive burst, toppling everything in my path. Glass shattered, chairs flew, and people were violently swept aside. In a deep demonic voice, I roared, "Get out."

Scattering like cockroaches, everyone scrambled for the exit. With the path now cleared, I made my way for the stairs. As I neared the top of the darkened stairway, a deep voice called out from above, "The lounge is closed tonight, private party."

Completing the ascent, I came upon another overstuffed bouncer. The music from beyond the door blared loudly, drowning out any screams from inside.

"Hey dip-shit, didn't you hear me? The lounge is closed."

I shoved the bouncer through the locked door, splintering it to pieces. Slumped over, on the corner of the bar, was Phillip. No doubt he had encountered The Chamber's famous vampire potion. In the corner across the darkened room were approximately ten freaks crowded around a table. The music was blasting, drowning out the destruction of the door and my arrival. As I approached the frenzied orgy, my suspicions were confirmed. Dee was the main course of tonight's freak show.

I grabbed the first guy in my path by the shoulder. He turned, and instantly realized I was not a regular member of his clan. "Who the hell let you in? Beat it, dickhead," he demanded. Hissing, he displayed a set of high-quality Hollywood canines. Behind him, I caught a glimpse of Dee, stretched out on a table, her face etched with fear. Obviously, they wanted her conscious for their sick little ritual. With her arms and legs bound, mouth gagged and shirt torn open, her conceded expression telegraphed her loss of hope.

Witnessing the assault, I snapped, rage racing through my veins. With the pressure of a hydraulic vice, I grabbed the douche-bag's face and began crushing it. As he screamed out in agony, I derived deep satisfaction, not only from the pain I inflicted, but the appealing sounds of splintering bones. His wails of agony instantly captured the attention of Dee's assailants. With all the prowess of an uncaged rabid beast, I attacked the eight men and two women, without discrimination or concern for injury. Bodies flew about like rag dolls, bones shattered like kindling twigs.

In what seemed to be only seconds, all were on the floor, leaving only a few capable of crawling for the door. My heart was surprisingly calm and my breath steady. In the aftermath, I realized this had to have been the force I used to kill Monique.

Without a shred of remorse, I turned and faced Dee for the first time, as a creature unknown, a vampire. Traumatized by the assault, she closed her eyes feeling only the security of my presence.

"I will be right back."

"Don't leave me," she pleaded.

"I won't. I have to call for help."

I walked over to the three freaks crawling for the exit. "Move another inch and I will rip your heads off and stuff them up your asses," I growled. I pulled my cell phone and punched up O'Reilly. Never thought I would see the day I had a cop on speed dial.

"Please tell me you are *not* at The Chamber right now. Every cop in the Quarter is headed that way. We've had reports of explosions, assaults, you name it," O'Reilly warned.

"Yeah, I am here, on the second floor. Call the boys off. I will explain when you arrive."

"Jesus, Brian ..."

O'Reilly did not have the opportunity to finish his rant. I hung up, eager to return to Dee, who was struggling to free herself. Tugging in vain at the restraints around her legs and wrists, she winced in pain and frustration.

"Hang on, let me get those. You will only bruise yourself."

Dee's predicament foretold a fate barely escaped. I wondered how many had suffered the same ordeal? After this, O'Reilly certainly would have enough probable cause to re-open numerous missing-persons reports.

My eyes were drawn to Dee's body, her pants partially removed and her shirt ripped open, exposing the same exquisite form Samantha possessed. Her flesh glistened with fear, the scent mesmerizing. Desire crept from a crevice in my subconscious mind, an inborn yearning to take her. Drawn from an ancient instinctive desire, like leading a wolf to injured prey, I savored the helpless victim. The instant I became aware, I focused my attention on freeing her. I untied her legs first. "Are you alright? Did they hurt you?"

"I'm okay. Is Phillip all right?" she asked timidly, afraid of my reply.

Bitterly, I reminisced on my own *Elixir of Love* experience. Peyote, ecstasy and God knows what else. Seeing Phillip in this state, I had to wonder how in the hell Isabelle had expected anything out of me other than her teeth in my groin that first night. "He will be fine in a day or two, but will have one hell of a hangover. I'm surprised they did not drug you as well."

"They were going to, but the guy whose face you crushed said he wanted me awake and pure."

I knew Phillip was alive, I felt his beating heart from across the room, pumping blood, thumping, like a tribal drum. Apparently, with the frenzy of my assault, a craving for blood, live blood, was becoming uncontrollable.

I untied Dee's left arm and then started on the other. As I rolled her arm over, the warm, gratifying sensation of blood began saturating my fingers. "You are bleeding." I inspected the puncture wounds on her wrist, watching in tantalizing fascination, as the crimson, sweet blood raced from the puncture and cascaded down her arm. Her veins swelled to my desire, answering to a silent craving.

I fought with every ounce of strength possessed. I could not do this. The pulsating thumping called like the Pied Piper. Intoxicated with the aroma of blood, incoherently, I finished untying her. I turned away, my body burning with a famine I never imagined possible. Frantically, I hurried to the bar and grabbed a bottle of Southern Comfort, hastily pulled the spout out, and tipped the bottle back pouring the liquor down my throat, until all of the golden spirits were consumed. Attempting to eradicate my newborn lust, I grabbed a bottle of vodka and poured it over my hands, washing Dee's blood to the floor, removing the temptation to taste her succulent juices.

Dee was sitting up on the table, silently absorbing the full carnage of my wrath.

I returned to bandage her wound. "Let me see." The sight and fragrance were overwhelming. My eyes rolled as her blood continued to flow. I wrapped the towel tightly. "Keep some pressure on it. It should stop soon."

She nodded without a word.

"Did one of them bite you?" Concerned of the wound's origin, I began to consider if any of my victims might be ... like me.

"No, one of them used a shiny tool, like some type of knife, just as you arrived."

"Did any of them drink your blood?" Worried she might contract a disease from one of these misfits, talking helped distract my instinctive beckoning.

"No. They didn't have the time. Thank God you got here when you did. I don't know what would have happened." Dee sighed as she rubbed her wrist.

I knew. '*People go missin in that place,*' Renaldo had warned. They would have raped her, drank her blood, and killed her. I was not about to traumatize her with that trivial information. "Come on, we need to get you out of here." Taking her by the arm, I assisted her off the table and wrapped my jacket around her.

"Damn it, Brian!" an angry voice cried out coming up the stairs. "What the hell did you do?" O'Reilly questioned, as he entered the room observing the bodies strewn about.

"Mitch, this is Sam's sister, Dee. Those assholes were preparing to rape and murder her. The guy over there on the bar is my buddy Phillip. He's been doped up with that peyote concoction I told you about. Seeing as how this is a crime scene now, you will have ample opportunity to find their stash of magic juices, and their blood supply."

"How about leaving the detecting to me, Brian!" Mitch snapped, appearing irked by the multitude of bodies strewn about, he pulled me away from Dee.

"Sorry, Mitch, I didn't have time to wait for the cavalry."

Mitch shook his head slowly as he surveyed the carnage.

"Sorry, Brian. It's just this whole thing is snowballing." Mitch slapped his hand against his face. "Shit, I meant to ask you earlier, what the hell happened to that rock star disguise you were sporting three nights ago at Utopia? I hope you know there's no way you're getting out of here without being recognized."

"My hair is not spiked and blonde?"

"Here's a news flash, you look exactly the same as the first time we met."

"Shit, I haven't seen myself in three days. Mirror issues, you know. This could be a problem." I took a moment to contemplate my next move.

"But on the bright side, the coroner has matched the blood from Monique's corpse to the samples we collected after you capped her in the basement *last* week. The coroner was quite impressed with her apparently functional canines."

I raised my eyebrows. "I had not intended for any of the bodies to be recovered by the police."

"Relax, Brian, the coroner is a friend. I needed some personal answers, not that I don't trust you. Another thing working for us, the coroner couldn't find a bullet wound in Monique's head to corroborate the witness accounts of you shooting her. So ... if we can find a way to look past how you mangled her body this week ... and her fang-infested mouth, we can probably write off last week's murder as no more than acid-induced, overzealous imagination from a few disreputable witnesses. Hell, I can probably sell it as no more than an ill-conceived propaganda stunt. This week's mess is a different story. The heat from my boss is building. I can't keep covering up all of your bullshit by passing the blame on these clowns."

"Relax, Mitch, I can handle your boss. Bring him to me tomorrow at sunset. I will persuade him this is not a routine police matter."

"I appreciate that Brian, but I think my boss will be much better served not knowing you personally." Exasperated, Mitch placed both hands on his cheeks. "I am not sure it isn't time for me to retire, again. My boss might be better served just thinking I am incompetent, rather than deal with all of this shit." O'Reilly gestured about the room as he shook his head woefully.

"It is your call." I looked back to Dee, who was rubbing her wrist. "For now, I would like to take my friends out of here. I will make sure Dee contacts you tomorrow and gives you a statement, so you can put these freaks away. You might have to wait a few days for Phillip over there."

"Just make sure she stops by tomorrow. I don't want any of these lunatics back on the street." Mitch pulled his radio out. "O'Reilly here, I've got civilians on the way out, let them pass. What do you want me to do with him?" O'Reilly asked, thumbing towards Phillip.

"We could leave him there; I don't think he would move for several days." The thought brought a partial smile, reminiscing the occasions I had done exactly the same after a blowout party. "But I do not believe Samantha's sister would find that amusing."

"We could, just to see how long it takes him to fall off his barstool," Mitch said grinning. "You want rescue to pick him up?"

"No, I'll take him with us. He will sleep it off in a day or two." I returned to Dee with a strained smile.

Dee, not fully recovered from her shock, was still leaning on the table.

"Are you ready to go? Can you walk?"

She nodded, but the confusion and fear still gripped her expression. I helped her with the first steps and ushered her toward Phillip. I hoisted him over my shoulder and led Dee toward the exit.

"Show off," Mitch mused as we passed. "Don't worry about this, I'll take care of cleaning up your mess, again."

Heading down the darkened stairs, Dee grabbed my waist to steady herself. Five cops were surveying the disaster area that was the main bar as we passed through. Amongst the suspicious stares, I overheard a whispered accusation, "That's him."

Out on the street, away from prying ears, my irritation returned. "Dee, what in the hell were you two doing in that place?"

"Looking for you." Dee spoke with trepidation. "Your buddy from Utopia said you might be there. Once we got there, the bartender said you had been a nightly regular. She told us to wait upstairs." Dee paused, and looked away from the intensity in my eyes. "I think they were going to kill me."

"That and more." I wanted Dee to understand the magnitude of the danger, to learn to exercise more caution when dealing with those people. I wanted all of them to leave New Orleans until I was done. Their return had complicated matters beyond my ability to cope.

"Brian, what you just did. How did you ... Sam said you were some kind of government agent, but I have never seen anything like that outside a movie. How did you do all of that?"

"All of what?" Playing innocent was never my strong card.

"I might be more traumatized than I have ever been in my life, but please don't take me for an idiot." Dee scurried ahead and turned, waiting to gauge my reply.

"Are you staying at your apartment?"

"No. Sam wanted to stay at your hotel, so Phillip and I got a room there as well. And don't try to change the subject. I am not as easily diverted as my sister."

"I would not call Samantha *easily* diverted."

"I am still waiting for an answer." Dee blocked my path, forcing me into an ocular inquisition.

"Can this wait until we get back to the hotel and I put Phillip down?"

"What's wrong, a little heavier than you expected?"

"Not really, I just need the time to make up a good story." I grinned and sidestepped Dee, accelerating my pace. Her sideways crab walk no longer sufficient to maintain the pace, she turned and scurried behind.

We covered the three remaining blocks in short order and passed through the lobby. It was Samantha over my shoulder, the big scene four nights ago, and now Phillip had taken her place. The self-proclaimed Mr. Low Profile, I was not.

"I should check in on Sam," Dee suggested, as we entered the elevator.

"She is sleeping, I checked in on her earlier, just before I went to The Chamber."

Eight doors down from my room, Dee slid the key into the lock. I carried Phillip to the bed and flopped him down.

"Now, you and I are going to have a little chat Brian." Dee took my hand and led me to the sitting-room sofa and pushed me down. She pulled a chair up close, interrogation style, slapped her hand on my leg, and stared me right in the eyes. "No bullshitting, what is going on?"

I knew it would only be a matter of time before she found out. It made sense to tell her everything. Maybe she could help me figure out how to end things with Sam.

"Do you know the full story of who I am, and why I'm here?"

"Phillip told me everything you wanted me to know." Dee replied.

"Then you should know everything that has transpired, up until the time you left." I paused. After this confession, there would be no going back. "Before I tell you, I want you to know, I love Samantha. I never wanted to hurt her."

"Go on, I am listening." Whatever effects Dee suffered from her ordeal, any lingering effects were vanquished by her desire to learn the truth.

"The night you left for New York," I began with a sigh, "I arranged to meet a very evil woman at Utopia, with every intention of killing her. I even had the New Orleans Police Department for back up. From that point, everything went wrong. Somehow, she seized control over my willpower, took me to a vacant house, where she," I hesitated, as I visualized the sequence of events that followed.

"You had sex with her?" Dee ascertained.

I frowned. Obviously even as a vampire, I could be shamed.

"How could you?"

"You don't understand, Dee, their willpower is incredibly strong."

"Oh, when it comes to sex, I am sure your desire is pretty strong too." Dee's berating tone showed no sympathy.

"Dee, let me finish."

"I think you are quite finished, Brian." She stood up and placed her hands on her hips. The conversation was over.

"Dee, I need to explain."

"What more is there to explain, Brian?"

"Damn it, Dee, the woman was a vampire! When she was done with me … she tried to kill me. But to her surprise, I was stronger and faster. I killed Monique, I killed her with my bare hands." I paused for the *coup de gras*. Dee's expression of shock was about to elevate to new heights. "Dee, I have become a vampire as well."

Dee's ghastly expression instantly changed, surprisingly to one of amusement. She took a step backward. "Brian, I don't know what to say. When Phillip first told me, and then I saw the video ... I believed these people were demented murderers, but not real vampires." Dee's speech was accelerating, her anxiety obvious. "Then tonight, those assholes, they all thought they were vampires. And now you confess to fucking and then killing a woman with your bare hands? What the hell were you thinking, getting my sister involved? You are out of your mind, just like those idiots at the club."

"Shhh," I suggested.

"I am not going to *shhh*. You need to get the hell out of this room and Samantha's life right ..."

Dee's eyes bulged in fear, her ability to speak interrupted, suppressed by a force unknown. "I told you Dee, the will of a vampire is strong. Take off my jacket," I ordered.

Unwillingly, she pulled the shoulders of the jacket back, and let it drop to the floor. "Refuse me, cry out," I taunted. The exhilaration of controlling the human mind so effortlessly was intoxicating. I circled Dee, as if she were prey. I leaned close and whispered in her ear, "Resist me."

"Take off your shirt," I commanded softly. Conflict raged in her eyes, but her body succumbed. From my experience with Angelique, I understood the absolute surrender forced upon her. Without buttons, the shirt fell quickly to the floor.

"Ask me to stop, or I might take more than your body." I flashed a sinister grin, exposing my glistening fangs. "Yes, they are quite real." I picked my Armani jacket from the floor and dusted it off. "Take off your bra," I ordered silently, my mind dominating her every effort to resist. Her eyes begged for mercy as she began to comply. "That is enough." Halting her involuntary strip, I maintained complete dominance of her free will.

I pulled my jacket back over her shoulders. "I hope you now understand, but you left me no option. Monique left me no option. I do not know how I survived, or how this happened to me, but it did." Upon releasing her, Dee gasped for air.

"If I had any clue this would happen, I would have taken Sam and run away from this place, forever." Dee gazed at me, fearfully, untrusting, as she pulled the jacket tightly around.

"Dee, you need not fear me. I had to prove it to you."

"How do I know I can trust you?"

"When you were tied to the table, helpless, half naked, and blood running down your arm," I paused, reflecting on the moment of such strong desire, "believe me, you can trust me."

"Good Lord, Brian, what are you going to do?"

"What I was planning, before you showed up, was to track down the four remaining vampires, kill them, and then, have a good friend return the favor. That is what I was planning. Needless to say, your arrival created a major hiccup."

"So what are you going to do now?"

"Well, pretty much the same thing, only I am going to have to say goodbye to your sister face- to-face." I turned away, wondering if there could be a compromise. "And just when I thought my life just could not get any shittier."

"Brian, you cannot tell Sam goodbye. She is in love with you. She was ready to stay here and die with you."

"Dee, for three days I have been tormented by the thought, but there is no *sailing off in the sunset* scenario now. Hell, I cannot even go in the sun. Tomorrow night, I will confess myself, and then I *will* tell her goodbye."

"You really don't know my sister very well, do you? She will not let you go that easily. Maybe there is some way to ..."

"Stop, Dee! There is no way she can be a part of my life. Ever! I am a vampire, the living dead. Tonight alone, I have already drunk two pints of blood and a fifth of whiskey, assaulted at least twenty five people, and almost made a late night snack out of my girlfriend's sister."

Dee raised her eyebrows to the last reference. "Did I miss something?"

"You will never know." Through all the strife, it was hard not to smirk at the thought.

Dee delivered an open palm punch to the shoulder, "Don't forget to add to your list forcing me to undress."

"While we are at it, even though it was three nights ago, let's not forget about Monique either." Wanting to solidify my case for walking away from Sam, I continued to tally any pertinent facts.

"Based on what you just put me through, I think that is one detail

Sam does not need to know."

"Which part? The sex thing, or the part where I killed her with my bare hands."

"Both."

"Dee, I won't lie to Sam," I insisted.

"This is exactly why you need to rethink this whole thing. You are a good man, Brian. Sam loves you, and you love her. There has to be some way to work through this."

"Dee, my life is now cursed. I cannot look at a cross, step in a church, or touch Holy Water. I will burn in the sunlight. Eventually, I will sleep in a coffin and I am sure to develop a most serious drinking problem. And eventually, I will be hunted, just as I hunt those responsible."

Listening intently, Dee considered the points, her eyes counting off options. "Samantha will not give you up so easily."

"That is why I need you in my corner, Dee. You need to be the voice of logic."

"I am in your corner, Brian. That is why I won't facilitate your plans. I think you can be different from the others. You proved tonight that you are not all evil."

"What if, just now, I had not stopped? There is no guarantee I will always be able to control myself."

"My sister would not be happy. Mainly, because twenty years from now she would look like crap, and I would still be gorgeous."

"God, you are so like your sister," I groaned. "Doesn't it bother you in the least, the thought of your sister with a vampire?"

"What bothers me more is the thought of Sam being with some jackass like Mike again. Talk about a vampire."

"Sun will be coming up soon." I headed to the door, glancing at Phillip passed out on the bed. "He been treating you all right?"

"Until a couple of hours ago, he has been wonderful. He has been worried sick about you, thinks this is all his fault. When this is over, I am going back to New York to stay a while. I believe your friend is deeply in like with me."

"He has always needed someone special, to put a foot up his ass and keep him in line. I honestly believe you are that woman, Dee." The thought made me smile, something far and few experienced over the past few days.

"Brian," Dee called following me out the door. "I know it might not seem like it, but there has to be a good side to all of this. Promise me, for Sam's sake, you will try to find it before you make any rash decisions."

I wish I could see a greater purpose, but for the moment, I was blind to it. I nodded my head, if only to offer temporary assurance. "When you are done with my jacket, would you be kind enough to leave it in my room?"

Dee pulled the jacket off and handed it over. Half dressed and damn proud, she grinned. I couldn't help but sneak a glance at her exquisite shape. "You *are* so much like your sister, in more ways than one."

"And in some ways, you will just have to imagine." She playfully closed the door in my face.

If she only knew how truly difficult it had been. To refrain from taking her body and blood was an epic test of resolve. Dee opened the door, and stuck her head out. "Hey,"

"Hey," I sighed.

"You keep a handle on that drinking problem and things will be all right."

I kissed her on the forehead and turned away. "Let me know when you find a support group for that."

CHAPTER FIVE

"YOU NEED TO see this, sir," the young man said, hurriedly entering Paul Watson's office.

Watson, senior officer in charge of retired agent management, was sitting at his desk scrolling through mounds of digital mail. Bald and weathered, Watson's fifty years of faithful service to his country had landed the desk job few had the stomach for.

"Let's see what you have, Agent Tanner." He scanned the image briefly, instantly recognizing the face. The image of the man had to be taken at least twenty years ago. "Where did this come from?"

"Peterson was clearing the main frame server's deleted waste files. He came across this in a hidden archive file that would have been scheduled for automatic deletion at midnight. He checks the file destruction system randomly, as a security protocol, and found this hidden file."

"When did this picture run the digital face recognition database?" Watson's temperament was even keel, his voice showing no undue concern. His calm mannerisms began to transfer to the much younger agent.

"Four days ago, sir."

"Do we know who ran it?"

"New Orleans PD, sir," Tanner's initial excitement was tempered by the monotone subdued demeanor of his senior agent.

"I suppose you have a name to go with this picture?"

"Yes, sir, New Orleans PD arrested a Brian Denman, who comes up as a ghost. I did some extensive research and ID'd him as Nick Gabriel. Here is his file," Tanner said, as he proudly handed over the documents. "He was permanently retired for over twenty years, the victim of a targeted hit."

"I know this man. We need to start a new case file. I want to know why Mr. Gabriel, or someone who looks like him, is a person of interest to the New Orleans PD."

"Well, sir," Tanner began, as he handed over a second manila folder, "it seems as though he is a suspect in a shooting at a night club in New Orleans. Before he could be booked on charges, he escaped. According to our sources, he may be involved with the murder of an unknown female victim, approximately twenty-four years of age. Currently, his whereabouts are unknown."

"And do we know how this particular file came to be scheduled for deletion without a red flag?" Impressed with the rookie's thoroughness, Watson studied the picture, waiting to see if the youngster had discovered the photo's age discrepancy.

"Two possible scenarios: the first, and most probable, is somebody inside the agency did it, either by accident, or intentionally. The second scenario is somebody hacked into the system and deleted the file from the outside. The data footprint appears to have been covered by someone very skilled in file manipulation. We also are having issues with the outside source theory; the moment New Orleans ran the image, we should have caught the red flag from the same software. For an outside source to have deleted the file before we caught it, they would have to be monitoring our system twenty-four seven. And there is no way that is taking place. That leaves us with the inside agent theory, sir. But at this early stage, we don't have evidence that points to anyone."

"Any chance this was some kind of computer glitch?" Watson asked.

"No, sir," Tanner reported, wondering if he had missed something.

"You did not find it peculiar Agent Gabriel was a notorious hack in his years of service?"

"No, sir, there was no mention of any computer skills in his files at all." Tanner knew something was amiss, but he had reviewed the file thoroughly, twice.

Watson opened the file and thumbed through a few pages. "Son of a bitch," he said as he shot out of his chair. His voice raised an octave and a decibel higher.

"Some smart-ass has replaced Gabriel's records with mine." Watson slammed the folder down on the oak desk. "Call in everyone for a meeting in one hour. Nobody goes home until I have answers. I want to know where and when Gabriel's records went AWOL. In his day, Gabriel was the best of the bad asses. I know, I recruited him. Somebody is fucking with us."

Watson sat back down and brushed his hand through the imaginary hair that had left him twenty years ago. Distant memories blitzed through his mind. "When we lost Nick we lost one of our best. With all of the facial recognition software in place over the whole country, there has never been one hit since his death. I want to know who is doing this and why."

There was an unsettling moment of silence for the rookie as Watson was lost in a blank stare.

"This picture; how did you manage to match it to Gabriel?"

"Well, because of the great lengths somebody took attempting to delete it, I figured with no matches, it was a sure bet the same individual had wiped the image from all facial recognition software protocols. The only hit was from ID badge photos taken in 1991. All other references to Gabriel were gone," Tanner said.

"The only problem, this photo is of a guy between thirty and forty. Gabriel, if he is alive, is near sixty. Any chance we have an offspring, or somebody inserted an old file photo just to fuck with us?" Watson asked.

Tanner's confidence took a slight hit, as he paused to collect his thoughts. "Computer says the match certainty is ninety nine point six percent positive. So unless Gabriel has had plastic surgery, we'll proceed as if somebody has breached our system, and inserted Gabriel's photo for unknown motives."

"Call Murphy in New Orleans. Have him pay a visit to the detective who worked the case. I want details before lunch. Get going, pronto."

Once Tanner departed, Watson rose from his desk, walked

slowly to the door and closed it firmly, listening to the solitary click of the latch. If he was alive, Gabriel had surpassed all the odds, the only operative to accomplish surviving a lifetime of top-level missions. Nobody with this clearance was supposed to retire.

"Nick Gabriel, why are you back from the dead?"

Reaching for his cell phone, he pushed speed dial number nine. The phone rang twice before a scrambled voice answered. "Compliance, Gabriel, Nicholas, New Orleans."

Watson hung up the phone. It was never easy to make the call to terminate an agent, much less twice. But there was an obligation to fulfill. Charged with protecting the dirty secrets of the nation he served, Watson knew this was the very reason he could never retire. He lived with the fear of the call: Compliance, Watson, Paul, Arlington.

Samantha woke from a most invigorating sleep, unlike any she remembered. Gazing around the room now filled with only distant memories, she wondered, had Brian actually been here holding her, or had it just been a dream born of desire and Ambien. Samantha yearned for the warmth of the morning sun as it filtered through the sheers, but her distress would not allow such simple pleasure. Then a most delicate aroma caressed her senses. Turning to the source of the fragrance, her eyes sparkled at the sight of a crystal vase filled with roses. Brian *was* here!

Samantha jumped from the bed and searched the room for luggage. Eagerly heading down to Dee and Phillip's room, she knocked on the door anxiously, anticipating her suitcase to be inside. It was after eleven in the morning. "Damn it," she groaned. Pounding harder before giving up, Samantha headed to the lobby for an extra key.

Samantha spotted Dee on the lobby couch, her back turned, sitting next to a man who looked familiar. She moved in stealthily to eavesdrop. Samantha listened intently as Dee described to Mitch O'Reilly the attack last night as she slept; the drugging of Phillip, the assault and threats of a sick ritualistic phlebotomy, and eventually, Brian's daring rescue. What followed was devastation beyond comprehension. Dee recounted, verbatim, her conversation with Brian back at the hotel.

Words echoed, then fused together as one taunting confession. *Brian is a vampire.* Over and over the words burned. Feeling flush, her body swayed near collapse, Samantha staggered toward the couch.

"Dee?" she called weakly.

"Oh my God, Sam!" Dee jumped from the couch and ran to her sister's aid.

O'Reilly followed Dee's lead, and helped stabilize Samantha.

Samantha collapsed in their arms. Once on the couch, Dee cradled her sister against her body. "It's okay Sammy, it's okay," she comforted, gently trying to reassure Sam.

O'Reilly knew he had enough information to charge the ten lunatics from the club with assault and attempted rape, supported by the discovery of the club's illegal cactus juice supply. Additionally, ten pints of blood were recovered from the crime scene, of which for the time being, O'Reilly was sure he could divert five pints to an unnamed Good Samaritan who was probably getting a little hungry.

"If you don't need me or have any further questions, I will give you some time alone with your sister." Compassion had never been one of O'Reilly's strong suits, but after what he had seen, he figured it was a good time to change his ways.

O'Reilly handed Dee his card. "Brian saved my life. So if you need anything from me, anytime, night or day, call me."

"Thank you," Dee witnessed the sincerity in O'Reilly's expression, too many times vacant in most men's self-indulging offers for assistance.

"How much did you hear?" Dee asked, as she rummaged for anything to help dry her sister's tears.

"Enough to understand just how screwed up everything is."

"First, I need to make sure you know everything I know. It's the only way you can decide where you go from here."

Painstakingly, Dee recounted all that she knew about Brian's transformation and the sordid details surrounding it. Over and over Samantha heard the word *vampire*. When Dee finished Samantha wrung her hands. "I don't know what to do ... I was ready to spend the rest of my life with him."

"Well, I would not jump to make any decisions immediately, but he does love you. That has not changed. The biggest change is his sleeping arrangements ... and his diet. But the guy is ready to end his life just to protect you from himself. And I have never met a guy I could say would do the same for me."

"What would you do?"

"I think we should meet Brian for dinner, tonight ... after sunset. He also has a little problem with sunlight." Dee allowed a reassuring smile to telegraph her belief things were not as bad as one might perceive.

Samantha returned the gesture. "Damn. So much for spending the rest of our lives on a remote beach soaking up some rays."

"I hear it is possible to get a pretty nasty moon burn, if you try."

"So you're all right, with Brian being a vampire?" Sam questioned, literally amazed at her sister's disposition.

"If he will love you, protect you, and treat you like you deserve, and, let's not forget, not drink your blood, then yes, I think I'm okay with it," Dee said with resolve. "We will meet him for dinner. Just give him a chance, before you decide to drive a stake in his heart."

"Dee, that's definitely not funny." Samantha wrestled a smile from her face.

"Yes it is, you're just upset your boyfriend is a blood sucker and mine isn't."

"Oh, I'm so going to kick your ass when this is all over," Sam moaned.

"Now that's more like it. There's my Sammy," Dee proclaimed happily.

CHAPTER SIX

THE SUN HAD not yet set as I awoke in my makeshift bed; a bathtub padded with extra quilts. Unable to rest comfortably, I began to wonder if there was something to that casket thing after all.

How am I going to explain this to Sam? I had mulled the question for the better part of the day. Unable to come up with a reasonable solution, I redirected my thoughts to Isabelle, who had forced me to consider the possibility my unnatural youthfulness was not the by-product of proper diet and exercise.

Isabelle claimed to be one hundred years old; yet she is not a vampire. How is that possible? She occasionally drinks blood, but she walks with the living. She is human, but, somehow interwoven with this vampire culture. *Maybe the book Daniel promised to deliver would yield the answers I desperately sought.*

I powered my phone on and reluctantly dialed the number, fully aware of the lecture to follow.

On the third ring a husky voice answered the call.

"Aunt Rena, it's Nick." Nicholas was my birth name. During my years at the CIA, I operated under many aliases. After I retired I continued the practice, as a way to keep everyone off my tail. In

Phillip's social circle I was known as Brian Denman. But I possessed many other identities, and as Mitch had discovered a few days ago, none traceable back to my true identity.

"Nicholas," Aunt Rena reprimanded, her thick Romanian accent emphasizing her stern disapproval, "it has been over three months!"

"Aunt Rena, I am sorry. I have been on a job." Vampire or not, I was reduced to the mischievous child she raised once again.

"Too busy for one phone call?"

"I need to see you, tomorrow night."

"What is wrong?" Aware of the tension in my voice, her tone became somewhat sympathetic.

"We will talk tomorrow. Can I see you then?"

"Nicholas, you know you don't need to ask," she reminded, "I will make your favorite pasta."

"You don't need to do that."

"Nonsense! The last time you came home you looked as though you had not eaten for weeks. I will make dinner, and you will eat." Her voice demanded compliance.

"Thank you," I replied. Having never won an argument, and already in her doghouse, I was at her mercy. "I will see you tomorrow, but it will probably be late. Don't wait up."

"Make sure you come hungry, Nicholas," she ordered, ignoring my request and then hung up.

The logistics of getting to New York quickly and avoiding daylight would be virtually impossible. I punched in Dee's cell number next.

"Hello," she answered, sounding remarkably similar to Sam, and cheerful.

The tone of her voice lifted my spirits. "Hi. It's me."

"How did you get my number?"

"Job-related benefits." If she only knew the information I had access to. "What do you say to Dushea's, after dark, say around nine thirty?"

"We will be there."

I hung up, and peeked out into the room. The sun had set enough for me to venture into the bedroom. A weathered book sat on the bedside table. Flipping through the delicate pages of the tattered book, I read with amazing speed the chronicles of the Ursuline

Convent vampires.

Written by an assortment of nuns, priests, and convent guards, the pages began shortly after the women were confined to the third floor in the mid-1800s, quarantined by the demands of the distrustful public. Turning the pages, I discovered how the eight innocent human women succumbed to the evil requisites of Monique and Angelique. Notations of the implementations of safeguards, personal thoughts, prayers, and a smorgasbord of human interaction, filled the pages in random detail.

And there, crudely confessed by a male guard on the pages of this historic document, was the account of cruel deception. The last remaining mortal woman was offered freedom by the guard in exchange for sexual favors. My pace slowed as I read, painfully sharing the emotional angst of a woman terrified by the fate which had already befallen seven of her friends. She heard the agonizing screams of life draining into the abyss of the undead; the raw fear of knowing each day might be the day the *others* would choose to satisfy their insatiable hunger with her blood. She lived with the fear that her baby, now growing inside, was condemned to death, before it would ever breathe life's first precious breath.

I briefly closed the book. *Man, that guard was a prick.* He knew what the deal was, and not only did he lie about his intentions, he allowed this girl to die, as well as his child, and then had the balls to write it all down. I opened the book again, compelled to learn more.

Her name was Sabine. She was the tenth vampire, the final transformation. The one who vanished without a trace.

Sabine was finally taken, feasted on, and born to the undead. She remained a recluse to her new sisterhood. Removed by a nun and two guards for childbirth, Sabine was returned to the confines of the Convent's third floor after the birth of her child, a baby girl. The infant was taken, leaving Sabine to presume her *unholy* baby had been destroyed.

I read on, saddened by the revelations of this tragic tale. For nights, Sabine cried out for her lost child ... the name I read hit me like a runaway freight train. *Isabelle.*

"Isabelle!" I shouted loud enough to be heard throughout the floor.

Isabelle. Was she the mortal child of an impregnated human

turned vampire during pregnancy? I had never come across any references to vampires giving birth. Could this be a coincidence? A renewed spirit welled within me. A purpose of good. I had to find Sabine, not to exterminate, but reunite her with Isabelle. Perhaps the daughter lost nearly two centuries ago.

Closing the book, a long-overdue exuberance swept through me. Was this Daniel's alleged *purpose* for me? I had to go *now*. I had to see Sam and explain everything.

I pulled the curtain back far enough to see the sun had set. It was time to go. I made a quick detour to the safe house after I exited the hotel. Instinctively looking in the fridge for a beer, I discovered Daniel had already stocked up my coffers. "Cocktail time." I raised the bottle mocking a toast. "Make mine a bloody Mary, or John, or bloody anybody, come to think of it."

Draining the bottle, I instantly felt invigorated, almost to the point of intoxication. The thought of another round crossed my mind, but how easy could the addiction become uncontrollable? Better to test restraint now, in the solitude of this musty office, rather than in the public eye, or worse yet, the public's neck. Sadly, for the first time in my brief unnatural history, I began to understand the urge to consume. The power it possessed within, and the restraint required to abstain.

Before the maître d' could offer her assistance, I breezed past, instincts guiding me. I found Sam at a table for two, a glass of wine in her hand. The tension etched on her face combined with an uncommon rapid toe tapping revealed her apprehension of our meeting. My pace slowed, all my logical reservations lined up to battle the love I still harbored for this vision of beauty.

"Sam." My voice was unrecognizably timid.

As she turned, her eyes glowed briefly, but were doused by the realization of what stood before her. Rising to greet me, her hug was less than enthusiastic. No doubt, any hug was more than I deserved. I savored the sensation of her warm body, pressed against mine. "Please sit," she said, quickly breaking contact while gazing to the floor.

"Sam ..."

"Brian!"

Interrupting what was sure to be another in the long series of babbling speeches I had become suddenly famous for, she abruptly looked up, boring deep into my eyes like never before. I did not know what to make of the intensity before me. If not already doomed, cursed, and dead, it might have even frightened me.

"I know everything. And I do mean *everything.* So you need to keep your mouth shut and listen to what I have to say."

"But ..."

"Shhh. You need to prove you know how to follow instructions, right now."

"Sam ..." I tried again.

Fearless in the face of the creature I had become, Sam pointed a sharp finger at me. "Don't! You will know when I want you to talk." Raising her hand to her lip, she twisted her index finger and thumb. The *lock it* command had been issued. "Understand?"

No woman, not even Aunt Rena, had ever put me in my place the way Samantha had. I had to look away.

"Oh no you don't, Brian Denman." She reached across the table and aimed my chin, redirecting my eyes to hers. "I only asked one thing of you when I left. Do you remember?"

I nodded silently.

"Considering your current circumstances, would you agree that you failed miserably to keep your promise?"

Again I nodded my head.

"You said you were going to kill vampires, but you failed to mention that would involve having sex with them."

"It was only one," I began to explain.

"Aht! Do not say a word. I did not ask for your commentary yet. Dee told me every detail. And, considering all of the circumstances, the fact you were under some kind of spell, you did still manage to kill this woman, with your bare hands no less, which makes me feel a little better since she fucked you ..." Sam paused, attempting to recollect her composure. "I won't say I am not royally pissed at you for having sex with her, but I am trying to get past that."

Sam sat back and sighed, her expression softened.

"Before I left, I knew what I wanted. I was willing to stay here and do whatever I could to help, even if it meant dying beside you." Again Samantha's expression strained as she leaned in. "Dee told me your plan, once the others are dead. I will not allow that. I still love you. I just don't know how to do this, but I do know we belong together. You are just going to have to figure out how to make it work."

Preparing to fire off a long list of damned good reasons, once again, Sam squashed the bug.

"Look at the mess that you got us into. You listen to me now. I have been thinking ... all day and I know there are going to be some challenges, like sleeping arrangements, meals, vacationing, and diets, but we can make it up as we go, until the day comes that it doesn't work. And I don't see that ever happening, as long as you quit having sex with other vampires ... and making my sister take her clothes off."

Sam turned her head, obviously finding some humor in Dee's plight; Sam tried to conceal a brief smile.

"And don't think you can use that mind control stuff on me later tonight, or any other time for that matter. I am way too pissed off right now for any of that nonsense. You have no clue how much I was looking forward to our first night back together. And you had better pray you have not contracted any nasty vampire ho disease."

I looked at her, expressing permission to speak. "Are you done?"

"Probably not, I'm sure I haven't covered everything," Sam vented, with a long sigh.

"Is it okay for me to talk?"

"That would depend on what you have to say." Sam swallowed the remainder of her half-filled wine glass hard. She reached for the bottle of Merlot and filled the glass to the top.

I looked down at the table before beginning. Even though she had found a way to make light of certain aspects of our predicament, my shame would not afford my eyes the honesty, and perhaps forgiveness, I knew her eyes would offer. Timorously, I raised mine to hers.

"For three days, I could never sort out where to begin, how to tell you. I am grateful you made it look so easy, even though I know it was anything but. Most importantly, I do love you. I will love you forever. From there, I do not have a clue where to go next. I am afraid. I just don't know what I am capable of, or how to make us work."

I reached out and took Sam's hands. "I don't think I can ever sleep in a regular bed again, I have an unnatural appetite for liquid cuisine, and any plans for a big church wedding ..."

"Did you just say wedding?" Sam was flabbergasted.

"Before you left for New York, yes. The thought might have crossed my mind several times."

"So church or beach weddings are both off the list?"

"Maybe a moonlit beach wedding." I smiled for the first time in a week.

Sam gazed in my eyes, the glare of persecution gone, replaced by a gleaming compassion. "You are such an ass," she said softly. "Why did this happen?"

"Do you believe in destiny?" I figured now was as good a time as any to test her level of tolerance.

"Yes." She released one hand and reached for her glass. "You're cold."

"Occupational hazard. No more sweaty sex."

"That could be a deal breaker." Her face lightened, acknowledging with my pledged love in her hands, she was ready for anything.

"I'll buy you a sauna." The burden was lifted, at least temporarily, as once again the woman I believed could move mountains, had returned to me. "Anyhow, you know how old I am?"

Sam nodded yes.

"Well I met a woman in New Orleans who claims to be over two hundred. Yet she looks about the same age as me. A journal from the Old Ursuline Convent was given to me. Some of the stuff written leads me to believe that this woman might not be as delusional as I first believed. There's a possibility that she is the child of a vampire woman and a mortal man, making her immortal, and yet not a vampire. So I began to consider, maybe she and I shared some kind of hereditary immortality."

Sam's forehead wrinkled with incertitude. "*Hereditary immortality?* What is that supposed to mean?"

"If we believe her story, she's old, but looks about the same age as me. I'm sixtyish, and until this week, survived all kinds of shit that would have killed most men. Neither one of us knows our parents, although mine are from Romania ..."

"Brian, I know where you are headed with this and that's just crazy. You keep yourself in great shape and have a disgusting case of baby face. You are not the only man to enjoy these youthful attributes. You are sixtyish; she claims to be over one hundred. She is from New Orleans, you are from New York. You were not immortal before that disgusting act with Monique."

"I am not so sure, Sam. When I arrived here, I had frequent premonitions about this place. And let's not forget, how many guys do you know who took a bullet to the brain, and lived?"

"A man in Brazil took a steel rod through his skull last year and lived. I saw the pictures on the Internet. So, both of you had a destiny to live, not immortality. Proof that you have a purpose beyond the life you were leading."

"Maybe so, but I just don't know. That is why I am flying to New York tomorrow night to see my Aunt. She is the only one who knows about my family history."

"You are leaving tomorrow night? And, what about the rest of the vampires?"

"They are gone, and until I can find them, I need some concrete answers."

"When will you be back?"

"I do not know. Mitch, along with Chuck and Jimmy, will continue to search for clues about the locations of the vampires. If they find them, they will let me know where they are. But until then, I want you to come to New York and stay at my home. You definitely have to meet my Aunt Rena."

"Are you sure?"

"All of my life, not always patiently mind you, my Aunt has waited for me to fall in love. I do not want the opportunity to make her happy pass me by."

"Then I would love to come with you," Sam said with a gleam, as she squeezed my hand a little tighter.

I rolled my eyes up at the ceiling.

"What is it Brian?" Sam asked.

"After all that we have been through, I need to ask for your understanding, one last time."

"At this point, I do not know what you could possibly say that requires *more* understanding."

"Well, when I left the CIA, I feared they would not let me live long.

I knew too many secrets. Guys in my specialized line of work usually did not live more than five years. I was the only one, to the best of my knowledge, to actually retire. After two quiet years, I thought I was in the clear. That is when the bitch capped me in the head. Initially, I thought it was a retaliation hit from my Colombian buddies.

"I woke up alone, in the hospital, in the middle of the night. I did not know who to trust. I called in Rob who helped me stage my death, and then I went dark. I developed a multitude of identities, just like the one you witnessed several nights ago. Nobody was looking for me any longer, so it was rather easy to stay dead to the world."

Sam looked eager to hear more. "And?"

"Nicholas Gabriel. That is my real name. Phillip does not even know it."

"Nicholas?"

"Or just Nick."

"Bri—Nicholas ... I have had all of the surprises I can handle on an empty stomach. Can we join Dee and Phillip for dinner now?" Sam took two great gulps of wine to finish her glass.

With a slightly embarrassed, awkward smile, Sam leaned across the table and kissed me on the lips. "Nicholas, I like that. A much more appropriate name for a sexy vampire than Brian, don't you think?"

"What in the hell have you guys been doing?" Dee crowed, Phillip propped against her, his mouth hanging open. "I was about to eat the candles."

"How is he?" I smiled, having personally experienced the misery of the peyote cocktail.

"In and out, still trying to sleep it off, Dee giggled.

"Apparently I will not be the only one sleeping with the dead tonight," Sam taunted. "Mom warned you about playing with strangers. Now look what's happened to poor Phillip."

"We will take a bottle of this," Dee said pointing to her wine glass to the waiter behind me, "and an assortment of appetizers. Pick your favorite three, and bring them as quickly as possible, please." Dee shrugged unapologetically. "I have not eaten since lunch yesterday."

Dee leaned in to the table, "Did he show you the fangs?"

"Dee!" Sam gasped.

"Did he do the mind control thing?"

"*No,* and he won't be doing that … ever!"

"Easy sis, it's not every day my little sister decides to hook up with a vampire. What will Mother say?"

I smiled politely as the sisters sparred as if I weren't there.

"Brian and I are planning to go to New York tomorrow, preferably on Phillip's jet. Do you think Phillip will mind?"

Dee looked to Phillip, whose head was back against the wall, mouth agape like a Venus flytrap awaiting prey. Dee grabbed the top of Phillip's head and nodded it up and down. "Phillip says it's a company jet, and since he owns the company, he is fine with that, but please don't leave it on empty."

As we shared a laugh, Phillip's eyes popped open. "Brian," he said with a groggy smile. His eyes rolled back and he slumped back to Peyoteville once again.

"They must have really juiced our boy up. I was not nearly this bad." I decided it was best to just join the girls' lackadaisical attitudes and forget about my problems for the evening. They were not just *my* problems, but Sam's and Dee's as well. So if they could put it behind them, at least for the present moment, then so should I.

The food, which only nights ago created such a wondrous festival of flavor, had lost its magnificent appeal. As the night wore on, Sam and Dee began to show signs of fatigue, I suggested we call it a night.

"Are we just supposed to leave you, so you can roam the streets?" Dee asked.

"Got nowhere else to be. Seems suddenly I have become quite the night owl."

"You could ask Sam to keep you company tonight, to make sure you behave." Dee gave us both a mischievous wink.

"I do not believe that is a great idea, at least not quite this soon," I snapped back.

"Oooo," Dee toyed, as Sam pouted. "If he's refusing your company, then we should insist he show you his fangs."

Sam whipped her head around to me, expecting me to oblige. Not ready to concede to the freak show exposé, I smiled politely. "Alright, have it your way ladies … Sam can come. But don't blame me if the vampire population increases by one tonight." I looked over at Phillip. "How in the world did you get him in here?"

"Believe it or not, he kind of walked." Dee laughed. "Sam and I will meet you out front," Dee said as she grabbed Sam by the elbow and led her away.

"You know buddy, in the old days I could have just left your ass here. Now look where all of this girlfriend trouble has gotten the both of us." I tossed Phillip over my shoulder and departed with stares, finger pointing, and laughs as we passed through to the street.

Renaldo, ever vigilant of his duties, immediately greeted our arrival with a hearty laugh. "Oh my Mister Denman, this is becoming a nightly ritual, seeing you tote somebody through the lobby. It's going to get pretty boring once you check out."

"Why on earth would I ever want to check out, Renaldo?" I asked smiling.

After dropping Phillip and Dee off at their room, I took Sam's hand and led her to our room. "We don't have to do this you know."

"I know." A nervous flutter in Sam's voice announced her reservations. "Back in the ladies room, Dee and I were talking about the night you killed Monique. You know, after you had sex with her?"

"You still remember that trivial ancient history?"

"Yes, I do." Sam's wrinkled smile displayed conflicting emotions. "Well in the process, you lost your cross."

Having never crossed my mind, the sudden realization vexed me.

"Well, O'Reilly found it where you ... did it, removed the evidence and gave it to Renaldo, who gave it to me." Sam was fidgeting with her hands, struggling with her words. "I gave it to Dee back at the restaurant. I told her I wouldn't be needing it again."

I had begun to slide my key card into the lock, but stopped as suddenly the fear of uncertainty gripped me. "Sam ..."

"Shhh," she ordered, as she guided my hand toward the lock. "Brian," she began and paused with a sigh, "Nick ... I am scared as hell, but whatever happens, as long as we're together ..."

"Shhh," I said, "One step at a time."

As I closed the door slowly, the soft solitary click of the lock sealed in the night and whatever ends it might bring.

CHAPTER SEVEN

SAM WAS DOING her best to prove even though I was a fearsome vampire, I still needed her. During the day while I rested in the bathtub, which at this point was becoming a matter of indignity, she took care of several matters. Phillip had finally returned to the world of the living so Sam had arranged to have the plane ready. Eagerly, she packed all my belongings and had everything ready by the door. As the sun was preparing to set, she waited quietly beside the tub for my awakening. As I pulled the covers off, my first sight in the dimly lit bathroom was most welcome.

"Thank you for not staking me," I said softly. "That means a lot."

"Thank you for not biting me; that meant more."

"I could get used to this."

"You had better get used to it, because I want every night to be as amazing as last night. For the rest of our unnatural lives," Sam said passionately, as she reached down and caressed my face.

"Sam," I said, almost pleading for her to refrain from the enticement.

"Shhh," she said, "One step at a time." Her smile was confident; her decision concerning our future was complete. "Phillip and Dee will be waiting at the airport. They're going back with us."

"In that case, we had better get moving." I needed to stop by the safe house first, and get a few pints *to go*. I was growing more confident in my ability to suppress the sudden urges to consume from the first flesh bag to cross my path. But knowing it would be at least six hours before I hit the streets of New York I needed an emergency supply, just in case …

Phillip and Dee were already on the plane, cozied up, and enjoying a glass of wine when we arrived. Phillip's eyes lit up as we boarded.

"Brian," he said, his smile cautiously enthusiastic.

I saw in his eyes a hundred questions and an endless barrage of apologies. I was not in the mood for either. "Don't get up. We can talk later. Just pretend we are not even here."

Moving toward the rear of the jet, Sam in tow, Dee called out with noticeable concern, "Sam?"

Letting go of my hand, Sam made makeshift fangs with her fingers and shook her head *no*.

We settled into the custom memory foam velour seats which were more like a love couch than a cramped airplane seat. Phillip's party bus; money well spent. Sam cuddled tightly, resting her head on my shoulder. "I'm sure that went over like a ton of bricks," she said as she turned her head and kissed my neck.

We had barely settled in when an escalating ruckus startled us. "No, I won't," Dee snarled before heading in our direction.

"Look here, the both of you." Dee said abruptly. "I might have condoned whatever it is the two of you did last night, but don't dare to think for one minute it's going to be your own little secret. Wipe those smirks off your faces and fess up!"

"Everything's fine, Dee. I'm fine," Sam said.

"Did you bite her?" Dee's expression was almost venomous.

"Not hard enough to draw blood, if that is what you are asking … and I am fine too, thanks for asking." Given our conversation yesterday, I was relatively sure Dee's interrogation was all in jest, or at least I hoped so.

Dee peered sharply.

"What?" Samantha blushed before pulling her blouse slightly

open. "I think he might have given me a hickey. Do you want to see that?"

"No, don't be gross. I just need to know if you ... you know," Dee paused, contemplating her choice of words, "are like him."

"And if I was," Samantha raised her eyebrows. "After all, wasn't it you who said I need to do whatever it takes to keep from losing him?"

"Never mind," Dee replied. "It's just when you got on the plane, you looked ... younger. Like a lot younger. I just had to know if it was because of, you know, him ... and not me just looking older than you."

"Dee, you already look older than me."

"You wish," Dee said with a cocky smile. She held out her makeup compact, angled the mirror in the direction of Samantha and checked for a reflection. "Just making sure," she sang. "Try not to make too much noise back here, and for goodness sakes Brian, please behave yourself." Dee turned back to her seat, hips excessively swaggering all the way.

"Sorry, I'm sure that was a little awkward."

Time to change the channel. "So what is going on with Dee and Phillip?"

"I think if she would drop her guard, she could easily fall in love ... like I did with you."

Love. If only I had never looked into those eyes—or seen those legs. But I did, and now all I could think to do was sit in silence and be grateful that I did look.

"Kind of ironic, don't you think?"

Apparently, my golden silence was not meant to last. "What is?"

"Here we sit on a plane, just like day one. If it hadn't been for your *golden rule* of not dating women you meet on a plane, I might not have been intrigued enough to give you a second thought."

"And just look where my lack of discipline and your second thought got us."

Without a flinch Samantha whispered, "Does it hurt?"

"Does what hurt? Becoming a vampire, or knowing I have completely fucked everything up?"

"I know you are hurting here, Nick," Samantha placed her hand over my chest. "Give me some time and I will heal your heart."

Samantha swallowed an imaginary lump. "How did it feel ... to die?"

"I am not entirely sure when I died. It wasn't at all like the movies. She did not bite me and we did not exchange blood ... none of that. But I think, maybe it happened in the bar, an hour or so before I killed her. There was this most intensely unpleasant experience, worse than the bullet in the head. My body felt as though it was burning from the inside out. And just when I thought it could not get any more excruciating, suddenly, it felt like a horde of demons sliced through my stomach, reached inside and yanked my intestines out, all at once and yet inch by inch, slow enough I thought the pain would last for all eternity."

Four days gone by, my words had detached from the reality of the pain, and reporting it was a mere matter of history. "Overall, a pretty damn unpleasant experience."

Sam choked back a tear. "I'm so sorry. I'm sorry you had to experience that ... and I gave you a hard time. I had no idea. I feel so selfish."

"Don't apologize. The life I lead, the pain I inflicted over the years. I had this coming. I decided God just threw you into my life to heap on the misery as punishment. Without you, I could deal with this easily. But knowing I have screwed up your life ..."

"If this is a punishment, then it was meant for me as well." Samantha took my hands. "Take me now, and I will endure the pain to be with you, to be like you, till *our* end. You know in your heart we were destined to be together. You know what you desire to do."

"Damn it, Sam," I said in hushed tones. "Just for once, couldn't you say the wrong thing? Couldn't you say something so incredibly stupid that I would know you had lost your mind?" The call of my inner demon was mesmerized. The scent of her blood, offered out of love, enticed the ancient evil within.

Sam peeked ahead. Dee and Phillip were preoccupied. "Do it now, so we can live out our lives as one."

Sam pulled her collar down, exposing the flesh of my desire, her artery seeking the silent cravings of my mouth. I knew this yearning, for I had battled the mystic of the vampire's seduction, only to fail, and fall into the darkness. Samantha was intoxicated by ancient evil unseen. "Sam," I said, as I rolled my head up and looked to the unseen heavens. If I took Samantha, my final damnation would be complete.

And the beginning of hers. What did I believe? What could I afford not to believe? Was there truly a purpose for any of this?

It would be so easy to take Samantha as my bride and live out a life of immortality.

But was it the right thing to do, or just what I wanted to do? The hour to ask God for the answers had long passed. I was solo on this one.

I looked to her, sadness engulfing my eyes. My mouth filled with saliva, dreaming of the oh-so tempting sweet taste of her blood filling my mouth and body. Her luscious blood, the craving for my quenchless thirst. We were destined for each other, thus, so too her blood. My lips parted, revealing my glistening white fangs. I took her hand and brought it to my lips. Brushing her soft skin against my face the scent filled my head with images of lost purity. She was willing to throw away her life, and soul, to share this damnation. Desiring to covet, keep her with me for eternity, never to age or suffer illness, my choice became clear.

"Please," Sam crooned, pleadingly with a tremble.

Silently, I prayed; "God, if this is wrong, stop me, please." Ironically, I never sought advice, gave thanks, or prayed for anything from God. Yet here at a spiritual crossroad, I sought out the only help Daniel professed I needed.

Without pardon, I kissed her delicate hand and placed it in her lap. "Not here, not now."

"You need to do it now, before I chicken out." Sam beseeched, her uncertainty cementing my resolve.

"That is exactly why I will not. You are not truly ready, and in all honesty, the only reason I would do it is out of selfishness."

Out of frustration, or relief, Samantha reclined into her seat with a sigh.

"If I am meant to do this, we will both know for certain. Besides, if I did it here, your sister would friggin' kill me with her bare hands."

Sam smiled at the thought, then turned her head to the window then appeared to lose herself in a myriad of mixed emotions.

We said goodbye to Phillip and Dee at the airport. Phillip had offered us a ride to my apartment, but I was not ready for the confines of a limo and a plethora of journalistic questions. With one final apology, hopefully the last, and a promise of some "quality time" together in the next few days, Phillip begrudgingly consented to part ways.

Sam was eager to be alone, as well as to see my place. The alone part would provide renewed challenges. I had to admit, I was looking forward to seeing my home more than ever before. The guest room had only one window, and an eight-by-ten closet. Wanting to avoid the entire casket scene and be done with the bathtub, I arranged to have a queen mattress delivered earlier in the day, with thoughts of converting the closet into an enclosed sleeping chamber. Gone now were the days of bathtub beds, my sleeping arrangements no longer befitting a new reality show: *Trailer Park Vampires.*

The cab pulled up in front of a meticulously detailed brownstone, standing apart in the dark, amongst the other residents on Sixtieth Street. Accent lighting illuminated the fine details of the building: Spotless stonework, flawless paint, and fully blossoming flowers adorning every window. Even the sapphire blue awning appeared new. The door glass was spotless and the brass trim polished to perfection. As we approached the entrance, an older, stout, cheerful doorman greeted us as he held the door open.

"Mr. Denman, so good to see you again."

"It is good to be home and to see you, Charles."

The entrance looked more like the foyer of the W hotel than the lobby of an Upper East Side brownstone.

"As usual sir, everything is in its place," Charles reported.

"It always is." I handed him five one hundred dollar bills rolled up tightly. I knew my mail would be sorted, my apartment immaculately clean, and my refrigerator well stocked. In fifteen years, I never came home to any unwanted surprises. Knowing I was returning late, Charles had returned to duty just to greet our arrival. A retired Navy chief, Charles understood the importance of details and loyalty. Working as an electrical contractor during the building's renovations, he took the job as doorman extraordinaire once the renovations were complete, supplementing his retirement pay and affording him the opportunity to live here.

Sam was silent, scoping out every detail of the lobby. "Wow, this place is stunning," she said, as she took notice of the exotic bouquets that filled the vestibule. "How much is the rent in something like this?"

"I hope there is nowhere else quite like this. I pay a small fortune to ensure there is not."

Sam looked at me to elaborate, as she ran her hand over the curved mahogany rail in the elevator.

"I own the building." The elevator doors closed silently, as the car lifted smoothly upward.

"Oh, excuse me. I had no idea my vampire boyfriend was loaded."

"I trust this does not change anything."

"Are you kidding me? I *was* worried about you not being able to work, and how I was going to afford your drinking habit."

The elevator doors glided open into the wide-open living area. "Oh my," Sam gasped as she took in the visual feast of my home. The openness of the living room, its light avocado green walls, with mahogany trim, white linen fabrics, sculptures, water fountains, artwork, and plants took her breath away. "Pinch me. I know this has to be a dream. I never envisioned your place *anything* like this." She walked toward the sweeping granite spiral stairway in the middle of the living room. "Where does this go?"

On my desk, across the room, I spotted the flicker alert on my Mac. Priority alerts were programmed for all of my devices, but I had not looked at my laptop since *the event*. My phone had suffered a much worse fate, smashed in a fit of rage the same day. At that junction, I did not think I would ever need a phone or computer again.

"I will show you in just a minute. I have some urgent business I need to attend to." Sam took notice of the object of my attention. "Feel free to explore," I offered.

"I'll wait on the couch. I prefer a personal tour."

"In that case, come on over."

"Are you sure?"

"Absolutely ... I think." I smiled nervously. Sam followed to my desk, and stood behind me. I swiveled the leather chair around and pulled her into my lap. Reading the encrypted message I tensed. "Are you sure you want to know everything?"

Sam pulled her hair back and tweaked her ear to listen. "We have made it this far."

I sighed, unaccustomed to confessions.

"The work I performed, for the CIA, it involved illegal information acquisition, physical intimidation, assassinations, and other numerous international crimes. There were maybe, four guys at a time that performed my level of work. They all died out in the field. It was dangerous, working under the radar, and way beyond the boundaries of internationally accepted law. I knew my clock was ticking, so I began weaving a network of identities and exit strategies. Twenty years ago, when my airplane buddy with benefits shot me, I assumed it was a hostile retribution for either my work in the Middle East, or Colombia. Even though I got shot, she did provide me the perfect exit, the chance to be dead and not have anyone look for me. I called in Rob. He staged my death perfectly, allowing me to disappear once and forever. But over the years I could not shake the feeling that maybe she was working for my own government.

"Not only does the CIA use facial recognition software to track the movement of our enemies, but their own people as well. Traffic and sidewalk cameras, ATMs, department store surveillance, you name it; the CIA is wired in and monitors it all with advanced computer systems. So I wrote a program, hacked their system and hid a file deep in the operating system. Internally, anyone in the office could pull my file and review records I falsified, but I blinded image recognition software to any electronic queries of my image. It worked perfectly, for almost twenty years ... until now."

"What happened?" Deeply intrigued, Sam perched on my leg as if she were ready to spring into action.

"New Orleans PD ran my picture, in an attempt to ID me after my arrest. Somehow the virus I created in the CIA's computers failed and now they know I am alive.

"What are you going to do?" Sam's tone revealed she understood the implications.

"Hopefully, I can put this to rest with a phone call." I opened my desk drawer, and pulled out a new iPhone and plugged it into the computer.

"How many phones are in there?"

"I don't know, maybe six or eight."

"I would hate to see your cell bill."

"I don't get one."

Sam leaned back just far enough to get a full view of my face. "I can't wait to hear this one."

"Okay, like I told you, I am quite the computer hack. I wrote an app for my phone. When I push this button, right here," I said indicating the button, "my phone dials into a random AT&T store. From there, it hacks into their computer and selects employees that are not working, uses their passwords and selects random unassigned phone numbers. My phone then uses the WIFI signal from my laptop to establish a fictitious point of origin for my calls. See, it's done already," I said as the computer flashed *upload complete*. "It takes a few seconds longer when the phone is new. I never upload the software until I am ready to use it."

Now, let's see who is at the bottom of this inquisition. I scrolled through the CIA database until I found the header *Agent Compliance*. "Paul Watson. Geez, this guy has got to be ancient by now. He hired me." Mumbling more than talking, I dialed the number.

"It's time to wake up Mr. Watson."

"You are calling him now?"

"Why not? More than likely he has probably already ordered me terminated. At this hour, home in bed, it won't give him the opportunity to run me down, not that I think he could." I showed the phone screen to Sam. "See, origin of call, Glasgow. It would take them at least fifteen minutes in the office to unscramble this call. With him home in bed, unless they are watching his line, it's not going to happen."

The phone rang five times before a groggy voice answered. "Hello?"

"Wake up, Paul. Do you know who this is?"

"No."

"You are looking for me, but you need to stop," I ordered.

"Nick?" the voice searched.

"Listen carefully, Paul. I have three server computers in various countries. Everything I know is stored on those computers. Everyday, I phone in a kill code that keeps them idle. If I don't make the call, they will auto dial at least one hundred and fifty different reporters and media outlets; they will email, fax and use recorded audio to tell everything I know."

"Jesus, Nick. Are you out of your mind?"

"Your first assassin missed twenty years ago. I will not afford you the opportunity to try again without paying an unbearable price."

"Nick, I don't know what you are talking about. But you do need to come in. We need to talk." This was no more than standard CIA bullshit stall tactics, undoubtedly; he was connecting the call to headquarters.

"No Paul. You need to call off the hit. You need to forget about me, forever. I promise if your man succeeds, you will not live long enough to read about it in the papers."

"Nick, it's too late for that, unless you come in voluntarily, immediately."

"I hope for this country's sake, and yours, Paul, you are wrong." I hung up the phone and looked into Sam's eyes. Sitting in my lap, arms wrapped tightly around my chest, I felt her trembling.

With her left hand resting over my heart, she sighed. "I am about to pee in my pants, and your heartbeat hasn't gone up one tick. Doesn't any of this bother you?"

"No," I stated simply. "In this building we are completely safe. So, are you ready to see the rest of your home?"

"My home?" Bubbling with enthusiasm, Sam headed toward the terrace.

"Let's start downstairs," I suggested. Heading down the granite spiral staircase, Sam eyed the heavy metal door impeding our progress. "As far as everyone else knows, this is where I live." Keying in the code on the control panel, the door opened, revealing a slightly less extravagant, but still tastefully decorated and furnished apartment.

Void of the lavish appointments above, as Sam toured, her hands explored the various textures of paint and wood. "This is very nice. I could be very happy living down here." Slipping into the kitchen, she opened the stainless door of the refrigerator to find it fully stocked. "Expecting company?"

"Charles. I told him I was bringing a guest without elaborating."

"So let me see if I understand. You are saying nobody, Phillip, or any of your past girlfriends have ever seen the apartment upstairs?"

"Not a single one," I pledged.

"I could see where any girl would be delighted with this apartment. But why wouldn't you use the upstairs apartment to really make an impression?"

"Up there, it is my private space. I have not felt the need or desire to impress anyone with what money can buy. Have you already forgotten what I told you on the plane?"

"You told me a lot of things when we first met. You really didn't expect I would believe any of your pick-up artist BS, did you?" Sam was suppressing a smile, egging me on.

"Just as a reminder, I was not trying to pick you up."

"Oh, don't I feel special now." Sam turned away, no longer able to conceal her amusement.

Through all of the drama of the previous week, remarkably, Sam's playfulness had returned. "You know, I have not told a woman I love her for over forty years, so yes, that does make you special."

It was Sam's turn to blush. "Can I see the bedroom, upstairs ... now?" Sam tugged forcefully on my arm, announcing her intent.

"I was saving that for last. I thought we would spend the rest of the night there, after you finish the grand tour. Maybe we can try to make up for lost time." It was my turn to smile. Although we had spent last night together, I was fearful of myself and of my love for her.

As we made our way up the second flight of stairs to the rooftop terrace, Sam took hold of my hand. "Nick, this is absolutely beautiful." Gazing out over the landscaping, cabana, fountains, and city skyline she breathed deeply the warm night air. "Can I ask you something else?"

"Anything."

"Were you born rich? Most government employees don't make enough for this lavish lifestyle, not to mention owning your own building."

"Buildings," I replied with a smirk. We walked over to the balcony and looked down to the garden below. I put my arm around Sam and pulled her close. The sheer warmth of her body brought immense pleasure.

"I met Chuck in Afghanistan on a job," I began to explain. "We were getting paid to eliminate a certain tribal leader. Chuck knew several other tribes, and warlords, that were willing to pay to see the cause through. So he sold the job out, several times over, unbeknownst to the other parties we were there to assassinate their enemies in the first place. Any job that got us close enough to the target, if there were any spoils to plunder, we took that as well. We never figured we would live long enough to enjoy the money, but we did. After I retired and met Phillip, he introduced me to a man who taught me how to trade and invest my money."

"Are you rich?"

"I do not have a definition for rich. All I can tell you is that there is nothing in this city I will not get for you, if you ask for it."

Sam turned to me, her eyes ablaze. "You, I want you. I want to spend our lives together. And when you are ready, I want to be …"

I shut her up the best way I knew how. I knew where she was heading. Besides, it had been four and a half days since our last kiss. Our lips met and the passion unfurled on the terrace. I picked her up and carried her to the cabana. Killing the terrace lights by remote, our clothes came off in random succession. All of the memories of our passion, which had faded into bitter regret, were born anew, as we made love on the rooftop, under the watchful eye of the heavens above.

As the night grew long, we finally arrived in the bedroom and collapsed on the bed, cuddled in each other's arms, barely clothed. Mentally and emotionally spent, it only took Sam about two minutes to collapse into deep sleep. I held her in my arms until dawn, then withdrew to the confines of my closet casket.

The day passed silently and I awoke to a new night of splendor. Even though I had slept on a mattress in a closet, it sure as hell was more dignified than the bathtub at the Maison Dupuy or any casket for that matter. Through the late hours of the night, I had taken the time to do some business as Sam slept peacefully in my bed. She became restless around four, so I rejoined her in bed and stayed there until dawn. Some time around five in the afternoon, she had joined me in the closet. Working as carefully as she could not to disturb me, she slid under the blankets and held me close. As she worked so diligently to not awaken me, I did not let her know she had.

Around eight thirty it was time to arise. Sam was fast asleep. I would have left her there, only tonight was dinner with Aunt Rena.

Kissing her softly, I stirred my sleeping love. "Sam, it is time to wake up." Even though the closet was pitch dark, I could make out her every intricate detail as she woke.

"You know, if we're going to make this work, you have to get a bigger closet. At least big enough for a king bed," Sam mumbled.

Sam cracked the door to ensure the sunlight had faded. What little light remained filtered in the room with the effect of a dull glow. Pulling back the blanket, revealing a long black silk lace gown, Sam rose and passed in front of the window, the remaining radiance highlighting her silhouette.

"I hope you brought something else to wear tonight."

"If you want, I can take it off." Sam dipped her shoulder, allowing a strap to fall.

"No," I objected. "You look great, but my aunt is a little more conservative."

"If you think your auntie would object, I did bring something a little less revealing. But I need a shower first, before we leave. Do you think you can show me how to work those fancy faucets?" Her tone and facial expressions oozed sexual innuendoes.

Vampire bad-boy girlfriend: Sam was obviously settling into her new role with gusto.

"I would love to, but I don't want to keep Aunt Rena waiting. And just for future reference, this is a perfect example where two alone can shower quicker than two together."

Sam sashayed close and poked me in the chest. "Chicken."

God, how her beauty was mesmerizing. I stepped even closer, getting my face directly in front of hers. I stroked her hair with my hand, allowing my lips to brush hers. Sam sighed heavily and her lips quivered.

"That is Count Chicken to you." I abruptly turned away; to the sound of an exasperated exhale.

"You will pay for that later mister. It will be a mighty cold night on your side of the closet."

"Before you shower, will you do something for me?" Heading out into the living room, I gazed over in the direction of the front door. As expected, Charles had placed a package on the ebony marble mail-stand by the door.

Sam came out of the bedroom as I reached the package.

Retrieving the box out of the gift bag, I studied Sam's form, her gown flowing, as she approached. This vision, it had to be a dream. At no time in my life had I ever experienced such grace and beauty.

"Stop right there," I commanded. Studying every detail, I closed my eyes and retraced every detail just created. I breathed the air deeply, drawing in her scent. Opening my eyes, beholding her once more, I shook my head at the unexpected twist of fate which led to this moment.

Taking her hand, I led her to the couch. Having hatched this harmless deception only several hours ago, I was suddenly ensnared in a moment of weakness. Sam was here, I was here, and a ring was in my hand. Caught in the void between logic and emotion, I knew my well-plotted course was true.

"Sam, my aunt Rena is over eighty years old. For the last forty years, she had waited, not always patiently, for someone like you to come along. You might say I have let her down, more than once. It would make her night, maybe even her life, if I could introduce you as my fiancée ... just for her sake." I knew the ice I was treading was thin. If not for my unfinished business and this certain ... undeadness, hell I might have been actually ready for the grand leap.

"Yes," Sam replied, her expression casting a sense of mockery, as if she knew an inside joke I had yet to realize. "For Aunt Rena's sake."

"Great." Happy Sam was willing to participate in the charade, I produced the blue Tiffany box. "I got this for you to wear tonight."

Sam's eyes grew wide. "When did you get this?" her eyes locked on the box. "Please don't tell me you keep these laying around like your phones."

"No. I woke up a friend last night who arranged to have it delivered today." I handed Sam the box.

"Woke up a friend in the middle of the night? Must have been a really good friend." Unwrapping the box, she gazed at the sparkling three-carat diamond nestled in the soft satin and velvet.

"Let's put it this way, Susan's commission made the late night intrusion worthwhile."

Sam stroked the sparkling diamond, and turned her attention to me. "Ask me."

The inside joke just slapped me in the face. "Samantha, sweetheart. I would love to. But marriage ... I cannot step a foot in a church ever again. And children? You deserve it all."

"Ask me," her words were soft, almost pleading, her eyes glistened with hope.

"Samantha, how could we? Imagine introducing me; 'Mom and Dad, I would like you to meet my husband Nicholas, the vampire.' I love you, but there is no changing what I am. Eventually, you will want more than I can provide. I do not want to ruin your life and future."

"The hell with a church wedding. You are my future, my life, my existence."

I sighed.

"Ask me," she implored. "Both of us could die tomorrow. I would not want something so right, to be the biggest regret of my life. Ask me now, Nick."

An answer for every question, the composure I lacked, decisive when I was lost, Sam delivered unquestioned love when I was blind. "Samantha, will you marry me?"

"Yes." she said softly. In one simple word, my eternal life was made whole.

CHAPTER EIGHT

I HAD JUST created an epic nightmare. Sitting in the back seat, Sam remained transfixed with the ring on her finger. "A little over the top, don't you think?"

I smiled politely. "You have been uncharacteristically quiet. Having second thoughts yet?"

"Needless to say, with our current circumstances, we are quite an odd couple. And if nothing about that should change, I will become old, gray, and wrinkled while you remain young and handsome. I might have a teeny-weeny issue with that. Picture us in forty years, people will think you're taking your mom out to dinner for God's sake."

Not quite the conversation I was expecting. "Well if that time should come, and I emphasize *if*, we will cross that bridge with a carefully planned solution, which will not involve sexual temptations or trickery of any manner."

"And if we never cross that bridge? You would be happy going for walks in the park with me and my walker?"

"Here is a news flash, Samantha. You are not the first sultry vixen to tempt me. The difference between you and the others? Your beauty flows outwardly, wrinkles will not change that."

"Nice answer, Romeo." Sam took my hand and placed it on her

leg, guiding it inside her skirt and up her thigh. "And if my legs wind up looking more like elephant legs, you would still be okay with that, Mister 'your beauty flows from within'?"

Like so many times in our short history, with my hand on her leg she had me on the ropes, and knew it. "You are not playing fair."

"I think we have had *that* conversation before, and yes, I will continue to not play fair," Sam stated boldly.

"Even after the years have passed, and regardless of your temptress ways, I will still love you and still my answer will be *no*."

Sam pulled my hand higher. It was time to change the subject. Vampire or not, she understood exactly how to exploit my weaknesses. "That is very nice dress. Conservative, yet it has a stealthy sex appeal to it. Where did you find it?"

"Bergdorf's, and I'll bet Aunt Rena will never suspect I have no panties on underneath either, would you?"

"Oh." Attempting to appear disinterested, the floor of the cab was an ideal hiding place for my wanting eyes. "And are the shoes new?"

"Yes, even though I bought them to go with some new lingerie, which you may or may not see later."

She was downright cruel, arrogant, and vicious, you name it. I was butter in her hands. Impervious to the hack glancing in the rearview mirror, with my hand remaining on her leg, she guided higher until it would go no further. "See?"

"That is enough!" I snatched my hand away. "You need to behave yourself."

"But I am behaving, like a woman who is madly in love, and cannot keep her hands off her guy."

I thought about her logic. She was behaving exactly that way. "Was there ever a chance for me?"

"Yes, but then you went and jumped off the balcony. You could have just let me walk away."

I smiled at the memory, reflecting on the circumstances. What were the odds, in just two short weeks, I would be engaged to a woman who I happened to meet on a plane bound for New Orleans. Engaged? I was not even supposed to go out with her, much less dance, sleep, and, especially, fall in love with her? How in the hell was I ever going to make this work?

"Nick?" Sam squeezed my hand, distracting me from my folly.

"Yes?"

"Are you all right with me telling Dee, and maybe my parents about us?"

One step at a time, a little voice reminded me. The cab pulled up in front of Aunt Rena's building. *But by all means, say the right thing*, the voice added.

"Absolutely, my love. Would you prefer to have Dee over for dinner tomorrow night, or go out?"

"Is it all right for Dee and Phillip to see your real home?" Sam asked, concerned with my apparent need for privacy.

"It will be fine," I reassured with a kiss.

I got out of the cab and extended my hand. Sliding out of the back seat, Sam's dress hiked up her thighs. Wrinkly elephant legs? Knowing I held the key for the fountain of youth, I grinned. Even though it was but a passing thought, the smile was snatched away by the unpleasant image of what must transpire for that to occur.

Opting to bypass the elevator, we trekked up the four flights. "Don't be nervous," I said, as I prepared to knock on the door.

"I'm not," she insisted in a winded huff. "Is there a reason why we avoided a perfectly good elevator?"

"Got to keep those legs of yours in shape." I smiled broadly. "And you are lying, I can sense your nervousness."

"I don't recall giving you permission to *sense* me?"

"Can't help it. It is a new instinct, just like wild animals sensing fear."

"Well you had better learn how to control yourself pretty quick, mister. I am a very private person."

"Save the speech for somebody that does not know you, sister."

I knocked on the door.

The heavy footsteps approached rapidly. Aunt Rena was two hundred fifty pounds of good-spirited, but stern, Romanian love. Although growing up in Romania, she was quick to point out she was actually Hungarian. That was one reason she hated her birth name, Roma. When we moved to America she changed her name to Rena.

The door flew open as she began to bellow in a deep Romanian accent. "Nicholas Gabriel, you are fifteen minutes late and ..." She stopped dead in her tracks, as if she had seen a ghost.

"Aunt Rena, how many times do I have to remind you to use the deadbolts?" I lectured, despite her sudden change in demeanor.

"Nicholas, who is your friend?" Her voice became timid, almost haunting as her eyes popped wide.

"This is Samantha, she is my fiancée."

"Your fiancée? Oh my lord! Where are my manners? Come in, come in." Grabbing my arm and yanking me in, she kept her eyes focused on Sam.

"Please, come in, dear. Dinner is ready, although Nicholas did not tell me we were having company. I just need a second to set an extra place." Leading me to the table, with a firm hand to the shoulder, Rena forced me into the chair.

"You sit here, darling," she instructed, as she pulled a chair away from the table. "I will set an extra place." Rena lumbered quickly into the kitchen.

"Can I help you?" Sam offered.

"No dear, you sit, I will be just be a minute."

China and silverware rattled as she hurriedly collected the necessary utensils. "Nicholas, you failed to mention when you called the other day, you were engaged."

There was an unfamiliar tone in her voice which I could not discern. "That is because I wasn't. It kind of happened today." I cut a playful look at Sam who continued to beam as she ogled her ring.

Rena reappeared with an extra setting and a bottle of wine. She set the dishes, poured the wine and disappeared back into the kitchen. It was amazing to watch her move at eighty-two years old. She brought out a large bowl of *mari e monti* pasta, truly one of my favorite dishes. "I'm not too sure how this will taste without garlic. I hope you plan on seeing a doctor about your stomach, soon." The antique mahogany chair protested as Rena dropped into her seat. "Nicholas, would you say the blessing?"

Me pray? Well now, this was awkward. We plowed into dinner with the enthusiasm of a pack of cannibals. Throughout my youth, dinner was not the time to make excessive conversation. It was the time to enjoy Rena's extraordinary culinary skills. It was the reason she felt locked doors unnecessary. As she had cooked for practically every neighbor over the decades, she was confident nobody would allow her to be harmed. On many occasions I had prompted her to move to a better location, but she always insisted this was her home and these were her friends.

Tonight, the greatest disappointment, as with all meals since the cursed event—all food had taken on a rather insipid flavor. Truly, I was a cursed man.

After dinner, we retired to her sitting room. Lacking the customary interrogation of my travels and work since my last visit, she focused most of the attention and conversation on Sam. Uncharacteristically fascinated by her, Aunt Rena intensely studied every aspect of Samantha. I had never observed this behavior before, and like the earlier tone of her voice, red flags were being hoisted. Not to mention, Rena was generally disinterested with almost everything I had to say outside of topics involving Sam.

Although her tone was overwhelmingly friendly, I felt her laser-beam focus was making Sam a bit uncomfortable. At brief intervals, Rena would cut her eyes to me with a most perplexing expression. The evening was getting late, almost eleven thirty, and I had not begun to broach the subject that led me here.

Rena, being a typical New Yorker, even at eighty-two, was usually good until about one in the morning. Patiently plotting my entry, awaiting the opportunity to break in, I waited, listened, deliberated and ... fretted. My questions would lead to hard answers. We might be here till sunrise.

"I will grab another bottle of wine," I offered.

Quite cozy in her favorite chair, spinning tales of New York, raising me, and generally things she had witnessed over the many years, Rena bantered on. I returned and poured out three full glasses.

"Nicholas, if I drink much more you will have to carry me to bed."

I knew this to be untrue. Rena could drain a barrel on the proper occasion, and never let on. "Aunt Rena, I need to talk to you."

"Isn't that what we have been doing?" Her trademark smile, known throughout the neighborhood, offered reassurance that all would be just fine.

Sam and I were sitting very close, holding hands tightly, as I embarked on my mission of discovery. "I need some answers, things I know only you can tell me."

"And so, please go on."

"Why am I sixty years old, yet only look half my age? Why have I been shot in the head and lived? Why do I cast no reflection in the mirror?" True, I knew the answer to the last question, but I was nervous and as such, the multitude of questions spilled out. Obviously, if she knew the answer to any of the questions, the rest would logically fall into place.

"Is this true?" Rena asked with deep concern. "You cast no reflection?"

"Yes, and I cannot tolerate daylight and ... I have developed an unnatural drinking habit as well."

Rena dipped her head in shame. Her jovial disposition instantly disappeared. "Nicholas, you are drinking blood?"

I nodded my head as Sam clenched my hand even tighter.

"Was this why you asked me to leave the garlic out of tonight's dinner?"

"Yes."

"And Samantha?"

"No, she is not like me."

"So the curse of the *Nosferatu* has found you after all," Rena said sadly. "We tried so hard."

"We?" I asked sharply.

"Your father and I."

"You and my father? All of my life, there has been some secret agenda you felt it should not be shared with me?"

"How much Romanian history do you know?"

"Oh, this can't be good. Vampires and Romanian history." Sarcasm laced my reply. I had *never* felt anger toward this woman until this moment. Learning she and the father I never knew had conspired to keep some dark secret from me ignited an indefinable ire.

"Shhh," Sam insisted. "This would be another one of those times to be quiet, listen, and try not to be a smart-ass. I am sorry, Aunt Rena, Nick has not been himself lately."

"It is all right dear. What I am about to reveal, I swore an oath to never divulge. Your father was to send for you when it was time. He was to be the one to educate you. But I fear your father was killed many years ago. No one has ever sought you out."

Looking intently, Sam and I waited for the story to continue.

"Do you know the history of Vlad Tepes, known to the world as Vlad the Impaler or more commonly, Count Dracula?"

"Just the popular tales, which really is not much." I answered. Sam shook her head *no*.

"Although he was cruel and sadistic, contrary to legend, he was not the vampire of legend. A great warrior and prince, but he was very much flesh and blood. In his early years he practiced in the ways of paganism, but later in life, he converted to Catholicism, to marry Countess Ilona Szilagy, cousin to Matthias Curvinush, King of Hungary. By way of his marriage to the Countess, King Matthias appointed Vlad to the throne of Wallachia. Countess Ilona bore Vlad two sons, Vazul and Vlad II," Aunt Rena said.

"There is no public historical documentation of Vazul's life, other than the recording of his birth. To my knowledge, I have the only written account of Vazul's life that exists." Rena rocked forward, creating momentum to help boost her from the sunken recliner. Effortlessly, she located the weathered volume from the massive bookcase that mantled an entire wall of her apartment and handed it to Sam.

"The accounts in this journal were written by my ancestors, and handed down through generations. It was our duty to attend to the royal family of Wallachia. I have been in possession of this book since 1948."

"Vazul Dracula was born under a dark curse. Unable to escape the pagan ways of his father's past, some believed his affliction to be a pagan curse in retaliation for his father's conversion to Christianity. Others believed the source was from God, in retaliation for the sins of Vazul's father," she said. "In the great wars, Vlad Tepes, while defending Wallachia from Muslim invaders, began his ritualistic consumption of his victim's blood. Whichever the truth, the malice of Vazul was evident from his earliest days."

She continued, "The child was hidden away, far from the prying eyes of a nation eager to have a prince unite the provinces into one strong, secure nation. As the years passed, it became clear that Vazul's cruelty far exceeded that of his fathers. Consumed with a thirst for power and blood, in a remote village in Transylvania, he created a secret society in the shadows of darkness. With the passing of his father, and several years later his brother, any hopes of containing Vazul's empire faded."

"The Order of the Dragon, a secret society, of which Vazul's brother, Vlad II, and his father were members, took on the task of reeling in Vazul's reign of terror. Truly, the sins of Vlad Tepes paled in comparison to Vazul's." Aunt Rena recited the history as if she were reading from a well-rehearsed script.

Continuing with the tale, she appeared to tense. "Rumors spread of the evil residing in the mountains of Transylvania, until a small militia of men, recruited by the Order of the Dragon, sought out Vazul and his cult. Knowledgeable in the ways of dealing with evil, they began to destroy the followers of Vazul."

She went on, "Vazul escaped the onslaught in 1640, and fled to Germany. There, in exile, a transformation began to occur. Feeding only out of necessity on nomadic travelers, he settled in a remote village in the Black Forest. Upon meeting a band of Romanian gypsies in 1669, he took one, Ileanna Kerlápoly, as his wife. Out of that union Levente Dracula was born."

"Vazul returned to Romania, alone, in 1695, in an attempt to regain control of the scattered vampire population, and take his rightful place as their prince. Believing if he could seize power over the murderous cult, he would gain favor with the Order of the Dragon, and eventually reclaim his family's right to the throne of Romania, a position he solely desired for his son Levente." Aunt Rena paused long enough to sip her wine.

Gingerly setting her glass down, she continued. "In 1701, although it was never clear who was responsible for his death, Vazul perished. With guidance from his mother, Count Levente grew into a strong and influential man. Taking up Vazul's quest to re-conquer the homeland of his forefathers, in 1732 he returned to Transylvania. Forging an alliance with the Order of the Dragon, he set about, not to destroy, but to convert his race into a peaceful tribe, capable of cohabiting with man. But not all were swayed to a peaceful existence with man. There were those who sought to wipe out the weaker race."

"The Count waged a private war that lasted almost two hundred years. Through the historical turmoil that existed in Romania, through both World Wars, Count Levente continued with his quest. After World War II, a new battle was waged. Communism spread throughout Eastern Europe, this fervor, unlike any invasion witnessed in the past. The Communists realized the threat of resistance any surviving members of the royal family presented. A secret genocide erupted in many eastern European nations. Any member of royal lineage, any person with a claim to the throne, was exterminated," she recounted.

"In 1946, Levente retreated to Germany, back to the region of his birth. He traveled with a small group of vampires, loyal to his cause, with intentions of building a resistance to the suppressive Communist regime, which had quickly spread throughout his homeland. Once safely in refuge in Hundsberg, Austria, The Order of the Dragon arranged a marriage to Elisabeta Dragomire of Transylvania and in 1948, she gave birth to Neculai Dracula." Acknowledging the name Neculai brought a gleam to her eye, as if a burden had been lifted.

"The Communist Party had learned of Levente's existence, and made his assassination a top priority. He was tracked into Germany, where the first attempt on his life occurred. Tragically, many of Levente's loyal followers perished in the failed assassination. Levente and Elisabeta, desperate for Neculai's survival, made immediate arrangements for their son's secret exile to America," she said.

"I was honored to be chosen for the duty of ensuring the infant's safety as he grew into adulthood. In order to protect Neculai, I was ordered to never disclose the origins of his family to him, until I was absolutely sure his safety was no longer an issue, or until the time *you* were old enough to understand the consequences of *your* family lineage."

"Please tell me I am misunderstanding you," I began, "you just insinuated I am Neculai, son of Levente, grandson of Vazul Dracula, great grandson of Vlad the Impaler. The original Dracula."

"Yes, you are correct." With a gleam in her eye and tone of pride, Rena appeared relieved, as if a burden had been lifted.

"That means he's a prince?" Sam asked, mouth agape, awaiting Rena's response.

"Yes, Neculai Dracula is heir to the throne of Romania." Rena turned to me. "It was your father's expectation, his dream, you would not inherit the full consequences of the curse without the consumption of blood, and one day would stake your rightful claim to the throne."

"Whoa. I do not think I could just waltz into Romania, announce

I am Nick Dracula, and expect they would bow down crying, 'Welcome home, we have been waiting for you!'"

"You would be surprised by just how many people would do exactly that. There are many who have waited. The old ways were not forsaken by all."

Sam just stared at me. I stared back. I opened my mouth to speak. With this new bombshell, I felt an apology was in order. Wordless, my lips moved.

"Shut up," Sam ordered.

Aunt Rena looked at Sam, amused with her spirit. "She is like your mother in more than one way."

"What does that mean?" I asked, wondering if I even wanted to hear any more revelations to this amazing and virtually inconceivable tale.

Rena opened the tattered book and flipped the pages toward the end. "This is your mother," she explained, handing over the open book.

The deafening silence lasted for about thirty seconds.

"Oh shit," I moaned, as I examined the faded black and white photograph attached to the page. If Samantha had a twin, this would be her. "If this does not completely ice the cake of lunacy."

Sam studied the photograph. "I am most definitely not your mother," she declared defiantly. "I know my parents, I have seen pictures of my childhood, and I have never been anywhere near Romania for that matter."

"Thank you honey, for quickly dispatching my newly unexpected incestuous fears." My smile remained anxious as the lump gradually dropped from my throat. I stared at the faded image of a mother long lost, never known, sadness filling my heart. "I can see why you could not take your eyes off Samantha."

"It is true, I was shocked, when I first laid eyes on her. For a moment, I was sure you were about to tell me your mother had found you." Rena paused briefly allowing the silence to gather our thoughts. "Tell me Nicholas, how long have you been a vampire? How did you come into the darkness?"

"That is what I was hoping you could help me with. It happened about a week ago, but to the best of my knowledge, I was never bitten. I thought you had to be bitten, and then drink the blood of your creator to become a vampire."

"Please go on."

Rena completely glossed over my interest in the how, and gestured for more with her hands. "I was in New Orleans, looking to rebuke a local vampire legend." Instantly Rena's expression shifted, as if she knew the answer. "The only problem: the legend was no myth, the vampires were real."

"You went to the Ursuline Convent?"

"You know about the Convent?" Just when I thought the revelations of the evening could not get any more bizarre, another bombshell detonated.

"It is where your father exiled two of his own." Rena paused; the weight of what was to follow was apparently a bitter memory. "Angelique and Monique."

"Oh, this can't be good." Sam leaned in closer, perching on the edge of the couch, if possible, more anxious than I to hear the ensuing tale.

"In 1792, your father married his first wife, Évike Szekeres, a Hungarian countess, in an attempt to win an alliance with his northern neighbors, and thus solidify his efforts to win back the throne. But while continuing his crusade, he met with a small band of nomadic vampires. This is where he met Angelique. They fell deeply in love. I believe if not for the arranged marriage to Évike, your father and Angelique would have wed. Angelique's cousin Monique was eager for Angelique to ascend to power, and upon their return to Romania, set out to bring Évike's life to an end. The attempt on Évike nearly brought about a war, thus bringing the marriage to an end. After Monique's failure to kill the Countess, she and Angelique were banished to America. Victor Tepes, your father's cousin, was to deliver the outcasts to America, where if they could prove they could abide within the laws your father set down, they could return in two hundred years. If they were unable to refrain from the ways of evil, Victor was to destroy them." Aunt Rena reached for her glass, but did not drink.

"Victor had sent word of the subsequent imprisonment of Angelique and Monique in the Convent. Victor was to wait in New Orleans, until the two hundred years had passed, then he was to free the estranged pair. There were no other communications from

Victor after 1891. It was presumed he perished." Rena sipped her wine, suddenly disheartened for no apparent reason.

"I freed them." I said with a grimace. "I do not know where Angelique went, but I killed Monique. She was a murderer and had to die." The blood filled images of Monique's death replayed like a high-definition movie.

"Then you served the will of your father, for she did not walk in the ways he set before her."

"I am relatively sure, before I killed her, I might have ingested some of Monique's blood. I was told it was a method used to control the will of the strong minded."

"Apparently, as you already possessed the genetics of the undead, all that was lacking was for you to consume the blood of a vampire."

Lucky me. Had I been Chuck, I would still be mortal. Albeit, with almost certainty, I would also be dead. My thoughts strayed back to Isabelle. "Tell me, how is it I was even born? I have never heard of vampires having children."

"Not a soul knows why two vampires are unable to reproduce. But like your father, your grandfather mated with a mortal. And out of that union, your father was born. And despite all of the legends, your great grandfather, Vlad, was mortal. The curse began with Vazul. Your mother was very much mortal when you were born. It was only after your birth that your father agreed to make her as one."

Sam huffed softly. "Well, sounds like your father knew how to honor the woman who loved *him*."

"Of all things your father desired for you, a life free of the curse was his greatest wish. It was your parents' belief, if you never consumed blood, you would not suffer the full effects of the vampire's curse. Through your childhood, everything they had hoped for became a reality. As you aged over time, it became evident only certain aspects of your father's immortality had been passed on."

"Then I ran into Monique." In spite of the belief my grandiose fuck-up could not possibly increase any more in magnitude, now all those years of planning, dreams for which my father died to protect, were ruined.

"So, if I am understanding you correctly, Monique, the woman who tried to murder Levente's first wife, over two hundred years ago, was responsible for turning Nick into a vampire?" Sam surmised.

"It would appear to be so," Rena agreed.

"And you believe Levente and Elisabeta were eventually killed by the Communists."

Rena's heartbreak could not be concealed. "Sadly, it is what I believe."

I stared at the bookcase, dumbfounded by the odd twist of fate. I knew Daniel would derive some spiritual satisfaction from these absurd circumstances. I killed the woman who attempted to murder my father's wife, but she cleared the path for him to eventually marry my mother. The same woman my father banished, committed the one vile act he desperately desired to avoid. And what about Angelique? On several occasions she referenced our intertwined fate. Could she have somehow known or sensed who I was? Was this the reason for her sparing my life?

I flipped through the pages of the book in silence. Sam looked on. I retraced the pages to the picture of my mother, running my fingers across the photograph, needing to feel her flesh. How unbelievably amazing it was, Sam's resemblance to my mother. And of all women to fall in love with. Turning the pages backwards, for the first time, I stared into my father's eyes. I felt his presence, his strength. I closed the book.

"I need to digest all of this. Do you mind if I borrow the book?" I gripped the bound leather bindings tightly. "I will bring it back in a night or two."

"That is fine, but please bear in mind, this is a historical account of your family's history, through the eyes of my ancestors. It bears a certain prejudice, from a perspective that is not always flattering to your family."

"I understand." I lightly slapped my hand on Sam's thigh. "Are you ready to go … Mom?"

Sam stood, teetering for a moment. "Thank you so much for the fantastic meal," Sam said. "Nick was right, you're a fantastic cook."

"You're welcome, Samantha, I look forward to seeing you for many more suppers."

"Me too." Embraced by my aunt with a full tilt, Romanian bear hug, Sam peeked over Rena's shoulder with a strained expression.

"Thank you," I said, as I considered the newly discovered depth of her service, "For everything." I gave her a hug and opened the door for Samantha, who breezed past leaving a chilly wake.

Sam rambled down the stairway, her heels clicking sharply. Not waiting, she shot straight for the lobby door and out to the curb, without a word.

I followed her out. "Are you all right?"

"Give me a few minutes. I thought I was about to throw up just now."

"I hope it wasn't the food."

"No, it was more like seeing your mom, who I resemble more than my own. This is a little too creepy. You will have to forgive me if I sleep in the other bedroom tonight, I mean tomorrow ... day. Damn, I need to talk to my mom, like now." Sam scrambled through her purse for her cell phone.

I grabbed Sam's arm, "Sweetheart, it is twelve thirty."

"One, please refrain from calling me sweetheart for at least ten minutes. At this exact moment, it might be highly inappropriate," Sam said in excited tones as she dialed. "Two, my parents are in San Francisco this week, so it is only nine thirty there. Three, that little mom joke was just sick. I mean really sick. I hope you know you are sleeping back in the bathtub tonight."

Sam held up her index finger giving me the mandatory shut your pie-hole cue. "Mom," she began. "I am fine."

Sam's eyes blazed.

"I just need to know something," Sam continued. "This is very, very important. You and dad, and all of my grandparents were all born in this country, right?" She waited for the answer. "As far as you know, is any of our family from Romania, or Hungary?" Again there was a pause. "It is a long story. I would rather tell you in person." Samantha's expression and posture eased slightly. "And one last thing, and you have to tell me the truth. Was I adopted?"

CHAPTER NINE

THREE MONTHS PASSED without any trace of Angelique, Celine, Gabrielle or Sabine. I had made two trips back to New Orleans in an attempt to pick up their trail. Returning to the Crescent City, all of the misery of my creation was replaced by some bizarre heartfelt homecoming. Born to the undead, my soul pined for the spirits who refused eternal rest. In all of its grandeur, New Orleans resurrected a spirit within I had allowed to be stripped away.

Between my crew in New Orleans and New York, we combed through piles of insignificant reports, news stories and web postings. If the remaining vampires were leaving victims in their wake, they were cautiously disposing the evidence. Nightly, I gazed over FBI and state police reports for missing persons and peculiar murders to no avail. It was as if they had vanished from the country. If she was still unaware of my father's death, Angelique had every reason to return to the homeland. If she had gone, quite possibly the others returned with her.

Back in New York, Samantha had taken both to the Manhattan lifestyle, and living her life predominately in the afterhours. She had told Dee, and then her parents, about the engagement, minus one major detail, namely, the Prince of Romanian darkness stuff. I was to meet her parents later this month, a meeting I had put off as long as possible. It was our intention to tell them about me now, as opposed to lie, and have them find out later.

Although her relationship with Phillip had turned serious, Dee seemed a little touchy over my relationship with Sam. Maybe it was the anti-aging thing, or the whole royalty deal, but whatever the case, something was amiss. Phillip, over the long distance relationship, convinced Dee to quit her job a month ago and move to New York, and spoiled her at every opportunity. Although he would not admit it, a proposal was in the air.

Most days Sam snuggled as we slept the day away peacefully. Admittedly, I missed her California tan as it faded into paleness. As she bemoaned her lost golden color, I kept reminding her it was better for her skin, and overall health. She kept reminding me if I would just go ahead and bite her, health would never be an issue ever again.

The CIA, now aware of my ability to hack into their systems, stood vigil against my intrusions. Continually I eluded their firewalls, but they were getting adept at detecting and shutting down my access portals. Any chatter about the agent assigned to terminate me was not on the CIA grid, so the possibility existed the director had taken care of the issue after I threatened his life, and exposing the agency's darker side. The alternate possibility: they did not give a crap and the hit was still on.

Hacking into Walsh's home PC, searching for signs of pertinent files, I found traces of military encrypted files, but they had been cleansed to the point of useless data trails. On a continuing basis, I continued to swap data within my files, delete photos, and continued to be a major nuisance to anyone involved with my case. Stealthily and painstakingly, I was collecting the sources of their back-up files. Once I was satisfied I had them all, I would send one final kill command to forever delete all records of my existence.

Although my body no longer required traditional nourishment, tonight, as accustomed, I accompanied Sam to explore the endless cuisines New York offered. The hunger I *did* experience did not compare to mortal hunger, but was more like having your supply of oxygen extinguished. When the hunger arose, I had to feed just as humans must breathe. One particular night while in Brooklyn, feeling as I was closing in on the scent of another such as me, the hunger became overwhelming. Too far from home on unfamiliar turf, my choices were limited; a human or the rat that scurried by. *What the hell, why not?* The difference between human and animal blood could be described as the difference between the best fire-grilled filet mignon and eating a month old moldy spam sandwich. Needless to say, my desperation level would have to be critical before doing that ever again. Acquiring human blood was not an issue. I had sources for my home supply and had no problem slipping in and out of hospitals, blood banks and morgues when traveling about the city.

Upon returning home from a dinner, Sam and I were greeted by the flashing light of my computer. Only the second occasion Sam had witnessed the beacon, she knew it required immediate attention.

"It's Mitch," I announced to Sam, as I studied the encrypted message. Back in New Orleans, logging countless hours off the clock, O'Reilly continued his diligence to locate the missing vampires. I dialed up his number from a special cell phone just for this purpose.

"Mitch, it has been a while."

"Yes, it has. Our coroner received a broad based request today, for information for COD's with remarkable blood loss, secondary to puncture wounds. Obviously they have a stiff of interest in Miami."

"Thanks Mitch, I will look into it and get back to you." Mitch understood the importance of keeping conversations brief and to the point. After I hung up, the image of Rob raced through my head. Punctured and bloodless.

The memory of his brutal death still stung bitterly. Finally, after months, a lead. Would it be Angelique, Sabine, Celine or Gabrielle, or possibly all of them together? It was entirely conceivable that another, perhaps one created by the others could be responsible. Whatever the case, immediate response was required.

"I need to go, tonight." Sam winced, knowing this day would come, as she watched me dial the phone. She also knew there was no way in hell she could tag along either. She waited anxiously for the opportunity to hear my plans.

"Phillip. I need the jet. Now!" There was no discussion on the other end. We had discussed this day in depth, on numerous occasions. He understood the potential mass casualties these women were capable of, and more so, understood his responsibility. "Miami. I need you to get me an apartment, with a walk-in closet, preferably in a room with no windows, and a car, tonight. Or you can rent a house, it does not matter. Have the agent have a key waiting at the airport."

Sam watched eagerly as I listened to Phillip's response. "Thanks, Phillip, let's hope this will be the end of this." I hung up and turned to Sam, who was not attempting to conceal her disappointment.

"I know we have talked about this, but ..."

"No," I said abruptly. "You are not going anywhere near any vampires, other than yours truly." I walked briskly to the closet, and pulled out a pre-packed suitcase.

"Do you have a half an hour or so, before you leave?"

"Not if you want me to be off the streets before sunrise."

"I am sorry, I knew this would happen eventually. But it does not make any easier for me to watch you leave. Look what happened last time I left you alone."

"Things are different now. I have no need for stakes, crosses, or holy water. There is nothing for me to fear."

"Twenty minutes?" Sam asked as she blocked my path to the door.

"Damn, woman."

"Well, we don't know when you will be back, do we? Is there anything wrong with one for the road?" Sam shifted into the role of the great seducer once again.

"No, as long as I am out of here by eleven," I said with a pronounced sigh.

"It is not like it is my fault anyway. You know the saying: 'An evening without Vlad makes a woman go mad.'"

I looked at Sam, who was trying her best not to smile. "How long have you been waiting to use that line?"

"Thirty seconds." Sam grabbed me by the shirt and pulled me toward the bedroom. "Come on lover boy, you're on my time now."

The flight down afforded me time to catch up on old business. "Paul, time to wake up."

"What the hell?" The groggy voice on the other end was not unaccustomed to getting calls at three in the morning. His tone dictated; it was definitely not appreciated.

"You are still looking for me. I asked you not to."

"Nick? Have you completely lost your mind? You've dug yourself in deep, buddy. Hacking the agency's computer system whenever you feel the need? The IT department is all over you now, and they are not going to let you go. You pissed off the wrong geeks this time."

"I know; I see everything they are doing. But I am not going to stay out until I am sure every last one of them gets the hell out of my business. I have been retired for over twenty years without incident. It's time for you to make me a ghost Paul."

"Nick, I can't ..."

"Paul," I interrupted, "I know what you can and cannot do. Make it happen before it gets ugly." I hung up the phone.

Testing my computer skills against the agency's best, and winning, was giving me a massive boner. I had gained access to the agency's network, and offsite back-up servers, as well as identified numerous flash drives containing my files. My kill virus was already written, and in just a few more weeks I would download it to the main CIA server. On the prescribed execution date, any system containing my files would be identified as a trojan. As soon as preventive measures were taken to quarantine the virus, my files would basically self-destruct. I was hoping this would finally bring an end to my association with Uncle Sam.

Thanks to Sam, I cut my departure a little too tight. As a result, upon arriving in Miami, the first light of day was breaking as the driver wheeled into the apartment complex Phillip had provided. Fully furnished and containing the few amenities I had requested only hours earlier, all of the shades were drawn in anticipation of my pre-dawn arrival. The interior bedroom had no windows, a walk-in closet and to my delight, a new mattress already trimmed with satin linens. Sam must have called Phillip after I left and made the arrangements. Thankfully, I would not be sleeping on the closet floor or in a bathtub tonight.

At the risk of seeming ungrateful, with nobody watching, I smiled broadly at my life. In truth, I was disappointed; my plans of eventually graduating to a bed had not come to pass, leaving me a nocturnal slumber dysfunctional.

One of my many peculiarities throughout my mortal life was that I never required more than two or three hours of sleep. Now immortal and all-powerful, I could not seem to function with less than six to seven hours in a confined space. Any lesser amount resulted in diminished capacities of my powers and survival instinct.

Shortly after sunset, I awoke to the sensation of lips, warm, sumptuous lips, lightly brushing my ear. First, a moist tongue, then the nibble of teeth on my earlobe. I groaned as her hand explored below my waist. Her lips traveled down my neck, with light delicate kisses, exploring my chest, then lower, my abdomen tensed to the sensation. My body arched in pleasure. *Did I not tell you we would be together again?* The words whispered in a sultry French accent chilled my ear.

"Angelique?"

I shot up, throwing my hands about defensively, punching nothing but air. I leapt from the mattress and flipped on the light. No rose, no Angelique ... just one hell of a boner. "Asshole," I barked at myself. "That is what you get for sleeping in. From now on, I am setting the alarm." I was not sure how concerned I should be about my dream. With no rose at the crime scene, I was relatively certain it was just a dream. But damn. Why was I dream-humping the woman I was here to kill?

It had been about five years or so since my last visit to Miami. All of the amenities that endeared the city to me had lost their luster. Great food, emerald green waters, sandy white beaches, and multitudes of hot single women no longer provided the same motivation. Being home to a vast population of illegal immigrants, Miami made for an inviting playground for my AWOL bloodsucking kin. Although it was probably pure futility, nevertheless, I held to a glimmer of hope my girls had yet to create more of their kind ... our kind.

Mitch had offered to travel to Miami to follow up on a lead, but I settled for all his intel by email instead. Our first break, a homeless man in the psych ward at Jackson Memorial, who was rather insistent on a diet of blood. On several occasions since his admission a week ago, he attempted to bite nurses, doctors, and even a janitor. True, it was not an earth-shaking break in the case, but after almost three months of nothing, a lunatic in the psych ward was the only place to start.

Before I left the apartment, I made a final check of the phase one CIA software bug. It was ready for the test. I would be running all over Miami, a town littered with security cameras. If it did not work, they would be on my ass in a matter of hours, if not minutes. I pressed the execute button, and watched as the progress bar uploaded the encrypted files, not directly to the CIA mainframe, but through Walsh's home PC. As soon as Walsh logged in, in the morning, bam, anyone who looked at my file would think Brad Pitt and I were twins. I regretted nobody would ever appreciate the pure genius behind a bug so complex, yet simple. When the full virus deployed in two weeks, after purging all hard drives of my life, the bug would literally eat itself.

An hour later I arrived at Jackson Memorial and studied the intel on my phone. Pierre Dupont. In a predominately Hispanic town, they managed to find the one French guy. Go figure. As Mr. Dupont was not a person of suspicion, hospital security was relatively lax. I signed in as a family visitor at the front desk, and was allowed to go straight to his room. I checked in at the nursing station, where the young nurse went to excessive lengths to explain why my *uncle* was restrained and sedated.

Upon light interrogation, I found out that "Uncle Dupont" had been visited by his niece, Celine Dupont, twice since his admission, the last visit being two nights ago. Even though a remote possibility existed this was the wrong Celine, I was generally jacked-up, not being one to believe in coincidence, and knowing the chase was back on. If she was following a feeding pattern, perhaps in an attempt to merely control his willpower, then it would be highly likely she would return within the next three nights. If I was unable to locate her before her suspected return to the hospital, then this would be a golden opportunity to nail her in just a few days. I politely thanked the nurse; left my cell number and some seed money to ensure a call, should my cousin return.

Through the heavily sanitized funk of the hospital, I perceived a trace of familiarity. Even though her visit was two nights ago, all doubts were instantly vanquished. Celine had been here. Entering Pierre's room, I found him fully restrained and unconscious.

"Pierre, didn't you learn anything in school? Bite a nurse and look what you get." Scanning his neck for any sign of the typical Hollywood bite wounds, I came up empty. On his left wrist, I found a single puncture wound. Celine had become wise in her ways. By carefully angling her bite, she was able to conceal the signature imprint of our race. "Your friend is a smart girl, Pierre."

I leaned into Pierre's ear. "Wake up, Pierre."

Startled, his eyes shot open. "Master," he winced, as he tugged at his restraints.

"Yes, Pierre, I am here."

"Why have you left me here?"

"Who told you I was to come? Was it Celine?"

"In my dreams ... the shadows. They whisper of ..." Pierre's eyes were glazed and distant as he spoke.

This was an unexpected wrinkle. Was this guy just whacked, or was there truly some all-seeing psychic highway for the undead?

"Has Celine spoke of this?"

"No. Celine is evil. She would hold me in bondage, for all eternity. She does not allow me to cross over, or to pass from the living. She enslaves me, to do her bidding."

"Have you seen Gabrielle?"

"I know Gabrielle. It was Gabrielle who delivered me to Celine. She claimed to love me. She told me our love would last till the earth ceased to exist. But she lied." Pierre's eyes became glossy as he recounted the memory. "Why she chose to leave me, I do not understand."

Celine's venom coursed through Pierre's body to ensure her dominance. But why did Celine take Pierre from Gabrielle? Was it jealousy? Maybe to stake her dominance over Gabrielle. If I knew, perhaps I could use the knowledge as leverage, pitting the two against each other.

"Pierre, these voices that come in your dreams. Tell me about them."

"I do not know. I cannot see them. The voices come to me in times of my darkest despair. They calm my fears, and give me hope."

"What fears do you have, Pierre?"

"That I will be left here, forever caged. I thirst for blood, but none is given. I yearn for the Gabrielle's touch, but instead receive only Celine's torment. I have begged to die, but the bitch is heartless."

"Pierre, I can grant your peace. But to do that I must first find Gabrielle and Celine. Can you help me?"

"I do not know where they live, only where they prowl," he offered. "South Beach, they stalk their victims, and there is no defense for their powers of seduction. My lust for Celine far outweighs my loathing of her."

Instinctively, I knew what needed to be done with Pierre. He only needed to be removed from Celine and Gabrielle's reach for a short period of time. They were feeding on him, but not to the death. In turn, he was ingesting their blood.

"Rest now, Pierre," I commanded. He closed his eyes, and drifted into a deep sleep. Tomorrow, I would have Phillip make arrangements to have Pierre transferred to another facility, far from Celine's reach.

I left Jackson Memorial and made the quick trip to South Beach. Having lived in the area for months, I knew all of the popular hot spots. Upon arriving, I decided to foot it up Collins Avenue, attempting to pick up their scent. The humid night air was void of any trace, which only meant they were not in close proximity. Unlike the hospital, the warm sea breezes would not allow scents to linger. I headed over to A1A, and strolled past the oceanfront restaurants and bars, my haunts from a life long ago. If they were in South Beach, they would eventually pass these streets.

Lacking any desire to eat, drink, or mingle with humans, I strolled over to the beach. The moon had just risen over the ocean, its reflection bright, rippling in the waves. The picturesque silhouette of the palm trees against the glow of the ascending lunar spectacle created an internal yearning for Sam.

Daniel had been right about more than I initially cared to admit. All of these strange events were interlinked in some unexplainable twist of fate. I no longer believed it was a mere case of accidental lust that opened my eyes to Sam. Her striking resemblance to my mother was not coincidence run amok. I stared off into the distant sky, lost in my musings. And me … the great grandson of Vlad Tepes. I guess somebody had to be. Setting free the very women my father condemned, what kind of odds could possibly justify that? One day … actually one night, Daniel and I would sit and have conversation concerning his spiritual interpretations of all of these supernatural quirks.

I sat under a tree, for what must have been several hours, listening to the rush of some tropical breeze caress the beachfront palms. Tuning out the hubbub of the nearby bars, the melodic symphony of wind and waves soothed my inner spirit. How I yearned for this nightmare to be over. Immortality, at whatever cost, held no appeal. I would prefer to grow old with Sam, knowing my life experiences were not limitless, but that each moment truly mattered.

Lost in thoughts of mixed emotions, I began to return to the realm of my purpose here. Through my own experience of refraining from live blood consumption for months at a time, and not killing any human, thus far, I considered the possibility of converting the remaining vampires into non-lethal beings.

A young couple consumed in passion walked by, oblivious to the danger in such close proximity. With her silhouette against the silver moonlight and the aroma of their arousal, ancient urges began to gnaw. I rolled my head back and gazed at the starlit heavens above. Intoxicated with the euphoria experienced from freeing my instinctive nature, I ignored the call to flee this festering desire.

A short time passed before another couple encroached on my territory. Drunk, and looking for a place to have sex, the scent of the woman's arousal electrified me. With the instincts of a wolf, unconsciously, I rose and began the stalk.

With so much more than physical attraction at work, I savored the thought of her sweet blood filling my mouth. Like fine wine, blood had its own unique characteristics. Many, but certainly not all, tasted quite pleasing. The permeating redolence of this young woman foretold of an exquisite culinary experience.

Appearing about twenty-five, the tanned blonde was dressed in an exceptionally short white skirt with a black sleeveless blouse. Her hair was silky smooth and cropped unevenly around her shoulders. Her date's attire, faux biker, screamed off-the-rack Walmart. His shaved head more a cover up for premature balding than badass. The frenzied need to feed was overwhelming, magnified by my increased sexual prowess. There was no earthly addiction to compare to the forces driving me. Not enough to simply have my way with her, feed off of and then kill the pair, deep within my very being, I wanted to belittle and dominate him, before the kill. Completely off the scale of any rational thoughts I had ever possessed, I was not a man, but an animal, starving for food, desperate to establish superiority.

From a short distance, I watched as they took a position on top of the stacked beach chairs, covered and stored for the night. From my position, I studied as their hands explored each other's bodies. Salivating, I ran my tongue over my fangs. His hands slid up her blouse, as she unbuttoned his pants. The internal forces driving me spurred me forward.

Hastily, she pulled his pants down. Sexual pheromones filled the air fueling my frenzied desires. Out of the corner of their eyes, they both seemed to catch the intruder's silhouette.

"Hey buddy, how's about giving us some room?" he asked, surprisingly polite.

Blazingly fast, I jumped on top of the chairs, just above her head. Placing my entire hand over his face and mouth I squeezed with a crushing force until he dropped to the ground. Her eyes pined with a fearful desire. With my free hand, I tore open her blouse. She quivered in anticipation, as I ran my hand over her chest and into her panties. I pulled her face close and kissed her sweet, succulent lips. Her veins rose to my calling as I moved to her neck.

"Take me," she begged.

After tonight, I knew the fate of the damned would haunt me forever for the murder I was about to commit. There was no choice. I was a vampire, fulfilling the curse of my forefathers. I opened my mouth and set my teeth to her neck. She moaned in aroused anticipation. With the first light puncture of flesh, her blood began to flow, filling my mouth. My eyes were fixed on the distant horizon and with the scrap of humanity left in me, I pleaded, "Please stop me."

CHAPTER TEN

WITHOUT PROVOCATION OR cause I stopped. Withdrawing my teeth from her flesh, as much as I desired to swallow the succulent blood filling my mouth, I spit it out. Her eyes searched mine, begging me to continue. I laid her down, beside her unconscious friend.

"I am sorry," I said in a timid voice, shocked by how quickly I had become completely unglued. In the native tongue of my ancestors, I chanted her to sleep.

I staggered away toward the ocean, disgusted by my actions, and fearing this newfound demon. The taste of her fresh blood resonated in my mouth. I was invigorated, with a greater strength than I had ever known ... yet I was wounded deeply. Did my love for Sam mean nothing? How did I instantly become completely incapable of controlling these primitive urges? How did I stop, in the midst of the greatest, most intense pleasure I had ever experienced? I fell to my knees at the edge of the surf lost in a myriad of questions.

Before New Orleans, the only faith I possessed was in myself. Obviously, I was way out of my league now. "Okay, you have my undivided attention," I roared out. "What in the hell am I supposed to do now?" I half expected an answer to thunder from across the vastness of the ocean. But no words came, no burning bush, seaweed

... nothing.

Twice since New Orleans, when all strength and discipline failed in the face of defeat, there had been only one unknown saving grace. "Daniel! I hope you are happy," I called out. If he were here, his shit-eating grin would be the size of Montana.

Suddenly a familiar fragrance drifted across the sands, snapping my neck in the direction of its origin. Celine was nearby. I traveled back to Ocean Drive, passing the unconscious couple I had terrorized only moments before. They would wake in an hour or so, he with a major headache, and she with a rather suspicious wound to her neck. Neither would remember my ill-mannered indiscretion.

Celine's scent grew stronger as I headed north. Half a block away, she sat at an outdoor table sharing drinks with two men. Appearing to be of Cuban descent, they were young and buff, one like a mastiff, the other a pit bull. Judging by the abundance of empty glasses on the table, they were looking to get Celine drunk. Having invested their hard-earned money on the effort, my intrusion would not be welcome.

I approached from the left, out of her line of sight. Having learned that vampires could mask their scent, I had practiced with Sam the art of camouflaging my unique aroma. "The city is different, as are the players, but the game remains the same. Does it not Celine?"

Celine turned slowly, as if the sound of my voice created some great discomfort. Recognizing my voice immediately, she feigned a smile of delight. "Why Brian, what on earth brings you to Miami?"

"I would love to say it was just you, Celine, but truth be told, I would love to see Gabrielle as well."

The more ripped of the two Cuban mutts butted in. "Who is your friend, Celine?"

"Not that it is any of your damn business, but I am her pimp. And judging by your attire, you cannot afford five minutes of her time, Romeo. Celine will be leaving with me now, and you two boys can go down to the beach and jerk each other off."

"Why don't you go jerk off, and we'll see to it she makes it home later?" the other asked.

Never having the patience for this kind of male pissing contest, I was ready to bash their heads together like cymbals. But not wanting to attract too much attention, I decided on diplomacy.

"Gentlemen, the discussion is over. Tell Celine goodnight, or get up off your asses and try to stop me. But be warned, I am in an exceptionally foul mood, and although I will not take any pleasure in it, I will shove these beer bottles up your asses one at a time." Placing my hands on each of their shoulders, I administered a crushing grip. Wincing in pain, neither attempted to rise.

Peering into their eyes with a deathly gaze, I gripped harder. "What's it going to be boys, get up, or goodnight?"

"Goodnight," growled the mastiff.

"Smart choice," I said, instantly releasing my grip. I grabbed Celine by the elbow forcing her from her chair. Her resistance was minimal as I led her away.

Celine smirked as I escorted her across the street, back to the beach, where we would have slightly more privacy. "I am quite capable of walking on my own," she exerted, as she yanked her arm from my grasp. "I am very surprised to find you are still alive, Brian. Tell me, where is Monique?"

"Monique underestimated my resolve. It was a very costly mistake."

"I see," Celine replied simply. "And are you here to kill me as well?"

"That depends. I told you in New Orleans you could not remain out here amongst the living."

"Why should it be for you to decide where I can or cannot exist? Monique was right about men. All you desire is power and domination."

Her snippy French accent irritated me. "No, Monique was wrong. I could not care less for how you live your life, only I cannot allow you to murder whomever you please. Only by a gross miscalculation did I set you free. But that is the core of my resolve, I must take you back to Daniel, or …"

"I will do whatever I please. There is nobody left to tell me how to live my life. I will not repeat Monique's mistakes," Celine proclaimed boldly.

"You already are. This is how I found you. And when they realize," I said, pointing to the inhabitants of Ocean Drive, "they will hunt you down as well."

"Oh, so you are doing this because you are concerned for my safety?"

"No Celine, I am doing it because I fucked up, and I will not have you mercilessly killing scores of innocent people."

"Well, you are too little too late for that," she sneered, with no apparent concern for the threat I posed.

Her arrogance stiffened my resolve. Her sarcastic French attitude pissed me off. "Well, there you have it. Your fate is sealed."

Celine stepped back and studied my attire. A thin white T-shirt and tan linen pants offered no camouflage for weapons. "From where I stand, it would appear the only thing for certain is your death. Monique was a fool to toy with you."

"I do not see Gabrielle, or the others anywhere nearby." Panning our surroundings, I was sizing up the proximity of potential witnesses. "Do you honestly think you can dispatch me all alone?"

Celine scanned the immediate beach area. We were far enough from the crowds and it was sufficiently dark for her to take action. I sensed her growing aggression as she drew near. "Dear Brian," she said, as a smile of arrogance encompassed her face. Placing both hands gently on my head, she violently twisted in an attempt to snap my neck. My head did not budge. With an increasing panic, she wrenched harder. Mystified by her inability to kill me, a growing look of fear eclipsed her confident smile.

I grabbed her by the hair and yanked her head back, while shoving her shoulder down, clearing a path to her neck. In our present circumstances, there was only one way to kill her. Without hesitation, I thrust my teeth deeply into her neck. Now fighting for her life, Celine flailed about madly, only to discover her strength was no match for mine. With my grasp firmly around her neck she was unable to scream. Her blood filled my mouth as I drained her body. As she wretched and convulsed, I could sense her life force passing to me. Celine's body ceased to resist and collapsed. I continued to drink until her veins ran dry.

I looked down in my arms at Celine's lifeless body. Despite the violent nature of her death, she appeared to be at peace. Unlike New Orleans, where revenge cleansed my malice, grief rained upon me. I had killed one of my own. "May God have mercy on both of our souls." I kissed Celine's forehead, sat down and cradled her in my arms. I phoned my driver and instructed him where to pick me up. Ten minutes later, the black Denali pulled up on Ocean Drive.

I picked up Celine's body in my arms and carried her to the waiting car. "One shot too many," I said to the driver, as he peered at Celine in my arms. There was no room for mistakes here. I placed Celine in the back seat and returned to the other side where the driver was waiting by the door.

"Spiritul de întuneric, Te implor. Posedă această ființă indisciplinat. Forja cuvintele mele asupra sufletului lor. Viața lor să fie a mea sângele nostru să fie una." I chanted until the driver collapsed into unconsciousness. Stuffing him to the passenger back seat, I took the wheel and adjusted the mirror. Briefly startled by the illusion Celine's eyes had opened, my heart pounded. I shook off the mirage and pulled away.

Unfortunately, the hunt for Gabrielle would have to wait until I dealt with Celine's body. I had decided on the flight down, the most logical and safe disposal method was to dump the body deep in the everglades.

I dialed my phone again. "Are you ready?"

"Man, I was born ready," the familiar voice replied.

"Meet me in thirty minutes. The package is ready for delivery." I hung up the phone. Expecting success, I had already selected a rendezvous location with an expert in hazmat disposal.

Considering my cargo, I pulled away from Ocean Drive and headed toward the causeway, back to Miami obeying traffic laws as if my life depended on it. There were a series of isolated abandoned warehouses just west of Jackson Memorial Hospital where I would hand off Celine's body without fear of discovery. One in particular I knew well, having used it several years back to set up a prominent politician with a nasty drug habit who held a vendetta against a wealthy client.

I knew I would have to exercise more restraint with Gabrielle and the others—if they were even here. Given the nature of her apparent friendship with Celine in New Orleans, it was a safe bet Gabrielle was somewhere nearby. Celine's death was hasty to the point of reckless, which could bring exposure. I would have to come up with a better plan for Gabrielle. First to extract information, and secondly, to find some scenario that would convince her to return to the Convent. My final option, which I now viewed as a distressing solution—find a more secluded location for her execution.

I arrived five minutes early for the pre-arranged meeting location on NW South River Drive. Pulling into the pitch-black lot, I killed the headlights. Chips of coral crunched under the tires as the Denali crawled to the far corner of the lot. Rolling my window down, I listened for signs of hostiles as I took visual inventory of my surroundings. On the opposite corner of the lot, I made out the silhouette of a black car.

A distinctly European engine purred as a BMW slowly approached. The windows were tinted almost as black as the exterior. As the Beamer pulled alongside, its driver's-side window glided down.

From the darkened cockpit, the deep voice spoke, "Brian, it's good to see you again, alive."

"Likewise Chuck. Nice Beamer." Chuck had never been one for sports cars. He usually opted for the more industrial modes of transportations, like Hummers and Jeeps.

"Yeah, it is. I ran into a little cash a few months back. So I decided to treat myself."

"Nice treat." I instantly concurred. A *little cash*. This was most likely his New Orleans payday.

Chuck opened the tailgate of the SUV. "Damn bro, she's too damn cute to be this dead. Who is she?"

"Celine. And trust me, she was as devious as she was beautiful."

"I gotta ask you. Why are all the vampires good looking? I mean except for you. Honestly, I haven't seen a butt-ugly vampire yet."

I sighed heavily at Chuck. No matter how intense the situation, his mind always revolved around one thing. "I don't know Chuck. I am sure if you stick around long enough you will eventually meet an ass-faced vampire or two."

"For sure. So what's the deal with the dude? You trying to get a two for the price of one on me?

"No." I studied the drivers face for any signs of awakening. "He is just out cold. I will take him with me."

"He ain't drunk is he? Cause I'll fuck you slam up if he pukes in my ride."

"No worries Chuck. He is just out cold," I explained as I shoved him in the front seat.

"Cold cocked him, did ya?"

"Something like that. Let's get this done." Chuck and I exchanged keys. "Here's the address," I said, as I showed Chuck the location where I would leave his car. "I'll leave the keys inside."

"Ten-four," Chuck confirmed.

"What's your plan?"

"There's this nice little place out in the 'Glades, way off the beaten path. Very desolate. It's pretty infested with gators. By lunch time there will be nothin' left of her."

I knew Chuck would be thorough. He always was. "Do you still have protection?"

Chuck smiled as he gripped the cross from under his shirt. "I'd show you, but rumor has it you've developed some strange allergy." He reached behind the driver's seat and pulled out his backpack. "Everything a vampire slayer needs and more. Jimmy and I figured because of what we did in New Orleans it might be a good idea to remain prepared until we were sure all them bitches were gone for good."

"How is Jimmy?"

"He's cool as can be expected. He went to LA to close out Rob's affairs and has been sulking around ever since."

"I should have called him. Ever since I got to New York, I just wanted to put New Orleans behind me, even though I knew there was still work to be done. I let you guys down and there's no way to make it right. I wouldn't have called you, except I need your help."

"You needed me? Dude." Chuck smiled broadly. "I always knew you cared." Chuck climbed in the Denali. "Brian, we all fucked it up. Rob is just as much on Jimmy and me as he is you. That's just life."

Chuck drove off leaving me in a cloud of sandy dust. Life, mine was always so black and white, now it was a sad carnival of irony. For years, I killed whoever stood in the way of accomplishing my objectives without remorse. Now, having evolved into a blood-drinking killing machine, I found the prospect of taking life unpleasant and immoral. Go figure.

I opened the door and began to slide into the Beamer. "Nice car *amigo*," a voice called from the dark.

The scent grew stronger. Three approaching Hispanics came

into view. At this hour, in this neighborhood, I knew trouble was not far behind. "I would love to stay and chat gentlemen, but I must be going."

"Wah, chu don' like our company?" one of the men murmured.

"It's not that guys, I just have somewhere else to be."

"*Amigo*, you can't just drive into my neighborhood and do business without obtaining a business license, you know," the first voice insisted as the other two laughed.

Obviously, they had witnessed the exchange from some hidden vantage point. "Sorry guys, it won't happen again."

"Chu right 'bout that, man. You leave us the car we'll call it even," the third insisted.

Killing them was not the best option, but a good ass-whipping was entirely different. Option three was to put them out, like sleeping beauty in the passenger seat. Deciding option three would result in the least commotion, I took a step closer.

The three circled tightly, crowding my space.

"You do not want to do this," I warned them.

"Oh yeah, we do," the first one stated.

"Spiritul de întuneric," I began to chant. Before I completed the first sentence, I felt a steely cold piercing of my abdomen. *Shit, they shanked me.* I felt a second knife rip into my ribs, higher up. Vampire or not, the penetrating steel burned.

Before a third assault could be launched, I sprang into a frenzied attack. The first guy's neck snapped in my hands before the other two had realized their friend was dead. Using only my CIA acquired skills, I savagely crushed the second guy's nose bone deep into his brains. The third guy barely had a split second to realize the grave predicament befallen his friends, before I had my hand around his throat. He slashed at my arm with his knife as I constricted his airway with a vice grip choke "Time to die," I said coldly. My hand clamped down until his neck snapped like a pretzel. Releasing his body, it collapsed to the ground, piling on top of his two compadres. I looked down at my lacerated blood-soaked shirt. "Shit, not another damn shirt." With my blood all over the crime scene, I could not just leave the corpses here.

I dialed up Chuck. "Turn around." I insisted. "I need you back here, right now."

I scuffed the coral around, hiding as much blood as possible while waiting for Chuck to return. The vast majority was mine. Although the pain persisted, the bleeding had all but subsided as the wound closed within minutes. Still standing after what should have been a mortal wound, twenty years of wondering how I survived a bullet to the head was answered in a painful experience.

An approaching vehicle's headlights dimmed, the rumble of the Denali announcing Chuck's return. Pulling up next to the corpses, he rolled down his window and stared at the carcasses.

"What the hell?"

"You left too early. These boys showed up for a party right after you left. They tried to convince me I should let them borrow your car."

"Looks like you convinced them otherwise." Hopping out of the Denali, Chuck caught sight of my blood soaked shirt, illuminated by the light of the open door. "You okay?" he asked as he nudged a corpse with his shoe.

"I have been better."

Chuck reached down and grabbed the stiff on top by the shirt collar and dragged him toward the back of the Denali. "How bout you Julio? You okay? Hey Brian, Julio says he can't talk right now cuz he's dead like a motherfucker."

"I suppose I could have just given them your car."

"Yeah, and I'd be loading your ass for the gator farm next," Chuck scoffed.

I grabbed the other guys by the waist and carried them to the tailgate and effortlessly slung them in. Chuck watched in awe of my strength. I grabbed the last guy at Chuck's feet and slung him in as well.

"Show off," Chuck moaned. "All dead?"

"Dead enough," I replied, concealing a smile. Prior to becoming a vampire, Chuck and I were evenly matched in strength, even though he held a considerable size advantage. After my transformation, my strength and speed were now magnified much to the jarhead's chagrin.

Chuck saw my constrained smirk. "You know, if you gave me your power, I would still be able to kick your ass."

I had his ego on the ropes and was not about to let up. "Really?

I don't recall an instance where you were ever able to kick my ass."

"That's probably because you were always unconscious afterwards."

"I will tell you what, leather neck, once we are wrapped up here in Miami, we can go down to the gym and settle things like men," I taunted.

"No thanks, Count Chocula. You'd probably just use one of those sissy-ass spells of yours, and then drink my blood."

Even though I was slashed, bloodied, and irritated with circumstances, once again, Chuck forced my smile.

"Are you done for tonight?" Chuck asked as he closed the tailgate. "Or should I just follow you around until sunrise? I hope you realize the price of the job just jumped up. I agreed to dispose of four skinny-ass vampire bitches, not a bunch of homies that just happen to be at the wrong place at the wrong time and piss off the wrong guy."

"Done for tonight," I claimed while dusting my hands together.

"Let's hope so. By the time you get my disposal fee, I'll be buying a Lamborghini as well." Chuck climbed back in the Denali and drove off.

I kicked the dirt around, covering the residual spillage, stripped off my shirt and threw it in the trunk. I looked down at the knife wounds in my chest and abdomen. Although the incisions were sealed, scars remained.

On the drive back to the condo, I woke the driver and explained how he had tripped and hit his head, knocking himself unconscious while helping me load Celine. I also explained how she had woken, and subsequently puked all over the backseat. I then told him my friend Chuck had agreed to take Celine home and clean up her mess while I drove the two of us back to South Beach. I gave him instructions for the car exchange to occur later in the day. At four in the morning, it was the best bullshit I could come up with and would have to suffice.

With less than two hours before sunrise, it was time for me to get off the streets. I returned to the condo to find my laptop flashing; the message short and simple. "Stay safe, love Sam."

"Shop safely. Don't forget your sunscreen, love N," I replied and then headed for the shower. Phillip had arranged for Sam and Dee to go to his beach house in the Hamptons in my absence. I hoped the distraction would help keep Sam's mind off of my business, for a while.

Six months ago I would have bet everything I owned that neither Phillip nor I would be marching down the path to marriage. And sisters to top it off. What were the odds?

CHAPTER ELEVEN

SUNLIGHT LEAKED FROM under the door, announcing I had risen too early. Having seen a vampire's reaction to direct sunlight and curious as to how I would react to indirect light exposure, I cracked the closet door, but prepared to slam it shut at the first hint of discomfort. Cautiously moving toward the living room, colors had faded to more of a gray tone with the waning of sunlight. The window was facing east, yielding a panoramic view of the ocean, the setting sun still reflecting on the turquoise sea. Stepping cautiously, one foot at a time, I allowed my body to acclimate to the sensations of the growing brightness. Inching closer toward the window, I sensed my body temperature escalate. Gazing out the window at the reflection of the golden waves, I experienced what mountain climber's term as snow blindness. As if staring at a light more intense than the sun, the brightness was screamingly unbearable. My eyes burned beyond description, as all details instantly vanquished in a flash fire of pain. Immediately, my head snapped away and I staggered a good half dozen steps backward, as my heart pounded uncontrollably. My reaction was not of any rationalized fear, but an instinctive primeval fight for survival. I shuddered at the thought of a full sun encounter.

Retreating back into the bedroom, sulking along the way, I sat down on the bed, forced to accept the vulnerabilities of my species.

I flopped onto my back and sighed deeply. "Well that was a pretty stupid idea," I grumbled. "Maybe I should try bathing in holy water next."

I laid in the growing darkness, staring at the details of the ceiling, wondering what Sam was up to. I knew what I would rather be doing, if not for the odious task before me. The bed was quite comfortable, reminding me of happier times, when I still enjoyed a good night's sleep in a bed. My mind began to roam, drifting in and out of consciousness, thoughts randomly approaching and receding to the melody of the sea below.

Visions of my father, in agony, trapped, clawing for survival, suffering immensely, but not crying out. How had he died?

Alert again, I checked my watch. It was past eleven. Unsure whether I had been dreaming, or in some alternate state of consciousness, the haunting visions witnessed would have to be ignored for now. The haunts of a life unknown were clawing my subconscious; my Romanian ancestors were beckoning me home.

I jumped from the bed. Romania would have to wait. Gabrielle had to be the sole focus and purpose tonight. If successful, I could be back in New York tomorrow night and the thought of that was quite calming on my dream-rattled nerves. Heading out the door, and down to Collins Avenue, I planned to walk the blocks of the Art Deco district hoping to pick up Gabrielle's scent. A hardy breeze was blowing out of the southeast, and thunder rumbled off in the distance announcing a storm's approach. With the direction and magnitude of the wind, I was unable to pick up any trace of my elusive vampire. The redolence of rain filled the air as thunder rattled the plate glass windows. Shards of lightning streaked to the ground only blocks away, scattering the remaining people on the streets like roaches.

With the torrential downpour advancing, now visible only two blocks ahead, I was no longer concerned with the danger of a lightning strike, but not relishing the thought of walking around soaking wet. I did not have to look far for shelter. Directly in front of me was a club named Havana.

With the clubbers once standing in line scrambling for shelter, I cruised right in courtesy of a bouncer in need of gratuity. I ordered a beer at the bar out of habit, more than the need to quench my thirst. A thirst that had certainly changed. Having already consumed two pints of blood stocked in the condo refrigerator courtesy of Phillip, I hoped to suppress my predatory desire that raised it's ugly ass head last night. For the moment, it was working.

The scene inside Havana was nothing out of the ordinary, a packed dance floor and bar, with booze and sweat flowing. The few tables and chairs scattered about were anchored by people with no intention of moving. Wanting a chair, I approached two guys trashed at a small table between the bathroom and dance floor, and I sternly ordered them to move. Meeting their gaze of stupefied defiance, I stared into their eyes silently warning them of their fate should they not comply. Within seconds they were stumbling away.

Checking the storm's progress on my phone, it appeared as though I would be rained in for an hour or so. I settled back and observed what I once considered to be the makings of a damn good night. I had probably been parked on the stool about forty minutes when a soft French voice called out. "If you wanted to find me, you should have asked Celine."

"Shit," I muttered, once again caught with my pants down. The voice sounded like Gabrielle's, but her scent was different. Could it be I had finally found Sabine? I turned, only to find Gabrielle, somehow looking more seductive than she did in New Orleans. Wearing an oh-so-short skirt, white blouse, and fire engine stilettos, she was dressed to kill, literally. Her skin was dark bronze, and her hair cropped short.

"Are you going to be a gentleman and offer me a seat?"

I stood up, took her hand, kissed it lightly, and led her to the remaining stool. "I apologize. I was distracted by the sight of you."

"I hope the distraction is a good one."

Her French accent so innocent, her secret affliction so lethal. In my relatively short time as a vampire hunter, I found it odd to not cross paths with any ugly vampires, as did Chuck. I was sure somewhere, there had been a buck-toothed, Neanderthal bloodsucker, but I had not witnessed anyone remotely close to this description as of yet.

"Oh yes, you are," I remarked. Gabrielle smiled shyly, but I knew she was anything but, and I knew what she was capable of. Assuming, as did Celine, she was unaware of my similar malady, I decided to play her game.

"Nice tan."

"It's spray-on. On my body it only lasts a day, but I like how it makes me look … like everyone else."

"You, my dear, do not need to look like anybody else. Your beauty is quite unique."

Gabrielle looked down toward her lap, concealing a gratuitous smile. I understood her desire to be like other women. The power possessed did not necessarily balance out with the unique abnormalities we both shared, and the feeling of isolation.

"Tell me Brian, how did Monique die?"

"What makes you sure she is dead?"

"I knew what her plans were. I told her she was a fool to toy with you. But she would not listen," Gabrielle explained. "The next night, when she did not return, I went to the house. Her blood was everywhere. The house reeked of her death."

"Speaking of scents, yours has changed. How on earth did you accomplish that?"

"You noticed. I am impressed."

I was having difficulty getting a read on Gabrielle. There seemed to be a duality, one side mildly timid, the other self-assured.

"But perhaps we should know each other better before I reveal my intimate secrets."

"Fair enough, assuming we get to know each other better." Turning on all the charm I could muster, I knew where this was leading. "So you knew Monique was going to kill me, and you chose not to warn me. Ouch. I would have warned you."

"For some strange reason, I believe you, Brian. But it was not my place to intercede, nor did I want to. Celine and I both knew there was a good chance you would kill Monique. Do not forget, it was Monique that made me what I am. It was her fault I have not seen the sun rise for over two hundred years, her fault I was imprisoned for so long. Because of Monique, I no longer enjoy the taste of food or have ever experienced love in my life." Gabrielle attempted to temper her tone. "I saw the way you looked at her, your Samantha.

You protected her. You would have died for her. Do you not think I would want to know this kind of love?"

"I understand."

"I came to your hotel again, the night after you killed Monique, hoping to find you. I wanted your passion, and was willing to die for it. But I could not find you. Celine insisted we leave New Orleans the very next night." Gabriel sighed. "And here I have been ever since, imprisoned by a curse I did not deserve."

Gabrielle's emotions poured out, maybe for the first time in two hundred years. And as much as I tried to remain objective, I could not help but feel pity.

"Celine did not return last night, and now here you are. I suspect you have killed her as well?"

I nodded my head, confirming her suspicions.

"I know I am no match for you ... so now the end comes," Gabrielle sighed. "I will join my sisters in the eternal hell."

"Not all of them."

"What do you mean?" her voice perked, enlivened with curiosity.

"Angelique and Sabine. They left New Orleans as well ...You did not know this?"

"I ... we thought you had killed them both. Poor Sabine, all she could think of was her child. She lost her mind with grief, over the child she never knew. She always believed her child had been taken to New York and swore if we ever got out, she would go there to find her. But we never saw Sabine after our escape from that dreadful place."

"I never saw her after the Convent, so maybe you're right, she bolted for the Big Apple."

Gabrielle shrugged, "What is this Big Apple?"

I let out an honest chuckle, amused by her ignorance of the modern world. "Just a nickname for New York. So, maybe Angelique is in New York, helping Sabine?" Wasn't this a picture perfect moment. Two vampires, hell-bent on killing one another, having a quiet conversation amongst the masses of unawares.

"I do not know. But what I do know; Angelique is obsessed with you. She commanded no harm befall you. It was Angelique's affection for you that spurred Monique's desire to conquer you. After our escape from the convent, Monique blamed her for everything."

I could come up with several damn good reasons for Angelique's apparent obsession. With my striking resemblance to my father, did she somehow know who I was, or was she just grateful for the freedom we provided? If Sabine and Angelique were in New York, suddenly Sam's safety was a major concern. If Angelique knew of Sam, which given our public outings, was almost a certainty, she could be in imminent danger. Shit. If I could somehow turn Gabrielle, she could prove a major asset in locating her sisters. My sisters. *My evil, bloodsucking sisters.* I had a poker deck of options before me. But which hand to play?

"Gabrielle, there is no need for you to die. If you will travel with me to New York, help me find Sabine ..." I reached out and took her hands. A surge of electricity jolted between our bodies. The identical sensation when Angelique kissed me, and when Monique seduced me. Instantly, Gabrielle's desires swooned, intoxicating me. I experienced her yearning for companionship, freedom, and love. Unfortunately, I was not able to conceal my reciprocal lust.

"I know what you desire," she purred.

I broke the grip and withdrew my hands. Quickly, I blurted out, "I have seen her daughter. I know where Sabine's child lives."

Gabriel's eyes lit up, as if a key to her salvation had been found. "And Sabine's child ... Is she like us?"

"No, her life is prolonged, as is yours, but she can move in sunlight, and does not share your thirst."

"My thirst? How little you truly understand," Gabrielle protested indignantly. "Take me to your home and make love to me. Then you shall know of my thirst."

In her eyes I witnessed a yearning two hundred years in the making. "I fear too many a young man has already made that mistake. I am in no particular hurry to join all the others."

"Celine's appetite, like Monique's, was insatiable and as such, she killed many. I have not fallen in their ways for fear I would become like them. I have never killed."

"Never killed?" My tone registered immediate agitation. "The Convent? His name was Rob. And he was a damn good friend."

Gabrielle reached out and took my hand. "He was already dead. I feared Monique's retribution if I did not follow my sister's example."

I digested her story, reliving the video in my mind; it was possible

Rob was already dead. "Obviously I can't hide my feelings from you. As you know what I desire, if I were to allow it, how do I know you will not kill me?"

"You are not like any other man I have known. You killed Monique, and all the others. My power is but a whisper of theirs. But if you fear me, then strike me down where I sit. I will not resist."

A momentary silence passed. To offer her life, appealed to the mercy I had begun to nurture for one of my own. Was this some kind of genetic predisposition I shared with my father's legacy?

"I will not take your life, but I cannot give you what you want."

"It is her? This woman, Samantha, who was with you in New Orleans."

"No." I snapped defensively, eager to remove Sam from any jealous homicidal thoughts.

"It is foolish for a man who lives the life you do, to be involved with a weak, vulnerable woman such as her."

I squeezed Gabrielle's hands tightly. "My relationship with her, or anyone else, can never be any concern of yours. If we can find a path, some mutual, agreeable course for you to remain free, you must promise to never seek her, or anyone I might be involved with … do you understand?"

Gabrielle donned a devious smirk, which suddenly gave me the urge to instantly finish her off. Her silent attitude was threatening, and at this moment, the only thing keeping her alive was her knowledge of Sabine. A minute or two passed, neither of us breaking the visual checkmate.

"Damn, I give up. We can go back to my place."

"I thought you would never ask." Gabrielle rose from her chair, her long slender legs leading her body toward me. She held out her hand for mine. "And, what about Samantha?"

"New Orleans is a long way away."

Outside, rain poured down in warm sheets saturating our bodies. Gabrielle jerked at my arm, unable to hide her anticipation. "Which way?"

"Let's wait for a cab."

"I don't see any, and I'm already soaked. Can we just walk?"

My primeval instinct guided my eyes to her white cotton shirt, clinging tightly to her braless chest. Acutely aware of my gaze,

Gabrielle pushed me against a wall and pressed her lips to mine. Her tongue was met with the iron gate of locked lips. All the efforts I had made to conceal my vampire nature would have been in vain the instant her tongue raked across my fangs.

Frustrated, she took my hand, and pulled it to her legs, guiding it up her rain-soaked flesh. Her voice quivered with my touch.

"You are going to have to wait a little longer, my dear," I explained as I took her hand and led her toward my condo ten blocks away. We had walked about two blocks in silence, my mind racing with conflict, hers racing on sex.

"If I consent to help you find Sabine, when would we leave for New York?"

"Tomorrow, just after sunset."

"Are we to fly? I have never been close to these machines that fly as birds."

"Yes, we will fly." After a brief chuckle at the notion, *machines that fly like birds*. I broached the burning question of the evening.

"What about the others? I can't leave anyone behind."

Gabrielle looked bewildered, as if I should already have known. "There is only me now. There are no others."

"Tonight you will stay with me and tomorrow we will leave for New York."

I quickened our pace as we sloshed through the monsoon. We arrived back at my condo and now I was clueless as what to do with a seductively soaking wet vampiress in the mood for romance. But I knew I could not let her out of my sight. Entering the condo I made a beeline to my laptop.

"Make yourself at home, I need to arrange our flight." Stroking the keys, I looked into the reflection of the window to see nothing. Then the hand touched my shoulder causing me to jump. Damn non-reflecting vampires. I wheeled around in my chair. Minus the six-inch Dante's *Inferno*–red bedroom slippers, Gabrielle was naked.

"I am sorry, I forgot you were soaked. You must be freezing. I'll get you something dry to wear." The sight of her silky flesh and perfect curves stirred the inner demon once more.

"Don't bother. I am always cold. Occupational hazard."

With a long slender leg, Gabrielle cut off my angle to the bathroom and wrapped her arms around me. I gave her a quick kiss, and pulled away.

"Cool your jets, girl. We have all night."

She grabbed my collar from behind with one hand, and my crotch with the other.

"My jets have been cooled for over two hundred years. Right now will be just fine." Her voice was oh so sultry, the kiss on my neck electrifying. This was not going well at all. I felt the firmness of her breast pressing into my back. Somehow, *not tonight dear, I have a headache*, was not going to work. Her hands were having their way, exploring my body, and my body's reaction was not helping convince her I was not interested. Gabrielle grabbed my hand and pulled it behind, guiding it between her legs.

Options? I could kill her now, even though I felt she would be of some value in New York. She groaned in my ear while guiding my hand. Sam would not be at all sympathetic or understanding to my predicament in the least. *Options?* With her free hand she stroked me.

Suddenly, like another gift from above, there was a knock at the door. I turned and put my finger over Gabrielle's moist lips. The driver? He did not know the apartment number. Chuck would know, but I did not believe he would show up at this hour unannounced. The cops? Possibly Phillip, or worse, given the fact Phillip knew the location of the condo, it could be Sam. I went limp. "I am not expecting visitors," I whispered. I took Gabrielle by the hand and led her to the bedroom. I opened the closet door and grabbed a shirt. "Put this on, stay in here and keep quiet."

I walked back to the door. The scent from beyond the door was unfamiliar. I breathed a sigh of relief knowing I did not have to explain the half-dressed vampire in my apartment. I opened the door, wedging my foot as a doorstop. One good look at his face and the overwhelming noxious odor and I knew, he was a vampire! He burst through the door, knocking me backward to the floor. Followed by two similar-looking lads. Suddenly I realized Gabrielle had been a very bad girl.

Bloodsucker number one looked like Billy Idol with a nasty crack habit. His face was gaunt, and white as bleached flour. His hair was equally white, spiked to comical proportions. Dressed in tight black leather, if I did not know better, I would have thought him to be a distasteful joke. His two Cuban sidekicks, with their slicked Ricky Ricardo hair, wearing cheap club attire, effortlessly scooped me off the floor and pulled me back until my head slammed against the dining room wall. Refraining from immediate retaliation, I decided to let this little drama play out.

Billy slowly closed the door, as if being shut in with these stooges was going to intimidate me. "Where is Gabrielle?" His tone was high pitched and grated my nerves quickly.

"She left."

"Fool," he said as he grabbed my cheek and squeezed. "I can smell her presence." Sniffing the air, he searched for the origin. "Gabrielle, come out. I want to talk with you."

Gabrielle did not reply.

With a forearm across my throat, I struggled for words. "Hey dipshit, I banged her. That's what you're smelling. You been stalking her?"

"I don't need to stalk. When Celine did not come home I followed Gabrielle out tonight."

"Stalker," I goaded.

"Gabrielle, come now or I will kill this man." He waited for a response, and got none. "I will not ask again."

Silently, Gabrielle appeared from the bedroom. Billy shook his head as he observed her attire. "Once a whore, always a whore."

I could only assume he was alluding to her life in France, over two centuries ago. But how did he know her history? "Don't call her a whore."

"Fucking a mortal! You are pathetic. I would kill you where you stand, but I want to know where Celine is."

"Gabrielle, I am waiting. Where is Celine?" he shrilled again, growing impatient.

"She is dead, Craven. I do not know how."

"How do you know for certain she is dead?" Billy gasped.

"Hey shit for brains, why not ask me?" I barked.

Billy turned, smiled evilly, flashed his menacing fangs and then smacked me across the face. "I will deal with you in a minute." He walked toward Gabrielle.

"How did Celine die?" he demanded.

"I killed her, fuck face!" I exclaimed. It was past time to dispatch the clown and pony show. I tossed the two Cubans restraining me across the room. With speed they had never before witnessed, I smashed a dining room chair and thrust the splintered legs through their hearts, impaling them on the wall. Without thought, I found myself in a most peculiar posture. Defying gravity, I clung to the wall, five feet off the floor, just like spider man. I snarled at Billy, fully exposing my fangs. He grabbed Gabrielle, and thrust her in front.

"I will kill her," he threatened.

"What do you think I am about to do?" I hissed back. Climbing down from the wall, I slowly stalked the retreating vampire and his hostage. I raised my arm out and with my palm turned slightly downward; my thoughts swooned, silently commanding Billy to submit. Reciting the ancient Romanian phrases of my ancestors, I struck fear into his very being. Picking up another splintered leg, effortlessly, I moved Gabrielle to the side.

With him quivering before me, he pleaded, "No, Master."

"How many more vampires are there?"

"None."

Coldly, I looked him in the eye. "You will thank me for this one day." I shoved the stake through his chest until it protruded out his back. I turned to Gabrielle, unable to conceal my disappointment.

She uttered the last word she would ever speak, "How?"

"*There are no others?*" I asked bitterly. I bit deeply into her neck as she thrust against my body. Like her scent, the taste of her blood was uniquely living. She cried out faintly, as her life began to pass through me. Filling my mouth with the greatest succulence ever experienced, I stopped, just before death would take her. Sweeping up her limp body, I carried her to the couch. With barely a breath left in her body, I placed her head across my lap and caressed her once vivid face, now sunken, and gray. Her weakened eyes, which only minutes earlier had been so vibrant, pleaded with me.

"Gabrielle, I am so disappointed. You lied. For starters, that was three *others.*"

Gabrielle struggled to speak.

"I will allow you to decide your fate. I will finish what I have started, or I will leave you this way for all eternity, making your imprisonment at the Convent seem like heaven. The choice is yours. But before you decide, you will tell me the truth."

Her body wrenched in unending agony.

"Yes, it is painful. I understand. I have left you just enough blood to sustain this miserable existence. But unlike humans, our bodies will never rejuvenate blood on their own. And you my dear are far too weak to feed on your own. In this state I will leave you, unless you tell me everything."

Gabrielle's eyes pleaded, seeking desperately for mercy through her excruciating pain. She moved her lips but was too weak to speak.

I raised my wrist to my mouth and bit lightly. Blood began to flow freely from the puncture. I lowered my wrist above her mouth, dripping precious drops of blood, restoring a fraction of her vitality. Weakly, Gabrielle raised her arm and guided my wrist to her mouth. As she nursed, traces of color returned to her skin and eyes. The veins in my arm began to bulge as my forearm turned a deep shade of purple. This newfound experience inflamed my eroticism.

"That is enough for now."

Breaking the bond, witnessing her tongue eagerly swipe the remaining traces of my blood from her lips, my heart pounded as I quivered with delight.

"Please!" she pleaded. "I need more."

"That is all you get, until you answer my questions and I swear, one more lie and I will take you right back down to the hell you just left, and leave you there."

"If I do as you say, will you still take me with you? Ten minutes ago, we were about to become lovers." With a crooked weak smile, she turned her face into my hand.

"Gabrielle ..." I pulled my hand away. "The only way this will work is from this point on we both have to be honest with each other." Her eyes met mine with a truthful acceptance. In sharing my blood, a fascinating bond had been established. Not since that first night in the Convent with Angelique had I experienced this kind of connection.

"You know I find you quite irresistible, there's no hiding that. But I love Samantha. My soul purpose for bringing you here was to extract information."

"So you lied?" Gabrielle accused.

"I have to eliminate the threat I unleashed in New Orleans, by whatever means necessary." Nuzzling her head tightly against my stomach, eyes still locked in mesmerizing desire, this moment, this kindred creature was more enticing than any fantasy, and I feared my inability to regain self-control.

"How long have you been like me?"

"The night I killed Monique. She did this to me."

"You are one of us. How is it you take the life of your own kind so easily? Especially when so few remain."

"I have a moral obligation, to my former race, to protect them from the predatory creatures roaming loosely due to my carelessness. Beyond protecting the humans, once I am satisfied vampires no longer pose a threat ..."

"I am no predator. I have killed no one. I have never tasted human blood," Gabrielle replied, defending her life. "The others fed on whatever blood the Convent guards gave them. But I knew if I drank the blood of humans, I would become as unholy as they had. All hope of ever returning to the light would perish. Angelique understood my choice, and together with the aid of the nuns, we consumed only the blood of animals."

"Gabrielle, I saw you drink Rob's blood." I felt like I needed to revisit the issue one last time for any inconsistencies.

Gabrielle reached for my hand and pulled it along side her face. "Please indulge me. No man has ever touched me so tenderly."

With the bond reaffirmed, I conceded and gently stroked my hand through her hair. "You were telling me about Rob."

"About your friend, I waited until last. He was already dead. I was afraid if I did not appear to join my sisters, they would leave me behind in the Convent. It is true, I bit him, but I never drank his blood." From what I knew of Angelique, Gabrielle's story was credible.

"One last detail, please explain why I have three dead vampires on my carpet."

"Craven, the one you just killed, he belonged to Celine. But he was not a vampire when I saw him last. The other two, I never met. "When Celine did not come home last night, they must have followed us as he claimed."

"And do *you* believe there might be more of these?"

"I do not believe so. With your words from the old world, I don't think he could lie."

"Gabrielle." I searched for words. I searched for feelings sprouting deep within. As my blood coursed through her veins, this helpless woman was now a part of me. Suddenly an overwhelming urge to protect her defeated all desire to harm her. Her eyes were so weak and helpless, and I knew her life was now my responsibility to change.

"If I allow you to live free, I have to know beyond all doubt, I can trust you."

"Tomorrow, we will go to your home and look for any signs that there might be more rogues."

Gabrielle affirmed with a silent nod.

"Then you will go to New York with me, to find Sabine and Angelique. If you help me do all I ask, and you can convince me you can exist without killing, we will discuss finding a mutual place where you can go free."

She nodded again.

"And one final point, the most important," I continued. "Choosing to take you along as a companion, not an adversary, I need you to understand, my attraction to you is apparently instinctive to our race, some kind of genetic attraction. I can sense your passion and desires and apparently you can sense mine. But regardless of my subconscious feelings, I am very much in love with Samantha. There will never be anything between the two of us."

Once again, she nodded.

"We have shared our blood, and forged a bond that will only be severed by death. I will care for and protect you from this day forward, but you must respect my relationship with Samantha. Is that clear?"

Her serene expression convinced me Gabrielle was no longer a threat. As I stretched her frail body out on the couch, a sense of shame cornered my inner bastard, regretting the pain I had inflicted. Tenderly, I placed her head on a pillow and headed for the kitchen. I hit the speed dial on my phone.

"Chuck, stop by in the morning. I made a fucking mess of the place." I was glad he had not answered. I honestly did not feel like a long explanation at the moment. Opening the fridge, I looked at my juice boxes. Normally, this close to sunrise, I would have a cocktail, but Gabrielle's blood proved to be a most nourishing experience.

"Drink this. Your strength will return," I suggested as I handed Gabrielle a box of A positive. It was quite fascinating, to witness the consumption of the life-giving blood, then like a plant parched from lack of water, her skin instantaneously began to turn from a grotesque shade of gray, back to the appealing, cottony, hues of white. Closing her eyes as she drank, that look of complete satisfaction swooned over her as the rich blood revitalized her veins.

The next several nights we canvassed South Beach and Miami for any clues or suspicions of any remaining vampires, but came up empty. Over those nights, Gabrielle shared her story; scraping for life in France as an indigent teenager, her hopes for a fresh start in New Orleans only to become a prisoner, then to watch, as one by one her friends were murdered while waiting for her turn to die. All of this shit, over two hundred years' worth, only to spend her freedom looking over her shoulder, waiting for the inevitable. Waiting for me.

Gabrielle was inquisitive of my life, both current circumstances and my former career. I found myself uncharacteristically open to her questioning. No doubt, being two of the same outcast creatures made the confessional much easier. I admired her beauty and grace, while fitting of her age, she maintained an almost girlish innocence, that was refreshing in so many ways. I found it peculiar, that another love could blossom in a heart, which for so many years remained barren.

Unlike Samantha, the freight train collision which dismantled my entire life, this one was of a singular simplistic affection, akin to a paternalistic relationship. Oddly, with Gabrielle being over two hundred years my senior, it was she who looked to me for guidance.

She knew so little of the modern world history, or physics, such as how planes fly. Her excitement was uncontainable over the flight to New York. Once there, she wanted to experience movies, Broadway, museums and even a ball game. It was in Gabrielle's exhilaration I found what should have been an obvious revelation. Being a vampire did not make me evil, nor did it her. The evil, which had been my life, was the misguided sense of duty. Duty to a career whose purpose was cloaked in dishonesty—the true adversary. Studying every aspect of this beautiful creature, I could not fathom the damnation of her soul. And I came to realize, if I truly believed Gabrielle could be turned away from Monique's homicidal lunacy and find salvation, then perhaps my future as well was not carved in stone.

Tomorrow night, I would be reunited with Sam. My unintended feelings for Gabrielle were playing into an internal debate over Sam's future. Even with my newfound revelations of good versus evil, there was absolutely no way I could ever take Sam's mortal life and deliver her into this world of unending darkness.

My homecoming; how it had been transformed from my expectations a mere six days ago. Armed with my newfound ally, my eagerness to resume the hunt was rekindled. Greater now, my desire to find Angelique, to have her explain our forever-intertwined fates. She had known something. But how? No longer did I feel compelled to destroy her or Sabine. With Monique dead, Angelique was perhaps the only person alive who could give a first hand account of my family history. A past which had shadowed my life, lurking behind, quietly protecting, and now reclaiming the son I was destined to be.

CHAPTER TWELVE

THURSDAY EVENING ARRIVED with renewed vigor. Gabrielle's giddiness overflowed into a contagion of youthful bliss that encompassed me. A simple mundane task, such as flying, exuded childlike excitement. Robbed of her youth, hell, two hundred years of life, her biggest hurdle to overcome would not be killing humans for food, but merely maintaining a low enough profile to remain off the radar.

I watched curiously as she downed a pint, wondering if she would be able to control her lust for blood. Questions, she had a million, about Sam and my perspective on mixed relationships. She appeared to understand my commitment for Sam to remain mortal. Confessing her desire to find a relationship Gabrielle conceded there was no hurry. "After all," she began, "I have already waited quite a few years, what's a few more?"

On the outside, I was quite pleased with her progress. But I knew, down deep, fear continued to weigh on her. The very same fear I possessed. I had new concerns as well. Phillip was going to freak when he discovered I was bringing a Convent vampire back with me. Up until this point, any acknowledgement could only be verified through betraying my circumstances. With Gabrielle, he would have a sacrificial lamb, absolute proof a race of vampires existed, and that the Vatican had orchestrated a cover up of *monstrous* proportions. The story would be a blockbuster, perhaps the greatest of his career.

Imagine the fervor created over vampires ... and the prospect of cheap immortality for all. I would have to forcefully pop his Clark Kent bubble by reminding him that he was an accessory to violating multiple international laws in obtaining a Convent vampire, and murder. But I knew Phillip. He would still try to sell me a story, one with well spun details, and expertly crafted alibis to alleviate any admission of guilt or wrongdoing. This would eventually allow him to parade Gabrielle before the unsuspecting world and solidify his place in history, not to mention, line his coffer's with unimaginable wealth.

Phillip was eagerly waiting our arrival at the hangar. I had phoned ahead and prepared him for the event. To try to conceal the nature of our new guest would undermine our friendship, and destroy the trust which it was built upon. Phillip's eyes seized upon Gabrielle, a reaction I was all too familiar with and fully expected from Captain Horndog. "You must be Gabrielle." His eyes absorbed her delicate features, head to toe, in an embarrassing display of gawking. "Will you please excuse us, just for just a minute?" Phillip found my elbow and tugged me off to the side. Once we were a safe distance from the group he began to rave, "Damn, Brian, you said she was hot, but I think you understated the facts, my friend."

"I never said she was hot."

"Okay, so you said good-looking, but shit, that is scorch'n hot over there," he exclaimed as he thumbed in her direction.

"First, Phillip, let me remind you, you are engaged. Secondly, she is a vampire. I see the look in your eyes, and I have seen it before. But I have to warn you, I will slam fuck you up if you try anything with her. She is strictly off limits, forbidden. You understand?"

"Easy, Bro," he said smoothly. "I love Dee. I would not screw that up. But geez, you can not honestly tell me you would not be doin' the bone dance with her if the opportunity arrived."

"I did have the opportunity, Phillip, and no, I did not. Their beauty is deceiving, entrancing, and at times, overwhelming. And, do not forget, deadly."

"Yeah, yeah, yeah," Phillip quipped. He chuckled as he obviously pondered the thoughts about to roll off his lips.

"So, do you mind if I tag along to your place? I cannot wait to hear how you are going to explain your new houseguest to Sam. I don't know what'll be more entertaining. You, desperately searching for the right thing to say, or her reaction."

I knew he was right about the looming confrontation. For two days I had contemplated breeching the subject with Sam. Had Gabrielle been just plain ol' butt-ugly, the introduction soon to occur would be a breeze. But she was drop-dead smoking hot. After losing her husband to a much younger, attractive woman, I was sure Sam would be hypersensitive to our new guest. Especially when I informed her Gabrielle would be staying in the downstairs apartment.

"Yes, I will let you keep Gabrielle company while I find a way to tap dance around that one."

"That is what bros are for," Phillip chimed gleefully. He took my arm and led me back to Gabrielle. "All right, let's go," he announced. "It's getting early and some of us have to be in our caskets soon." Phillip smiled at his misguided humor as he led the way.

As we headed to the limo, Gabrielle took a hold of my arm and pulled herself near enough to whisper in my ear. "Just good looking?" she asked with a smirk.

It was four in the morning and I had hoped, maybe even prayed, for Sam to be asleep, to postpone the inevitable showdown. But Sam must have been listening for the elevator; she enthusiastically flung herself into my arms, leaping from the floor and wrapping her legs around my waist, planting a big wet kiss on my lips.

Phillip cleared his throat, eager for the showdown to begin. "Where's mine?"

Sam peeked over my shoulder as Phillip approached, Gabrielle by his side. "Phillip!" she exclaimed. "What are you doing here, at this hour?" She slid back to the floor and immediately cast a suspicious gaze on Gabrielle.

"Let's go in," I suggested.

I closed the door softly as Sam, Phillip and Gabrielle entered in order. The time to cut the chase was here. "Sam, this is Gabrielle. You two have already met. She is here to help me find Angelique and Sabine and will be staying in the guest apartment beneath us for a while."

Sam thoroughly inspected Gabrielle. Had we not had the encounter in New Orleans, and if Gabrielle had ranked somewhere below a seven, I was sure things might have gone better.

"Wonderful," she quipped as her expression foretold of an imminent private conversation. "Phillip, would you show her the apartment? I need just a moment with Brian."

Gabrielle followed Phillip to the spiral stairway. Once they disappeared from sight, Sam took me by the hand and led me into the bedroom and closed the door.

"Is this why you were in Miami so long?"

The tone of Sam's voice was foreign to me. Obviously subduing what might have otherwise come out as a scream, I began to gauge the depth of her ire. Aunt Rena would surely be amused at my predicament.

"Yes." My reply was uncharacteristically timid. "After I disposed of Celine, I found Gabrielle. She was willing to help me search for and clean up the clan Celine had begun creating."

"And how did you persuade a vampire, who was hell-bent on killing us, to suddenly switch allegiances?"

"It is a little complicated. Can we discuss it after she is settled in and Phillip is gone?"

"Did you sleep with her?" Sam's tone was sharp and resentful.

"No!" Don't lie, no more half-truths, I reminded myself. "Well, kind of, but not sexually. I had to keep an eye on her, to make sure I could trust her before bringing her back here to New York," I was on the ropes and knew the knock-out punch was looming. "She slept in the closet with me."

"Trust her?" Sam squawked. "Damn it, Nick, she is one of them! Did you forget she would have killed me in New Orleans had you not intervened?"

"No, I don't believe she would have. From everything I have learned about her, I believe Celine was the problem. Apparently, Gabrielle has not bitten a living human in the two hundred years since she has been a vampire."

"Learned? From who? Gabrielle? What would you expect her to say? You were there to impale her. She would have told you she was a Girl Scout in France before she was kidnapped by the evil Celine," Sam spoke in condescending tones, not entirely sensitive to the ears of our guest below.

"How on earth did you find out about the Girl Scout thing?"

"Don't you try to make light of this, Nick," Sam snapped.

"I am sorry honey!" Unsuccessfully, I tried to give Sam a hug.

"No, no. Don't you dare patronize me with that honey crap, Nick. And don't you think you can do that vampire mind thing on me either!" She paused to reload her ammunition.

I gave her my best dopey, *I am so sorry* expression.

"You know, I thought I was an important piece of your life. I thought you might consider calling me to discuss this, before bringing a stray person, a vampire into our home." Sam slowed her pace, attempting to regain composure.

"I am truly sorry, Sam. Believe me, I have spent many hours deliberating how to tell you. I knew if I told you about it while I was in Miami you would have been just as bad, if not worse than you are right now. If you knew I was sharing a closet with her … but I swear nothing happened or will ever happen between Gabrielle and myself."

"Ever is a long time." Sam's tone changed from offensive to sullen. "The two of you might have forever. I don't."

"Sam." Raising her hand to my lips, I kissed it, "What is really going on?"

"Well, you probably have not noticed, but she is quite beautiful."

"And?" I prodded.

"Well, thirty years from now, she is still going to be beautiful, and so will you. And I am going to look like a two-legged Shar-Pei grandmother. A hundred years from now, I will be dead and buried, and the two of you will still be goddamn beautiful."

"Okay, so this is more about she is a vampire, I am a vampire, and you are not?"

It was Sam's turn to avoid eye contact, but my hands gently guided her face back to me.

"Samantha, if I was not a vampire, one lifetime is all we would have. No matter how much we would want to cheat that, in no way does it justify bringing this curse down on you." I watched as her eyes begin to glisten with emotion. "I love you now, and I will love you when you are old, wrinkled, and gray. It was not your beauty that attracted me, true your legs might have played a part, but it was your spirit that knocked me off my feet. And I have envisioned the day, when your time comes, I will take that journey with you. This world will have no meaning for me without you in it."

Sam sniffled, "And you don't think when I am old and gray that you won't find her beauty irresistible?"

"I am going to confess something, Sam. I hope you can understand it better than I do. Gabrielle and I are the same creatures. We may be all there is of our kind remaining. The feelings I hold for her are instinctive. It is like the love you have for Dee. We are one in the same family, rooted through a common curse we both would give the world to be free of. And even though she is hundreds of years older than me, I love Gabrielle like a daughter."

Sam looked confused. I could not blame her. "But you killed the others? Where was all of this one family love for them?"

"Before I became one, vengeance spurred me to kill. Afterwards, in Miami, I took Celine's life more in self-defense. But Gabrielle ... after nearly killing her, I literally held her life in my hands, the decision for her to live or die was mine alone to grant. But for her to live, she needed blood. My blood. And as my blood coursed through her veins, we became one family. For her to die now; a part of me would perish as well."

Sam was speechless as she absorbed my confession. I took her hands and pulled her close, wrapping my arms around her. She offered no resistance, but did not partake in returning the affection. Telling her I loved Gabrielle was possibly a strategic mistake, but I wanted to be honest with her. She had to know regardless of the consequences.

"I swear to God, Nick, if you are lying to me, I'll put a stake right through her heart."

"Everything all right in there?" Phillip called out. "I know it's been almost a whole week, but I hope you two aren't busy getting busy just yet."

Sam pulled away and smiled. "Just so you know, I had plans for you tonight, but I guess it will have to wait for now. Just so you know …" Sam slowly unbuttoned her shirt, revealing a black lace brassiere.

I looked down. Black pumps. A devilish smile crossed my face. My girl knew how to take care of business. Profiled and exploited, I was such a pushover.

"And the panties? I guess you will have to wait till I find myself in the mood again to find out about them." Taking my hand she led me to the door. "Let's not be rude. Time to go meet your immortally good-looking little vampire daughter." With her swagger back in gear, Sam sighed, opened the door and led the way.

I lagged behind, enjoying the view. Yes, it was good to be back home.

"Is everything all right?" Phillip and Gabrielle were parked on the couch making small talk.

Sam smiled at Phillip. "Never been better." There was a hitch to her tone, indicating a remnant of disapproval.

Perhaps Gabrielle's position on the couch, seated dangerously close to Phillip was the issue. It might have been Gabrielle's slender long legs, exquisitely displayed by her *über* short skirt, which Sam's eyes now trolled up and down.

"Gabrielle," Sam began.

Gabrielle cut her eyes up to Sam. Her expression reassured me she knew her place. This was Sam's turf and she was a guest. I sensed no animosity as she awaited the pending instructions.

"I am not accustomed to having another woman living in my home, especially one as adorable as you. So I must insist you follow just a few rules."

Gabrielle nodded, awaiting instruction.

"First, you are sitting next to my sister's fiancé. That would make him strictly off limits. If you catch him cheating with anyone else, including yourself, that person needs to die. Secondly, the men who frequent this home are horn dogs, so two things to remember; your skirt can never be shorter than mine, and the puppies need to go back in the doghouse. Bras are not optional in my home around these boys."

"I am sorry, but in Miami—" Gabrielle began to explain.

"Well sweetie, you are no longer in Miami, and you are not a hooker. Tomorrow you and I will do a little shopping. Come with me, I will show you your apartment."

As Gabrielle rose, Sam inspected her once more, this time from head to high-heeled toe. In exasperation, she shook her head and muttered. "We'll see how skinny you stay after a week or two of Junior's cheesecakes."

Clueless to Samantha's reference, Gabrielle smiled cordially.

"The downstairs apartment is yours. We live up here. I don't mind if you visit, but please be considerate of our privacy. If you would like to come up, call first."

The girls disappeared down the stairs. Phillip looked over to me with a shit-eating grin.

"Do not even think about it!" I knew where his twisted mind was headed.

"What?" Phillip exclaimed. I was just going to comment on how well Sam was taking it. And by the way, she looks great tonight, as usual. Sorry your little coming home party had to be interrupted."

"She does look great," I conferred. I looked at my watch. It was nearly five.

"You had better get home. We can talk tomorrow night."

Without further discussion, Phillip headed to the foyer. As he opened the door, he turned, smile still plastered across his face, "You know ..."

"Goodnight, Phillip." I gave him a final nudge out the door and closed it.

Though the alarms of bad judgment were sounding in my head, I allowed Sam and Gabrielle to venture out, unsupervised. I was not sure if the warning bells were fear for Sam's safety, or her ability to purchase clothes in every store the girls frequented. As they returned home with assistance from Charles, they set a multitude of Sachs and Bergdorf bags in the foyer. My subconscious groaned and silently mused; *"Bite her, once she's dead she will not need all those clothes."*

Gabrielle hugged Sam and headed to her apartment below with only a small collection of bags. Sam took the opportunity to pour a glass of wine and snuggle up close on the couch. Sensing my dismay,

Sam nibbled on my ear. “Don’t blame me. You were the one who brought home a stray, and without any clothes I might add.”

Sam silently studied the grid maps of the city on my laptop as I plotted my search for Angelique. After a silent moment she spoke softly. “You were right to spare her life,” Sam confessed with confidence. “She is a good person.”

“I know.” I folded the laptop down and smiled. Sam was ready to talk, and work would have to take the proverbial backseat for now.

“I am sorry I doubted you.”

The subsequent kiss on the cheek was enough to ensure her confidence. “I am sorry I did not call ahead to warn you. That was wrong of me. By now, you might think I would know you well enough to understand just how phenomenal you are.”

“Count Tepes, if you think for one second your flattery is somehow going to convince me to part with one shred of my clothing, or entitle you to any sexual favors, you are sadly mistaken.”

I raised my finger to my lips. “Gabrielle does not know. I am still Brian to her. I think it is best for now if I remain that way.”

Sam leaned back into the couch and crossed her arms. This posture of contemplation I had quickly, but begrudgingly become accustomed with: a thinking woman. “Last night, you told me you loved her, and I get that now. But every time you have been less than honest with me, look at the trouble it’s caused. And how can you expect her to be honest with you, if you are not honest with her? You must tell her.”

I turned to Sam and smiled that uncomfortable smile while shaking my head. “You know, before I met you, I was never wrong.”

“Need I remind you, a lot has changed since then?”

The derogatory nature of her inquisition only twisted the dagger of my flawed intentions deeper. Regardless of my power, I could count on Sam keeping me grounded with the occasional slice of humble pie.

“I’ll go get her,” Sam offered.

I held Sam’s hand, restraining her efforts. “She is on the way.” The bond created infusing our bloods had continued to strengthen. Evolving into some sort of occult ESP, I could practically dial into Gabrielle’s mind on demand.

Within seconds her footsteps on the stairs announced her

approach. "Yes, Brian," she called as she reached the top step.

"Please come join us," I said.

"Grab a wine glass," Sam suggested. "Even though you won't enjoy it, I am going to need some help with this bottle. Brian is never much help when it comes to wine."

Without concern to Gabrielle's unnecessarily close position to me on the couch, Sam poured a second glass. Attentive and appreciative, Gabrielle digested the many jigsaw pieces I had chosen to omit over the past few days. As the hours passed, the conversation drifted from my thoughts to more of Gabrielle's grand inquisitions. As dawn approached I walked Gabrielle to the stairs. Hugging me affectionately, her eyes met mine in an embrace of admiration. "I am honored that you have allowed me into your family. I will protect Samantha with my life." Beaming with gratitude, Gabrielle pulled away and descended to her apartment below.

I smiled back at Sam, who sincerely returned the gesture. Although Rob had been dead just a few months, the voice of his unique wisdom echoed in my mind. *Just when a woman appears completely content, you can damn sure bet it won't last. Run away.* I looked to the terrace, then back to Sam, who continued to smile. Opening the terrace door, a cool breeze rushed in. I closed it quickly. "Sorry, Rob, not this time."

The following months folded neatly into a year. My search for Angelique and Sabine continued without reward. The few clues that lead me to Celine and Gabrielle were nonexistent. While Phillip and Dee married, Sam patiently continued to wait. Gabrielle, with Sam's assistance, joyfully made up for the lost years, experiencing all life and knowledge the Big Apple could serve up.

I walked the streets of Manhattan almost nightly, although it was more out of habit than belief in success. My demeanor refused defeat, but reality continued to whisper. Had the time come to surrender my quest?

CHAPTER THIRTEEN

A BUSINESS MEETING with a couple of prospective investors on a brisk October evening brought me to the Village. Seviche and a cold brew at Panchitas was a perfect escape from a night at the opera with the girls. Although there was no nutritional value in the meal, my palate had slowly grown to enjoy the taste of food once again. With the days growing short, it was now possible for us to venture out much earlier than the long drawn out days of summer. The theatre, ballet, and all types of events, even ones as painful as opera, were now within the realm of attendance. Gabrielle was equally enthralled with football, basketball, and hockey. So occasionally, Sam would share her with me.

After a most productive dinner meeting, I chose to walk the streets of the Village. I had systematically trolled these avenues on three scripted missions, all with the same abysmal results. Originally, my plans were to head back to 82nd Street where I ended my search the previous night, and continue north, but the meeting proved just enough distraction to alter my course for the night. The Village remained one of my favorite sections of the city to lose my cares and simply veg out.

Wandering aimlessly, I had abandoned my purpose for the evening and chose to simply admire the urban beauty of this infamous neighborhood. It was early October and leaves were rapidly loosing their silky texture, giving way to a withering crispness proclaiming autumn's victory. As a brisk northerly wind forced its way down the narrow lane, the utterance emitted through the brilliantly colored festival whispered the call of their youth departed.

The autumn of life; for trees, it's a bittersweet hibernation, followed by the promise of resurrection in the spring. For my human counterparts, it is what ever you believe the afterlife holds. For me, I would never suffer that fate of aging, or disease. Shipwrecked in the eternal summer, eventually I would suffer the incredulous pain of witnessing Sam wither and die. Though time marched on, my resolve had not weakened. My curse was never to be her destiny.

I turned randomly off Bleecker Street onto Thompson and headed up the deserted street. Although it was just past one, it was unusual to see a block completely deserted this early in the night. With the wind in my face, I was blinded to the scent stalking from behind, closing in with each meandering step.

"And thus the prophesy has been fulfilled," the soft French voice announced.

"Angelique," I replied, without turning to face her.

I felt her breath on my neck. "I know why you have come."

A whirlwind of thoughts caravanned through my mind. How in the hell did she find me? And what was I going to do with her? Now kindred beings, I sensed her soul as never before. But was she aware of the change in me?

I turned slowly, not wanting to tip my hand and put her on the defensive. Our lips were close enough to touch, our eyes engaged in the grips of a lost passion I knew not the origins of. Her lips trembled. I reached out and gently cradled her jaw. Partially out of instinct to prevent her from sinking her teeth into me, and partially because my mind craved to feel the silkiness of her skin once more.

"Why have I come?" I whispered, as I allowed my hand to slide up her jaw, caressing the back of her neck.

"To destroy me, as you destroyed the others."

"If you believed that, then why didn't you kill me when you had the chance?" Exploring the eyes of the one who had spared my life on a multitude of occasions, I perceived an air of shame as she abruptly broke contact and turned her head away. Immediately, the notion she had killed many, or created an uncontrollable legion over the months since leaving New Orleans drew a lump to my throat.

"How many, Angelique?"

She glanced back without turning her head, apparently confused by the direction of my question.

"How many have you killed? How many have you made like you?"

In silence I studied her profile when suddenly it occurred to me, this face I held had been my father's lover, the father I bore a striking resemblance to. Ironically then, the very first time Angelique laid eyes on me, she must have thought I was my father, or a blood relative, but she never said a word. Two hundred years of waiting, and not even a flicker of emotional response. How in the hell did she do that? Was that the reason she felt obligated to protect me?

Turning again, fully gazing into my eyes, I witnessed a passion ... but it was not meant for me. It was directed to the one who had passed over two hundred years ago. My father.

"I am sorry," she replied without provocation. "If it is your desire to end my life, I must share something with you first." She held out her arm for me to take. "Please."

My curiosity was sparked. If she believed I was here to destroy her, why did she not attack? I took hold of her arm and we headed back in the direction from which I had arrived. "Are we going to see Sabine?

"Sabine?" Angelique popped. "Then she is not dead?"

"If she is dead, it was not by my hand. The last I saw of her was in the Convent."

"I have not seen her for over six months." Angelique drew slightly closer as we meandered to the empty street.

"If you believed I was here to kill you, why did you seek me out?"

"In short time, you will see." With the faintest hint of a smile, I sensed her calming.

Never being a fan of circuitous questions, I decided to broach the subject. "Can you take me to Sabine's home?"

"No. I have never been there. She arrived before me, and we have crossed paths only on rare occasions. I know she blames me for her fate." Angelique hesitated, gauging her next words. "I can only tell you she has taken a mate. Other than that, I do not know much of her life."

Taken a mate! Three words of damnation I sure as hell hated hearing. And to ice it, she had not been seen in over six months.

"But even if I knew where to find her, why should I tell you? You bring nothing but death to our kind."

Angered by the new revelation I snipped, "Angelique, you know of my work. If I had wanted to kill you, you would already be dead."

"The others are dead because they were weak and foolish. I am neither. Had I not sought you out, you would still be searching."

We turned into a moderately styled brownstone. "This is my home."

"It may interest you to know ..." I paused briefly, reflecting on the wisdom, or lack of what I was about to reveal, "You and Sabine are not the only ones left alive. There is another."

Angelique immediately let loose of my arm and turned with a gleam in her eye. "Who has eluded Brian Denman, last of the great vampire hunters?"

The tone of her voice was hard to read; genuine joy, or mockery. "In time I might tell you, but sarcasm will not earn you the needed brownie points."

"Brownies? They are very messy, they get stuck in your teeth."

Befuddled by her expression, I was hoping she was inferring to the chocolate snack, and not the little girls running around the city selling cookies. "I think it is better if we leave that one alone." Entering the lobby, it was not plush by any means, but at New York prices, it had to be at least three grand a month. Pretty steep for a two-hundred-year-old, unemployed vampire. "This is nice. Do you mind if I ask how you afford it?"

"That is quite rude, you asking." As her tone continued, it occurred to me, she was being playful. "I would never be so presumptuous as to ask where does your money come from ... for all of the nice clothes you wear."

"You are right, but I never claimed to be a gentleman. In fact, I am quite the opposite," I proclaimed, as the elevator doors leisurely confined us in close proximity. The car creaked and groaned as it ascended ever so slowly. A stray and uninvited memory of Sam, and the elevator at thc Maison Dupuy invaded my focus.

Angelique stared intently at the buttons, as a smirk worked

across her face. "You like these slow elevators. Yes?"

Shit, the one instance I dropped my guard and she was in my head like a wildfire. The door opened as slowly as it closed. "After you," I insisted, without reply.

Angelique turned the keys to the door and lead the way in. "Please come in." A young woman, perhaps in her mid-twenties, was sitting on the sofa reading a book.

"Angelique, you are back early." The slender young woman closed her book, rose and gave me a lightning-fast inspection.

"Yes, Krista. I'm back for the night. You can go home early if you like."

Eyeballing me a second time, Krista looked at Angelique with a restrained smile of approval.

"This is Mr. Denman."

Krista extended her hand, "Nice to meet you." After a quick cordial shake, from across the back of the couch, she slid her shoes on. "I will see you tomorrow night, at the usual time." Grabbing her book, then her jacket off the arm of the sofa, Krista moved past as she cut her eyes to me once again. "I am glad you finally took my advice," Krista whispered to Angelique as she passed out the door, closing it behind her.

Angelique smiled at me. "She is a sweet girl. Very trustworthy."

"Considering your predicament, she would have to be," I deadpanned. "Does she know about your affliction?"

"No," Angelique headed to the kitchen. "Can I get you anything?"

"No thank you, I am fine."

Rattling glasses in the kitchen, Angelique reappeared momentarily with a wine glass filled with a thick crimson beverage.

"O negative?"

"A positive," she replied. "I find it to have a much deeper, full bodied flavor."

"Do you mind?" I asked, as I gestured to a worn armchair beside a mahogany leather couch.

"No, please do have a seat." Angelique took a seat on the couch. "You are welcome to sit over here," she offered as she patted the leather cushion next to her.

"This will be fine for now." We looked at each other awkwardly for a moment, each having something to say, but neither seeming to know exactly what to say.

"Angelique," I began, as I studied the moderate furnishings of her home.

"Yes, Brian?" The anticipation in her voice was obvious.

"Actually, my name is Nicholas." I turned to gauge her reaction.

Her eyes popped ever so slightly at the revelation, but she withheld any comment.

"New Orleans ... I was plagued with curiosity. I was killing your friends, and yet not only did you choose to let me live, you actually tried to protect me, to some degree. I asked myself why, many times over. But in returning to New York, I believe I discovered the answer."

Angelique gazed with anticipation. "Please go on."

"While in New Orleans, I heard references to the Count several times. I now know why he banished you, and Monique. I know at one time, the two of you were lovers, and I know he held you accountable for Monique's failed attempt to kill his wife."

"Bravo, Bri—Nicholas. I see you have done your research."

"Oh, but I have not told you the best part of my theory, not yet."

"And?"

"After several months of diligent work, I uncovered a staggering fact. My theory of why you could not bring yourself to kill me. I bear an uncanny resemblance to your former lover, Count Levente Tepes."

Angelique's lips parted as her face lengthened. "I think maybe you should go now."

Indeed, as I had learned from firsthand experience, vampires are not heartless. Hearing his name, I had served up an emotional dagger, right through her heart. "So, I am right?"

Speechless, she nodded while staring down at her wineglass. Softly, she began, "I ... we were in love. But Levente was consumed with returning the Tepes name to the throne of Romania. The Countess was of Hungarian royalty. He loved me, but I did not fit into his grand scheme of uniting our two countries. That is when Monique plotted to kill the Countess, believing Levente would then take me as his wife. As we were cousins, this would give Monique access to power she so deeply craved. I gladly would have waited for the Countess to die a natural death, but Monique's lack of patience became my ultimate punishment.

"When you arrived at the Convent, at first glance, I was sure my eyes, after all the long years, were deceiving me. After entrancing you, your true purpose became clear. But the mere resemblance to the Count was so overpowering, I could not bring myself, or allow the others to bring harm upon you."

"Wow," I exclaimed. "It's a damn good thing I did not get my looks from my mother's side of the family."

"So good fate was on your side. Your father must be a very handsome man."

"Was. He has been dead a great many years." Not sure the confession was intended for Angelique or myself, but verbally acknowledging his death to Angelique forced unexpected sadness. "I should fill in the story, after your exile. After you were banished Countess Szekeres returned to Hungary, Monique's attempt on her life bringing an end to the marriage. Two hundred years passed before Levente married again, this time to Elisabeta Dragomire of Transylvania. At this time, the world had new enemies; one of the greatest was Communism. In an effort to ensure their domination over all the countries they conquered, they systematically hunted down all remnants of the royal families in their ever-expanding empire. Elisabeta bore Levente a son during this era, but to ensure his safety, they sent their only child to America, out of harm's way until it was safe for his return. The exact date is unknown, but it is presumed Elisabeta and Levente perished sometime in the fifties.

"The child grew into manhood in America, his dark lineage unbeknownst to him. His name, Neculai Tepes. The aunt who raised him called him Nicholas."

Angelique's head snapped to attention, her eyes eagerly searching mine. "You?"

"Yes, Levente Tepes was my father."

Angelique's mouth gaped open. "How can this be?"

"As it appeared my grandfather discovered centuries ago, a vampire can reproduce when mating with a mortal. But you might have already known that fact back in my father's day, or certainly discovered it after Sabine's pregnancy."

"What do you know of Sabine and her child?" Angelique's tone was bitter, as if the missing child had been her own.

"I know the baby's father was a Convent guard. I know he took her away, keeping her safe from becoming like Sabine. I know she grew to be like me, immortal, but not cursed."

Awaiting full disclosure, Angelique's anticipation was evident.

"I know her name, and I know where she is living."

Once again, I became aware of Angelique's attempt to enter my thoughts. Her frustration was evident with another failed attempt.

"I know what you are trying to do and I promise your skills are not diminishing." I smiled, revealing for the first time my glistening razor sharp fangs.

"How did this happen?" Aghast by the sight before her, she recoiled into her chair.

"If she were not dead, you could ask Monique. But as she is quite deceased in the full Biblical sense, that conversation will prove quite difficult."

Angelique's wineglass slipped to the floor, splintering into tiny shards. Covering her mouth, tears welled in her eyes.

"It's all right, Angelique. Although I much prefer my old teeth, it's not as bad as it looks."

"I ... I am so sorry. It was you father's dream, that he would have a mortal son, one that might break the Tepes curse. And now, even in death, I have failed him once more."

There was a deep-rooted expression of sorrow, one not quite befitting the grief she claimed, one of a peculiar nature that shadowed her obvious grief.

"I need to show you something," she replied stoically.

Rising from the couch, she stepped over the broken glass, and reached for my hand. Guiding me to the short hallway, she softly opened the bedroom door. The light from the hallway illuminated a crib in the corner. "Come."

Sleeping quite peacefully under a quilted blanket was the silhouette of an infant.

I looked to Angelique, appalled by my twisted thoughts running amok. "Angelique, what have you done?" I whispered. "To whom does this child belong?"

Ignoring my question, her faced glowed as she gazed down. "Is he not beautiful?"

Fully absorbing the details of the sleeping child, possibly for the first time in my life, I began to study its details. A serenity existed unique to all babies not yet burdened by the cruelties of the world. In hushed but sterner tones I repeated my question. "Angelique, I must know where this baby came from."

"He is my son, and now it appears, the grandson of your father. And you, Nicholas, you are his father."

Instantly her words broadsided me like a freight train; the Maison Dupuy, the rose on my bed, memories flashed before my eyes. In the night, she had come to me; spellbound I did as she commanded. I was dumbfounded, only able to stare ... at my son.

In all of my wildest dreams did I ever contrive parenthood as a personal option. Having never known my father, the dynamics of that type of relationship were never experienced, and therefore never known to be lacking. Sam and I certainly had never even broached the subject of children in all the months we had been together. Shit! Samantha. True she had proven to be the most understanding and accepting woman I had ever known, but surely, if there were a straw to break the camel's back, this might prove to be a log of bone-crushing proportions. I continued to study the child, so serene, so mine. I was so screwed, literally. Still, at a loss for words, Angelique kindly broke the silence.

"When I laid with you, I did not expect this to happen." Angelique was smiling at the baby, unabashed by her actions. "When I first laid eyes on you, all of the emotions of two hundred years came rushing back. The passion we shared, I so desperately needed to relive the fervor.

"Relive?" I quipped. "I hope my father was not comatose when the two of you ... you know."

"You were not comatose. Although you have no memory of it, in fact you were quite the contrary. That is why I returned to your hotel."

"Returned?" I asked, my voice escalating. The dread of yet another confession to Sam loomed.

"The Convent I have already explained. Your hotel happened because I wanted more. And now, here you are."

"There is no next time," I interrupted sternly. "I am with someone."

The baby stirred at the harshness in my tone. Focusing on his obvious discomfort I had created, I calmed my voice. In the gathering silence, he drifted back into peaceful sleep.

"What is his name? Whispering again, I looked into Angelique's eyes with a hodgepodge of newly discovered emotions. I desperately wanted to hold her, to experience the passion she claimed we shared, and suck the life from her all at the same time.

"I gave him his father's name," she said with a proud smile of satisfaction. "To honor the man who ended two hundred years of misery."

"Brian," I called, as I looked down at my child. Suddenly, an unexpected wave of joy and pride swooned over me. "Angelique," I began, redirecting my attention away from the baby. "I am sorry if I sounded harsh, but I am committed to another woman."

"Committed, or in love?" Angelique was searching my expression, or tone, for any doubt looming in my reply.

"Love."

"Then I am happy for you, Nicholas. It is true I knew the day would come when our paths would cross again, and I had fantasized our being together, as one family. But in light of who I now know you are, it would bring a great dishonor to your father, to pursue his son."

Angelique's words poured true from her lips. Without having to rely on my vampire intellect, I could see it in her eyes.

"But I cannot undo what has been done. So it is with great desire I pray you will allow our child to be a part of your life, to allow your father's legacy a chance to be realized. But I understand the difficulties this may present with your current life, so if you refuse I will understand."

"He is my son. How could I not be a part of his life, despite being an unwilling participant in the act of creation?"

"You were quite willing," Angelique offered, smiling slyly.

"Okay, unconscious then."

Angelique chuckled at the memory only she was privy to. "This woman of yours, she must be exceptional."

"That she is. In more ways than you could imagine. Although this little revelation may prove to be quite the test of her fortitude."

"If she does not understand, please know, you are welcome to return here."

The baby stirred again.

"I should go." Kissing my fingers, I lightly touched the baby's forehead. In a most content fashion, he sighed deeply as Angelique looked on with pleasure.

Following me to the hall, Angelique propped her face against her hands and leaned on the door. Whether by design or not, her thoughts opened to me without reserve. Experiencing her longings for the love lost and hurt, over what she dreamt would be, I could not help but pity this beautiful woman before me. As with Gabrielle, there was a kindred love that was undeniably unstoppable. "We still have much to discuss, but I think there's been enough bombshells dropped for one night."

Angelique nodded in agreement.

"Angelique, I hope you will believe me, I no longer have any desire to harm you, or Sabine. But I also have to make sure things are put right. I cannot have humans dying because of my gross negligence in New Orleans."

Angelique placed her hand gently on my shoulder. "Nicholas, your father dreamt of a peaceful coexistence with humans, a vision I too shared before I was banished. We both knew the path to this goal was a child of two worlds. One that would dispatch the fears and mend the bonds of a broken nation."

"Fix a broken nation? What a head-trip; Nicholas Tepes, deliverer of the vampire race. Now, all four of us."

Angelique looked down the hall to the bedroom. "At least five," she said with a warm smile.

"Is he?" The sudden realization of his potential predicament caused my dead heart to skip a beat.

"I think he will be exactly like his father. Handsome, brave, strong, immortal, and enjoy a well-cooked cuisine."

A wave of relief blew through me. "Would it be alright at some point in the near future, if she does not run away, or scour me with holy water, to bring Samantha over?"

"I would hope so. If he is to be part of your life then logically, she will have to accept him as well." Angelique placed a hand on each of my shoulders. "Nicholas," she began. My name rolled off her lips in tones so inviting they made me feel like melting butter. "I never wanted to see you harmed in this way. You will never understand how badly it hurts. Your father would have been devastated. I will live with this failure the rest of my unnatural life."

"Angelique, as a wise man once told me, none of what has transpired has been by accident. It is as it was meant to be. My destiny. I am a vampire for a reason, to fulfill a greater purpose, other than my own perceived happiness or misery."

"You have talked with Daniel, haven't you?"

"You have had that same conversation?"

"With him, his father, and his father's father." Apparently, the memory brought a certain degree of happiness as she smiled broadly.

The aspect of three generations of "Danielisms" created a similar reaction for me. "So what do you think ol' Daniel is doing now?"

"Eating pineapples. He always wanted to go to Hawaii."

"I hope he brought lots of sunscreen. He was whiter than you." Sharing a laugh at Daniel's expense, I marveled at how at ease I had become.

"Me? Have you looked at yourself in a mirror lately?" Angelique quipped.

"Thanks to Monique, I don't suffer the mirror's benefits or vanities any longer."

Sensitive to my father's dreams of breaking a generational curse, Angelique's smile vanished as rapidly as it arrived, the result of my mindless joke.

Instinctively I pulled her close, bringing her face snugly against my shoulder. "It is all right. Kids rarely turn out like their parents dream anyhow. Together, we will find a way to fulfill my father's dreams, all right?"

Angelique pulled away, again tears filled her eyes. "I am sorry. This is just so very hard for me. I loved him more than you can know. And you, in many ways, are just like him. You will accomplish great things, just as he would have."

I kissed her cheek. "I will see you soon, we must find Sabine." I turned to leave.

"Nicholas," Angelique called in a sullen tone just as I reached the elevator.

The emptiness in her voice bade me to continue on my path. Counterintuitive to the disaster I knew awaited delaying my departure, I turned.

Angelique steadied herself in the doorway, tears trickling down her cheeks. "I can't help but love you," she said in broken words.

"But apparently this continuing breaking of my spirit is just another punishment I must endure."

As she sank to the floor, I resisted the overwhelming urge to return to her side.

"Your father married Countess Èvike, it was a decision for the good of our country and our people. After Monique's failed attempt on her life, we were sentenced, then sealed in a casket, and placed on a ship bound for America for a crime I had no part of. Out of heartache, I accepted my fate. Two hundred years I waited.

"It was you who freed me, not only from the Convent, but from chains of a life void of passion. You gave me a child." Angelique looked through the ceiling of her apartment toward the heavens. "I know I have not earned forgiveness, but every night I pray he will lift this curse and allow me to love as I once did." She bowed her head down. Tears cascaded from her face, dampening the black fabric of her dress.

"Angelique." I could not go to her without compromising everything I felt for Sam. If I held her now, I would be lost in the barrage of emotions I felt for this woman. "We have a bond which exceeds the boundaries of my love for Sam and I will not pretend I know quite how to handle it. In as much as you love me, I love you as well. In part, it is instinctive to our race. The rest, hell, I do not have a clue. But I promise you, I will do everything I can to set you free."

Angelique looked up, her expression of understanding afforded me the emotional opportunity to leave.

"I will see you soon." Leaving her apartment the need for a drink hit hard. In the old days, beer, and lots of it. Tonight, AB positive.

CHAPTER FOURTEEN

FRUSTRATED BY THE continued string of events that were out of my control, yet I was responsible for, I yearned for the old days. *Kill the bad guys*; accomplishing the purposes of my making held a calming satisfaction I could never recreate elsewhere. I was frustrated ... and thirsty. Thirsty for something a little more exotic than my home supply, I don't know why, but the rarer the blood, the more euphoric the experience. I headed off to the blood bank at Sixty Seventh and Second Avenue.

A faint light omitted from the window of the interior stairwell leading to the refrigeration unit on the third floor. Before ascending the wall, I noticed the steel door was not completely secure. Pulling it open quietly, I detected muted voices from above. Creeping into the vestibule, I ascended, gliding step by step up the dusty stairwell. At first glimpse I counted five men and three women, all dressed in the costume rejects from the movie *The Lost Boys*. The one perched on the highest step took immediate exception to my presence.

"Can I help you?" Immediately, all of his companions veered around, alarmed by his stern inquisition.

Aroused by the aroma of blood filling the stairwell, I continued my ascent. I was ready to feed, and these fools were in the path. "You do not belong here, leave now."

A gauntlet of idiots cradling half emptied donor bags all looked to the top of the stairs for their leader's rebuke. Apparently, they had already pilfered the refrigeration unit.

"No," the lanky fellow at the top hissed as he flashed a rather genuine looking set of pearly spikes. "You need to leave while I am feeling generous."

Sensing his mortal insecurities, I realized I had stumbled into the New York chapter of the Freakazoid Breakfast Club. "Wrong place, wrong time ... last chance to get the hell out."

"Ooooo." As he taunted, several laughed in allegiance. "I tell you what, skank, if you get the fuck out of here right now, I might let you live."

"Yeah, get the fuck out," several others echoed.

One thing I never tolerated well was phonies. Disrespectful phonies I loathed even more. I marched right up middle of the club meeting, forcing several to remain seated as I passed. Grabbing King Douche by the throat, I elevated him off the floor, then slammed him against the wall. One of the more ignorant pawns began to rise to his defense. A swift sidekick to the head sent him careening down the stairs, the collateral pin action collecting a few of his bros in the process.

I stared intently into Count Fake-ula's terror-filled eyes. I forced his mouth open, exposing his rather elaborate, high-priced dental work. Just as I broke off the first artificial fang, two more of the goon patrol scurried to his defense. With a sweeping motion of my hand, they tumbled down the stairs head over heels.

"Douche bag, you want to play games, might I suggest zombies next time. This undead thing, not very wise ... unless you are." My eyes went black and as he caught a glimpse of the evil upon him, terror filled his.

"Go home." Releasing my grip, he dropped to the floor. "If I ever catch you here again, make sure your organ donor card is filled out."

The scent of fear, or maybe it was urine, permeated as they scurried down the stairs, dropping the bags of blood en route. Unsure if they would call the police, I decided to deal with their leftovers and get the hell out of Dodge. Both bags were A positive. Damn. My craving for AB would have to wait until another time.

There was no time to cry over the spilled blood pooling on the steps. Feeling rather pissed off that a bunch of clowns compromised one of my favorite watering holes, I poured the contents of the first bag down my throat as I pulled the rusty metal door closed behind me.

Sadly, there was a time not too long ago, I would not have considered ever sharing a beer with any of those fools, let alone blood. But I had to consider; what in the hell would drive an individual to want to be like me? Not solely because of their loathsome need to pretend they are something they are not. Maybe they too shared a lineage that beckoned them beyond reason. Quite possibly, as on other recent occasions, I was wrong. But what about the hygiene issues, damn those guys were just nasty. Draining the second bag, I smiled at the notion; "Nicholas Tepes, King of the Trailer Park Vampires." At least I didn't lick the stairs. I clutched the last bag of blood, unopened, unspoiled and guiltless. "If the shoe fits, wear it well," I mumbled, choosing to finish, rather than save the last bag.

The imaginary conversation with a beat cop, explaining my pint to-go brought a smile to my face as I looked down Second Avenue. As the night was not quite half over, I considered continuing my search for Sabine, mainly as a means to avoid the inevitable confrontation soon to occur. It was time to face the hangman.

Arriving back to an empty apartment, I took a beer out on the terrace, reclined in the chaise and enjoyed the beauty of the night. Staring out over the Hudson River toward the Bronx, a soothing October breeze blew through my hair. From inside the apartment I heard the laughter of Sam and Gabrielle as they entered.

Feeling the breeze blow through the apartment, Gabrielle looked to the terrace and smiled. "He's waiting for you." After nearly a year, she knew when it was time to excuse herself. After hugging one another Gabrielle made her way down the stairs.

Sam stood in the terrace doorway, her arms spread as if to block any attempt to escape. The smell of her scent aroused my attention. Turning to lay my eyes upon her, she was every bit as inviting as the first day I laid eyes on her.

"Should I slip into something more comfortable?"

"Not tonight, Sam, we need to talk."

The guilt-burdened tone instantly triggered a concerned expression as Sam made her way beside me. "What is it, Nick?"

"I learned things tonight, things I had no suspicion of. Things that may ... will change everything."

Samantha crossed her arms, her posture suggesting she was bracing for the worst. "Tell me."

Samantha had endured many bombshells in our relatively brief love affair. Never once did she falter, but this time I sensed might be the end. "I found Angelique tonight, or to be honest, she found me."

The mere mention of Angelique's name seemed to stagger Samantha. She threw a hand on my shoulder and steadied herself. "Is she dead?"

"No. No she's not ... It would appear, according to Angelique ... while I was in New Orleans, on more than one occasion, she had sex with me." I swallowed the words with difficulty.

"I know." Sam spoke softly, with unexpected assurance.

Shocked by the revelation I was not sure if I should speak, or just shut up. "I have known for a while." Appearing not to want to relive the story, Sam gauged my reaction as she sighed. "Do you remember this past summer? That waitress down in SoHo? The one you were being overly flirtatious with?"

"I remember." Sam's cold shoulder for almost a week after the incident was a lesson hardly forgotten.

"You made me feel so vulnerable. I was upset and mad, so Gabrielle and I went out several nights that week."

"I remember that as well."

"One of those nights, Gabrielle told me about New Orleans. About Angelique's boasting of her incantations, and of her conquest. She said, against Angelique, no man stood a chance. Then Gabrielle told me about Miami, how you rejected all of her attempts to seduce you. Gabrielle told me this to unequivocally convince me of your love."

"Gabrielle had to convince you?"

"I know you love me. But thanks to you, I still have all the mortal limitations a woman can ask for. And there are still times when I see you look at other women, and I cannot help but think you are tiring of me."

"You know Sam, you have dealt with more bullshit than I ever could have asked for. And I wish that was the full extent of the situation, but it is not." It was too late to turn back and probably too late to bite her, for all that was to follow to be forgiven. I inhaled deeply.

"It would appear, when Angelique left New Orleans, she did not leave alone." Knowing my next breath might be the last before the fall, I savored it. "Angelique was with child … my child."

"A baby? Your baby!" Sam's temperament was impossible to gauge. "Are you sure?"

"Yes, I saw him tonight, for the first time."

"Stay here, don't you move. I need a bottle of wine." Sam got up and headed to the door. Just beyond the threshold, she turned and threw her hands into the air. "Don't you dare fucking move."

Sam turned and made a beeline into the kitchen. She grabbed a bottle from the rack and pulled the cork. Inspecting a wine glass in the light, she observed her hand trembling. "This will not do. Not tonight buddy boy!" she grumbled. She opened the cupboard drawer, grabbed a twenty-ounce beer mug and filled it to the top. She gulped the wine until the glass was half empty, then topped it back off. She set the bottle down and began to return to the balcony. Before she had taken two steps, she turned and grabbed the bottle. "This little puppy won't live to see the sunrise."

Returning to the balcony, beer mug in one hand and wine bottle in the other, Samantha chose a chair just out of reach. Refusing to look even close to my direction, she stared out at the city lights.

"Sam."

"Nick. This is what is known as shut up and listen time … again." Taking another big swallow of wine, without making eye contact she began in a most solemn manner. "For two years, I envisioned a life beyond all of this mess. A day, or night, where all of this crap was behinds us. Maybe a day when *we* … might start a family. And right or wrong, I let myself be careless, more than once. And nothing happened. Never even one damn day late." With tears were flowing freely, Sam took another long drink. "So I went to a doctor, and you know what? The bastard had the nerve to tell me I had better chances of being a mother if I adopted."

"Sam." I began to rise, ready to offer as much comfort as I could give.

"Don't," she demanded, raising her hand for me to halt. "I feel so isolated sometimes. Gabrielle and you have this common thread, a bond. And now Angelique. And the one thing I wanted to give you most, I can't. But she did. I don't think I can do this. Not anymore."

"Sam, I am so sorry."

"No," she said sharply. "You do not have to apologize for anything, anymore. I am not mad with you. You certainly did not set out for this life either. It's just the way things turned out.

"Sam," I said as I reached for her.

"Please don't try to rationalize this away. I think we both know …"

"Okay. My turn," I interrupted.

Sam resisted my attempt to remove her wine mug.

"Please." She pulled her mug back and cradled it to her chest like a security blanket.

With her hands occupied I turned her face toward mine, but her eyes looked away. "Look at me."

Samantha retreated deeper into the chair sensing my will entering her mind. "Please don't do this."

"Then look at me."

Begrudgingly she turned her eyes.

"I know I have told you on many occasions you are the only thing that matters. I will leave this all behind, the city, Phillip, Dee, Gabrielle, Angelique … and even my son. Right now. Say the word and we can leave and go search for that deserted beach. And as long as you are with me, I will never regret it."

Sam sat quietly for minutes, searching my eyes, longing for the answer to her angst.

"I told you not to use that mind-control stuff on me," she said sheepishly after a prolonged silence. The corner of her lip turned up, as a familiar smile could not be restrained. "Nick, you can't leave this behind, not yet."

"We have to leave. It is the only way for us to survive. Chuck and Jimmy can come and finish my work."

"No," Sam said with determination. "We can't leave. Not like this. You have to finish this. You can't just up and leave, not with a son here. I won't let you. I won't go."

"Sam, it's all right."

"No, it's not. But I will tell you one thing Nicholas Tepes, you get your ass out there and you find Sabine, and you put an end to this. Because you do owe me one hell of a vacation."

She was right. But I owed her more than a vacation, I owed her a wedding.

"Tomorrow night, I will go back to Angelique, and see if she can give me any other information that will help me find Sabine. I will not rest until she's been found."

"You're going back to Angelique's tomorrow night? You are not going anywhere near that woman without me, mister. Besides, I would like to see him."

"Brian?"

"Brian, what a nice name. I used to be crazy about some guy with the same name."

I looked at Sam and smiled at her ability to move beyond yet another clusterfuck of mine.

"What happened with Angelique, you know that's date rape. The fact you have an heir doesn't forgive her crime. But, if she can manage to keep her filthy paws off of you, I think we can get through this."

A well-timed autumn breeze swirled around the terrace, neutralizing the cool air I forcefully exhaled, feeling once more I had dodged another bullet.

"Nick, I don't want to be on the outside looking in anymore. I want us to share everything."

"Sam, we have been down this road too many times. I would rather tell you goodbye and never see you again, than to share this curse with you."

"You say cursed, I say privileged. Curses are of evil. But you are not evil, Nick. All I have seen from you is good intentions, and good actions. And look what you have done with Gabby. There is not a shred of evil anywhere in her body. And I desperately want to be like her. Then we can truly be one."

"Sam, my father believed if there is to be any hope of salvation, it had to be through selfless acts and deeds. If I make you a vampire, it would not be for good, it would be out of a desire to feed my needs. If there is to be any hopes of breaking this curse, I have to do what is right by others, not by me. That is where reconciliation lies."

Samantha sipped her wine and looked away. The same answer she had grown to hate was the only one she knew in her heart to be right.

"I can only think of one thing that might help. And it's long past due, but it's something we both wanted not too long ago. I think it's time we set a date."

Sam's expression perked up. "Are you sure?"

"I was sure the day I asked you, and nothing has changed since that day."

Sam leaned and hugged me tightly. "Are you sure? I know we were going to wait till this was all over."

"Yes." My voice was soft, but my conviction was firm.

"Well so much for angry make-up sex."

"Is it too late to try to piss you off again?"

"Say Angelique's name one more time tonight, and you might. On the other hand, after Gabby and I pull a vampire on your bank account and suck the cash out of it on this wedding, you may be just a teensy weansy bit upset." Sam playfully smacked my cheek softly, got up and ran into the apartment. "Better get busy Count, the way I see it, you're gonna need to live forever just to pay for this wedding."

"Oh I am about to get busy," I called out as I waited briefly, and then began to stalk my prey.

CHAPTER FIFTEEN

MERCENARIES, ASSASSINS, AND soldiers; no matter the label, we are all the same. Guns for hire. Outside of killing for a living, for the most part we are very much like ordinary people.

We get up, get dressed, usually eat two or three meals a day, maybe watch television, some even like to read. We get up, go to work, and punch the proverbial time clock, just like everybody else.

Louis was an assassin, and a damn good one. Never missed a target, never any collateral damage. He was methodical and patient, with the virtues of any true craftsman. He never took a job where a single opportunity was the only option. There were always multiple plans for the kill. A missed mark was the kiss of death.

Louis located his mark two days ago. He studied his options, sought out the perfect location, set up his shot and waited. For two days he waited by the window, mostly eating peanuts and mostly just waiting. The shells accumulating by the window were occasionally swept away by the sole of his size thirteen tactical boots.

Louis, aka the Laser, was dialed in, focused, and ready. It was nighttime, just past nine o'clock. Laser chewed a mouthful of peanuts with a mechanical rhythm, when suddenly he spit them out. He grabbed his night vision scope to verify what he believed to be his target. The mark was on the move, and headed right at him. Louis turned his ball cap backward, and grabbed Terminator, his sniper rifle. Tonight was the night, it was payday. Tonight he would finally be free of this elusive target, who had somehow managed to remain off the radar for months despite Louis' best efforts.

Making the turn down Third Avenue, Sam and I were headed to a dinner meeting with Dee and Phillip to discuss our plans. From there the highly anticipated, yet agonizing trip down to the village for Sam to meet, and square off with, Angelique ... and meet my son.

In my former career as a sniper, I extracted a morbid pleasure from the sound of the bullet as it raced from the barrel, the slicing of the air as it made its way to the target, and the final thud of impact. I could sense them; looking back, that awareness must have been rooted in my vampire DNA. It was that same keen sense that alerted me to an incoming projectile. The firing had been muffled by distance and silencer, and mostly lost in the urban noise. But as it approached, there was no mistaking the signature song of my craft. Just as I braced for the impact, Sam cut in front of me to look at pictures of a tropical destination in the window of a travel agency, pictures of a life she was eager to begin. Just as I reached for her, the bullet found a target.

"Nick!" Sam screamed out in agony, as the bullet burst out the front of her chest, passing through.

"No!" I yelled. Sam collapsed to the ground, her precious blood spilling all over the sidewalk, covering me in burgundy spray of death. "Sam!" I screamed out upon deaf ears. The bullet had passed through her heart, dealing a deadly blow instantaneously. "No!" I shrieked again.

Bystanders were screaming and running for cover. Before I had time to react to Sam's dire situation, the sound of another bullet sizzled through the air. This one finding its intended target, striking me in the chest. "Call the police. Somebody killed that lady," a woman cried out as she ran.

The impact of the bullet knocked me off my feet. The pain in my chest was immense. Instinctively, I lunged to Sam. There was no movement, no breath. "Baby, stay with me. I can't do this without you," I cried.

Appalled witnesses stood barely a block away, but there was only one hope, one chance to save her life. No longer concerned with the consequences my actions might bring, I bent over and bit into her neck, nearly draining the blood that remained in her body. I sat up and ripped the flesh from my wrist and held it over her mouth. My blood spilled out the corners of her mouth. "Sam, baby, I know you can still hear me. You have to drink!" Her mouth filled with my blood, but she did not swallow. Her lifeless body limp in my arms, I screamed out toward the heavens, "Noooo!"

Seconds later, another bullet pierced the air, this one finding its mark in my skull. I careened backward as the bullet crashed out the backside of my head. Falling back, I visualized the shot. On a fire escape three blocks down Third Avenue was the shooter. I hit the concrete hard.

I lie in a pool of my blood, brain, and bone fragments. I had to get up. The source of my remaining strength and focus was unknown to me, but I rose nonetheless. I looked down at Sam, still lifeless. The shooter had already disappeared into the window from the fire escape. He had witnessed the result of his skill. No doubt, the pride in accomplishing his mission outweighed the collateral damage that was Samantha.

I stared one final time at Sam. Rage instantaneously consumed me in a manner I had never experienced. Without thought, I left her behind and covered the three blocks to the fire escape outside the realm of human perception. I shot straight up the wall, bypassing the fire escape completely.

Inside, the shooter was busy packing his bags. He never saw or heard my approach from behind. I looked at his phone sitting on the table. The sent text message read simply, "It's done."

"It's done? Motherfucker, her name was Samantha!" I screamed. Grabbing him from behind, I threw him into the wall like a rag doll. Large chunks of plaster showered the floor from the force of impact.

"It ain't done! Not yet bitch." He groaned as I yanked him from the floor and hoisted him into the air. Terror filled his eyes. Instantly, I snarled, revealing my glistening bloodthirsty fangs. I desperately wanted him to taste raw, unbridled fear in the last remaining seconds of his life.

He tried to throw a punch, but I grabbed his hand and twisted until his wrist snapped in two. He screamed out in agony as shock waves of pain rocketed up his arm.

"You have seen your last shot with this eye." I plunged my index finger into his eye and pushed until the eye disappeared from the socket. He continued to scream out in agony. I slung him down to the floor. "You careless piece of shit! You killed the one good thing in my life."

My rage-filled assault was suddenly interrupted by a pounding on the apartment door as sirens screamed on the streets below. I dropped the shooter to the floor and stormed to the door and flung it open. "Do you mind! I am trying to fucking kill somebody." I slammed the door shut on the appalled Samaritan. It suddenly occurred to me, the shooter had an employer, and with revenge in the air, I could not afford to stay and savor the moment.

He was crawling to his bag when I stepped on his back. I pulled his arm to my mouth, which rolled him over. "I just watched my fiancée die. Now it's your turn." I bit viciously into his wrist, quickly drawing off the vast majority of his blood, leaving only enough to sustain his slow, faintly beating heart.

His eyes searched mine in terror. "Yes. Now you understand, don't you? You know how it feels to have your life leave your body." I drank of few more precious drops. "Why did you have to put her through that?!"

He could not answer. He did not possess the strength to respond at all. I swallowed again, knowing full well every organ in his body was aching for blood. But there was none to give. Death would wait, but a few agonizing minutes. I dropped his arm to the floor. I bent down and stared into his one remaining eye. "Yes, this is what death feels like." His eye stared blankly. I bent down to his ear. "One day, we will meet again. And on that day in hell, I will rain my misery on you for all eternity." I whispered.

I climbed out on the fire escape and stared down the Avenue before climbing to the roof. Police surrounded Sam's lifeless body. Six blocks in the other direction, an ambulance cried out, as it rapidly approached for no other purpose than to transport my love's corpse to a harsh steely cold slab, in some lonely city morgue.

Shameless tears for Sam streamed down my face, the incredible pain of my injuries outweighed by the breaking of my soul. I looked up to the heavens. "I have no reason left to live, and you have nothing left to punish me with, I guess we're both kind of screwed now."

Two police cars skidded to a stop five floors below me. Decisions had to be made. I did not have the time to be arrested for the grisly carnage two floors below. I no longer cared if I found Sabine. I had no need for Gabrielle, Angelique, Phillip, Dee … or my son. Angelique would take care of him. Having learned my history, I was sure she would do right by the family legacy. There was only one last piece of unfinished business that would not wait beyond tonight. The shooter was CIA. I knew the exact origination of his orders. Before the sun would rise, the blood of Paul Watson would be on my hands.

I desperately wanted to return to Sam, to hold her body, just for a while. But with a bullet to the head and chest, and the growing multitude of cops, I knew it would be prudent to disappear until my injuries healed. Monique's fractured skull looked virtually normal after only one night, with any luck mine would heal just as quickly.

I took one last look down the street to Sam's body. In all of my rage, any opportunity to feel her spirit pass was lost and now she was gone. Even though the bastard killed her, if she had witnessed my actions, she would have been appalled. She always found a way to forgive even those who might not deserve it, especially me.

Appalled or not, it was time to take care of business in Washington. After Director Watson was dispatched, it would be time to call on Chuck's services one final time. My time amongst the living had no further purpose. Sadly, I held no illusions of any spiritual reunions with Sam. The eternity I earned in hell was of my own creation.

CHAPTER SIXTEEN

RETURNING TO MY home, unable to use the main entrance, I crawled up the ally wall to ensure my arrival remained a secret. Climbing over the terrace wall, I stared blankly at the chair, where just last night I had held her close. That chair, where for the last time, all my shortcomings were forgiven. The chair where I realized what mattered most.

Through all the bullshit of my self-serving sense of purpose, the one thing that had remained a bright and constant point of peace for me was Sam. Unbridled, unconditional love, no more. This chair, the balcony, this apartment, would never experience the joy of her presence, smile, compassion, and love ever again.

I stood beside the chair, her scent veiling the fabric like the fragrance of a spring rain caressing a field of wildflowers. I picked up the chair, bitter and angry, and hurled it over the balcony and fell to my knees, weeping uncontrollably.

On the blood-covered sidewalk of Third Avenue, Samantha had been pronounced dead on the scene, her extraneous injuries bewildering the coroner beyond fascination. They had loaded her body in the back of the meat wagon, preparing her for a rendezvous with the butcher of investigative necessity.

Back on the scene, forensic specialists were busy recreating the event and collecting evidence. Thanks to my unrestrained intervention in his departure plans, detectives had already found the body of Louis the Laser, and were busy trying to understand the nature of his injuries. A massive city wide APB was put out for the missing man, an eye witness, shot by the same assassin, first a victim, and after the discovery of Louis, now a suspect.

As the ambulance was about to depart, Angelique, wearing a hooded sweatshirt, approached the driver's door. He looked to the woman standing by his window. As she lowered her hood, her beauty instantly mesmerized him.

"Wait," she implored. "I think that is my sister in the back. Please let me see her."

"I'm sorry lady. You'll have to come down to the morgue for an ID. Go see one of the detectives over on the sidewalk. They'll tell you what you need to do."

"Let me see her, now," she demanded in forceful tones.

"Geez, alright. Help yourself lady, but I got to tell ya, she ain't too pretty anymore," the driver replied in monotone submission.

Climbing into the back, she could feel the eyes of the young paramedic trolling over her features as she gazed upon the lifeless corpse. Before he could ask a question, she announced her intentions.

"I am here to help this woman."

"Lady," the paramedic scoffed, "I hate to tell you this, but your friend is dead. There is no way she is coming back."

The door slammed open to my apartment and Gabrielle rushed in. "Nick!" she cried out anxiously. Spotting me hunched over at the top of the spiral stairway with my face buried in my hands, she rushed to my side.

"Tell me it's not true!" she urged, as she sunk down and wrapped her arms around me. For the first time in her life, in my extreme anguish, my thoughts had been revealed to her. From across the city, my torment jolted her like a surge of electricity.

"My God, what happened to you ... to Sam?" As I wept openly,

Gabrielle submitted to the crushing grief as well.

Verbalizing the events, retracing every detail, so vivid, yet so dreamlike, brought the harsh reality to life, a finality that I had yet to absorb.

Gabrielle sunk into an instant state of depression. As a young prostitute in France, Gabrielle had never had a role model the likes of Samantha, who became a sister and friend, sharing her ways of wisdom and strength. She had convinced Gabrielle beyond any doubt that she could accomplish any goal she set her mind to.

So we sat on the cool marble steps, two vampires embraced in a cradle of pain, a pain that would endure for all eternity.

The buzz on the street amongst the detectives at the crime scene had erupted into confounded hypothetical bantering over the preliminary findings. Samantha, victim one: shot dead, a set of odd bite wounds that matched the bite wounds on victim two; apparently the sniper, found mutilated, three blocks away. The third victim, who appeared to have created the injuries to the neck of victim one, was shot twice, once in the head, as reported by eyewitnesses, and then went missing so quickly, nobody could account for his disappearance.

Bullet fragments, bone, blood, brain matter, a gun, and fingerprints were methodically being processed by the veteran staff of CSIs. In this neighborhood, only the best would work a case like this. Detectives were busy collecting video evidence from several surveillance cameras that lined Third Avenue between the two crime scenes. Once the bodies arrived at the morgue, the DNA samples would hopefully reveal the freakish nature of the lacerations and punctures on the victims.

Angelique ignored the words of the young paramedic. "Drive," she demanded, to the man behind the wheel. Pulling away from the crime scene, Angelique watched the clueless circus of humanity disappear from sight.

Angelique looked at the handsome young man sitting in the

back with her. "Return to life, no. But to live among the dead? That remains to be seen." Buttons flew about as Angelique ripped Sam's shirt open. "What is your name, young man?"

"David." Awestruck in the presence of a force he could not begin to understand, his dumbfounded expression hardly instilled the confidence he could tie a shoe, much less save a life.

Inspecting Sam's body, Angelique found the bullet hole and the puncture wounds from my failed attempts at resurrection. Realizing what I had attempted to do, she opened Sam's mouth only to find it remained partially filled with blood

"David, cut off her bra."

"Hell no lady, I am not going to lose my job over some kind of freak show."

Angelique held up her index finger, a talon about three inches long grew out of the end. "David, if you want to help save my friend, I will need a little more expedient cooperation out of you." Angelique slid her finger under the bra and sliced the center.

"What the hell are you, lady, some kind of alien?"

"No, David, but if you do not do everything I ask from this moment on, in a more timely obedient manner, then perhaps you will wish an alien was all that I was."

Angelique's razor sharp talon sliced through Samantha's skin, tendons, and muscles like a scalpel. Pulling her flesh apart, her lifeless heart was exposed below the ribs. Not one globule of blood spilled, as virtually every drop had been consumed by me. Angelique slid her finger through Samantha's ribs until her finger punctured, then penetrated deeply into the heart.

David watched in frightened fascination.

"David, this next part is vitally important. Her life depends on you. David!" Angelique snapped, as David was unresponsive. "You must pay attention. This next part is crucial. In a moment she will breathe, gasp out, and choke. You must hold down her head, and force her mouth to remain shut. She must swallow the contents of her mouth."

"You ... you mean the blood?"

"Yes. She will fight you, but you have to be stronger. She cannot be allowed to exhale. You must not fail me."

David nodded. He grabbed Samantha's head firmly. "You do

realize I am holding the head of a dead woman, and you have your finger in her chest, and outside of some kind of miracle from above, I'm gonna be fired and you will be packed off to Bellevue, right?"

Angelique ignored his typical trivial human skepticism and focused all of her energy on Samantha. *"Pierdut spiritul, timpul nu a venit pentru trecerea dvs. A reveni la acest cadavru. Insufle viață ultima respirația,"* Angelique chanted. The medieval force possessed by vampires flowed through Angelique's finger directly into Samantha's heart. Slowly, and faintly, the organ responded to the bidding of its new master.

The beating heart meant nothing without a spirit to drive it. Angelique knew this all too well and summoned Samantha's spirit from the world of the dead once more. *"Pierdut spiritul, timpul nu a venit pentru trecerea dvs. A reveni la acest cadavru. Insufle viață ultima respirația."* Other than the rhythmic beating, there was no sign of life.

Angelique would not allow thoughts of failure; she had seen this done by the Tepes himself. Again she demanded, *"Pierdut spiritul, timpul nu a venit pentru trecerea dvs. A reveni la acest cadavru. Insufle viață ultima respirația."* Still nothing happened. "Breathe!" Angelique screamed.

Sam's body jolted to life, then convulsed in agony. David, although pummeled by fear, maintained his grip on Sam's head and mouth. Gasping for air, she inhaled deeply, her body contorting with violent seizures. Instinctively she fought to break free of David, to open her mouth and cough out the fluid that filled her lungs. David hung on with all his strength, withstanding the onslaught of her desperation.

As suddenly as it began, Samantha's body collapsed lifeless, except for the slow, soft methodical beating of her heart. Angelique removed her finger from the delicate organ.

She smiled an expression of timid confidence. "You can let go now, David."

Angelique leaned down to Samantha's face. Caressing her skin, she whispered in her ear. "Do not be frightened by what will transpire. We all must die to live."

I had not been home thirty minutes when the phone rang. Undoubtedly it was Phillip calling to harass me over being late for dinner. Gabrielle was kind enough to answer the phone. "Tell him we won't be making dinner," I said before she had answered.

"Hello Phillip," Gabrielle answered in her soft French accent. "No," she replied in a stressed tone. "Phillip, I do not know." She listened as Phillip babbled on. "He is here."

Muting the phone as she crossed the room, Gabrielle handed it to me. "He knows."

"Phillip." I struggled to maintain my composure.

"Brian, what the fuck man?"

"It was a motherfucking assassin, Phillip. Sam stumbled right into the shot. She was dead before she hit the ground." Tears flowed freely as I visualized the scene again. "There was nothing I could do."

"Geez Brian, half the cops in the city are looking for you. They got your face on some surveillance video from inside a jewelry store you passed."

"Does Dee know?"

"Are you fucking kidding, man? I don't know how to begin to explain this. She is going to lose it, big time."

"Bring her here. I will tell her."

"We will be there in twenty minutes. And Brian, stay put. Do not go outside. We're gonna have to get you out of the city, tonight."

"Trust me, Phillip, there's not a chance in hell I am going back out there tonight." With my head looking like it came straight out of a B-film horror flick, there was no going anywhere without risking an outbreak of pandemonium.

"They are coming here?" Gabrielle appeared confused by the revelation for apparent reasons.

"Yes. Why wouldn't they?"

"Not many people have seen the likes of your head. Had I not seen the damage you inflicted on Monique, the site of you might have put me in shock. I would suggest you get cleaned up. Phillip and Dee do not need to see you like this."

I walked to the mirror on the wall. "What? I look the same." I looked down at my white linen shirt, now stained almost entirely dark crimson. I felt my head. The bullet exit wound in my forehead had almost closed, but I could only assume my skin remained black and blue and grotesquely swollen.

"No, I will see them as I am." I plopped down on the leather couch. Bitterness had replaced any shred of decency. I stared at the mirror across the room, the same mirror that for months held the reflection of Sam cuddled next to me. Now this was nothing but an empty couch.

Samantha's body jumped to life, flailing wildly against restraints that confined her to the gurney, her body writhing in burning pain. She vomited the contents of her stomach, screaming out in unfathomable pain. Angelique observed in quiet, self-congratulatory satisfaction, most pleased with her accomplishment. David had pinned himself against the side of the bus, seized in a magnitude of fear he believed impossible to survive.

Samantha continued to fight with all of her energy, the life in her body giving way to the undead. After several minutes of futile resistance, she collapsed again.

"Take off the restraints," Angelique ordered silently. David submitted without hesitation, as if the order had been given aloud. Unexpectedly, with the successful resurrection and some higher connection to the spirit world, Angelique's powers had grown expansively. Again she tested this newfound surge in the energy of her thoughts on the driver. "Take us to the Village, corner of Houston and Thompson Street."

The knock to the door startled me. I was hoping Phillip and Dee would magically not show up. But here they were, just after eleven. Gabrielle answered the door. I sat dumbfounded on the couch. As they approached, my disheveled look from behind forewarned of dire news.

"Nick, my god, what happened?" Dee cried out. The lack of hair and skull made it impossible to hide the severity of the incident.

She rounded the front of the couch and took in the full visual nightmare that was my face. Phillip gasped in repulsion.

The tears were streaming down my face. I could not contain my raw emotions.

"She's gone, Dee. Sam's dead," I cried.

"Nick? What happened? Where's my sister?" she shrieked as her knees buckled.

"We were ambushed. A gunman shot us. I could not save her." The words burned my lips as they passed, the all-powerful vampire completely helpless, the futility of a lifetime so ill timed.

Dee fell to her knees, took my hands and sobbed out, "No, no, not Sam. Oh god."

Gabrielle dropped to the floor and hugged Dee from behind, offering what little comfort she could render. Through Samantha's and Gabrielle's friendship, Dee had grown almost equally close and the comfort offered was beyond the realm of my current frame of mind. Phillip looked over the girls huddled on the floor and mouthed, 'we need to talk.'

With her head securely cradled in Gabrielle's lap as the minutes passed, Dee's hysterical crying began to wane. I excused myself and asked Phillip to follow.

We walked into the bedroom, Phillip trailing closely behind, inspecting my head.

"God Brian, how in the hell are you even alive?"

"Haven't you heard, Phillip? Short of cutting my head off or driving a stake through my heart, I am fucking immortal."

"Look, I don't know if there is ever going to be a good time to bring this up, but there's some shit going down that is going to require damage control beyond anything I can provide. Is there anyone I can call?"

I sighed. I did not give a shit about damage control. I was ready to die, my reason for living having died with Sam. "What is it, Phillip?" My tone was terse as I considered the task for my final few days.

"Okay, I have sources all over this. Stuff that would make unbelievable headlines for a special edition in the morning. First of all, the shooter, the cops are way freaked out by his COD. Secondly, they have you on a surveillance video. The story we received was you appeared as a flash or even a glitch on the tape, until they played the video in slow motion. Want to talk about freaked out? They can't even begin to estimate how fast you were moving. And as if that were not enough, another video has your ass launching up the wall of the apartment like some kind of rocket."

"I really do not care if they know about me now, Phil. Fuck 'em all. You have everything you need to run a great story, all the way back to New Orleans. Go for it, man. It will make you an immortal in the publishing world."

"Fuck that, Brian," Phillip said indignantly.

"Nicholas." Phillip had never taken to my true name, but instead chose to call me by the only name he had known, up until a year ago. "Please use my real name."

"Nicholas? Whatever. You need to get off your pity party for now. There are people that count on you, Gabrielle for starters, whose life stands to get screwed if you don't make things right. She's got a life that depends on your little secret, and if you don't fix this, she's gonna get fucked. Whatever you are planning to do with yourself, I can't change. But make no mistake, if you leave her exposed, they will crucify her. You know they will."

"Phillip, I am most certain you can manage to take care of Gabrielle's future with what I am leaving behind."

"I already told you, this is over my head. They have seen your face. They may know what you are, or at least have some sort of idea by now. For all we know, they might be on the way here. I'm gonna need your help putting it right," Phillip implored. "Come on, man, Gabrielle loves you. Sam would not have let you bail like this."

Phillip was right. Sam would have put her foot up my ass already. "How soon can you have the helicopter here?"

Phillip checked his watch. "Thirty minutes."

"Do it. I need to get down to Washington, tonight. There is a man who can make this all go away." The very man I intended to kill might have earned a suspended sentence, until he cleaned up the bullshit mess he made.

Phillip dialed his phone and barked a few brief instructions to the voice on the other end. "It's on the way. So what next?"

"You guys get the hell out of here, just in case the cops show up. I may not be back tonight, depending on the hour." I turned on the shower water and began to strip. "Bag this stuff up," I ordered as I tossed my clothes out of the bathroom to Phillip. "Get someone in here tonight to clean this place top to bottom. Wipe the prints clean. Anything with blood, pitch it. Have Gabby stay in her apartment downstairs, or take her to your place, until we know everything's cool. With any luck, I can plug the damage before the cops show up."

"Roger that." Phillip's phone vibrated, drawing his attention to an incoming text. He stuck his head in the bathroom. His eyes were instantly drawn to my back where the wound had yet to heal from the first shot. "God Brian, how bad does it hurt?"

"It hurts like a bitch, only difference ... I don't get to die like everyone else."

"Shit," he exclaimed. "Sam's body has not shown up at the morgue yet. And they are unable to locate the ambulance."

"Doughnut break or wrong morgue I would guess. Whatever, let me know when they find her," I said as I stepped into the shower and closed the door. In the confines of the shower, I watched as pools of blood spiraled down the drain; the last traces of Samantha I would ever know.

CHAPTER SEVENTEEN

THE AMBULANCE PULLED up to the corner of Thompson and Houston. "Stop here," Angelique willed the driver. "David, if you want to live beyond tonight, you will never repeat any of what you have seen, do you understand?"

"Yes," he replied. The sheer force of Angelique's demand would become a commandment etched in David's subconscious.

"Samantha! Get up," Angelique ordered.

Dazed and confused, Samantha rose.

"We need to leave now." Angelique took Samantha's hand and led her from the ambulance. Sam was oblivious to the fact her shirt was torn open and her breast partially exposed.

"Wait." David took off his EMT jacket and put it over Samantha's shoulders. He snapped two of the buttons, covering her incision and breast, which was rapidly healing and no longer exposing her heart "We can't have you running all over the city like that."

Appreciative of the gesture, Angelique gave David a kiss on the cheek. "Thank you."

Angelique took Samantha by the arm and led her into the village, toward her home. Samantha struggled to walk, the instability of her legs caused by the traumatic changes to her body. "Where are you taking me?" she asked.

"I am taking you to my home." Guiding Sam with almost every step, she thought about the lost love in her life. Only an hour ago in his moment of desperation, Nick's angst pierced her like an arrow; his cries for help so powerful, as if she were there beside him. Her awareness of Nick's pain was so acute, to experience his undying love for this woman, after all that had transpired with the Tepes family, she knew she could not allow Samantha to perish. Arriving at the crime scene, she sensed the presence of her ancestors, coercing her to do the right thing, regardless of her feelings. Ancestors or not, she owed it to Nicholas for all the havoc she had precipitated in his life.

After walking in silence for a block, Sam asked weakly, "Who are you?"

"Save your strength. Once we are safely inside I will tell you everything.

Sam felt so strange. The colors of the night, vivid and renewed. The scent of the city had changed, each odor no longer a conglomeration of disharmonious smells. Each tree she passed had a unique fragrance. Pedestrians a block away had their own individual redolence. The stain on the sidewalk was the remnants of pumpkin ice cream. Suddenly, overwhelmed by the onslaught of sensory perception, Samantha's stomach convulsed, and she vomited.

Angelique shook her head in amusement. "I hope you are almost done with that. We will be in my apartment soon."

"I'm sorry. I don't know what is wrong with me. My stomach is quite queasy and I feel as if my skin is burning up. I think I must be coming down with something. Maybe I should go home."

"I do not think that would be wise," Angelique said, as she held the door open for Sam. The elevator ride was silent, Angelique contemplating her next move and Samantha trying to get a handle on the lapse in her memory. As Angelique unlocked the door she looked back to Samantha. "Do you remember anything of tonight?"

Sam struggled for the answer. The time spent dead had done its damage, but the process of rejuvenation was well underway.

"I was ..." Sam began, but her words stalled as she lost her direction. "I'm sorry, but what did you say your name was?"

Unsure of Samantha's reaction Angelique hesitated, but she knew the truth would soon be out. "My name is Angelique."

"Do I know you?"

"Indirectly, you do."

Sam thought in silence as pieces of her memory returned like bits of a jigsaw puzzle.

"I was walking with Nick. I remember Barbados." Blankly, Samantha rubbed the phantom pain in her chest where the bullet had passed through. "The next thing I remember is throwing up outside."

"Samantha, what I am about to tell you might seem quite impossible, but trust me, considering the events of the past few years ... well you will understand." Angelique unbuttoned the paramedic's jacket.

Slightly uncomfortable being undressed by a strange woman, Samantha nervously allowed Angelique to continue. She looked down at the state of her shirt, missing bra and disfigured chest and moaned. "Oh God."

Angelique traced her fingers across the wound. "This is nothing. It will heal within days."

Appalled by the scar that remained, Samantha pulled Angelique's fingers away. Unaware of just how bad the scar had been, her hands trembled as she inspected the wound.

"You were walking with Nick," Angelique began. "You were shot first, then Nick. But bullets do not harm our kind. You on the other hand were not so lucky. You died instantly."

Samantha had pretty much lost most of her glowing skin color with the transformation occurring, but what little was left departed with all haste as Samantha began to faint.

Catching her mid-fall, Angelique led her to the couch and laid her down.

Sam studied Angelique's features as she gradually regained her composure. "You are Angelique ... from New Orleans, aren't you?"

With an air of pride, Angelique replied, "I am."

"Where is Nick?" With a tinge of panic in her voice, Samantha recoiled from Angelique.

"After you were killed, he was shot several times while attempting to revive you. In his desperation, he attempted the one thing he thought might save you: the curse of the vampire.

"Where is he?" Sam asked urgently, sensing the worst may have befallen him.

"For the time being, all I know is that he is safe. But in his rage he was very careless. He savagely executed the gunman that shot you and potentially exposed our race to the world."

"Our race?" Angelique's words resonated as Samantha's brain assimilated the many fragments of information beginning to return. "You said I died, how am I here?"

"Nicholas has been a vampire for less than two years. Although he possesses great power, he is ignorant to the ancient ways of our people. I have been a vampire for over three centuries. I know many dark secrets from our past he has yet to learn. I resurrected you from the realm of the dead Samantha, into the life of the undead. You are as they say in Romanian, *înviat*. You are now one of us."

The words passing from Angelique did not register initially. What she had wanted most from Nick, but was never given, was suddenly hers from the woman she feared the most. She looked at her hands, then pulled her shirt open again. In the few minutes that passed, the wound had healed considerably more.

"It will soon be gone," Angelique assured Samantha as she touched her hand.

"I am having a difficult time believing this is anything but a dream."

"This is no dream," Angelique sat down on the edge of the couch beside Samantha and brushed her finger over Samantha's lips before gently parting them. She took Samantha's hand and guided her fingers lightly over the razor sharp fangs. Startled by the discovery, Samantha flinched back into the couch. Angelique smiled as she pulled Samantha's fingers away from her mouth and then guided the trembling hand into her own mouth.

Samantha stroked the fang, exploring its glossy and honed profile. Pricking the tip, Samantha shuttered with trepidation.

Angelique withdrew Sam's fingers and kissed her hand sensing her fear. "It is quite alright. In short time you will feel at home with our ways."

Rising from the couch, aware of Angelique's peculiarly strong sensual prowess, Samantha decided the methodology deserved a little separation.

Angelique honed in on Sam's uneasiness. "It is alright Samantha. You will find there are many advantages to being a vampire. Many new experiences, some of a more passionate nature."

"No thank you. I am fine just like I am," Sam said nervously. "Dead or undead, but strictly straight, I like men just fine, thank you," she continued awkwardly. "Nick, I like Nick."

Angelique laughed at Samantha's awkwardness. "You are too sweet. I was just toying with you."

Samantha looked at Angelique with cautionary eyes, uncertain of her sincerity.

"I apologize. I cannot remember what it was like for me. It was so long ago. But I am sure you have questions. I will get us a couple of drinks, then we can talk. I will tell you everything you want to know." Angelique disappeared into the kitchen. Within a minute, she reappeared with two half filled wine glasses.

Samantha took the glass and brought it to her lips. The strange aroma warned her it was not wine. "This is blood?"

"Naturally, what else would you have us drink?"

"I feel like I should talk to Nick before I do this."

Samantha's reluctance was not entirely unexpected, so Angelique took a sip to set an example. "What have you to fear?"

"My humanity," Samantha quipped.

Not wanting to force the issue, Angelique smiled and chose an alternate tactic. "So Gabrielle is here, in New York?"

"Yes she is."

"And the two of you? Are you friends?" Angelique asked, curious of the relationship.

"Very good friends," Sam added proudly.

"So you have no fear of her?"

"She has never made me feel uncomfortable, so no."

"Then I hope you will allow me to be a friend as well, Samantha," The two shared a quaint smile, before Angelique took another sip. Reflecting on bygone memories of New Orleans Angelique sighed. "Gabrielle never wanted any of this, and once she was turned, she clung to the hope, my hope, the hopes of Nicholas's father, to return to the path of the righteous one day. Initially, she abstained from blood drinking, praying the curse would be lifted. But all it did was make her frail. And so she shared in the vulnerabilities of our race, but none of our strength. In vain, she kept her vigil, for almost two hundred years. So tell me, does she still refrain from human blood?"

"No, she found it impossible to survive on the outside without proper nourishment. But like Nick, she is vigilant over her consumption, and would never take a live victim."

"And the blood, it makes her stronger?" Angelique hoped the logical sequence would encourage Samantha to partake in the blood that would expedite the healing process. "You my dear are weak. You are vulnerable. If you do not trust me, then do not drink. I will not be offended. But make no mistake, your ability to protect yourself is far from developed, and like Gabrielle so many years ago, you are prone to an entire new set of dangers, like the sunrise for example. You are easy prey for hunters."

"Hunters?"

"Men are predatory in nature, particularly these men of New York. They feel they are superior, with the need to conquer women, by any means. Some use force, some use drugs, and some just use good old fashion suave. For the most part, I find them mostly uncivilized and distasteful."

Sam looked down at the burgundy beverage in her glass. She was a vampire now. It was time she develop the ability to act like one. She put the glass to her lips and slowly tipped the crystal back. Her intentions were to have just a sip, but the need deep within her would not allow her to stop, until all of the thick rich blood had been drained from the glass.

"It is good, yes?" Angelique asked, as she witnessed Samantha's first call to blood. She knew what her reaction would be, before she even picked up the glass and where this unquenchable thirst would lead, if not tamed.

"I want more," Samantha stated firmly.

"No Samantha. Our race is like that of sharks. A shark only knows to swim, and to eat. They have no level of self-control. A vampire can be a most dangerous creature. For like the shark, all they do is feed on the weak. If you do not learn to control your instinctive urges, and quickly, you will become hunted, as your ancestors were."

"My ancestors?"

"You are a vampire, all that have come before are now your family. You will find the spirits of your ancestors guiding you from time to time.

"But if we are all family, why did Nicholas kill the others?"

Thinking back to the memories of her fallen sisters, Angelique frowned. "Nicholas did not know his heritage, and was driven by revenge and righteousness. But you see, once he began to understand his place, he could not bring himself to destroy his own kind."

"He did kill Celine, in Miami, after ... you know."

"Celine was as devious and power hungry as her master. I am sure Nicholas's motivations were in proper accordance with his father's ways, as they were when he killed Monique. Like any family, there is always an element whose needs supplant the common good of us all. These rogues will always be a threat to our survival."

Emergency lights illuminated the street outside the apartment. Angelique moved to the window and observed a police cruiser passing slowly below. "They are looking for us Samantha."

"Who is?"

Angelique smiled broadly. "I think the authorities might want their victim's body back."

"Victim's body?"

"Samantha, less than an hour ago, you were the innocent victim in a brutal murder. A young paramedic witnessed your resurrection from the dead. I am sure the police are not happy with the fact your body is missing. I think it would be prudent for us to leave as soon as permissible, and go to your home. I do not want to bring any trouble to my door."

"The baby."

"Yes, the baby." Angelique's confirmation was buffered with an air of surprise.

"Can I see your son?"

"I see he has told you." Angelique huffed at the unexpected and awkward request. "Samantha ..."

"Angelique, please call me Sam."

"All right, Sam. Please understand, although Nicholas is the father of my child, the two of you are bound in a destiny beyond my vision. As such, you must also learn to assume the role as Brian's mother. Although I might feel slightly uncomfortable, even jealous, I knew the night I revealed his birth to Nicholas, that in time, you will assume a much greater role in his life."

The unexpected invitation caught Samantha completely off guard, all of the apprehensions she had held concerning Angelique instantly vanished. "I don't know what to say."

"There is much to learn, for all of us. Apparently, this child is heir to the throne and as such, we must all nurture and protect him with our greatest abilities."

"Are you...?"

"It is the right thing. Come, we will see him." Angelique led the way to the sleeping child's room. "I have a nanny who stays with him at night, when the need arises." As they entered, the young girl popped a watchful eye over her book. Krista, the nanny, was seated in a recliner reading a book by mounted light.

"This is my friend Samantha. Sam, this is Krista," Angelique whispered.

"Hi," Krista replied, straining to see in the dim light.

Sam was amazed, even in the darkness, every detail of the room shown as if the lights were on. Odd, Sam thought, that the room was decorated in the typical manner of any ordinary boy.

"What were you expecting, a coffin?" Angelique whispered.

"I'm sorry, I wasn't ..."

"It is alright. I should apologize. Your thoughts are as open as a book. It was rude of me to intrude. In time I will show you how to prevent that."

"I wish you would, certain people take liberties whenever they feel the urge." Samantha smiled broadly. *Wasn't he in for a big surprise?* She walked over to the crib and gazed in.

Looking down at the child, the crushing jealousy she felt only one night before was washed away, not by any instinctive maternal bond, but a deeper, darker source. A source growing, guiding, and shaping the renewed life inside.

"You feel it, don't you?" Angelique pointed out. She already knew the answer. Cautiously, she had monitored each and every emotion Samantha had experienced from the moment of resurrection.

"How did you ... never mind, it's that thing again, right?" Sam whispered.

"As I said, you have much to learn. For now, we should leave." Angelique turned to Krista. "I may not return tonight."

"You girls go have fun. Brian and I will try to stay out of trouble."

Angelique looked at Samantha's distressed attire. "This will not do at all. Let's go to my closet and pick something out. We can't have you walking all over Manhattan looking like the star of one of those zombie B movies, can we?"

Samantha smiled, and followed Angelique's lead. Angelique disappeared while Samantha slid the hangers, looking for something to wear. She looked down at the remains of what had been one of her favorite shirts. Simple white cotton, unbutton just enough to keep Nick's attention. She looked at her jeans, which had only been worn once before tonight. Damn if they weren't ruined as well.

Having already sized up Angelique, Samantha decided her clothes should fit just fine, well almost fine, maybe one size smaller, she thought with a frown. She pulled a dark blue pair of jeans off the hanger and a black button up shirt. Simple enough. Happily, the jeans slid right on. Samantha looked for a mirror to inspect for any unwanted muffin top. With her bra in shambles, she decided for the trip home to forego borrowing any personal lingerie. Covering her breast with the shirt, she crossed the hall to the bathroom for inspection.

"Well damn." Samantha stared back at the empty mirror. "I guess makeup is out of the question." Not that she thought Gabrielle needed any, but certainly this was the reason why she never used makeup. Samantha looked down at her stomach and breast as she buttoned the shirt. Things looked ... firmer, the few wrinkles in her hand ... gone. Pressing her breast and lifting she smiled. "Well hello, this more than makes up for the mirror thing."

Angelique suddenly appeared with another glass of blood and smiled at Samantha's discovery. "It had its advantages."

"I'll say. Guess I won't be needing to lift the pups anytime soon."

Angelique laughed. "No, the only purpose for a doctor from here on out is an occasional snack."

Samantha turned to Angelique with a bemused expression.

"I am kidding." Angelique placed her hand on Samantha's shoulder. "But tell me, Sam, what do you see when you look at me, or Gabrielle, or Nicholas?"

"Beauty."

"And that is how you will be perceived, without makeup, fixing your hair, without any effort whatsoever." Angelique straightened Samantha's collar. "You are quite beautiful, but understand this, your outward appearance is combination of self-perception and inner beauty. If you choose, you can be quite monstrous."

“I wish I could see, just one last time.”

“You get used to it,” Angelique chirped. “I got you a drink for the road.”

As she handed the glass over, Samantha took her hand. “Angelique, I will never be able to express my gratitude.”

“I am sure over the next hundred years or so, you will find a way.”

CHAPTER EIGHTEEN

THE SQUAD ROOM was abuzz with speculation. The shooting, although not remarkable as a murder, was circumstantially remarkable. Captain Patrick had four detectives in his office, and was dutifully reciting the riot act.

"What in the hell do you mean we've lost the victim's body?" he screamed out.

"Honest to god, the paramedic claims she got out of the bus on Houston, and headed into the Village, with another female who had joined them at the crime scene," Detective Lennar struggled to explain. They all knew when Patrick was on the warpath somebody would have to face the ire of the captain and Lennar drew the short straw. The fact she was an overall great detective and attractive did nothing to defuse his rant, which was directed at her.

"How in the hell does a woman who is beyond any reasonable doubt, dead as a doornail, get up and walk away. And who in the fuck let a civilian go along for the ride?" Patrick bellowed.

"It was the driver. He let her in. The paramedic in the back, David Pearson, claimed this woman did some kind of voodoo ritual, talking in some foreign language, and the vic just popped back to life."

"Was she or wasn't she dead at the scene?" Patrick grilled in derogatory tones as he stroked the top of his thinning hair.

"They don't get no deader Captain," Lennar responded assuredly, with her hands on her hips.

"Who else knows about this, this Jesus Christ wannabe?"

"Besides the five of us, just the paramedics, who we have in interrogation two.

"So please tell me, what in the hell else are you four Bozos doing about this clusterfuck?"

"We've got ten squad cars and twenty foot patrols in the Village, with more on the way. We are canvassing the crime scene neighborhood with pictures of our mystery Spiderman, trying to get an ID on him. The second stiff, the shooter, is at the morgue getting prepped as we speak. Miller is going down for the autopsy."

"This guy in the morgue? He's the one we believe the bullet proof spiderman mutilated?"

"Yeah, Flash Gordon and Wolverine wrapped up in one guy."

"You know, all of this shit is giving me an ulcer. And you know how I hate fucking ulcers." Patrick turned his back on the detectives and stared out the window. "This freak show had to be staged. I need you to find out how they pulled it off before I see the Chief of D's in the morning, because if I tell him we've got mutants on the streets of Manhattan, he's gonna send me to Bellevue."

"There is one other thing Captain." Lennar hesitated, before continuing.

Patrick wheeled around, glaring at the detective.

"The shooter, we think he's a pro. The equipment he was packing, the shot he attempted, only a pro would have tried it. Special forces, CIA, something, but I am pretty sure when his people find out he's dead and his mark isn't ... we won't be the only people looking at this."

"How much does the media know?" Patrick growled, knowing the answer about to follow.

"They're all over it, boss, except the fact our victim has gone missing."

"Shit, that means we've got maybe until sun up before this goes national. I need this closed tonight." Patrick, with his face blazing and veins bulging, slammed his fist on the desk. "Call in whatever resources you need, just get it done."

The detectives all stared in silence, as if waiting for their boss to collapse from a stroke.

"What the hell are you waiting for, somebody to put their size twelve up your ass? Get the hell out of my office, and find that stiff, or start thinking about which parking lot you want to patrol!"

Having finished my shower, and changed my clothes, I put a ball cap on to cover my rapidly healing, but still grotesquely disfigured skull. I returned to the living room. Dee was curled up on the couch, intermittently crying, but obviously feeling the effects of something Phillip had given her. Gabrielle had rounded up all the dishes and placed them in the dishwasher, bagged my clothes, and boxed my refrigerated blood supply.

Phillip was busy wiping down anything he could think of with fresh prints on it. "The helicopter will be here any minute," he reported, upon seeing me. "We have a car waiting out front."

Gabrielle returned to the living room and touched Dee on the shoulder. "We need to go now."

"We'll be at my place, until we hear from you. Do you have any idea when that might be?" Phillip asked.

"Tonight, maybe tomorrow night. I am not sure." In no mood to think about timetables, I stared blankly at a home that now seemed foreign.

"The cleaners will be here in an hour or two. I'll have your juice at my place when you get back. If we are not there, have Julio let you in. I'm sure Dee will want to find out whatever she can in the morning." Phillip put down his cleaning rag and sighed.

I placed my hand on Phillip's shoulder, and ushered him to the door. "Keep her away from the cops, no matter what, until you hear otherwise from me."

"I'll have my people keep tabs on whatever they find out and call you."

"No, don't call. I'll check in with you when I can." Pushing him to the hallway, I grabbed the doorknob. "Thanks, Phillip, you have been a good friend."

The defeated tone in my voice brought his foot to the door blocking its closure. "Been? No, don't you even think about going there. *Are,* we *are* good friends. And we are going to get past this, somehow."

"Yeah, I know. I will see you when I get back." I heard a helicopter approaching. I went over to my desk, unlocked the drawer and got Loretta out. I grabbed her muzzle. "One last job, baby," I said as I turned off the light and stared back at my empty home. This house would never be the same again.

CHAPTER NINETEEN

IN A WORLD laden with communication technology, it is amazing how very often failure encroaches at all the wrong times. Phillip's cell phone battery was sending warning shots of imminent battery failure, Gabrielle rarely carried a cell, and Dee was out cold, lying on her purse.

The last text Phillip received from his sources ended with: cops searching Upper East Side for Spiderman. The part of the message Phillip did not get was more important. *Cops searching the village for two women; one brunette, one blonde. See attached files.*

Had he gotten that piece of the text, he would have known the cops were searching for Samantha, her body missing, and some mystery brunette. Had he gotten the files, Gabrielle could have identified Angelique. But the message never came.

Nicholas was on his way to Washington, and Phillip on his way home. It was just past two in the morning and had been one hell of a long day. Phillip sat there, looking at his wife. He knew tomorrow would be the worst day of his life. There would be no consoling Dee. Phillip was ill prepared to deal with tragedies; unpleasant circumstances he could not delegate away. He looked at Gabrielle staring out the window. So incredibly beautiful he thought. So powerful. He looked back at Dee, and a smile crept across his face. What a scoundrel he had been until he met her. She rocked his world in a way no woman ever had, or could ... not even this most seductive vampire, sitting immediately across from him.

Gabrielle was aware of Phillip's roaming eyes and wandering thoughts. "Phillip, your attention is waning. If you want, I could make her sleep all night, and the entire day."

"Gabrielle! That's not what I was thinking. I'm sure in my sick little twisted mind, there are at least a dozen ways to justify what you think I think, but fortunately, I'm not thinking anything of the sort. I have a heart. And this woman holds the key to it."

Gabrielle turned to Phillip and smiled. "I know, I just wanted to make sure you were still worthy of her love. Now that Sam is gone, I must look out for Dee." Gabrielle straightened her skirt, and stroked Dee's hair. "Thank you."

"For?"

"It is nice, to be admired, even if it is strictly platonic."

Phillip sat back and welcomed a congratulatory broad grin. He was a changed man indeed. He was not far removed from the day where he would have spared no expense to get a woman like Gabrielle, even if only for a one night stand. Now he could admire, without the desire to have a sexual encounter for the solitary purpose of his own shallow, self-gratification. *Oh god, is this the first sign that I'm getting old?* he mused.

"No, just the beginning of maturity," Gabrielle chimed in magically.

"Hey, you stay out of my head, you little eavesdropper," Phillip quipped.

Gabrielle chuckled and looked down the almost deserted, long, lit streets of Madison Avenue.

Sleep, for humans and vampires, is a most wonderful thing. For both species, it can be quite unsettling to be woken from a deep sleep. A confusion exists, one that would immediately follow an intrusion into an individual's deepest disconnection from reality. To a trained ear, the sound of a silenced Beretta firing across a darkened room might likely produce it. The impact of the bullet striking the headboard and the smell of a singed feather pillow beside your sleeping head would definitely do it.

That was Paul Watson's wake up call. The first shot, confusion; the second, the heat of the shot felt on the side of his head, then fear.

"What the hell?" he cried out into the darkened room.

A third shot grazing the tip of his ear; pain.

"Jesus!" he screamed as he cupped his ear.

"Paul, what's going on?" The wife cried out in a panic.

I watched in amusement as he fumbled frantically for the nightlight. Neither could see me perched on top of his dresser from across the room. Suddenly the nightlight flashed on, and the two gazed in terror as they processed in the image before them.

Watson fumbled for his glasses. "Nick?"

"Yes, Paul, it is. Are you surprised to see me, alive?"

"What in the hell are you doing? Have you lost your mind?" he screamed.

"Save your breath, Paul. If you are trying to alert your bodyguards, they are taking the rest of the evening off." In the old days I would have simply snapped their necks. But not deserving my wrath, thanks to Angelique's incantations, they would live to serve another day. "And don't bother with the silent alarm. You remember, Paul, I always cover the details."

"Why are you here? What do you want with me?" As he cupped his ear, blood trickled through his fingers.

"Paul," I jumped off the dresser, crossed the room, and hopped onto the footboard of the bed, perching like a falcon. "I have no time or patience for this stupidity." I tossed his cell phone to him, the inbound text still reading: It's done. "We both know who sent this."

He examined the text then laid the phone down. "Yes."

"And we know what he is referring to. The only problem is, Paul, it was my fiancée." My tone was terse. "She was the only thing in my rotten life I ever loved. Now she is gone, Paul." My tone was just a pitch below a scream as I pointed Loretta in direction of his wife.

"Don't!" he pleaded, as he leaned over to shield his wife.

"Get over yourself, Paul. If my only purpose was revenge, you would have already seen her die."

"Nick ... please. You know how the game is played. It was just protocol. No agent, with the knowledge you possess, has ever been permitted to retire. We can't risk an agent selling services to the highest bidder, or worse, be captured and tortured until they start coughing up national security secrets."

"I promised you, Paul, things were secure."

"Secure? You, better than anyone, should know how dangerous a captured agent is. You've seen the results. Nobody in your department has ever retired. Over the last thirty years, only four, including you, did not die in the field. It is quite regrettable, but mandate forty seven requires any agent with intimate knowledge of covert ops be terminated for the sake of national security." Watson cited the policy as if he were reading from the manual. "You were never meant to live."

Hearing the words from a friend and mentor, I felt a painful shock, as if the bullet had just now struck my head.

"I am truly sorry about your fiancée, it was not the intent. But it's policy, just plain business. There was a day you understood that better than anyone."

I lowered Loretta. Paul breathed a cautious sigh of relief. "I can take torture, Paul. I can take a lot more than you give me credit for." I jumped to the floor and walked up his side of the bed. I handed Loretta over, grip first. With a shaky hand, he instantly aimed her at me. I grabbed the silencer and pulled Loretta to my chest. "Shoot me!"

"No, Paul," his wife objected frantically. "Call the police."

"Do it, Paul. You have already killed me more than you will ever know. Finish the fucking job!" He flinched. I saw the fear. Pathetic desk jockey. The pencil pusher had never spent one day in the field, never did a day's dirty work personally. He only made the call.

"Come on, Paul, time to man up. You need to know what it feels like, just one time. Do it," I implored.

"No, Paul," his wife pleaded.

His hand relaxed. I knew he did not have the balls to do it. I grabbed his hand forcefully, and pointed Loretta at his wife. "Damn it, Paul, I swear to God, if you don't do it, I will kill your wife by your own hand." He struggled against my strength feebly. Training the gun back at me I growled, "Last chance."

Loretta kicked, and with a muffled thump, a single bullet pierced my chest. The force of the shot was enough to send me tumbling backward. “Shit, that really hurt.”

An incredible pain rocketed throughout my chest as blood pooled through my shirt. Paul’s wife screamed out in horror. I opened my shirt exposing the gaping hole left by the point blank shot. I grimaced a smile. I stepped back toward Paul. He pointed Loretta back at me, hands trembling uncontrollably.

“It will not do any good, Paul. Much as I would like to die, I cannot. I got into some pretty heavy shit, some downright ungodly, supernatural shit. What you see is the end result. Beat me, shoot me, torture me, it just does not matter. There is no enemy I fear anymore. Send me to the gates of hell, they will open wide and welcome me home.”

Aghast, he stared as the bleeding from my wound subsided and the flesh began to mend. “Why are you here?” he murmured as he contemplated the unfathomable spectacle.

“It is your good fortune my original intentions have changed.”

“How so?” Watson answered in a timid voice as he lowered Loretta.

“It is pretty simple. Clean up the mess your shit head made in New York. His body is at the morgue, as should be my fiancée’s. I do not give a shit what you do with his, but I want Samantha’s body delivered to a destination of my choosing so I may lay her to rest properly. The cops are looking for me. They have surveillance video and other evidence. In short, I need you to make all of the shit that went down tonight disappear forever, understand?”

“Then what?”

“That is all. I disappear, you destroy any remaining files on me. You will never make any attempts to locate me … forever. In short, I die along with all of the evidence of last night.”

Paul nodded, confirming his task. He wrote the manual on cleanup duty; mounds of records and evidence vaporized with a magic stroke of his wand.

“Just so we are sure there are no misunderstandings, you need to know this, if I ever have to return to address anything, I will hold you, your family, and any of your friends personally responsible. And I will not understand, and I will not be forgiving. Do you understand?”

“Yes.”

I snatched Loretta from his grip. “I want New York cleaned up by dawn. Am I clear?" I tossed him his cell phone. "Make the calls, Paul, the clock is ticking."

Sam and Angelique stealthily weaved their way through the streets of Greenwich Village, avoiding the obvious multitude of police present. The pair headed northeast, across NYU, and finally hailed a cab on Broadway. In reflective silence, the pair stared out the windows as the cab rolled up Third Avenue, eventually passing the scene of the shooting. Several CSI units remained, scouring for evidence, corralled by an abundance of yellow crime scene tape, stretched out only three hours earlier. Sam gazed curiously at the assembly, wondering why she suddenly felt uneasy.

"This where you died," Angelique said somberly.

Sam touched her hand to the glass of the cab as they passed the blood-stained sidewalk.

"Your spirit parted from the body you now inhabit, not the same body as the one it left behind. Nicholas began the transformation; I completed it, and summoned your spirit back. Although you are like us in many ways, your spirit began a journey that none of us have made. In time, you will teach us from your experiences."

"I honestly don't think I'm qualified to teach anything." Her death was all a blur, certainly no memories of any spiritual journey worth repeating. As they passed the crime scene she languished to be held in Nick's strong arms. She hoped the emptiness she was experiencing would be filled by his touch once more. "We should stop here, and walk the rest of the way," Sam suggested. Pointing to the cabbie, she whispered, "If we're on the news, he doesn't need to know where I live."

Waiting for the cab to disappear, before they began the four-block trek, Angelique studied her surroundings. "This is a nice neighborhood."

"Nick worked his butt off for this. I hope tonight does not jeopardize everything he's accomplished. He is very fond of our life here."

Angelique abruptly stopped, and placed her hand on Sam's shoulder. "Samantha, I must apologize, for what I did in New Orleans."

Sam looked oddly at Angelique. After all of the insanity of this night, Angelique's date rape of Nick in New Orleans was the furthest thing from her mind. Last night, there sure would have been a discussion. In New Orleans, they were just two ordinary girls, well at least one, pining over the same guy. Okay, Angelique cheated, twice, and got pregnant, but it all had to be water under the bridge.

"Angelique," Sam hesitated, "you do not need ..."

Angelique chuckled. "Remind me when we have a minute, I have to show you how to close your thoughts."

"So you already know?"

"Yes, your emotions are strong, and you are broadcasting them like you have a megaphone. It is most difficult for me to block what you are thinking. But I do need to apologize. It was wrong of me, regardless of you, to take advantage of Nicholas, or of any man in that manner. I allowed my cravings to control my actions. These are dangerous situations for all of us. Our very existence depends on our ability to control our emotions ... and desires, no matter how strong."

"I have so much to learn. I'm going to need a lot of help." Samantha pointed to the brownstone immediately ahead. "This is our home."

Samantha was apprehensive about seeing Nick. Surely he had suffered for her death, and now he would have to deal with her resurrection ... all of it. As the elevator door opened she found it odd the apartment was mostly dark, with only the study desk dimly lit. "Nick?" Samantha called out. "It doesn't look like anybody is home," Sam announced as she stepped out of the elevator and walked in. Angelique followed, gazing at the spacious, well-furnished apartment, quite different from her home. "Your home is beautiful," Angelique commented, as her fingers glided over a contemporary marble sculpture adorning the living area.

"This was all Nick's work, I think. Seems he has an eye for design, in addition to his other skills."

"Most fascinating," Angelique said as she studied a Chagall hanging near the stairwell. "His taste in art is not unlike his father's."

Samantha reached into the desk drawer, pulled out a new cell phone and dialed Nick's number. On the counter in the kitchen, another phone began to ring. Sam turned eagerly expecting to see Nick had magically appeared from the back of the apartment. Eyeballing the phone, her heart sank. She could not remember the last time Nick left his phone behind. "Something is wrong."

Distraught, Samantha dialed Dee's phone, as she checked the time. The empty ringing echoed through the speaker. "Come on Dee, pick up." If everyone truly believed she had been killed earlier tonight, then there was no way somebody would not answer their phone. Sam dialed Phillip's number as panic built. Surely he would answer. Dee had often complained how he was on call twenty four–seven. Once again, one unanswered ring, echoed by another, and then another. Samantha's heartbeat accelerated.

"Something is terribly wrong. Nobody is picking up their phones."

"Maybe they have gone to sleep."

"Not Nick. And Phillip always answers his phone, no matter what time it is. No, something is definitely wrong." Sam paced to the stairs and then back to the desk, as Angelique observed in silence.

"Do you know why I was shot?"

"Probably the same reason they shot Nick, whatever that might be. All I know is his anguish, both physical and emotional, was so strong that it summoned me, and guided me to you. But he was already gone when I arrived."

"The police were looking for us. Maybe they have picked up Dee and Phillip. Maybe Nick is with them as well," Sam guessed. "What should we do?"

"We should do nothing. If the police are looking for you, or more specifically, your body, and me, the last thing we should do is waltz into the precinct to be detained until sunrise."

"Well, I can't just stay here, and wait, and hope they are all all right. What if the killer was looking for them as well? What if they've been shot?" Vampire or not, Samantha's stomach was knotted with concern.

Angelique thought briefly. "We can try your sister's home, but we should hurry. One of the most important things you must always bear in mind, sunrise is no longer a thing of beauty. It is not forgiving. The sun's rays will scorch your flesh like an inferno that will not turn loose of you. You must always be conscious of this and allow sufficient time to return to the safety of your casket."

"You sleep in a casket?" Sam was surprised to discover a vampire that followed the customs of old legend.

"Yes, I do," Angelique replied in a righteous tone. "Are you telling me Nicholas and Gabrielle do not follow tradition?"

"No, we don't," Samantha confessed with a slight stutter, suddenly feeling awkward of their sleeping arrangements. "Do you want to see?"

As they approached the bedroom, just beyond the door, a tall unkempt man entered the apartment from the private elevator. "As there is no door, can I come in?"

Samantha and Angelique froze, surprised by his sudden appearance.

"My name is Detective Logan, I know it's late, but I have a few questions, if you don't mind. It doesn't look like you were headed off to bed anyhow, not with the elevator unlocked. Are you expecting company?"

Angelique cut a sharp look at the detective. She did not trust the police, especially one as scraggly as this.

Sam, much more diplomatic, put on her warm and inviting face. "It is late, detective. What can I do for you at this hour?"

"Can you tell me your name?"

"It is Samantha," she replied, intentionally omitting her last name.

"Do you have a last name Samantha?" Annoyed by her deliberate vagueness, his tone was demanding.

"I do, but it is late, and until I know what business this concerns, I have no intention of sharing much more information."

At two in the morning, Logan was in no mood to put up with any shenanigans. "How about if I drag both of you down to the precinct first, then I'll think about letting you in on what this is about."

Angelique, ready to deal with the detective on her terms, inched closer. She was in no disposition to tolerate his arrogant and dominant attitude. Sensing Angelique's aggression rise, Samantha interceded, moving her body between Angelique and the detective.

"Detective, unless you feel an overwhelming need to falsely arrest us, we are quite fine remaining here."

"Oh, I am quite sure I can find enough probable cause to arrest you," he said as he inched into the foyer.

Samantha thrust her hand against his chest. "Do you have a warrant to come in my home?"

Logan was infuriated by her obstinance. Throughout his life, he was accustomed to using bully tactics to accomplish his goals. He was not about to let two Upper East Side ho-ho's get in his way of solving the case tonight. Logan grabbed Samantha's hand. "That's assault lady, now you are going for a ride." Pushing her to the wall, preparing for a cuff and frisk, he began to break into his Miranda rights recital.

Sam immediately pushed Logan back to the doorway. "Assault? You do not enter my home without a warrant."

Logan took two steps back and drew his Glock. "On the floor, bitch," he ordered.

Angelique's smile broadened. If this pathetic man only knew what he was actually dealing with. Instinctively intimidated by the initial appearance of a gun, Samantha stepped back and cowered in defense.

"I said, on the floor, both of you."

Samantha began to drop to her knees, but Angelique stood defiantly, smiling all the while, happy he had not made the call for back up. Logan was going to thoroughly enjoy taking these two down. "Are you deaf lady, or just stupid?" Logan waved his gun in Angelique's direction.

"Samantha, get up. This ignorant little man can bring you no harm." Angelique began walking slowly in the direction of the detective. "As I told you, there are a great many things for you to learn."

"Lady, one more step and I will drop you," Logan warned, his voice suddenly lacking the confidence of his previous demand. Logan took aim.

Before Logan could pull the trigger, his hand was left empty by Angelique's light-speed reflexes. She thrust him back against the wall, elevated about a foot in the air, with her hands compressed around his throat. Instantly his face turned red, as Angelique glared in contempt.

"You insignificant worm of a man. Tonight is indeed your lucky night, for you will live to see sunrise again. Angelique snarled, exposing her razor sharp fangs. "Yes, you know what I am. In your deepest fears you know what I will do"

Logan's eyes filled with terror as Angelique explored the depth of his fears. Telepathically, she filled his mind with dreadful images, death beyond realms of human comprehension.

"Yes," Angelique purred, "You can feel the pain of your lifeless body passing to the abyss." Angelique turned and smiled at Samantha, lesson one in progress. "You will forget our paths ever crossed or I—will—kill—you, not just once, but a hundred times, each much more painful than the previous."

With his mind invaded by Angelique's visions of morbid atrocities all he could do was plead, "Please, no ..." The words escaped from the python-like grip of Angelique's hand. Tears rolled out of his eyes as his body trembled with fear.

Angelique released Logan without warning. He dropped to the floor and gasped for air. Angelique crouched down next to him. "If you would like to leave and live out your days without my attention, now would be the time. But I warn you, if you bring trouble, there will be nowhere to hide and no mercy offered."

Logan rose to his feet, then stumbled against the wall and into the elevator. "See to it that your people do not feel it necessary to call on this place, ever again," Angelique warned as the elevator doors closed.

"That was amazing," Sam exclaimed. "Aren't you worried he will return with the entire police department?"

"No, he will not return. You will learn in time, how to strike fear so deep in the mortal mind that it will permeate for years in the subconscious mind, creating the most dreadful nightmares."

"I know those dreams."

"In time, you will learn to conquer them."

Captain Patrick grabbed the phone on his desk at four twenty in the morning as two federal agents swiftly approached his office.

"Thanks for the heads up, but I think you're a minute too late," he said as he hung up the phone. He had somewhat expected a federal intrusion as potential roadblock, but certainly not before regular office hours.

"Gentlemen," Patrick called out, as he stepped out of his office to greet them. Had he had adequate warning, he would have slipped down the back stairs to buy his detectives a few more hours of investigative time. But cornered like a rat, he prepared for a dose of federal jurisdictional bullshit. "What can the NYPD do for you?

The two feds looked at each other, the taller, younger of the two, nodded to the older agent. The dark-skinned black man with cotton white hair and gold rimless glasses cleared his throat. Unexpectedly soft-spoken, he introduced himself. "I am special agent Reid, and this is special agent Wilson. We should talk in your office."

"Agent Reid, I have no secrets from my squad. I assure you, whatever you have to say will be fully disclosed to each of them as expeditiously as possible."

"Very well sir. We are here concerning the murder investigation assigned to your precinct. Your investigation involves an undercover agent, and matters of national security. I have in my possession written orders from Homeland Security demanding you hand over all evidence, including all forensic reports, evidence, corpses, suspects, and witness list. In essence, absolutely every shred of information you have collected connected with this investigation. You are also ordered to cease-and-desist any further investigation into the matter. Any evidence collected from this point on will be handed over immediately upon its discovery. There is to be no discussion, leaking of any details, or any further inquiries into this matter, by you, or any one within the New York City Police Department. Do you understand these orders as presented?"

"Agent Reid, I understand the positions of Homeland Security completely, but let me make one thing clear. Two murders, that we know of, took place within my jurisdiction. I have an obligation to make sure criminals are brought to justice. If you have a loose cannon out there, I will not turn my back on further criminal activity. If I find out at any time you or your department have compromised the safety of my city, or integrity of our judicial system, I promise you, I will hang your ass out to dry. Do you completely understand my position?"

Reid stared down Patrick for a good thirty seconds without speaking a word.

"You don't want to play this game," Patrick stated firmly. "Not in my house."

"Fair enough, Captain," Reid answered.

Patrick bellowed out, "People, I want all files, records, memos, emails, anything relating to the mutant murders, on this desk." He pounded on the first desk just outside his office to accentuate the location. "Within ten minutes. So move it, people."

Patrick leaned in toward Reid's ear. "The female victim looked like an innocent bystander. I don't know what kind of federal bullshit went down tonight, but just between you and me, somebody will go down for her murder."

Patrick turned and strutted into his office, slamming the door in his wake.

I walked the streets of Arlington in a stupor. The sun would be rising in a few hours and I had not made the call to the helicopter. It was past four, and I did not want to talk to Phillip or Gabrielle, and certainly not Dee.

A sickening depression had set in. One the likes of which I had never experienced. I was tired. Tired of life. The thought of walking the streets until sunrise crossed my mind. An excruciating, agonizing death was no less than I deserved. To burn for my sins seemed quite appropriate.

But there was work still to be finished. I needed to go back to New York, and put my finances in order for Gabrielle, Angelique, and my son. I needed to make sure Watson had put the investigation to sleep, that no further complications would arise for my friends left behind. Just one or two miserably painful days to wrap things up.

I called the pilot. The next call was more painful, not in the favor I was about to request, but reliving the failure that created these circumstances. The phone rang three times. On the fourth ring, a grumpy voice answered. "It's me. Remember the job you promised you would do?"

As expected, without question, the voice replied, "Yes."

"It is time. I will send you the location. ASAP."

There was a silence on the other end. I was not sure if my message was heard, or if signal was lost.

Very uncharacteristically the voice simply asked, "Why."

"It is complicated. Just do it. You owe me that much. Instructions will follow." I hung up the phone.

Never once had Chuck questioned orders. After Miami, he thought circumstances had changed, that his obligation to fulfill the task would be forgotten. For Chuck, killing came easy, but this time ... He had sworn an oath, and with the request he knew something had gone dreadfully wrong. But what?

Chuck jumped from bed and threw on his clothes. A deep sultry voice moaned from the opposite side of the bed. Chuck looked over to the naked woman lying there, mostly unconscious from the binge drinking earlier in the night. His drinking; methodological escapism from the emptiness. Hers: he didn't care. They had a good drunken fuck. He thought about Brian and Sam. *What the hell, Brian?*

He finished lacing his size fourteen sneakers, and tossed on a clean t-shirt. Opening the closet door, Chuck grabbed the duffle bag, pre-packed and ready to go. He checked his phone for texts, sure enough, it was already there ... one word, *Apple*. Chuck was headed to New York. He grabbed the pre-packed FedEx box from the top shelf. Looking through a directory, he chose a pick-up location in Manhattan, and scribbled it down on the shipping tag. He grabbed an envelope containing a large amount of cash, and his car keys, then flipped off the lights. The blonde in the bed rolled over and moaned. Chuck thought about waking her, but they had enjoyed a good fuck, and that would have to be enough. He walked out the door, quietly pulling it closed as he passed. Time to put personal feelings aside. Time to go to work. Time to kill his friend.

CHAPTER TWENTY

THE SUN HAD finally set. Samantha had anxiously awaited the new nightfall, unable to sleep. Phillip's apartment had been unoccupied, and much to her chagrin, she had conceded to return to Angelique's apartment for the day. She was ready to find Nick ... and her sister. She could not wait to tell them she was alive. Sure, cynics would complain she was now the living dead, but she never had felt this vibrant ... and powerful.

Angelique awoke shortly after nightfall. Her needs were not as pressing as Samantha's. She began her usual routine of tending to her child, which generally included spending three or four hours with him before sending him off for bed. Angelique had considered keeping him up through the night, but she was unsure about putting him on a schedule that would preclude him from interacting with children his age. To this point, he was mortal in most aspects, just as his father had been.

Samantha did not want to interfere with Angelique's routine, but she was becoming anxious beyond the point of containment. She was not entirely comfortable about venturing out alone, so she patiently waited as Angelique went about her motherly duties.

With all of the transitions and events of the previous night, Samantha had absentmindedly left the cell phone back at her home. As

Angelique did not own a phone of any sort, Samantha was becoming impatient from being disconnected. Eventually, at five past eleven, Samantha decided to voice a small protest.

"Angelique, I need to see my family."

Angelique, while changing Brian's diaper, smiled at her new friend's manufactured anxiety. "You can go without me. Just try to avoid any major interactions with people, as much as possible. It is imperative you remain aware of your shortcomings. If you notice somebody focusing on your lack of reflection, you must concentrate very hard. You can force them to look away, like I showed you last night. And mind your strength, you are stronger and faster than any human you will encounter. Try to ensure that remains our little secret." Angelique picked up Brian. "Give your step-mom a kiss." She held the baby out for Samantha to coddle. "With that in mind, I suggest you start by simply walking out the door. Take your time. At any time if you feel uncomfortable, you can always come back. I will remain here tonight."

"Do you really think I am ready to go out there?" Samantha hugged the baby tightly and kissed his cheeks repeatedly. With so many caveats to consider, Samantha's nervousness was uncharacteristic for her ... or a vampire.

"I am confident you are ready," Angelique reassured as she retrieved Brian.

Samantha turned and headed to the door. She looked back to Angelique.

"Go," Angelique insisted.

Sam closed the door of the apartment, the clicking latch announcing her departure into the uncertainty of a new life. "Oh boy," she said softly. "I thought this would be a lot easier."

The cool autumn air distracted her self-doubt momentarily. So many scents. The world of night exploded in vivid hues. "This is so beautiful," she spoke softly. Whereas last night, everything seemed to run together in confusing heaps of incoming stimulation, tonight things seemed to process in some type of auto sort. Sam could hear the conversation of four women half way down the block, all wearing different perfumes. And in a single instant, she knew which one she wanted.

In a panic, she turned and hurried back into the apartment. The urge to feed had swept over her, taking her completely unprepared. She quickly re-entered the building. Her heart was racing and she was out of breath, as if she had just sprinted around the block. "How in the world did Nick and Gabby do it? How did they manage to fight off the incredible urge to feed?"

Samantha recomposed herself, taking in several deep breaths. There were only two viable options. The first was to go back upstairs, cower in the apartment like a child, and maybe have a pint to stave off the desire. The other choice was to suck it up and force herself to be more than just another bloodsucking night crawler. She wanted to make Nick proud.

With one final deep breath, Samantha headed back into the breezy cool night. To the right was uptown, her home. Phillip also had a smaller place uptown, although he and Dee spent most of their time in the large apartment he owned down past Wall Street. After last night's encounter, Samantha decided it would be more prudent to head downtown and see if they had returned. If so, they could help her reconnect with Nick.

She thought about hailing a cab, but the thought of dealing with a cabbie without Angelique's assistance was not appealing. At least not yet. Pondering the whereabouts of her friends, Samantha quickened her pace, which was already exceptionally fast, but effortless to maintain. As she zigzagged the streets to the Lower East Side, she approached the vicinity of the Brooklyn Bridge. A familiar scent drifted through the air. As a mortal it was almost undetectable prior to her transformation. It was the scent of her own kind, the uninhibited scent of a vampire. She looked around curiously.

Sam pressed on toward Phillip's.

"I don't know you," an eerie voice called, uncomfortably close behind.

Sam reeled around. "Should you?"

"I know all of our kind, which demands I inquire, who are you?" The lanky, scruffy young man approached.

"I am no concern to you," Sam said, then turned to walk away. She knew she was no match for any of her own kind. She did not know how to block her thoughts. She did not know how to defend herself. She knew what it felt like when Nick invaded her mind, and wanted to ensure this stranger did not have the opportunity to do the same.

The gangly vampire did not attempt to restrain her, but jumped alongside and began to walk with her. "I am Maltor. And it is very much my concern when another enters our home."

"Well Maltor, I am Diane. And as I told you, I am no concern to you, or your clan. I am here to see an old friend. Then I will leave." Sam felt his attempt to enter her thoughts. In doing so, he revealed himself to her. "Milton Powell," she barked. "That is very rude."

"I am sorry," he replied timidly.

Sam perceived his deficiencies concluding that this less-than-confident man was as newly minted a vampire as she.

"Very well ... Maltor. I am here from New Orleans to visit my family, who are not like us. I have no intentions of infringing on your territory, or partaking in the blood of the living on my visit."

"Very well. I hope you understand, I must ask these questions," he said with a slight smile.

"It is good you protect your family." Samantha realized she had either stumbled on Sabine's family, or possibly another sect created by her.

"Is your family nearby?" Instantly, Samantha felt as though her prodding might cause alarm.

Maltor did not seem to be concerned with her intentions. He pointed to the bridge. "We live in Brooklyn."

"As I do not wish to offend your family, I will remain a good distance from your territory."

"It's okay. But if you happen to stay in town a little longer, I would love for you to meet my family. We always have a sentry here. Tell them you are my friend and they will bring you to our home."

"This trip is short, but perhaps the next time I will." Happy to be escaping without an incident, Samantha turned her head as she began to walk away and called out, "Thank you, Maltor."

Gangly on the outside, nerdy on the inside. So vampirism did not change everything for everyone. With the discovery of Maltor, it was a small conciliation to know not every female vampire that might cross Nick's path would be drop dead gorgeous.

Phillip stood by the window, staring out at the East River. Twenty-four hours had passed, and it was just past midnight, and there was no word from Brian, or the pilot. Dee was lying on the couch, her head on Gabrielle's lap. As he was never good at uncomfortable moments of extreme emotional anguish, he was thankful for Gabrielle's assistance. And as far as he could imagine, things could not possibly be any worse than this. Samantha was dead, her body missing, the news of which he would eventually have to share with his distraught friend, if he ever resurfaced. Phillip's source in the police department had informed him the case was shut down by Homeland Security, America's version of the Nazi SS. Things were destined to get worse from here. He cringed as a new volley of sobbing began from the couch. "Dee honey, you need some sleep. Let me get you an Ambien," Phillip suggested.

"No, I need to work through this," Dee insisted. "I have to get it together. Mom and Dad will be here tomorrow. I have to be strong for them."

Gabrielle looked at Phillip and with a slow nod of her head signaled she was capable of putting Dee to sleep.

Phillip shook off her proposal. Even though he honestly could use some sleep himself, he needed to honor his wife's wishes. The events of the last two days had left him depleted beyond sanity. "Okay, baby. I just thought you might fare better tomorrow if you got a little sleep."

It had barely been two years since they met. Two years ago, when she looked into his mischievous eyes and thought there's no way this guy's for me. Casanova playboy, immature, and totally uncommitted to anything of moral value, except his business, he was never supposed to be anything more than a weekend fling. Now she could not imagine any guy better equipped to fill his shoes. Dee wiped the flow of tears from her face and sat up.

"Phil, why don't you take an Ambien?" Dee walked over to the window and snuggled to his side. "You need the sleep as bad as I do."

Phillip cracked a weak smile, and shook his head. "I will sleep when you do."

"Both of you go lay down. I will get you if anything happens," Gabrielle offered.

As they headed to the bedroom, Dee's knees buckled and she fell into Phillip. "I feel so weak."

"As you should be. You have not eaten all day." Phillip wrapped his arms tightly around Dee's waist.

Dee steadied herself with his shoulders. "Would you carry me if I asked?"

"Tonight, and the rest of your life ... if you asked."

"You're such a suck-up, Phillip." Dee faked a smile; it was the best she could manage at the moment.

Gabrielle smiled at the pair. Quite the couple to envy; kind-hearted, playful, generous, and sexy, all wrapped into one unified soul. They had forced Gabrielle to set her bar high when seeking companionship, which to this point was why she had no man in her life.

"If you hear any news, no matter how small, come get me," Phillip instructed.

As they moved toward the bedroom, the sound of Dee's feet shuffling across the hardwood floors was disrupted by a knocking. All three turned their attention to the door. At this hour, it was either the authorities or Brian, Phillip thought. If the police had found and ID'd Samantha's body, they would have waited until the morning to call. Phillip's office would have sent a text message. "Please God, don't let it be Homeland Security," Phillip whispered as he moved toward the door. Brian's familiar face would be most welcome, he thought. Phillip unlocked the two deadbolts, and began to address the overdue friend he hoped was on the other side. "It is about damn time you showed up."

Had Phillip been an older man, a massive heart attack would have been in order. He muttered the only word he could manage to assimilate, "Sam?"

Dee's eyes flew open wide. On the verge of collapse, she staggered her way to the door. "Sam?"

Dee pushed Phillip aside making her way to her sister. "Oh my God!" she exclaimed as she hugged her tightly. "I don't understand ... how can you be ...?"

Sam pushed away from her sister. An incredibly searing pain penetrated her chest. She pushed away farther. Initially dumbfounded by the excruciating pain, within seconds she realized the source. Underneath her shirt, Dee wore the sterling cross that once protected Nick. He had insisted Dee and Phillip wear them, knowing at least two vampires potentially remained in the city.

Cursed by God. Okay, so maybe one of Nick's reservations against converting her was somewhat justifiable.

"Dee … your cross." Momentarily stunned by the pain in her chest, Samantha turned her head away while collecting her wits.

Gabrielle rushed to the door, instantly recognizing the scent of another. "Samantha, how did this happen?"

Dee and Phillip were oblivious as to Gabrielle's insinuations, but Samantha understood immediately. Wired by this new bond, Gabrielle's intentions were crystal clear. Lowering her face to the floor, shamed by the event completely out of her control, Samantha confessed solemnly, "I am a vampire."

Appalled by her confession, or in shock from seeing the resurrected dead, or completely physically and emotionally spent, Dee and Phillip were lost in an unresponsive stupor.

Accepting the news as if Samantha had just confessed to buying a new purse, Gabrielle chirped, "But of course you are." She grabbed Samantha by the arm, as she had playfully done so many times before and led her in. Sensing Samantha's needs, Gabrielle led her to the couch. "Sit. I'll be right back."

In silence, Dee sat beside Samantha while Phillip remained standing in front of her with his arms crossed. Feeling weak and disoriented, Samantha was fearful of the sudden changes within her body.

Gabrielle returned from the kitchen with a glass of deep burgundy blood. "Drink, you will feel much better. I promise."

Samantha did as instructed. Within seconds, the effects of the blood had rejuvenated her strength. "Thank you, I guess I didn't realize what was wrong."

"Yes," Gabrielle confessed. "You are new to this. Everything we are comes from the blood. If we deprive our body of it, well you understand now, don't you?"

"She just drank blood!" The raw emotional hemorrhage Dee had suffered over the last twenty-four hours, including the total lack of sleep, erupted into an ear piercing screech. "Phillip, please tell me I'm not dreaming … or haven't completely lost my mind."

Ignoring her sister's temporary meltdown, Samantha closed her eyes and enjoyed the sensation; streams of energized blood passing through the veins of her body. She drew in a deep breath, and gradually opened her eyes.

Giddy with Samantha's situation, and already knowing the answer, Gabrielle felt compelled to ask, "It is better than sex, yes?"

The thought of sex, slapped Samantha back to reality from her euphoric high. "Where is Nick?"

"Nick?" Dee asked in a scratchy tone. "He's out wreaking terror and havoc on those responsible for your death. You are dead, aren't you? I don't believe you understand the magnitude of what's taking place here. You are dead and Mom and Dad will be here tomorrow to help plan your funeral, even though we don't know where your body is. But that's because you're here and not in the morgue where you're supposed to be ..."

Phillip placed his hand on Dee's shoulder. "Honey, you are hysterical. She is alive, sort of."

Samantha grabbed Dee's hands, her pulse racing uncontrollably. Gabrielle, seeing Samantha's concerned expression, walked behind Dee, placed her hands around Dee's forehead, and began to whisper in hushed tones in her ear. Almost immediately, the tension in Dee's body released, her eyes rolled back into her head, and she slumped over.

"Everything will be fine. I just gave her a Romanian sedative."

Within a minute, Dee's eyes popped open and searched her sister's eyes. Tears filled the darkened sockets. "Oh God, you are really alive."

"In a loosely defined sense of the word, yes."

"How, how did it happen? Nick saw you die. The police said you were dead. We saw the news."

"I don't know exactly how any of it happened. Angelique told me I had died and that Nick tried to save me, but he couldn't. Somehow Angelique, through Nick's thoughts, knew what happened and where to find me. She resurrected me with some ancient ritual that brought me back from the dead as a vampire."

"Are you sure?" Phillip asked.

Sam parted her lips. A new set of glistening white fangs adorned her otherwise perfect smile.

"Things could be worse," Gabrielle chirped happily.

"Oh my God," Dee sighed. "You are."

There was a brief moment of silence as each gauged the other's reaction. Dee tossed her cross and hugged her sister forcefully. "I can't begin to tell you how happy I am you're alive, even if you are a vampire," she said, as she pulled back to look her sister in the eyes.

"Everything is going to be fine, Dee, different, but fine."

"You have to tell me everything," Dee insisted eagerly.

"Whoa Nellie, not so fast," Phillip interceded. "Dee baby, you have to get some sleep. Sam can give you all of the details later."

Samantha looked at her sister's distraught face. "Phillip is right, Dee. Get some sleep. We can talk tomorrow."

Phillip took Dee by the hand and helped her to her feet. Samantha grabbed Phillip's hand before he could lead Dee away. "Phillip, where is Nick?"

"Things got pretty ugly last night. It seems that the police had several videos of Brian, running at speeds well beyond human capacity and climbing a brick wall like Spiderman. The man who was suspected of the shooting was savagely murdered. Needless to say, your boyfriend is the number one suspect, even though numerous witnesses testified to the injuries the shooter inflicted, which they claimed no man could have survived. Then, to ice the cake, your body went AWOL. That is just enough special circumstances to warrant a full-blown media circus. Brian said he knew a man in Washington who could fix things. He flew down there last night. I have not heard from him, or my pilot, since."

"No phones?"

"*Nada*," Phillip answered. "I have a guy watching your home and by the way, so do the police, but he has not shown his face yet. And I do not know where in the hell my pilot or my helicopter got off to."

"I have to find him," Samantha said with an air of desperation. "If he knew they were watching our home, where do you think he would he go?"

Phillip thought but a second. He shook his head. He knew he would get a major ass-kicking from Brian if he let the secret out of the bag, but to hell with it. After the events of the last two days, Brian would just have to get over it. "About five blocks from here, there is a vacant building on the river. He bought it about six months ago."

"Are you sure? Nick never mentioned buying any building to

me."

"Quite sure. It was supposed to be a surprise wedding gift for you." Phillip had a sinking ship sensation. He knew how much Brian had looked forward to the day when Samantha would finally get to see the finished project.

"What's the address? I need to see if he is there." Sam asked eagerly.

"You know, to be honest, I do not know. But I can take you there, as soon as I get Dee to bed."

"Don't think for a minute you're going without me, Mister Wilder. I might be exhausted, but there's no way I'm going to miss my sister's coming out confession."

"I will go as well," Gabrielle chimed in. "The streets are not safe tonight, even for a vampire."

Nick stared out the picture glass window at the reflections of the city, shimmering on the waters of the East River. "You are late," he announced, without turning to greet the man approaching from behind.

"Sorry man, I waited for the blue light special at Kmart for vampire stakes and mallets, but you might know, those were the two items they never put on sale." The familiar voice was laced with sarcasm. "I didn't want to overpay, you know how thrifty I am. I hate paying too much for stuff I don't plan on using but once."

I could not help but smile, just a little at the idiot. "So?"

"I had to buy them here. It's nothing I want to be seen traveling with. Just imagine the scene at TSA," Chuck waved a black leather bag containing the necessary tools. "So, I see, Mr. Smith, you are a vampire hunter. Do you prefer oak or ash stakes for the kill?"

"Yeah, yeah, whatever." I interrupted what was sure to become a drawn out over dramatized recounting of the entire experience. "Can we just get this done?"

"Whatever boss," Chuck snapped back, with a hint of seriousness as he surveyed the open loft. "Nice building, is it yours?"

"Sam always enjoyed the river. I bought this and was fixing it up, kind of a wedding present." I looked out over the river to Brooklyn. How much I desired to see Sam's face light up the very first time she saw her new home. In the window's reflection, I saw Chuck moving nearer.

"Well since you are not going to be needing it anymore, wanna give me a good deal on it?"

"Sure." I knew Chuck would not appreciate the passionate hours spent over every painstaking detail created thus far, but what else was I to do with the place?

"How many days will it take to do the real estate transfer?"

I knew what big man was doing. I walked over to the architectural designer's table. I grabbed a pen and scribbled instructions on a piece of paper. Chuck looked on as I wrote.

"Done." I handed him instructions to give to Phillip. I basically had willed Phillip all of my possessions, relying on him to disburse them to the designated people on the list I had prepared. "There's a briefcase over there," I pointed to the weathered brown leather case sitting by the window. "Take it with you. Tomorrow, if you follow all the instructions explicitly, this place will be yours."

Chuck glanced around the half completed loft again. "Brian, I don't think ..."

"Chuck, do not try to change my mind, it is made up." I had already prepared for this debate in my head. Chuck was like a brother, and although I knew he would follow through, I knew he would not do so without exhausting all other options.

"Listen, if I'm going to do this, then you have to hear me out. You are the closest thing I have to family, and I ain't gonna do it, unless you convince me otherwise." Chuck dropped his bag on the table heavily. "I know you're hurt'n man, Sam's gone and there ain't nothing that's gonna bring her back. But you're not the first to lose a loved one. People move on, they do get over it. And you, I mean come on, Brian, you're like the man that's got it all. You've got money, looks, you're smart," Chuck paused to inventory his memorized list of possible attributes. "You've got more power than any man that walks the planet. You can have any woman you desire. And, as a bonus, let's not forget, you're fucking immortal."

"You are right, my friend, except the one woman I loved most is gone."

"Gone," Chuck quipped. "Don't take this wrong, Brian, I don't mean to belittle Sam's death. Sam was awesome, but there are others to fill her shoes. Hell, somewhere out there, in time, you'll find one or maybe even two that will rock your world. Trust me, I know. And to top it all off, you have all eternity to find them."

I sighed. He was right, from a purely logical point of view. But Sam's blood was on my hands. There was no getting over that, and I had all eternity to remember it.

"Chuck, I know you will not understand this and until I met Sam, I didn't either. Until it happens, you can't." I collected my thoughts. "You and I have known many women, no doubt. But what happens between two people, takes place on different levels, mentally, emotionally, spiritually, and physically. But typically, at least it never did for me, it never encompassed every aspect all in one. If you take every sappy love song you have ever heard and wrap it into a feeling, it is only a fraction of how I felt about Sam." Tears formed, but an underlying bitterness cut the flow, and suppressed the watery results. "I can't breathe without her. There is no rest, no peace, no color in my life. I see no potential for joy in anything, ever again. I am terrified of what I will surely become without her.

"And do you think this is what Sam would want you to do? If the shoe were on the other foot, is this what you would want her to do?"

"Of course not. But it was my love for Sam that made this fucked-up life of mine tolerable. I have to fight my instincts every day. I do not drink blood merely because I need the nourishment, I crave living blood like a heroine addict yearns a fix. Every waking hour, I battle the urge to feed on humans for the mere pleasure of it."

"So if you are ready to end your life, then end it like a rock star. Go out and do what it is you were born to do. There are a lot of bad people out there. Take as many as you can, before they figure out how to kill you." Chuck pulled the stake and mallet from the bag. "This ain't no way to do it. You're a soldier, man. Go out like a soldier."

"I am tired of killing, Chuck. How many have we killed? I don't want to kill anyone anymore. I don't want to be anything. I am just worn thin by death."

"All those tyrants we dusted, look at all the lives we saved, all the good that was accomplished. We killed to keep our country safe."

"We killed to serve a political agenda generally unknown to us. They told us to kill, and we did ... not because of the agenda, but because we liked to."

"You think it was all bogus?" Chuck asked, his temper starting to show.

"Enough was."

"What is that supposed to mean?" Chuck bled red, white and blue, a Marine to the core, and any mission, legit or not, as long as it was sanctioned by Uncle Sam it was righteous by his book.

"Come on Chuck, you had to know the difference between night and day ops, and back in the day we could care less. But remember, I told you how I terminated American operatives, simply because I was told to. Guys like you, Rob, and Jimmy because they had allegedly gone bad. I know better now, we weren't meant to survive and now there's guys like you and me, looking to take us out. This whole game we played, the one that cost Sam her life, in the end is all about corporate American bullshit.

"Come on, Brian, that's fucked-up nonsense ... and you know it." Chuck objected forcefully.

"Colombia, 1994, remember that trip?" I knew I had to push Chuck's anger if I was going to ever get him to comply with the purpose of this visit.

"I remember them all," Chuck replied sharply. "We lost a few good soldiers that day," he said somberly.

"We were set up. None of us were supposed to return from that mission."

"Bullshit," Chuck said defiantly.

"Think about it Chuck. We got hit with sniper fire long before we reached the coke lab. And not by randomly hired guns, those guys were good. When did we ever run up against shooters like that day?" I pointed out.

Chuck thought long and hard.

"How many guys do you know older than you? There aren't any. Last night we got ambushed by a CIA assassin. And the psycho plane chick, she was a spook hitter. I got proof last night. It's not a random thing, it's fucking company policy. All the shit in your head is information Uncle Sam can ill afford you ever sharing, with anyone. You'll have a target on your back one day, just like me, my friend."

Chuck stood in brief silence. "Motherfuckers!" he proclaimed grimacing at the thought. "Our own people wasted you and Sam last night?"

"Yeah, I got it straight from Paul Watson's mouth last night. I called you from DC after I left his home."

"I hope you wasted that piece of shit."

"That is exactly what I had intended to do when I flew down there. But you know, it would not change a thing. And to be honest, Chuck, I have already killed enough people for ten lifetimes. I am over it. It's my turn." I held my hands out. "You can't see it, but there's too much blood here to turn back."

"Do you mind if I go kill the prick? We barely got out of Colombia alive."

"It is time to let it go, Chuck. Take your money and disappear. If you need a thrill, take up base jumping or something dangerous."

Chuck extracted the mallet and stake from the bag. "Hey Brian, why don't we spend a couple of days together, have some beers and raise some hell. I'll bet Jimmy will come out for one last throw-down. Then we can do this crazy shit." Chuck fingered the tip of the stake, ensuring its point was sharp to his satisfaction.

"We had our sendoff in New Orleans, Chuck."

"I know, but I'll bet a few days to rethink things will clear your head. You need to grieve, then you need to laugh. We do this now, it's just over man, no turning back."

"I appreciate the love, Chuck, but I knew back in New Orleans this day would come. I did not think the road traveled would have been this painful, but it is what it is." I sat on the floor and then laid back. "Just do it, Chuck, no regrets."

"I don't guess there's any chance you might, you know ... share that vampire immortality stuff with me, before you go?" He had a sheepish grin, but he was not kidding.

"Just get this over with Chuck. I am tired." I knew if I ignored his request it would avoid another lengthy delay in the inevitable end. "Do you want me to roll over?"

"Nope, only a pussy would stake you in the back." He knelt down at my side. "I thought about that all of the way out here. If you were terminal, I would do it, and I know you would do it for me. So no, I don't have a problem looking you in the eye."

I took his hand grasping the stake and guided it over my heart. "Right here."

"Hey dipshit, I know where it is, I shot enough guys in the heart to know."

"Well do me a huge favor, bro, smack it hard. I really prefer if you did not have to whack it three or four times. I am sure it's gonna hurt like hell."

Chuck looked away one last time and took a deep breath. "You know something, Brian? There must have been something to that golden rule thing. I mean think about it. Both times you fucked a girl on a plane you got totally screwed."

"Thanks, Chuck, I'll keep that in mind as you're killing me. I appreciate that, bro."

"Last chance," Chuck declared, as he raised the mallet, and clenched his grip. The muscles in his biceps flared as he prepared to strike down with a mighty blow. "Brian, I'll see you in hell one fine day. Tell Rob I said hello."

"I almost forgot," I interrupted. "There's an Iron Key flash drive on the blueprint table. There is all kinds of interesting information on it. Use it wisely."

"What's the password?" Chuck sighed, annoyed with my interruption.

"Politicians, drug dealers, and girlfriends." This was a catchphrase we had used many times over the years, which always prompted the same response.

"Fuck em all!" Chuck replied with a scoffing laugh.

"There you go." I smiled at the last half of the catch phrase we had used so many times over the years, and befitting of tonight. How many times we had both sung it out loudly, even in the bleakest of situations. I knew these would be the last words I ever spoke. "What else are you gonna do on a Friday night?"

Chuck cocked his arm back, but hesitated. Just as his arm went into motion, my eye caught a glimpse of the elevator call button illuminating. Someone was here. I did not want to leave Chuck with an unpleasant predicament, especially if the police had tracked me down. Chuck's arm was driving downward, the mallet targeting the head of the stake. With reflexes much faster than his, I threw my hand up, blocking Chuck's forearm.

Inertia. Two granite forces on a collision course. Something had to give. Bones splintered as the mallet connected with its target.

CHAPTER TWENTY-ONE

"SHIT," CHUCK GRASPED his arm and wailed as the mallet tumbled across the floor.

"Elevator," I coughed spitting blood, the pain rocketing through my chest. Still clutching the stake, I looked down to the source of pain. Penetrated and bleeding, I knew from experience, my end would be quick. I looked back to the elevator.

Whispering profanities, Chuck disappeared from sight as the elevator drew near. With my eyes trained on doors, I could smell the humans.

The doors parted, and Phillip and Dee were appalled by the sight of me on the floor, stake in my chest, blood on my shirt. Gabrielle appeared from behind. Simultaneously, they gasped.

"Brian," Phillip screamed, while Dee cried out, "Oh God, no!"

Next I saw what I thought was an angelic vision— Sam peering around the door. With an expression of morbid fear etched on her otherwise perfect face, this phantasm was nothing but a cruel reality of hell's welcoming committee.

"Nick," Sam cried out as she pushed her way past my stunned friends and ran to my side.

"No!" she cried again as she stroked my face.

Surely in the clutches of death, my last glimpse of life was a bittersweet vision. Sam appeared more youthful, and if it were possible, more perfect than I remembered. My eyes searched every aspect of her face, committing each and every detail to memory.

As Sam's tears cascaded down, she caught the slightest movement of my eye. "Nick!" She shouted. "You're alive?"

"No, Sam. If you are with me, then we are both dead." Was this just beginning my eternal damnation, nothing but a sadistic trifling? Better to drive her away now than spend millenniums being tormented.

"Of course he's alive," Chuck called out from across the room. "The asshole broke my arm, if anyone cares," he added, in dramatic tones. "But what the hell are you doing alive, Sam?"

Chuck's words hit me like a bucket of ice water. I gasped for air. Sam looked down, grabbed the stake and pulled firmly. I arched my back in agony, as she withdrew it from my ribs. Apparently, as Chuck began to swing the mallet, the collision of our arms redirected the razor sharp spear through my ribs and into my lung—missing my heart.

Blood pooled on my chest and Sam placed her hand over the wound. I was speechless. The woman was dead in my arms one night ago. And there was nothing I could do to save her. Now, here she was saving *me.* I gritted my teeth in pain, but allowed her name to pass my clenched teeth. "Sam?"

"Don't talk," she instructed me. "Help me," she cried out, not knowing if my wound was fatal.

Gabrielle jumped in to assist, pulling Sam's hand away and studied the injury.

"No," she began. After further examining the wound, her signature impish smile returned. "This will not kill him." She placed Sam's hand over the wound. "Keep the pressure firm."

Sam's face instantly shone with relief.

"I hope you know I would not do this for just anyone." With her fangs, Gabrielle lanced her wrist and brought it to my mouth.

Sam smiled coyly, realizing I was not only dazed from the injury, but bewildered by her presence. "It was Angelique," she said. "Angelique brought me back."

With a mouth full of blood and a hole in my chest, the best I could do was to silently ask, "How."

Her smile dissipated, instantly replaced by a hint of shame. "You were right to believe I was dead. I was, for a time. You were gone, when Angelique came to me. She resurrected me ... for you."

I labored to speak as the hole in my chest had yet to seal. "And *she* made you a vampire?" My tone, what little I could manage, was unjustifiably cold.

"No Nick, she only saved my spirit. You were the one who consumed my blood. But I was dead and unable to receive yours. When Angelique brought life back to me, it was your blood that filled my mouth and coursed my veins. As if I wasn't already bound to you, I am more than ever now."

Her words penetrated my confusion. Samantha was a vampire. The overwhelming urge I fought so hard to resist now existed in flesh and blood. Rather ironic, my desire to keep her human led to her death, and my desire for her not to become a vampire was what saved her. My eyes searched hers. The depth of her chestnut eyes, vibrant ... and yearning.

In the instant I searched for the truth, Sam sensed my conflict.

Bewildered by her newfound skills, I searched her eyes for answers.

"Angelique has taught me ... a few things." Telepathically, she experienced my confounded reservations. Pulling her hand away from my chest and Gabrielle's from my mouth, she moved her lips close to mine. "Kiss me, Nick."

This was not a request. Her thoughts proved to be stronger than the words my ears perceived. She reached around my neck and pulled me up with a strength that she had never possessed. I was in no position to offer any resistance. Our lips met, and all of the sensations of two years of bliss unfolded within my body simultaneously. It was Sam! All doubt and confusion dissipated within an immeasurable instant. And she knew it.

"Oh geez," Phillip moaned. "Get a room."

My heart pounded like an earthquake. Breaking off the kiss, I gasped for air, still reeling from my injury. Sam peeled back, her expression forecasting concern for the severity of my wound.

"We need to get out of here, now," she suggested, quietly.

Feeling the breath of her words on my ear, unsuccessfully I tried to spring to my feet. Though it had substantially slowed, blood continued to trickle down my chest. In a swooping motion, Sam effortlessly lifted me off the floor.

"Whoa," Phillip exclaimed, amazed at her ease of effort.

"There is no way you get to carry me out of here," I whispered. "I can walk." As my feet hit the floor my body nearly collapsed had it not been for Sam's vastly improved reflexes. "Okay, let's get out of here," I said weakly as Sam propped me up.

"Wait just one damn minute, Nicholas Tepes," Dee announced loudly. Begrudgingly, I stopped in my tracks, and turned around. "Nobody is going anywhere! *Yet.* Somebody is going to explain to me exactly what in the hell is going on. Right now!" Dee's voice quivered.

Chuck approached Phillip, Dee, and Gabrielle, holding his wrist. "Nicholas Tepes? I don't know any Nicholas Tepes, but Brian there," he said pointing at me, "just broke my arm." He waited while everyone looked in my direction. "I was about to put that stake through his heart, until you showed up."

Gabrielle suddenly recognized Chuck from New Orleans. I had never sensed any sort of aggression from her, until now. A swooning rage was about to explode all over Chuck.

"Gabby, it is alright. I asked him to come. He has only ever done what I asked of him."

"Why?" Nearly growling, her body posturing for an attack.

As Chuck studied Gabrielle's face, his eyes lit up. It had only been two years, but suddenly the memory of her face appeared in that dirty, damp crypt. It was Gabrielle and Celine who had pursued Chuck and Jimmy through the French Quarter. The haunting terror, a fear that had yet to dissipate, suddenly illuminated his eyes.

Gabrielle searched his thoughts and uncovered his fear. "Yes, you do remember me," she proclaimed as she stared into his eyes. Feeling her absolute power Chuck looked away.

"Brian wanted to die," he announced while staring down. "He told me he'd rather spend his life in hell than an eternity on earth without Sammy. I tried my best to talk him out of it, but he insisted."

Sam looked at me, hers eyes glistening with love. "I understand." she said softly. At once, she understood my undying commitment and love for her. She understood why I had wanted her to remain mortal. She understood that without her I could not exist. She understood a depth of unending love she never knew existed.

"Why don't we all go home, and get some rest," I suggested. "We can get together tomorrow night, and sort all of this out."

"You cannot go home," Phillip warned. "The cops are watching your place. You are wanted for murder."

"It will be all right, Phillip. I can handle the police. There are no victims left. Even the shooter has disappeared." I smiled at the efficiency of my former employer. "I am willing to wager, you will not even be able to find one shred of evidence that any crime took place last night."

Phillip looked at me with an eye of admiration. "Man, if only ..."

"Come on, let's get out of here." I pushed the elevator button as I looked back at my frazzled friends. Gabrielle broke the silence as we neared the ground floor. She elbowed Chuck softly in the ribs. "The night is still young, would you like to take me out for dinner?"

"Gabby!" I said sternly, giving her an implied warning.

"It's fine, Nick. I understand," Gabrielle replied, confirming she understood my concern. "No biting; I promise."

I gave them both a forbidding gaze.

"I know what you are thinking Bri—Nick, but I promise I will play nice. I promise not to stake her, as long as she behaves *herself*."

Holding on to Sam as we rode down, she looked at me with a puzzled expression. "Phillip told me you own this building, that you recently purchased it. Why didn't I know anything about it?"

The restrained smile that shone across my face was one Sam had grown accustomed to. "I bought it ... for a wedding present. I thought you would like a condo with a view of the river. I was refurbishing the floor we just left, the rest was going to be yours to decide what to do with. I thought you would like a place, new to both of us. You know, our home."

Sam smiled broadly. "This is my building?"

"Yep, all yours."

"So, if I was mad at you, I could throw you out?" she continued playfully.

"Yep."

"Well, from now on, you had better watch it, mister. I was only shacking up with you for a place to live in Manhattan. This changes everything," Sam warned.

"I am sure it does," I agreed. The bell chimed, as we reached the ground floor. "I think I can walk by myself now, Princess."

"No, I think you are not capable of anything on your own ever again. And in case you did not hear the news, I am a countess, not a princess." Sam leaned into my ear and began to whisper, "And one other small detail, which might have escaped you, I am a vampire too."

"I know," I said with a sigh of exasperation. "But you are not a countess until we are married," I reminded her.

"That's what you think."

Dee looked at Phillip as they walked through the lobby, just behind us. "Nice wedding present, don't you think?"

"Thanks a lot, Nick," Phillip called out from behind. "Now I am going to have to buy Mrs. Trump here a building of her own."

I turned, continuing to support my weight with Sam's help. "I'm sure she'll be happy with a check, Mister Moneybags."

We all had a laugh at Phillip's expense. As far as materialistic possessions were concerned, both Dee and Sam were happy living for experiences over valuables. Sure, they loved to shop with the best of them, but it was more about the time spent with friends than the purchase itself.

"Okay servant boy, let's see if you can walk now."

My legs wobbled as I separated from Sam. Her attention was lost in the vast lobby atrium. Three of the exterior walls were glass. The elevators backed up to the fourth wall. In the center of the room was a large waterfall fountain, with a rock-pond expanding out to both sides. The scent of fresh topsoil and cedar mulch filled the room, as the landscapers had only delivered it two days prior. The garden was void of any plants or trees as they were scheduled to be delivered later in the week. All of the gray and brown stone footpaths were freshly laid, outlining the paths that would ultimately wind through the atrium. Sam imagined the finished product, as she gazed about the room.

"This is going to be beautiful," she exclaimed, as we passed outside into the crisp night air, collectively taking in the view of the river. "The driver can drop you guys off, after he takes Dee and I home," Phillip offered.

"I'm hungry," Chuck announced, mainly in Gabrielle's direction. "I know you don't need to eat, but would you like to tag along?"

“As you have promised not to, how did you say it, stake me, yes I would like to tag along.” Gabrielle winked at Sam and smiled, then directed her attention back to Chuck. “Will your arm be alright?”

“I’ve had worse.” Chuck held his arm tightly. “Hey Denman, wait till you get the bill for this one.”

I shook my head, while locking the door to the now uninhabited building. “Sam and I are going home.”

With everyone leaving, Chuck and Gabby watched in uneasy silence as the car pulled away. “So do you eat food?” Chuck asked timidly.

“Generally I prefer active Marines, but in a pinch, a retired one will suffice.”

Chuck stopped in his tracks. “You going there before I’ve had my first beer. Damn, it’s gonna be a long night.”

“Do you still want to kill me?” Gabrielle’s asked without searching Chuck’s mind for the answer.

“Looking like that? Not hardly. Besides, Brian, I mean *Nick*, explained the way things are. So I’m cool with you.”

Gabrielle, had she been human, would have blushed at Chuck’s flattery. “Are you sure your arm is alright?”

“Honestly, it hurts like hell, but it’s nothing a little tequila can’t numb.” Chuck looked at Gabrielle out of the corner of his eye as she walked along side. She did not look as menacing as he remembered. As a matter of fact, to the contrary, she looked downright inviting. Remembering Brian’s claims of vampire mind reading, Chuck decided it was better to talk than to think. “So Brian, uh Nick, tells me you can read minds.”

“We can, some better than others. I have the gift, but I only use it when I feel threatened. I find it rather rude to invade a person’s private thoughts without provocation. Besides, if I knew everything someone was thinking, life would become quite boring.”

“So how’s that work?”

“Well your brain sends out thousands of electric signals. We have sensory cells, much like sonar, which can read these signals. Not only what you are thinking, but what your mind is telling your body to do. But, like putting a key into a lock, it takes concentration to accomplish. Imagine trying to insert a key in a locked door as you sprint past it. We must be focused on our target to thoroughly assess the thoughts."

"And you don't feel threatened by me?"

"Nick felt it was safe for me to be with you. That is all I need to know. Everything else, I would prefer to learn from you without an unfair advantage." Gabrielle had to purposefully look up to make contact with Chuck's face. As she did Chuck looked away quickly, feeling she had caught him, *checking her out.*

"So Nick tells me you are a friend who can be counted on ... and as he put it, a killing machine." Gabrielle was not in the habit of vague conversation. When she wanted to know something, she simply asked, sometimes rather bluntly.

Chuck cut his eyes to her, but turned away quickly as he saw she was still focused on him. "Do I make you nervous, Monsieur Chuck?" Gabrielle prodded, amused by his obvious discomfort. Thus far, he was not at all what she expected. Killing machine? Not hardly.

"All right," he began as he stopped and took her gently by the arm to face him. "I am not complicated like Nick. I'm just a guy. I like to eat, drink, work, and have sex with beautiful women. I'll admit, I find you very attractive. But I know if I look at you, my thoughts are gonna run to the gutter, cause that's the kind of guy I am. The only difference is, most women haven't got a clue what I'm thinking. You on the other hand, if you choose, can know everything I'm thinking. I don't like opponents with unfair advantages."

"So I am your adversary now?" Gabrielle, curious as to Chuck's reasoning was tempted to take a peek inside his head, but decided to let the events unfold naturally.

"No, no. It's not like that at all, I'm just some kind of control freak. Surprises can kill ya in my line of work." Chuck wrinkled his eyebrows, struggling to get the words to reflect his thoughts without thinking them first.

"So if I understood some of what you just said, if you look at me, you will think about fucking me, and you are afraid I will read your mind, and it will make for an awkward evening." Gabrielle was thoroughly enjoying dismantling Chuck's confidence.

"Bingo." Glowing red as a tomato and well aware of it, Chuck chose to look in a store window for a quick distraction.

"Well, why don't we just leave it with the understanding that you are a guy who likes sex, you find me attractive, and would like to have sex with me. I think if we mutually admit to the concept, we can dispense with the awkwardness."

If this woman was going to spend the night dissecting his brain, Chuck was going to need a shit-pot full of tequila to survive the evening. "Okay, sure," he began, trying to regain his confidence. "I'll admit when I look at you the thought crosses my mind. I'd have to be some kind of altar boy not to."

Gabrielle smiled even deeper. He was beginning to shine just as Nick had described him, raw, edgy, a rough and tough teddy bear. In her year in New York, she had never heard a confession of admiration quite as poetic as Chuck's. Not having taken a lover after her liberation from the convent, Gabrielle began to consider the possibilities. The sudden consideration of actually having sex wrinkled her edge. Time to change the subject, she thought. "So Nick says when you are in the field you are the most dangerous person he knows."

"No less than your friends," Chuck asserted.

Gabrielle was taken aback by the accusation. Her smile quickly dissipated to a frown. "I have killed no one."

"I saw the video," Chuck declared. "Don't get me wrong, at that time, I wanted nothing less than to track down all of you, and make your death as painful as possible. Rob was a good friend. But that's what war is all about, kill or be killed. And you people were just trying to survive. I can't fault you for wanting your freedom. But damn, your friends were some evil bitches."

"I am sorry, I alone could not save him. Nick has shared many stories about Rob ... and you." Gabrielle's frown deepened as the images replayed in her mind. "I know how much he meant to the both of you."

"He was a good friend to us all," Chuck reflected solemnly. "But you are right about me. It's what I was born to do. It's what I have done all of my life, and most likely what I will die doing."

"That seems sad, to spend your life in such a destructive manner, only to inevitably succumb to violence. Do you not feel as you have no other purpose in life?"

"Purpose, me? You might say I'm some kind of adrenaline junky,"

Chuck explained with a smile. "I don't know if that counts as a purpose. Killing isn't a purpose, just a means to an end that sometimes goes with the turf."

"And the thought of dying does not concern you?"

"Well, when I get up every day it's typically not one of those things I think about. But we all got to go one day, well except maybe your kind. It's not like I've got people depending on me anyhow."

Although he was smiling, Gabrielle heard the emptiness in his tone. "So there is no Mrs. Chuck on the horizon?"

"Are you kidding," Chuck laughed uncomfortably. After a prolonged silence waiting for a rebuttal, he mused *why not*? He decided to turn the focus on Gabrielle. "How 'bout you? What's your story?"

"No. I was never fit for a husband or boyfriend. In France, I was orphaned and became a prostitute at the age of fifteen. I am not proud of my past, but the choice was mine alone. So as you say, I own that."

"Prostitute?" Chuck attempted to make light of Gabrielle's confession. "So you had sex for money to survive. Big deal. I killed people to survive. People have sex all the time, and believe me, it ain't never for free. So you charged for what some women give for a hidden agenda. In my mind, that makes you smarter ... and more honest than most."

Gabrielle looked at Chuck with an awkward smile. The big oaf's logic was not far removed from the truth. Rugged and handsome, awkward yet honest and a closet full of skeletons; Gabrielle considered Chuck, the man who nearly drove a stake through her heart in New Orleans, as maybe a guy, the first, that could help break the bonds of shame and guilt. In renewed silence they strolled aimlessly through lower Manhattan.

"Alright!" Chuck called out, breaking a prolonged silence. "Mexican Cantina, dead ahead," he said, pointing out a restaurant in the next block. As they neared the restaurant, Chuck felt the urge to clarify his position. "You know, Gabrielle, you need to give yourself a break. In case you're not aware, I will tell you. You are damn hot. Too damn hot to spend your life without a good man. I mean, Nick and I have killed a lot of people. I think that's a lot worse than sleeping around for money. So should Nick give up Samantha just because he's been a bad boy?"

Gabrielle shook her head indicating she agreed with Chuck's logic.

Chuck stopped his relentless march toward the Cantina. He propped his chin in his hand, and began an impromptu examination of his companion. "I'm not usually attracted to skinny, two-hundred-year-old, ex-hooker Frenchy vampires, no matter how radiant and seductive they are, but if I were, I'd say you got it going on, Gabrielle."

Gabrielle smiled sheepishly. Not to be outdone, she added, "You know, for an obnoxious, Neanderthal, killing machine, you are not too bad yourself, Mister Chuck."

Sitting on our rooftop garden, Sam was attempting to rediscover the distinct taste of her favorite wine, while I nursed a beer. I intently studied every feature of her reborn body. She was the same woman I loved, but different. Minor imperfections were gone. Her hair rustled in the breeze as she surveyed the garden, taking in every detail through eyes that now appreciated the new beauty of the night.

The night air was brisk, with a moderate breeze blowing through the shrubs and greenery that lined the rooftop balcony. I missed the revitalizing sensation brought on by brisk autumn nights like these. I missed those bitter winter days, when the warmth of the sun cut the chill that stiffened my body. I missed the sweat that ensued during the heat of passion.

"You do realize, this changes everything," I said, interrupting the serenity of the moment.

"Like, you won't need to find a new wife in forty or fifty years?" Sam replied gleefully.

"Besides that. By the time you are able to go to a clothing sale, all the good stuff will be picked over." Cursed or not, I was elated to have her home again.

"I just think you're upset that you will not be able to pull any of your mind-control vampire antics on me anymore." Sam swirled her glass vigorously, attempting to derive more flavor from the grapes.

I could not help but laugh. Becoming a vampire had not altered her wit in the least. But she needed to understand the implications of her new life. "There is so much I need to teach you. There may come a time when we are hunted, not because of my former career, but because of what we are. One day, the humans will find out. I never wanted your life to be ... the thought of you being ..."

"Killed," Sam exclaimed, completing my thought. "I've already got that one covered. And being human was not any great advantage there. I think if we agree that sooner or later, somehow, some day, we are both going to die, we will be able to enjoy what we have, and what I have become, so much more. So stop worrying about me. We will figure this all out, one day at a time."

Yep, still the same old Sam, but with a new paint job.

"And right now," she said, as she stood up, and set her wine glass down, "I want to see how this new equipment functions in the bedroom." She took my hand and pulled effortlessly, lifting me from the couch.

"Let me tell you something," I said, giving a tug of resistance. "Gabrielle has had two hundred years to acquaint herself with her skills. She had instruction from Angelique, who has been the undead for almost twice as long. Don't overrate your abilities. I see that gleam in your eye."

"That gleam, is the gleam of anticipation. After kissing you earlier, I realized things were different, in more ways than one. I think for tonight, you had better strap in for the ride of your life." That kiss, I thought, was indeed different. It was a most tantalizing kiss. My blood was now Sam's, her sensations were mine. And the overwhelming nature of just one kiss, brought about more concern than anticipation.

CHAPTER TWENTY-TWO

NIGHTTIME RETURNED, UNLIKE any awakening ever experienced. The euphoric fatigue remaining, after last night, bordered lethal. Take the strongest sensation of the human body immediately during climax, expand it throughout the entire body, then multiply it by two, because we shared each other's sensations. I vaguely remembered Sam collapsing in my arms as we spontaneously fell into unconscious bliss.

I glanced over, delighted to see all of her appendages intact and no sign of blood anywhere.

"Can you think of one reason why we should remotely contemplate leaving the bedroom ever again?" Sensing I had awakened, Sam purred softly, without opening her eyes.

"Man's got to eat."

"Wimp," Sam teased, as her eyes remained shut. She stretched out her arm to my head, and began running her fingers through my hair. As if in slow motion, her eyes opened, and a glow encompassed her face. "It's sad, humans will never experience sex like that."

"A simple thank you would suffice."

"Watch it, Mr. Vampire man. You are not the only bat in the tree." Sam attempted to contain a giggle, but lost out.

"That may or may not be, but currently, I am the only one you know."

"See, that just goes to prove you do not know everything." The playful look on her face warmed my cold heart, a feeling that had escaped me for the majority of my life. As I rolled to my side to face her, the ache in my chest reminded me of my near call with true death last night.

"Why my future little countess, what ever do you mean?" My curiosity was piqued as I propped up onto my elbow.

Sam chuckled. "I know something that you don't."

I rolled my eyes in the back of my head. "It has happened on very rare occasions."

"So what is it worth to you?" she asked, as she stopped with the head caressing, and unexpectedly yanked my head toward her face. The wisp of her breath was enticing. No longer the warm flow of breath, but rather equivalent to a fresh breeze of autumn air, she began gently kissing my face, with a quiver of anticipation in her lips. "I know it has only been twelve hours, but what do you think? Round two?"

"How about you tell me about the other vampire first, and if I deem the information to be exceptional, I will consider allowing you another episode of orgasmic pleasure."

Sam kissed me quickly, and pushed back. She climbed from bed and paraded naked across the room to the picture window. "I know you are watching," she said, without looking back. She opened the curtains, revealing the splendor of a crescent moon, suspended on a cloudless night. I studied the curves of her body, noting subtle changes since her rebirth. "If you stare any harder, I fear you will set my body on fire."

"Just admiring the artwork, baby."

"Last night, on the way to Phillip's, I happened across a vampire, near the Brooklyn Bridge. He was some kind of sentry."

"Why didn't you tell me about this earlier?" I barked, as sense of missed opportunity altered my playful mood.

Sam wiggled her feet into a pair of black leather pumps and ever so deliberately began strutting toward me. "Do these shoes make me look fat?"

"Sam!" I said, objecting to any delay in a full report.

"Nick, first things first. If I find you pleasing, Mister Vampire man, I will tell you everything … later."

Sam knew how to pull my strings from the very day I met her, and becoming a vampire did not alter her methodology one drop. Only after she had had her way with me, did she consent to return to the subject I deeply desired to learn of.

"His name is Milton, but he goes by Maltor. I think his job was to watch for potential threats to his family, which I gathered was across the Brooklyn Bridge."

"Sam, why didn't you tell me sooner? Don't you realize he might be able to lead me to Sabine? Remember her? The last person keeping us here."

"I'm sorry, Nick. But my priorities have changed. It's just ... I no longer possess the same sense of urgency as before. For the first time in my life, the clock's not ticking. It's not like you were in any shape last night to do battle with the forces of evil. And let's just say for argument's sake, you went after Sabine and something bad happened ... everything we experienced last night would have never been."

"Samantha, dear, following that logic, we would never get out of bed again."

"We could get out of bed and leave now, and never look back. Leave all the human strife behind, just you and me." Her eyes searched mine; looking for just a hint I would agree.

"Sam," I began.

"What would be wrong with ten thousand nights, just like last night, anywhere we wanted it to be?"

"Just leave everyone behind, just like that? Dee, Gabby ... you could do that?"

"You've been doing that all your life, haven't you? They're all grown ups. I don't think they need us to babysit."

"That was me, a very long time ago. I have changed."

"I wouldn't call two years ago long. And yes you have. You love me, and I love you, at least I think I do," she said with a grin. "It's not like we'd leave forever."

"If there is a colony in Brooklyn, it is only a matter of time before it is exposed, just like New Orleans. In time, Gabrielle, Angelique, and my son, would be hunted down. If it were not for my contacts in Washington, we would already be a full-blown media circus. The only way to prevent that from re-occurring is to find Sabine, and contain whatever damage she may have created. Then, maybe we can finally be free."

"Nick, I am scared for you, for us. I have had a premonition, and it is so much stronger this time. I ..."

"Shhhh," I said, as I put my finger to her lips. "I will be careful."

"That is what scares me. Look what happened last time you were careful."

"Okay, so I am a vampire, you got killed, and now you are a vampire. Is there a problem somewhere? As I remember, you were begging me relentlessly to become one."

"That's not what I'm talking about." Sam backed out of my reach, disapproving of my sense of humor.

"Hey, at least we are both immortal now."

"Nice try spin doctor, but given a choice, I think I would just as soon prefer to grow old with you and live out our days to an end. It kind of adds a need to live each day to the fullest, don't you think?"

"Look who's spinning the topic now. You know I couldn't live with even one person dying because of New Orleans, at whatever cost. Maybe before I met you I wouldn't care, who knows? The point is, now I do." I jumped out of bed and pulled on my jeans and a tee shirt. "How about if we start by finding out exactly what is going on across the river? As a compromise, I will even call in some additional help and try not to be such a cowboy this time."

Still naked, Sam stood, put her arms around me and kissed me. "How about we go for a stroll, talk more about this grand scheme of yours and find a bite to eat." Sam giggled as she pulled away. "Bite to eat, get it?"

We never ventured to Brooklyn that night. Maybe my sense of urgency had dissipated as well. The evening was spent exploring our new common denominators. We laughed and loved more carefree than ever before. As the night grew late, I ushered Sam on to sleep. Watching over her, waiting for sleep to come, my mind churned formulating plans. After several hours of wasted time, I gave up and decided to take care of business.

It was ten in the morning, and Sam was sleeping peacefully. My instincts told me a phone call was in order. Mitch O'Reilly was pleasantly surprised to hear from me. I briefly explained the situation in New York, and asked if he would consider assisting with my well-laid, completely off the cuff plans. Mitch had not been back in the city for over ten years, or out of New Orleans for an equally long time. It took all of my negotiating skills and a pound of bullshit to persuade the crafty old detective to agree. More so than any other reason, Mitch claimed after I had left New Orleans life had been, as he put it, "as boring as waiting for a dog turd to turn white."

CHAPTER TWENTY-THREE

AT THREE IN the morning, sitting by the hangar waiting for Phillip's jet to arrive I reviewed my plans. I had enlisted Chuck's services to scout out our targets, for what I hoped would be the final chapter in this tale gone wrong. It wasn't hard for him to locate the brownstone in Brooklyn where a clan had formed. From Sam's description, he located Maltor near the Brooklyn Bridge, and waited for him to lead him to the hideaway. Judging by the number of people that returned to the brownstone at such irregular hours, as opposed to any other building on the block, Chuck projected that there were about twenty potential hostiles.

In New Orleans, ten female vampires, who had not stepped out in the world in over two hundred years, basically tourists went up against me and my seasoned crew of mercenaries. Truth be told, we did not fare well in that skirmish. In all honesty, we got our asses handed to us. Thirty Brooklyn vampires? Even if they weren't vampires, just being ornery Brooklyners would be bad enough.

But they weren't ordinary. Departing at night and returning before dawn for three consecutive nights, Chuck witnessed their numbers increase. Pulling a missing persons file, Chuck had identified two of the women and three of the men.

My worst fears were realized; an unchecked and careless

explosion of the vampire population would inevitably lead to exposure, carnage, and the extinction of a race. *But whose?*

The jet wheeled in front of the hangar and powered down. I leaned against the black Denali eager to see my old friend. Mitch was my kind of guy, hard as steel, but he knew when to bend. Whatever it took to get the job done. Mitch popped through the door first followed by Isabelle. I had not been sure he would be able to convince her to leave the French Quarter. By her own admission, she could not ever remember leaving the crescent city.

Who I saw next was unexpected. Daniel followed Isabelle down the steps. "My friends, welcome to New York. Daniel, Mitch ... Isabelle, it is so good to see all of you. Thanks for coming."

"I understand you are nearing the end," Daniel said as he clasped my hand.

"Possibly, but it might not come easy."

"If it were to be easy, should I not have stayed in New Orleans?"

"Daniel, Mitch, I have much to share, but please excuse me for a moment. I need time with Isabelle."

"Take all the time you need, Brian, as of six hours ago, I'm on the clock."

"Thanks, Mitch, so glad you decided to come to the party." I did my best to mimic Mitch's trademark sneer, but judging by his reaction, I fell short of the mark. "Hop in the car, we will join you shortly."

"Isabelle." I barely got her name out before I found myself wrapped affectionately in her arms. The silky texture of her skin and scent aroused memories of the confused longings I held with each encounter in The Big Easy. Half-breeds; both of us were lost in a world we didn't quite belong, our kindred spirits' yearning made perfect sense.

"I have missed you. New Orleans has been so barren since you left me there."

I pulled away enough to gaze upon her. Not one single feature of her face had changed. A tear has collected in the corner of her eye. I placed my hand against her cheek and brushed it away. "Isabelle. I have discovered why you are the way you are, but until a couple of days ago, I hesitated to share all that I have learned."

In her eyes I saw the curiosity, but also betrayal, for denying my feelings for her.

Although they existed for both of us, strongly I might add, I had failed to yield to the desire of a kindred creature. "You know, until I became what I am, I never believed in any of this. I believed you and your friends were all living in some type of freak show fantasy world. But now, at least I know the truth about you."

For all of her life Isabelle had often questioned her own sanity. The seemingly endless barrage of a semi-lucid past could never be explained. All of her memories could not possibly be grounded in reality, as many people had told her over the years.

A cold breeze blew Isabelle's hair off her shoulder and she shuddered. I pulled my jacket off and wrapped it around her. "You and I are one in the same. We shared a common genetic thread. I thought you were crazy when you claimed to have lived for so many years, but in fact I live with the same anomaly. True you are much older than me, but basically neither one of us have aged a day since our mid-thirties. For you, that has been somewhere over two hundred years, for me, about sixty five."

Even as I began to explain our anomalies, the innocence resonating in her eyes only spoke of desire. I knew what she wanted, and if circumstances were different I would have relented. But maybe the information I was about to divulge would prove enough distraction to douse her fire.

"Our parents, specifically your mother and my father, were vampires. Your father and my mother were mortal. The result was children with immortal lifespans, but lacking the need for blood or the specific weaknesses of the vampire race."

"How do you know this?"

"My aunt told me after I returned home from New Orleans. Once she learned I was a vampire, she shared the secret of my ancestors. Once I learned of my heritage, I began to understand the reasons behind your behavior."

"Brian, why didn't you contact me?"

"Because I just wasn't sure. I am still not one hundred percent sure, but there is a chance we may have located your mother. The legend of the Convent claims one of the ten had a child, but that child was taken away. Whether you are that child, I can't say for sure. But I did learn the mother's name."

"And you found my mother ... are you going to kill her like the others?"

"No. Things have changed." I released an exasperated sigh at the magnitude of that statement. "I have changed. If this woman is your mother, her name is Sabine and she is here in New York."

"You have talked to her?" An expression of jubilation exploded across Isabelle's face, one that I doubted anyone had ever seen.

"No. But this is why I brought you here. I believe she came to New York looking for you. I am not sure why she thought you were here, but nevertheless she did. She may be in a situation that would require the persuasion of a long lost daughter to resolve. Apparently, she has created a large colony of vampires in Brooklyn. We really don't know much at all about them. But even though we have not seen Sabine as of yet, we believe she is with them."

Another stiff breeze gusted, as Isabelle held her thoughts while a jet landed. "I enjoyed flying. I have seen planes for years, but never thought about going on one. And now here I am with you and we are about to find my mother."

Her childlike exhilaration was invigorating. Much like Gabrielle, there would be so much to experience outside the realm of the sheltered life she once led.

"We should join the others, it sounds like there is much work to be done," Isabelle suggested.

I opened the door of the Denali. The sight of Daniel and Mitch, sharing Phillip's scotch, brought a smile and a welcome feeling of confidence. The battle for Brooklyn was about to unfold. My crew: a suddenly love struck jarhead and two cronies ready to die for the cause, or maybe from heart attacks. Hoorah.

Impatience; whether it was an unknown number of vampires holding up inside a relatively secure building in a densely populated neighborhood, or the need to resolve Isabelle's overdue reunion, I felt it was time to bring this saga to a conclusion.

As much as my own body craved sleep during the day, I would forgo the vital rest. I knew this would be my best opportunity to take them unaware. Therefore I would proceed peacefully to the brownstone just before sunrise, as they were retiring for the day. I would assess the enemy's motives and counter any remaining resistance with extreme force. As in a few past military ops, my tactics did not meet the approval with the majority of my subordinates. The women were furious, but none had experience in battle, and vampire or not, their welfare could not be the focus of my concern. They certainly would be no match for a brownstone full of ornery Brooklyn vampires.

Chuck had rounded up three former team members, but none were happy to provide back-up. Should Chuck and I fail in our primary initiative, plan B was much more to their liking. Blow up and torch everything. Phillip, Daniel, and Mitch on the contrary were quite happy to occupy the command center and provide intel and communications. Phillip had procured an empty apartment directly across the street from our targets.

With the team at their post, we were ready to launch the covert urban assault. I knew the odds were stacked against us, but a larger assault group would certainly remove all hopes of any peaceful resolution with minimal civilian casualties.

Chuck and I slowly approached up the car-lined street an hour before dawn. Nolan and Andrews, two former Seals I had worked with on several missions, stood ready by a moving van we had rented the day before. Chuck nodded to them as we passed in silence. I gave a slight wave to my friends watching from the third floor of the apartment across the street.

"We are green." I reported to the team.

Outside the brownstone, two sentries studied our approach. In Chuck's advance scouting, he had observed them outside the building during the daylight hours. Assuming our targets to be of reasonable intelligence, I was sure they had enlisted a few mortals to assist in their protection during the daylight hours. As we drew near, I spotted the distinct bite wounds of a vampire on one's neck. I knew our two goons were under the control of some undead authority beyond the weathered oak doors.

"Hey Boss, is Jessica Jones in da house?" Chuck asked.

"Beat it jerk-off," the Hispanic one barked.

Chuck and I surveyed the street one last time for any witnesses. Both guards were on the ground in an instant. Andrews and Nolan appeared quickly, and dragged the bodies back to the moving van.

"You sure you are ready?" I asked Chuck.

"As ready as you will allow me to be. You know, I could be a hell of a lot more help if you'd share that curse of yours with me."

"Chuck, I thought we had buried the issue. I can not make others like …"

"You can, but you won't. Let's just say for argument's sake, your purpose is to make others like you. Peaceful cohabiting vampires, who would never dream of storming a building in the dark of night with intentions of annihilating an entire …"

"Boys, knock it off," Sam piped in on our ear buds. "Let's focus on the job, so we can get the hell out of Brooklyn."

"Sho nuff Miz Vampirella. Now that you're on his team why worry about ol' mortal Chuck."

"Don't worry Monsieur Chuck, I will be there for you," Gabrielle said.

Chuck sneered at me mockingly.

Chuck and Gabrielle, the ultimate odd couple. Where their relationship was headed, none of us could begin to imagine. But in three short days, I had witnessed a transformation in the pair that warmed my soul.

"Hey team," Mitch cut in from his rooftop vantage, "I hate to interrupt the Jerry Springer show, but the clock has begun ticking and you've got forty eight apartments to clear."

"Roger that." I looked at my smart-ass Jarhead friend. "We will finish this conversation later."

Chuck cut in front of me and headed up the steps. "If I'm still alive," he said over his shoulder.

Inside the lobby a single sentry stood by the elevator.

"Who let you in?"

"Carlos cleared us to relieve you guys." Chuck said as he went straight for the guard.

"I don't know any …"

Chuck was having way too much fun with this job. He dragged the unconscious guard past me to the front door. "You sure you don't want to sit this one out old man?" Andrews and Nolan had taken up position at the front door and were ready to dispose of Chuck's handiwork.

"There will only be a couple more of these pushovers, then it's gonna get dicey. So how about a little more serious attitude buddy?"

"Hey Gabrielle?" Chuck whispered on his mic. "Promise me if we fall in love, you won't turn me into a puss-ball like this guy." Chuck winked at me as he moved toward the stairs.

"You got us. Phillip?" I asked softly as I ignored Chuck's banter.

"I see Chuck clearly, and it looks like two warm bodies on floor two, and one on floors three four and five, all near the stairs. Other than that, everyone else is damn hard to make out."

"Daniel?"

"I'm at the front door, in the lobby across the street," he reported. "If any of your kind show, I'll take them down just like your buddy in New Orleans.

I cringed at the memory of Jimmy sprawled on the ground, courtesy of Daniel's marksmanship. "Chuck, watch the stairs." I ordered as I began to unlock the first apartment. Thanks to some pretty nasty persuasion techniques, Chuck had convinced the building owner to cough up his master keys. One by one, I entered the ground floor apartments, six in all, only to discover rotting corpses in most. From my initial search of the ground floor units I could surmise whomever we would encounter above, they had no interest in living peacefully amongst their neighbors.

"Chuck ..."

Chuck was startled by my stealthy reappearance. "Dammit! What are you, the ghost of Rob? I could have broken your neck."

"Chuck, stop, it's bad. I found nine victims. I think we've stumbled into a house full of Monique's."

"Oh, that bitch." Chuck appeared a little uneasy. "What's the call?"

"The call?" Sam interrupted from her position in the command post with Phillip, Gabrielle, Angelique and Isabelle. "The call is you get the hell out."

"Negative. We are proceeding. Allen, stand by." Paired with O'Reilly, Stanley Allen was ready to fire Molotov Cocktails via grenade launcher from the roof across the street. Once day broke, the vampires would have nowhere to run. One way or another, they were going to burn in hell.

Allen, a Star Wars nerd radioed, back, "Copy that Gold Leader."

Speaking of daybreak, the hour of dawn had arrived. Chuck and

I moved to the second floor. While Chuck disposed of his handiwork to our team waiting out in the street, I checked the apartments of the second floor, working slow and methodically, leaving no closet unchecked. Seven more bodies. NYPD was going to have a field day with this. There was absolutely no way Paul Watson would ever be able to make this go away. From this day forward, the world would know of our existence.

Nolan and Andrews kept busy cleaning up the sentries. Thus far, they were all mere mortals under the spell of a master being.

The third floor held only two victims, and still none of my brethren. Upon arriving on the fourth floor, I did not need to search. Instinctively, I knew exactly where to look. My hopes of a peaceful remediation were gone. The massive casualties told me these vampires only cared about one thing, feeding. The victims had been a cross section of young and old and men and women. If any had been spared, they were surely amongst the living dead now.

Chuck and I entered the apartment, Chuck behind me, his cross easily visible.

"Shit, don't this take you back." Chuck whispered as we studied the two caskets.

"You take the right, I will take the left. Let's do this quick." Chuck turned his back to me and I pulled two stakes from his backpack. Raising the lids simultaneously, the woman before me groaned and stirred ever so slightly. Unlike New Orleans, I took no time to consider her beauty, or lack thereof. I raised my stake, no mallet needed, and prepared to strike.

Nolan's words, "We've got a problem," buzzed in our earbuds, just audible enough to wake our intended victims.

As quickly as she opened her eyes, I sealed them shut forever with the driving force of an oak stake through her heart. Chuck, on the other hand, was not so lucky. His vampire immediately lunged from the casket and pinned him to the wall. I arrived with Chuck's stake and delivered the fatal blow from behind. As I pulled him away, Chuck finished him off with speed and precision, severing the head with a powerful swing.

I took two deep breaths as I studied the severed head and then gazed at Chuck's wild-eyed look of satisfaction. Turning my attention to the voice of the untimely interruption I asked, "What's up?"

"We had a beat cop. He passed by, but I think he's onto us." Nolan reported.

"Roger that," Mitch replied. "He pretty much took off after he cleared the block. I'm gonna head down to the street and roll out the NYPD welcome mat."

"We should pick up the pace, bro. You know where to find them, so we need to quit looking for any possible survivors and get on with it," Chuck suggested.

It was just before eleven and we had covered half of the floors. Chuck had estimated thirty hostiles, including eight potential warm bodies. Seven of those were down and one remained on the next floor. With two vampires dead, if Chuck's count were accurate, twenty vampires remained. As we moved up the stairs I began to feel the growing presence of a multitude of evil directly above.

Three squad cars arrived within seconds of each other. O'Reilly had barely had time to set up by the front door, replacing Nolan and Andrews, who had pulled back to the moving van. Holding his badge above his head, he called out to the officers who quickly surrounded him.

"Mitch O'Reilly, New Orleans PD. Who's in charge here, boys?"

"Never mind who's in charge, you wanna tell us what's going on here chief?" Joe Bonelli, with seventeen years of working the neighborhood, took exception to O'Reilly's air of superiority.

As several of the cops headed up the steps of the apartment, Mitch turned and warned the group. "Hey don't go in there, the buildings not secure." O'Reilly leaned in exceedingly close to Bonelli. "We have a situation here, but if you go in, the entire operation could go boom."

"Hold up guys," Bonelli called.

"While you and I talk this out," O'Reilly began, "how about getting the guys to pull their squad cars back. I don't want to spook our perps up there if it's not too late."

"Do it," Bonelli ordered. "Davis, get the Captain on board. Looks like we've got a situation here." Bonelli straightened his holster and cut a glare at O'Reilly. "Okay O'Reilly, what the hell is going on up there?"

"I'm here on assignment from New Orleans with the DEA. We've got a CI on the inside who may be compromised. Currently, we have two agents inside sweeping floor-by-floor looking for our girl. So far, all is quiet. If you guys go storming in that's gonna change."

Bonelli studied Mitch's face, looking for a tell. "Dispatch, hold all units back one block," he ordered into the radio. "Davis, you find the Captain yet?"

Chuck had taken out the last of the guards and moved on to search the left side apartments. I had moved on to the back apartment on the right, where muffled voices could be heard from within. Placing my hand on the doorknob, I turned it gently and slowly pushed the door open.

Instantaneously, three vampires turned and studied my approach. Just beyond them, restrained on a table appeared to be an unconscious woman.

"Yo, what's up?"

I sized up my options against the three. The mouthpiece was a monster, six feet eight and three hundred pounds. He would not go down easy. The other two were goons, a mere nuisance I would deal with before tackling the mountain of doom.

"Yo, why you covered in blood, bro?" Joe White Castle put his finger into my blood covered shirt. "Damn Al, this shit's fresh."

Al, the monster, moved from the rear of the table, but stopped short of leaving it unattended.

"Vincent send you down here?"

Attempting to get a better view of the restrained woman, I moved deeper into the apartment. My progress was arrested by Joe, who obviously did not realize how much I despised having hands laid on me.

Unable to make a positive ID, I switched tactics. "Vincent wanted me to check on Sabine."

"Bullshit. Don't nobody but me and Vincent check on Sabine." Al's aggressive tone forewarned there was no time left. "Angelo, go see what's up. I think this motherfucker is trying to pull something."

Angelo and Joe, or whatever their real names were, had just breathed their last breaths. I snapped my forearms to the floor and two stakes slid from my sleeves to my hands. Joe first, just because he had no manners, then Angelo; within a second both were dead on the floor. My favorite kind of dead.

"Motherfucker, what are you … some kind of fucking vampire hunter?" Al began to charge in my direction.

I coiled, then lunged and followed through with a crushing two-legged kick high to his chest. Al crashed backward and stumbled over a chair. Just as he was rising to his feet, I grabbed his greasy ponytail and pulled with all the energy I could muster. Gathering just enough momentum, I swung him wildly in front, then shoved him through the curtain-covered window sending him crashing into the glass. One last well timed kick and he tumbled over the windowsill and fell five floors to the street below. I peered out briefly to see him sprawled in the street, the tree filtered sunlight forcing my retreat away from the window.

He rose, only to discover his body was drenched in sunlight. With his flesh beginning to singe, he turned and began to sprint toward the shadows at the end of the block. Before he had covered ten yards, an indistinct thud halted his progress. Looking down, a wooden arrow had pierced his heart from behind. As he dropped to his knees, his body burst into flames.

"Now there's something you don't see everyday," O'Reilly chuckled. Before his words resonated in Bonelli's ears, a solitary gunshot rang out. O'Reilly, unfazed by the gunfire, continued to chuckle as Bonelli ducked for cover.

"Damn it, who fired that shot?" Bonelli called out on the radio.

"I did. There's a guy across the street from you with a crossbow. I think he fired the arrow that killed that guy. He ducked back into the building, but I think I winged him," an excited voice reported.

"Williams, you and Sturges get over there and secure that building, now." Bonelli ordered. "Dispatch, we need backup and a bus. Got one perp down."

O'Reilly remained out in the open, laughing in the direction of the flaming corpse. "Well that certainly made my day worth getting out of bed for. Thanks, Brian," he chirped into the com.

"Get over here you crazy fuck," Bonelli motioned to O'Reilly.

"Just a minute son," he said to Bonelli as he moved away. Redirecting his attention to the floor above he spoke into his com. "What's that? You've got Sabine?" O'Reilly looked up to the fifth floor window and then back to Bonelli. "Okay, I'll do my best." O'Reilly walked nonchalantly back to the younger cop. "Looks like they found our CI. My man is bringing her down, but she's been injured. Before you go and storm the building, The DEA would really appreciate it if you let them clear out before everyone starts blasting."

"You've got until my backup arrives." The neighborhood was filled with screaming sirens of approaching squad cars. It would not be long.

"I could've done that."

I turned to see Chuck standing in the doorway with his arms crossed. "Shut up and get over here."

"Is that her?"

"Yes it is. Help me cut her loose." I began slicing the nylon ropes on the right, while Chuck started on the left.

"What's wrong with her? Why's she all tied up?"

"Apparently they've been feeding on her. She barely has enough blood to sustain life. It's pretty damn painful." Finishing with the rope, I moved up by her face.

"A vampire running on empty. That's kind of funny, don't you think?" Once more in the midst of dire situation, Chuck extrapolated humor from whatever source he deemed appropriate, this time a Jackson Brown song.

"Sabine, I am Nicholas. We are going to get you out of here." I reached across her body and grabbed Chuck's hand. "This will only sting a bit." I lanced his palm with my knife and blood began to flow.

"What the hell man? First you break my arm and now you stab me?" Chuck screeched.

I put his hand to her lips. "Drink this, it will help you recover." Sabine parted her lips, allowing the steady flow of blood to enter her mouth. I looked back at Chuck, "Trust me, I know what I am doing." Chuck pulled back on his hand, but I did not allow it to budge. "Trust me."

Sabine opened her eyes, her gray flesh began to turn. I pulled Chuck's hand away and then began feeding her with my blood. The running footsteps forewarned of approaching company from the stairs. "Chuck, go deal with them." Chuck positioned himself in the hallway just beyond the opened door, as an impromptu rescue party arrived.

The two vampires that entered almost stumbled over the bodies of their fallen brethren. "What the hell is this?"

Before he finished his question, his head was rolling on the floor, detached via Chuck's machete. In a moment of, look what I did, Chuck temporarily forgot what he was dealing with. The singular follow through of his assault brought the blade behind him and then over his head creating a vertical strike on our second vampire, splitting his skull straight down to the nose. He was not happy.

Blood spewing in all directions, instantly he shoved Chuck to the floor and bit into his neck. Chuck howled in pain. I flew across the room and knocked him against the wall.

Of all the gore I had witnessed in my life, none compared to this. With his head lopped in halves, he rose from the floor and stood before me with a laugh so sinister I knew it would fill my nightmares for years to come. At this point I had to believe he thought I was human, because he continued to laugh without attacking. I felt a stake enter my hand from behind.

One might think, now with two brains, he might have been smarter. He was still laughing as the stake pierced his heart then pegged him to the wall. For just a second, I wanted to be like Chuck, to find some witty recant as his life departed. But in all honestly, the vision before me was just too damn disturbing.

"Hey man, help me up, I'm fucking dying down here."

I reached down and pulled Chuck to his feet.

"I hope that fucker didn't have rabies." Chuck held his hand over his neck and picked up his machete. "Ain't this some shit, a couple days in New York and I'm all fucked up. I need to get back to Colombia where it's safe."

"How about for now, you just get Sabine downstairs to the

lobby." I helped Sabine to her feet and walked her to the door. She did not possess the strength to make it down five flights of stairs. "This is Chuck, he will get you out of here. If you do what he tells you, everything should be fine."

Sabine's eyes were sullen and suspicious. She looked to the sunshine streaming in the broken window and pulled away. "There's not much time. My friend will carry you down and cover you before leaving the building. I don't have time to explain, but I have found your daughter. You must go now if you hope to see her."

Without a word, Sabine took hold of Chuck's arm. He swept her from her feet and headed for the stairwell. "You gonna take the lead?" Chuck asked.

"I'll go down to clear the way, but then I will double back. I'm going to find this Vincent the others spoke of, I need to know what he knows."

"Fuck him, let's get the hell out of here and blow this place to holy hell."

"Nick, don't do it," Sam implored over the com.

"Get the hell out of there, O'Reilly commanded.

"Brain ..." Phillip began to join the chorus of *the job is done, get the hell out.*

I pulled out my earbud and stuck it in my pocket. "Have Phillip initiate exit B." I closed my eyes and felt the presence of approaching evil. "They are coming, we need to go."

By the time Chuck reached the outer door, the street was full of cops trying to enforce a perimeter. Two news crews were frantically jockeying for position on the block just beyond the yellow and black crime scene tape. Lieutenant Michaels had just arrived on the scene and was busy barking out commands. O'Reilly had taken position between parked cars, slightly out of plain sight.

"O'Reilly, I'm at the door. Am I clear?" Chuck asked.

Mitch surveyed the chaotic circus. "Not hardly," he scoffed.

"Get me clear, I need to get Sabine to the apartment, pronto."

"Negative Big Guy. The albino cross-bowed the bloodsucker you guys threw out the window. The cops are all over command central.

Phil, Daniel, and Sam, hell the entire crew may all be in custody by now."

"Shit, I got to do something with this girl. Tell the cops we've got to get the CI off the streets ASAP. Suggest the lobby of a building where the sun's not shining."

"Ten-four. Stand by." Mitch sighed deeply and headed for the Lieutenant. This was about to go over like shit Slurpee in a blender with no lid.

"Lieutenant Michaels," Mitch called as he recognized the commanding officer.

"What the hell? Who let this lunatic in?" Michaels threw his arms in the air in exasperation and waited for someone to reply.

Joe Bonelli knew his lieutenant's tone all too well. More so, the lump in his throat knew it better. "Lieutenant, this is Mitch O'Reilly."

"I know who this is. This is Mitch Fucking O'Reilly, formerly of the 7th precinct, formerly of the NYPD. Would somebody please arrest this man or shoot him? Either will be fine with me."

"Lieutenant, before we go for a romp down memory lane, I've got a situation here," O'Reilly explained.

"You've got a situation? You are in my jurisdiction, Mitch, which makes it my fucking situation."

"Walter! Save it for later. I've got a deep cover CI. I need to get from this building to that one across the street, right now. Then it's all yours."

"It's all mine right now Mitch." Michaels looked down the street as the reinforcements piled in.

"If you're planning on storming the building, I've got intel you're gonna need to know before you go in."

Michaels grunted forcefully. "Let them out, Joe," Michaels instructed Bonelli.

"All units stand-down. We've got two agents coming out," Bonelli radioed.

"All's clear Chuck, proceed to the lobby across the street," O'Reilly relayed in his com.

Chuck, drenched in blood, burst through the doors with Sabine in his arms, her body concealed by a blanket from the early afternoon sun. Running as best as he could, he crossed the street and disappeared into the apartment.

"I want two men on those two," Michaels instructed Bonelli. "Then I want ten guys at the door ready to take this building." He turned back to O'Reilly. "What the hell was all that about?"

"Walter, have your guys stand down. They will get massacred in there."

"You tell'n me ten of Brooklyn's finest can't take care of this business? What's in there?"

"You've got a cult in there with at least fifteen members, the likes of you've never seen before. I've got one guy still on the inside. He says they've killed every civilian in the building. One hundred of your best are no match for them."

Michaels got on the radio. "Is SWAT on the way?"

"Two minutes," a voice replied.

"You might want to get your guy out, Mitch. If what you say is true, as soon as SWAT gets here, we're going door to door and floor to floor ... and there won't be any trial dates necessary for those pricks."

"Walter!" O'Reilly grabbed the Lieutenant by the arm and pulled him aside. "This is going to sound completely insane, but guns won't do any good. They are not human."

"Bonelli," Michaels screamed. "Get this deranged lunatic across the street and hold him with the rest of the circus he brought to town."

"Walter, you have to listen. They are vampires." O'Reilly implored. Bonelli grabbed him by the arms and as he was led away he screamed out, "Walter, they will slaughter them all."

"You're damn right we will." Michaels replied. "Where's my SWAT?"

"And who was the brainchild that decided I should not have been woken up?" Vincent peered out the window to the street below. Even with his dark sunglasses on, the brightness of the afternoon sun burned his eyes. He turned back and stared menacingly at Sylvia and Peter. Running his hand along smooth finish of his cherry casket, Vincent's ominous eyes warned of a festering rage.

"Len thought ..." Peter began.

"Len thought, now Len is dead along with Al, Angelo, and Turek, and my fucking wife is missing. Additionally, all of our security is gone. You'll forgive me if I seem a little cross, but apparently while I tried to get a little sleep, somebody was completely butt-fucking us and you morons were probably too busy fucking each other to notice."

"Vincent ..." Sylvia began to explain.

"Were either of you idiots aware that there is a legion of cops preparing to storm the building?"

"We were just about ..."

"Oh shut up and listen. We have a few more hours till sunset. Gather everyone down on the third floor. As the cops work their way up, make sure none of them ever leave. I want them all dead, every last one. That should back the NYPD off long enough for the sun to go down. When it does, we leave."

"Vincent, we should stay with you." Sylvia began to approach their chosen leader, but Vincent held his hand high. "So you can protect me? I think I've had all the protection I can stand. Go down and kill the cops, slowly. One of them is bound to know what happened to Sabine. Do not come back without an answer."

The sacrificial lambs entered the building, divided and began searching the ground floor apartments. Over the radio, they reported the tragedy from inside the building, breaking the spirits of all who listened to the barbaric details. So many gray corpses. Apparently, all had suffered from a multitude of bite wounds, in some ritualistic act of cannibalism.

Phillip had switched channels on my com, enabling me to know the progress of the SWAT team in the building. In my search for Vincent, I had gotten pinned down on the fifth floor as numerous vampires headed down to welcome New York's finest. For better or worse, Vincent was my priority, and the welfare of the cops below could be of no concern at this junction.

The floor grew quiet again, I guesstimated roughly twelve to fourteen vampires passed. If Chuck's intel was correct, I would face minimal resistance. I returned to the stairs and cautiously headed up. The first echo of gunfire stopped me dead in my tracks. Two more steps and my progress was halted by screams of agony. Too many screams to be ignored. This massacre had to stop.

Arriving from the rear of the attack, I was able to pick off most of them one by one with the stakes from Chucks backpack. Consumed with the buffet of fresh blood, the first five vampires I encountered on the fourth floor never saw me coming. By the time I reached the lobby only two police were left alive, both suffering from multiple lacerations. I sat on the bottom step and watched as they struggled to crawl to the door. Having witnessed the viciousness of the assault, I could not help but reflect on Rob's death. All of these people, these innocent victims, were all of my making. The repercussions of this day would have long-reaching consequences for years to come.

Night had fallen, and I knew it would not be long before a second wave of cops stormed the building. Turning my attention to departing this macabre crime scene, I headed back up the stairs. By the third floor, I sensed the solitary presence of another. Upon reaching the eighth floor, I knew he waited in apartment C.

The door was slightly ajar and creaked as I pushed it open. Standing beside a casket and looking through parted drapes at the spectacle on the streets below, he ignored my arrival. If Marilyn Manson had an ugly twin, this would be him.

"You must be Vincent."

"Yes," he replied in mellow tones, while continuing to gaze below. "And are you the one responsible for the death of all my friends?"

"I am."

"I guess that makes you some kind of lord of the damned?" He turned slowly and stared into my eyes. "Tell me, how does one man manage to kill so many?"

I offered a cordial smile exposing our dental similarities.

"And you are the source of my missing wife?"

"I merely offered Sabine the opportunity to leave. She was more than eager to accept."

"I find it rude for a stranger to interfere in the marital affairs of others. How is it you came to us?" Vincent crept alongside of his casket, fingers trailing on the glossy wood surface.

"Maltor seemed more than eager for us to become acquainted."

I studied his motion and his hands. I could not read any premeditation to strike, but the human nature I once possessed warned his rage would not long be contained.

"Maltor, one would have thought a stock broker would have been a most excellent vampire," Vincent laughed smugly. "You, however, appear to be a most outstanding vampire. How is it I have never heard a word of your existence?"

"My existence is of no concern to you. But what you have done in this building is the utmost concern of mine. Your very actions endanger the lives of those who prefer to remain in seclusion, living peacefully amongst the human world." Vincent was blocking his thoughts, that much I knew for sure. Skilled to a lesser degree of our ways, I knew his play was imminent.

"Coexist? Surely you are kidding me. Humans are weak by nature's standards. Take away their weapons and they would never survive in the wild. No my friend, it is not time to hide our identity as a coward, but to wake the humans to the reality of a new master race. And give them a choice, you know what most will decide; we are the master race." Vincent spread his arms as if I were to behold some magnificence that would stem the confrontation.

Vincent had methodically circled the room and was now at the door. If he were planning on running, the chase would be short. "All I see is a murderer, with no purpose but self-fulfillment."

"You know, I have learned much about vampires since meeting Sabine. It was a shame she thought as you did. It is why she had to be punished. But as she made me, I must have her back." With reflexes as fast as mine, Vincent pulled a semi-automatic pistol and fired the hollow point round into my head. As I fell backwards, he fired several more rounds all striking my head and chest.

I was on my back in excruciating pain as he picked up the stake I had concealed in my sleeve.

"What do we have here? Oh, was this intended for me? Vincent stood over me, feet straddling my hips. He touched the tip of the stake. "Damn, that's sharp." Licking the blood from his fingertip he smiled broadly.

I could not move or reply. Although the wounds he inflicted were temporary, my body was wracked in unfathomable pain, again. Having endured so many catastrophic injuries over the last week,

I was ready to clock out, permanently. The only issue in the way; I needed to kill this douche bag first.

"Well, time's just about up. Too bad mere bullets wouldn't do the trick. I hope you won't think it ill-mannered of me to use your own weapon to kill you." Double fisted, Vincent raised the stake high above his head. "On behalf of all my friends, fuck you."

Just as Vincent's arms began to strike down, the bloody point of a spear ruptured through the front side of his chest.

"Not today, asshole, nobody kills my fiancée without permission," Samantha screamed from behind. Vincent grabbed the front end of the stake as Samantha continued to shove it through. With the tip of the spear nearing my face, Samantha pushed Vincent's lifeless body to the side. Gazing down at me, Sam's expression was of dire concern. "Oh Jesus, look what a mess you are. Can you move?"

Moving just a fraction was all I could muster. "Sam," I mumbled weakly.

"You know, somehow this just doesn't qualify as being careful or safe. If you weren't already such a mess, I would wear you out, Nicholas Tepes." She put her hand behind my head and raised it up. "We don't have much time, can you stand?"

With three bullets in the head and three in the chest, standing was an unachievable concept. I gurgled my reply, which came out in the form of a bloody moan.

"God Nick, you are such a mess." Samantha shook her head as she studied the shambles of my face. "Do I need to get all the missing pieces?"

I weakly moved my head side to side, indicating no.

"Sam, time to go," Phillip radioed.

"I'll have him down in five minutes." Sam sighed deeply as she raised my chest off the floor. "It's a damn good thing I love you, but you are gonna owe me a new outfit after this."

Effortlessly, Sam lifted me off the floor and cradled me in her arms. "Did I forget to mention I've been working out? You should try it sometime, when you're not all busy getting shot up and bleeding all over my clothes."

CHAPTER TWENTY-FOUR

TO SAY THE next hours of my life were a blur was a colossal understatement. I drifted in and out of consciousness; my body taking hours to recover from Vincent's well placed shots. "It's about time you woke up."

Although not exactly the voice I expected to hear, Chuck's voice was a welcome relief nonetheless. "Where are we?"

"About an hour from Romania."

"Where is Samantha?"

"They're all sleeping. I got the Brian or Nick, whatever the hell you're calling yourself, watch." Chuck laughed. "I gotta tell you, this has been one hell of a ride, dude, thanks for letting me tag along. I thought New Orleans was gonna be tough act to top, but damn ..."

"How did we get out?"

"Shit man, so the cops had us all locked up in the apartment, acting like a bunch of bad-asses. Then that hot little piece Angie goes over and knocks 'em out cold with that spell she used on you. She goes out in the street and the next thing you know, the whole fucking neighborhood is like some Venetian Garden, statues everywhere. Then, Sam comes busting out the door with your pussy ass in her arms. Wait till you see the pictures, bro, we got to go buy you some nice pink panties after that one."

Rubbing my face I inspected the damage with my fingers.

"Don't worry Nicky, most everything has healed. It only looks like you have two extra assholes on your shoulders now. And don't worry, if they don't heal I'll buy you a nice werewolf mask when we get to town."

"Chuck." I really didn't know what to say. My head still felt like scrambled eggs. "Who's with us?"

"All your favorite vampires, Sam. Gabby, Angie, and dude, speaking of Angie, holy shit, you're a dad? How cool is that?"

"Where's Phillip?"

"Mitch and Phil stayed in New York for damage control. Phil's got Izzy and Sabine on ice getting some quality bonding time. He put Daniel on a plane south. But enough of those guys. What's it like bang'n a vampire, you big whore?"

I rolled my head to the side. Only Chuck could force a smile from my otherwise aching face. "It's like fucking with a lamp cord shoved up your ass."

Chuck shrunk down in his seat, uncharacteristically cringing from his words. "Hi Sammy, I didn't hear you coming."

"Obviously." Sam stuck her head in between the seats. "How are you, baby?"

"I'm fine, but Nicky here is about as worthless as a one legged mule."

"Chuck, you're in my seat. Why don't you go watch the others sleep?" Sam stuck her face close to Chuck's and smiled, revealing her fangs.

"Oh sure, flash your fangs and play the bad-ass vampire card. You know, I won't be mortal forever, then you won't be pushing ol' Chuckie around anymore." Chuck tried to maintain his stoic expression, but a smile cracked on the corner of his lip.

Sam gave Chuck a kiss on the cheek. "How about giving me a little time with our patient?"

"Okay doc, but if the plane starts to rock'n, I'll put that shit up on YouTube." Chuck headed to the back of the plane as Sam cozied up beside me.

"That was too damn close Nick. I think it's time we go find that island now."

"You know something, I believe you are right. I don't know why I feel compelled to do this, but before we fly off into the moonrise, I have to go home. But I promise you, although the history lesson will be interesting, it will be by no means anything to write home about."

CHAPTER TWENTY-FIVE

THE ROADS TO the ruins, by New York City standards, were bone-jarring similar, but void of traffic. Lacking New York cabbies, thousands of pedestrians, the glow of a million luminous light bulbs, and noise, there was an undeniable charm to the trek through the mountains of Romania.

Not since Miami had a visit to the ruins of my family's castle been on my agenda, but somewhere in the state of delirium, I was informed by Phillip, this was my chosen destination for our flight of necessity.

So here we were, Sam, Angelique, Gabby, Chuck, and myself, approaching Dracula's Castle. Thankfully, Phillip and Dee had agreed to keep my son in the city until we decided just exactly where in the world we belonged. I had no premonition of what to expect, or why I would have chosen Romania as our initial sanctuary from the pursuit of the NYPD, but here we were.

Angelique pointed out many details of the countryside, in the light of a three-quarter moon, as if it were yesterday, not two hundred years ago. It *had* been my experience through natural life, a woman's recollection of distant memories were thoroughly preserved, when the memories involved wrongdoing by a significant man in their life.

According to Angelique, at the height of our power, my family made use of several castles in Romania. Forsaking her suggestions as to the sequence we should follow to tour my homeland, I instead followed Daniel's advice. Although we left him behind in New York, the few but critical lessons he taught in New Orleans still resonated; close my eyes and follow my instincts.

However my instincts did not lead us to the castles of modern folklore. The ruins of Poenari would have been the last place Angelique would have suggested, yet this was the very place my heart called.

Climbing the steps of the ruins at night was not an issue, except for Chuck who whined and complained every step of the ascent. Although I attempted to stress the need for stealth, Chuck continued to bemoan his lack of vision as we passed through the darkened forest. In our hasty departure from the States, the thought of equipping Chuck with any para-military devices never crossed our minds.

Upon reaching the clearing where the castle stood hauntingly before us, Angelique sighed with a heavy heart.

"This is all that remains?"

Moonbeams filtered by the clouds sporadically illuminated sections of the great ruins.

"That's more like it." Finally able to take in what light was available, Chuck forged to the front to gaze at the mystical view before him. "Bro! This is your crib? I gotta tell you, if there ain't a shitter in there, we're gonna have a problem."

Angelique, Sam and Gabrielle joined Chuck at the front, briefly before Gabrielle took up the lead on the final set of steps leading to the ruins.

Samantha turned back to me, "So what now?"

"I don't know. Let's just go to the top and see what we find."

Sam stroked the side of my head tenderly. "And what if nothing comes?"

"Then we go back down and wait until something does." Normally, the caress of her hands would have drawn my attention away from the task at hand, but tonight the forces that guided me here would not be denied. Gabrielle, Chuck, and Angelique were already well on the way to the entrance. "I know what you are thinking. But right now, we have all the time in the world. We certainly can't go back home any time soon. And if nothing comes of this, at least we can check Romania off our bucket-list of vacation hotspots."

Sam forced a smile. "I just worry you're searching for something that may not exist. And I hate the thought that you might spend the rest of your life with some void that cannot be filled."

"Sam …"

"Hey old man, you need me to come drag your ass the rest of the way?" Chuck called from the top.

Almost as quick as his words echoed out, Sam and I covered the distance between the woods and our companions.

"Fucking showoffs," Chuck rolled his eyes. "Don't think for one minute you'd be any match if I had some of that vampire shit."

"You know, Chuck, the whole reason we parked way down the valley and hiked in without lights was to remain stealthy. But now I am quite certain if anyone is up here, including the dead, they will not be surprised by our arrival."

"If you boys care to quit bickering and join us, we can maybe get this done before the sun comes up." Angelique and Gabrielle turned and continued on past the vacant guard office. Samantha snickered and pushed her way past and followed the pair over the wooden bridge to the final set of stairs.

"Dude, in the old days you never would have let a chick lead you around by the pecker like that." Chuck turned away and followed Samantha.

Chuck was doing his very best to needle me into submission. He was certain beyond all doubt that he should join the brethren of the undead, and was irritated with my decision denying his opportunity. I waited for all of them to complete the climb, leaving me alone in the silent darkness. In solitude I began climbing the stairs as the late autumn wind whispered through the naked branches, stripped clean by the frigid November frost.

As I reached the ruins, a lone wolf bayed in the distance, perhaps the spirit of my kinfolk welcoming me home. Alone, with new family dispersed about the remnants, I stroked the gelid stone walls attempting to connect with whatever spirit had driven me here. As I looked out over the snow-frosted peaks surrounding the castle, a vision of a renewed Poenari filled my mind. As I roamed through these visionary passages lined with fine Persian tapestries and armaments from multiple centuries of battle, the aroma of torch flames filled my nostrils as shadows danced from the abounding light. Entering the north tower, the voices of guards echoed from above. Passing through the tower, I entered a grand banquet room, and before my eyes could partake of its grandeur, I was immediately drawn to a magnificent portrait of a most beautiful woman.

The Countess Ilona Szilagy; my great grandmother's portrait stood before me in all her radiance and beauty, glowing as if her eyes lay upon me for the first time. As I reached out to take her hand the vision vanished in a cloud as Samantha called my name.

"Nick, are you all right?"

I turned to see my friends, bewildered by my dream-like enacted movements.

"She was here, just now."

"Who," Gabrielle asked.

"My great grandmother." Needless to say, as I studied the reality of the crumbled stone surrounding me, the materialization and subsequent vanishing of a grand dining hall staggered my consciousness like a good upper-cut.

"Her portrait once hung here, right where we stand," Angelique began. After Vlad II's death, his brother, your grandfather, returned to claim the family castle. Their portraits stood beside each other, in this very space.

"How could Nick have known that?" Gabrielle asked.

"Maybe he was here as a child, like some kind of flashback," Samantha speculated.

"No," Angelique began. "Nicholas was born in the late nineteen forties. According to history, this portion of the castle was destroyed by an earthquake in the late nineteenth century. The tower and grand hall all perished into the Arges River below.

"More like one too many bullets to the head. If you ask me." Chuck snorted at his joke, his sense of humor not necessarily shared by the rest of the group.

Gabrielle punched Chuck in the shoulder. "You would not find it so funny if it were your head."

"Why do you think her image appeared to you here?" Samantha asked.

"It was here, the secret passage began," Angelique explained.

"Spiraling deep into the mountain, it led to a grand chamber where we rested. There were other chambers as well, rooms filled with the treasure of the Tepes family, ancestors from ancient times. I always hated that passage, dampened stone that seemed to never end, so dark and cold. I always feared it would collapse, and we would be trapped for all eternity."

"And now it is gone, along with all of its secrets," Gabrielle concluded.

"Perhaps not." Angelique turned to the opposite side of the ruins and pointed. "There was another passage that led to the opposite side of the mountain. A thin slate covered its hidden entrance, one that could be crushed by the force of a hammer. It is possible the way to the chamber might be found, if it did not collapse in the earthquake."

"Back down the mountain, and rummage through the forest again, in the dark? Maybe I'll hike back to the van and wait," Chuck bemoaned.

"Is Mister Grumpy Pants whining?" Samantha seized the opportunity to retaliate for all the grief Chuck had dealt out over the past three days.

"Hey, you turn off your night vision and see how much you like running around the woods practically blind. If somebody had thought to bring my night-vision goggles I'd be kicking y'alls asses all over the mountain. Hell, a flashlight would do."

"Take my hand, Chuck, I will lead you." Extending her hand, Gabrielle winked at Chuck.

"Damn it, Gabby, nobody leads a Marine around, no matter how irresistibly sexy they are." Even in the darkness of the pale moonlight, Gabrielle's blush was apparent. "I'd just as much prefer heading back to the van and wrestling some of those crazed wild dogs we passed on the way in."

"Look, we have about four hours before we have to be back on the road. So let's make this quick as possible. Angelique, please lead the way." I began walking back toward the bridge without waiting for any more commentary from Chuck.

About half of the way down Angelique veered from the stairs and headed into the woods. "Only once did your father show me the entrance, but it was in this direction." Upon reaching a shallow ravine Angelique looked back to the top of the mountain. "The entrance was in a crag, such as this. We followed it until the castle first came into view. It is fortunate the leaves have fallen otherwise the view is obstructed."

As we trekked through the ravine, I was captivated by the rugged beauty of the late autumn skyline. After nearly twenty minutes, the silhouette of the castle revealed itself. "There, through the trees," I pointed.

Immediately, we scattered and began searching the mountain base for a smooth slate matching Angelique's description. Amongst the Alpine undergrowth, dirt and leaves, the few stones that fit the description proved a false glimmer of hope.

"Maybe there is another ravine," Samantha suggested.

"Perhaps, but this just feels right." Angelique continued to search to the left and the right.

"Hey does anyone mind if the village blind man chimes in?" With no objections, Chuck continued. "Angie says the last time she was here was when the castle was still intact. Right?"

"Go on," I prompted.

"So how tall was the castle before it collapsed? Seems to me, if I could see through all this damned darkness, with the tower being much taller, I would have seen it long before we arrived to this location."

"And all this time everyone assumed all you could do is beat people up or kill them. Chuck, you are amazing," Samantha praised.

Gabrielle affectionately pulled Chuck closer. "That's my jarhead."

"All right, all right. Do not inflate his head any larger. We will never get him in the cave once we find it." I turned and retraced our path in, keeping about twenty feet above the base of the ravine. Tapping each stone with a large rock I had found, I silently paced off the return trip. With Sam and Angelique about fifteen feet above me, and Gabby and Chuck below, we methodically searched the hillside.

Other than the crunching of leaves underfoot, the wisp of the wind, and the occasional clacking of rock on rock, the night had grown silent. Within two hundred yards from where we initially searched, the echo of rock on hollow rock stopped us all dead in our tracks. Further up the hill, Samantha struck the stone slab again, confirming the echo. Just as before, the sound resonated with a unique clacking.

I ran up the hill, followed by Gabrielle with Chuck in tow. Studying the slab, my decision was to either shatter the rock or attempt to unearth the edges and preserve the hidden passage. One choice would expedite the process, the other was time consuming and possibly an unproductive waste of time if the stone could not be dislodged. I checked my watch as my heart raced with anticipation.

"We need to preserve the integrity of the entrance if possible, to keep it the hidden." I grabbed a broken branch and start excavating the perimeter.

Sam, Gabrielle, and Angelique joined in as Chuck stood by watching. "I'd love to help, but I still can't see a fucking thing."

"Fine Chuck, just watch our backs," I instructed.

"Would love to do that, but Godzilla could sneak up and I'd never see him coming either. Guess I'll just stand here and look pretty."

We all snickered at our beleaguered friend's incessant whiny humor. While digging in the dirt, Sam stole the opportunity to give me a peck on the cheek. "I hope you know you're going to have to pony up for manicures for us girls tomorrow."

"Good luck finding an all-night salon in this neighborhood." I smiled and returned to my task. Within thirty minutes the edges were unearthed and defined.

Chuck appeared over my shoulder with a thick branch about eight feet long. "Step back, Doctor Jones, and let a professional show you how this is done."

"Thought you couldn't see a damn thing out here?" I quipped.

Chuck's smirk was intended to annoy. "That was payback. It was kind of nice to sit back like Pharaoh and watch all of y'all *superior* beings do my dirty work."

Gabrielle, standing uphill from Chuck looked him in the eye and then playfully punched his chest.

Chuck drove the branch into the ground and rolled a large rock under it for leverage. Without much stress, the large slab gaped open. The ancient darkness sealed within would not allow much sight. Having been sealed for at least one hundred and twenty years, it was blacker than black.

Inside the confines of the tunnel I knew our presence would now go undetected. I extended my hand like a surgeon awaiting a scalpel,

"Flashlight, Chuck."

"You mean my flashlight? Maybe you should try feeling your way around for once."

With a stern look from Gabrielle, Chuck handed it over with a huff.

I shined the beacon into the tunnel. Darkness as far as the eye could see. "Anyone want to stay behind?"

With no takers, one by one we squeezed by the stone and entered the seemingly endless passage. As Chuck entered he allowed the stone to close behind him. The passage extended far beyond the beam of the mist-shrouded light. Without a sound to be heard, I led my companions through the rough stone walls deep inside the mountain.

With much anticipation in her voice, Angelique broke the silence, "I think it should not be much farther."

After nearly fifteen minutes we finally arrived in a grand chamber. Without our light, even with such keen night vision, it would have been impossible to witness the magnificent chamber, its vaulted ceiling rising about twenty feet above. Scanning side to side with the flashlight, I illuminated the six arching marble pillars dividing the room in half. To the right, a solid stone wall covered with tattered tapestries; to the left, two smaller archways, another passageway, and two more archways.

Angelique headed to the center of the room where an oak cask stood. After removing the lid she dunked a cloth-covered club into the barrel. Mounted on the pillar beside the barrel she found an antique flint lighter unlike any I had seen. With two strokes, she lit the torch and placed it in the holder on the opposite side of the barrel. "Gabrielle, would you and Chuck be so kind as to light the remaining torches?"

Samantha and I moved to the first of the four archways. The chamber behind was roughly twelve-by-twelve feet. Evenly spaced were two finely trimmed rosewood caskets. Angelique joined us while Gabrielle's and Chuck's efforts gradually increased the illumination.

"These caskets do not bear the markings of your family lineage." Angelique moved between the boxes, her hands gliding down the surfaces as she passed. "As there is no life within, I suggest we allow the inhabitants their peace."

"Who else would be in there?" Samantha asked.

"The very last time I shared this hall with your father, his companions occupied these caskets. Never did more than eight vampires occupy the grand chamber. There were other areas within the tunnels for sleep, but in this space only his closest confidants were allowed their rest."

Chuck and Gabrielle rejoined us as we moved to the second antechamber, again with two caskets.

"Holy shit, Brian. This is just like New Orleans all over, except now everyone is a vampire … except me …" Upon seeing all eyes trained on him, Chuck complained loudly, "Hey, don't nobody get any ideas. I ain't some kind of Juicy Juice pack."

I could not help but roll my eyes at Chuck. After all the grief I had endured over Samantha and every other misstep he witnessed, his time was due.

Angelique moved past the smallest of the five archways, which led to another darkened passage. "Down this passage lies the vaults of what once was your family wealth and several smaller rooms for the caskets of visitors and then the stairway back to the castle."

The third archway was sealed by means of stone and mortar. "This room was traditionally reserved for your father's closest friends and confidants. It makes no sense why it would have been sealed." Angelique quickly moved to the last archway. "Oh no," she cried.

Inside the final room were remnants of two caskets, splintered and charred into a pile of rubble. We all stood in the midst silently, each mired in the reflections of what might have been.

"You know, I hate to bring this up, but being a reformed vampire killer, I would have to guess this is where they killed your father, probably by staking, then decapitation, and finally by roasting."

"I think Chuck may be right." The finality of a lost love weighed heavily as tears flowed down Angelique's face.

Samantha hugged Angelique as we all stood in silence for what felt like an hour. It was no major surprise that it was Chuck who finally broke the silence. "At the risk of sounding insensitive, what's next? We could … maybe check out the treasure room."

Gabby and Sam cut a glare of audacious disbelief at Chuck. "No, he's right," I said. "We've got about an hour and a half to get out, cover our tracks and get back to the van, unless we plan on camping out in here tonight," I suggested.

"Camp out here? *Tonight?* I believe Sam forgot to scoop up the better half of your brain off the floor back in New York. If we stay here, *somebody or something* will find us."

"You're right." Hearing Chuck as the voice of reason, I grimaced. "Chuck, take the ladies and see what you can find. I would like a little solitary time."

Sam looked at me sympathetically, grabbed Gabby's hand and headed to the adjacent narrow passage. "Let's go."

They filed one by one down the narrow passage leaving me alone with the ghost of my past. A solitary chair sat positioned in front of the sealed arch. I shuffled my feet as I made my way to the lone piece of furniture. It creaked as I sat and immediately I regretted sitting, as I was sure the antique was about to collapse. As I stood to rise, a current of electricity jolted my body and my knees buckled. Falling back into the chair another vision appeared. Samantha was sitting in this very chair, surrounded by a dozen men. No, it wasn't Samantha, it was my mother. Although it was only a vision, the crosses held high in their hands seared my eyes as if I was actually surrounded. Torturous screams rang out as I shielded my eyes and retreated in the darkened recesses of my mind. From the hidden alcoves, I watched as the men taunted my beautiful mother, tortured her with showers of holy water before finally driving a stake through her heart.

In my darkness, I sobbed as my mother's body fell lifeless, bound to an unknown eternity. Still seated in the very chair my mother had faced her execution in, my lamentations echoed throughout the hall. Joined by a deathly chorus, certainly not of any angels' making, I wept freely over the brutality of her death.

Sam was the first to return in a near panic. "Nick, what's wrong?"

Still mesmerized in the vision, I could only watch as the blood pooled by her legs as the wailing continued. But it was not my voice alone. There was another voice sounding out its tormented agony.

Surrounded by my friends, I opened my eyes and stood. "I have just witnessed my mother's death," I mumbled as I search the room. I pulled on a torch mounting on the wall and wriggled and pulled until the steel bracket broke free. With all eyes on me, I stumbled back across the room until I faced the sealed arch. "My father did not die in the ruins of his casket. They left him to die, behind this wall. They forced him to watch her death." I began scratching away at the mortar with the sharpened edge of the steel.

Chuck followed my lead and broke another torch holder from the wall. Digging alongside me, we steadily chipped away at the filament bonding the stones. Within an hour we had our first glimpse inside. Upon seeing another heap of charred wood, I suffered again, to visualize the horrendous death my father must have suffered.

As Chuck and I continued the scrape away, Sam placed her hand on my shoulder. "Why don't you try this?" She and Gabby had gone back down the passage and found a marble bench, probably weighing at least four hundred pounds.

"I don't need to sit, but thank you all the same."

"It's not to sit on, silly. If we can throw it hard enough, it probably will break the wall down. Or you could just keep digging for the next ten hours." Samantha's hands were on her hips, and her expression of *I can't believe you didn't figure that one out* was somewhat demeaning.

"I knew that." I backed away from the wall. "I would ask for your help, Chuck, but you are probably exhausted from moving that stone door."

"Look bitch, just chomp down on my neck, right now, and I'll show you how much damage a bad-ass vampire marine can do."

"Chuck, if I no longer believed we might need you as a mortal, I might just take you up on your request. But things being what they are, if you will step aside, Sam and I will give it our best."

"Best this." Chuck grabbed his groin. "Don't give me that 'I need you alive' bullshit. You're just scared all the chicks will dig me more once I'm a bloodsucker. You're afraid of a little competition, bee-otch."

"Fine, Chuck," I sighed. Grab the side with Sam and let's do this." Samantha was already in position as I scratched out a line on the floor. Joining Samantha, Chuck and I took up our positions, lifted the bench and backed up about ten feet. "Let's rock it backwards, then run to the line and toss it," I instructed. Running forward at a rather slow human pace we hurled the bench, which crashed into the wall with a thunderous boom.

Although the results were not as I had hoped, we did manage

to create a hole just large enough for me to snake my body through. Twisting and turning, I managed to enter the musty chamber. I walked over to the remnants of what once had been at least one casket if not more. I stared down at the rubble and then to the back wall. Why on earth all of this overkill? I bent down and rubbed my hand through the ashes. Perhaps as part of their cruelty, my mother was forced to witness the death of my father.

Chuck stuck his head through the wall. "You know, if there's nothing in here to see, I don't see any reason for us to get our clothes all dirty just to hang out with you. Besides our window to get the hell out is closing fast, so unless you brought some hot dogs for the sleepover, you might want to think about packing it in."

My disappointment was evident as I turned and sighed. I was not sure what I expected, but after my visions, somehow I expected something more. Just as I made my way back to the hole, a pile of refuse in the left corner or the chamber caught my eye. Upon touching the pile it shifted and fell to the side causing me to startle and jump back. There, amongst the rags, was flesh and bone so withered it appeared to be mummified. I knelt down to inspect the remains, but as I turned its head, I thought I detected a wisp of breath. I pulled down the lower eyelid only to find an eye wrought in agonizing death. The eye appeared to be staring back, and then came another wisp of breath.

"Chuck, get your ass in here."

Chuck stuck his head in again. "What the hell is that?"

"Just get in here," I demanded.

Being slightly larger than me, Chuck faced great difficulty getting through the hole. "I hope you realize if I get stuck, we are both fucked."

Once Chuck finally twisted through, Samantha stuck her head in. "What is it?"

"A body maybe. Stay back, just in case," I warned.

"In case of what?" Sam asked.

"I don't know, just in case."

"Maybe I should go back out there with them, just in case," Chuck offered as he studied the gory remains.

I rolled the head back and felt for breath. Nothing this time. "I need a hand."

Chuck held his hand out. "Which one?"

"Either will do." I sliced it with my fingernail creating a stream of blood.

"What the hell?" Chuck complained as I pulled his hand to the mouth of the body. "Damn it, I'm tired of being your pincushion every time you think somebody needs a drink."

The drops of blood pooled on its lips and ran off its cheek.

"You didn't honestly expect that thing to be alive did you?"

Disappointed I released Chuck's hand. As I laid the head back against the wall a leathery tongue parted the lips and painstakingly slid across the flesh, from left to right.

"What the fuck, Brian?"

I pulled Chuck's hand back to its mouth.

"Not cool man!" Chuck objected.

With every drop, lifelike features began to return to what I had initially mistaken for a corpse. The eyes weakly cranked open and a frail hand took Chuck's hand and pulled it closer.

"If I get fucking rabies or AIDS from this ..."

I gauged as best I could, and somewhere just under two pints I pulled Chuck's hand away. What clearly now was a man gasped as though I had just removed his source of oxygen. "Easy now, let your body recover, just a bit."

"Is everything all right in there?" Gabrielle called from the main hall.

Before I could answer, unknown garbled voices seeped through the hole.

"Nick?" An air of panic peppered Gabrielle's voice.

I motioned to Chuck. "Get out there."

I gazed down at the frail skeletal man before me. Tearing my own flesh, I offered my wrist. "Drink, slowly."

As hostile tones reverberated, I pulled my hand away.

Chuck stuck his head back in the hole. "Dude, better get out here."

"Rest here, I will come back for you." Upon reaching the main chamber I was confronted by two unknown men.

The taller of the two, a husky man with a long brown beard and weathered face stepped forward. "So, the prodigal son has returned."

"Excuse me?" I searched his mind, but he effectively blocked my attempts. I sensed this man was not a vampire. But having never encountered a mortal so skilled at sensory evasiveness, I warily approached.

"Neculai Tepes, did you think your actions in New Orleans and New York would go unnoticed? We always knew the day would arrive when the son of Levente would return home. And I must thank you for showing us the secret passage into the mountain."

"Who are you?" Angelique asked as we slowly surrounded our uninvited guest.

"Ah yes, proper introductions. I am Alexandru Korzha. My brethren and I, as our ancestors before, have held the honor of protecting the fine citizens of Romania from the predatory nature of such beings as yourself."

"The Order of the Dragon?" Angelique surmised.

"Yes. And sadly, if Daniel had stood by his sworn oath we would not be in this predicament."

"Well, the way I see it, if you turn your ass around and leave, we don't have a problem," Chuck suggested.

"If you already know about us, then you should know we bring no harm to humans," Gabrielle asserted.

"Yes, the self-proclaimed peaceful vampires ... such as your father. Would you care to guess how many innocent villagers perished in the wake of his ... abstinence? You see, sooner or later, by your very nature all of you kill. And when you kill, things like New York happen."

"We fought to protect the humans," Gabrielle objected.

"You killed to control your turf! And you, Neculai, you killed your own kind. What hope is there for a man who would take so many of his own?"

Gabrielle inched uncomfortably close and Alexandru produced a shiny silver cross in one hand, and pistol type spray device, no doubt linked to a tank of holy water, in the other. We all withdrew and shielded our eyes. "As you can see, we are well prepared. Tonight, after you passed through the infrared sensors, the call went out, as it has so many times over the years. The Guardians of the Arges have prepared for years to finish our forefathers' work."

"I only see two scrawny guardians," Chuck said.

"My comrades have gathered just beyond the tunnel. But I could not seal your fate without first confronting the heir of the Tepes family."

"Seal our fate?" Without looking at Alexandru, Samantha inched nearer.

"Unless you want your beautiful skin seared away, I suggest you stay back."

Although she had yet to experience the excruciating pain of sunlight or holy water, Samantha chose to heed Alexandru's warning.

"So tell me, Neculai, how did you find your father?"

"My father? Are you are referring to the pile of dust and bones beyond that wall?" Alexandru's identification of our mystery man nearly dropped me to my knees. "If those lifeless remains were my father's, then the evil of your forefathers was unquestionably cruel beyond compare. And rest assured, they equally earned a seat of honor in hell."

"Sixty plus years behind that wall. How long do you think he suffered before he succumbed to starvation? No doubt you have many years to experience the answer first hand," Alexandru, boasted as he slowly began backing toward the tunnel, revealing a detonator in his hand. Alexandru bowed without taking his eyes off of us. "And this, Count Tepes, is where we say, *la revedere.*"

"Fuck this nonsense," Chuck said as he began to approach Alexandru.

Alexandru held the cross high and began dousing Chuck with holy water.

Chuck cowered and bellowed, "No, no, it burns." Lunging forward he grabbed Alexandru's neck and smiled, "Hey dick head, I ain't no fucking vampire." With a violent scissor twist of his arms, Chuck dropped Alexandru to the floor, his neck broken, then relieved Alexandru's companion of the stake he wielded. Undoubtedly, the fearless vampire killer had never imagined the pain inflicted by impaling a stake through the heart, until now. "Shit, that looks like it really hurts," Chuck taunted as he released the body to the floor. Chuck looked back at my incredulous expression. "What? Too extreme?"

"No, I just don't know if there's enough time left."

"For what? A memorial service? How about this? Ashes to ashes and dust to dust. Alex and his chump buddy are dead, now can we hurry the fuck up so I can get a chicken sandwich and go get in bed."

Chuck snorted, turned and spit in Alexandru's direction. "Rest in peace, pricks."

I had witnessed Chuck's methodology many times over the years and his actions as such were somewhat anticipated. But even after Alexandru's confession of intent, Chuck's brutality appeared to traumatize the girls in various degrees.

Angelique slowly stepped over Alexandru's body and placed her hand on my shoulder. "Is it true? Did you find your father's body?"

"If what he said is true, I have found my father, and he is alive."

"Yo Brian," Chuck called out. "I hate to interrupt a Hallmark moment, but we are already about twenty minutes behind schedule. Sunrise is coming bro. Unless you plan on waiting for Alex's buddies to show up for a send-off party, we've got to get the hell out now."

"Give me a hand," I exclaimed as I rushed back to the hole. "We have got to get him out."

Chuck grabbed my shoulder. "Do you think it's wise? We don't know who in the hell is really in there."

"I won't leave him here, no matter who he is." I climbed back through the hole. The man was hunched over on all fours. "Can you stand?" With no reply I helped him to his feet. His bones felt as though they would crumble within my grip. "We must leave, now." Too weak to resist, and apparently unable to talk, I decided to lift him through the jagged opening. With Chuck's help from the other side, I guided his body into the grand hall. Climbing out of a once impenetrable prison, I found Angelique standing over his hunched up body.

"Levente, is it you?" she asked. "Levente, speak to me."

With no reply and sunrise racing against us, I scooped him up once again while searching his eyes for answers. Immense suffering and emptiness filled the blackened orbs. I placed him gently in Sam's arms. "I need to be up front with Chuck, just in case we have a welcoming delegation waiting outside."

Throwing caution to the wind, we doubled our pace back through the tunnel. Just as Chuck was about to barrel out into the forest, a glimmer ahead caught my eye. I grabbed Chuck's shoulder and pulled him back just as a searing thud echoed into the cave.

"Oh fuck," Chuck bellowed in pain. "I've been hit."

Yanking him back inside the passage, I searched over his

shoulder. In the dark cover of the forest I counted three men, all with crossbows. We retreated to a point where our assailants were no longer in clear view. I turned my attention to Chuck, an arrow planted firmly in his shoulder.

"Ah shit man, this hurts. Pull that fucker out, Brian. Damn Jimmy's curse. He put this on me for not bringing him along."

"Nick, what should we do?" Gabby asked as she tended to Chuck's injury.

"I don't know. They've got night vision and can see us coming. I could not tell how many were out there beyond three. But the longer we wait, the more might show up, and sooner or later they will come in after us. But going out there is suicide."

Sam looked toward the entrance. "Alexandru was prepared to entomb us in this place, so let's grant him his final request." She pointed to explosives that had been planted at the mouth of the tunnel. "It will buy us time."

"In time, we will end up like our friend here," I pointed out.

"No, we can eat Chuck," Gabrielle chirped as she pulled the arrow out of Chuck's shoulder and licked its tip. "He is rather tasty."

"Hey, nobody eats Chuck." Chuck applied a rag to his wound.

If we went out against those skilled hunters, surely not all of us would survive. And we did not have the luxury of time as Sam pointed out. Her idea was the only viable answer. "Everyone get back to the main hall. Gabby, bring me the detonator. I'll wait here and make sure they do not follow us in."

Within minutes Gabby returned with the detonator. "Okay, let's get the hell out of here." Sprinting back to the main hall, I pressed the trigger and the mountain rumbled with a mighty explosion behind us. Fire and dust pursued our retreat until we cleared the tunnel. Once the aftershock had cleared, I returned to ensure the path was indeed sealed.

Returning to the great hall, I found everyone comfortably stretched out across several tapestries strewn on the floor. Angelique, speaking softly, was attempting to solicit any response from the gnarled and shriveled man. Gabrielle and Sam were tending to Chuck's injury, as the overgrown ham-bone played the wounded soldier routine to the max.

Directing my attention to Angelique I knelt down beside her.

"Anything?"

"I wish I could say. There is nothing about him I recognize, no features or scent, and he is completely unresponsive."

"He needs more blood, living blood."

"I ain't dead yet. Don't think I can't hear you talking about me. And forget it, between the pint or two Count Mummy already sucked out of me, and the arrow I took for you, I'm down about fifty percent, Jackeroo. That is … unless you want him to finish me up and make me one of the crew. It sure would help my shoulder heal a lot faster."

"Chuck …" I could not begin to gather my wits enough to make a logical rebuttal.

"Hey if you're hungry, or need to feed 'Ol Prune Stick over there, might I suggest Alexandru and his butt buddy. I don't think they've got any immediate dinner plans." Wounded and trapped, Chuck refused to let the dire situation get the best of his spirit.

"Even if there were a way out, it's too late tonight. We should rest now, and later tonight we can explore the old castle stairway. Perhaps it can be reopened," Angelique suggested.

Lacking any other viable plan, or suggestions to the contrary, we silently agreed. I snuffed the torches and the chamber fell into darkness. Sleep did not come easy for any of us. The events of the night and the uncertainty of what lay ahead was far too daunting to allow peaceful slumber. Through the course of day, my mind drifted through stages of tranquil dreams and horrific nightmares. Our guest, actually it was we who were his guests, appeared as a kind stranger and then as a tyrannous villain. On occasions as my breath quickened and my heart pounded me into consciousness, I would part my eyes only to discover him still on the floor, gray and feeble.

Frozen in darkness, the chamber remained oblivious to the passing of the hours, or the suns intentions for the world beyond. It was in this abyss where sleep finally claimed its exhausted victims. It was here, in this world where no mortal, or vampire, can resolve to control their destiny, these words drifted across the ancient, misty chamber; : *Odihnă ușor pe fiul meu. Calea pe care caută viața în sufletul tău.* (Rest easy my son. The path you seek lives within your soul.)

Five percent of the writer's profits will be donated to Canine Companions for Independence. CCI provides highly trained assistance dogs for individuals with disabilities, free of charge. For more information, please visit www.CCI.org.

www.ingramcontent.com/pod-product-compliance
Lightning Source LLC
Chambersburg PA
CBHW030425310726
48979CB00009B/1612/J

* 9 7 8 1 6 3 3 9 3 3 4 9 1 *